"I WISH YOU WERE THE FATHER OF MY BABY."

Casey's self-control failed and he looked down at Mary Kate, his lips just inches from hers. "What?"

"Don't be so surprised. You'd make a terrific father. I watched you with those kids today. Don't think I didn't see you giving them piggyback rides between rows."

"I'm a journalist, not Mr. Rogers. I don't know anything about kids. I was never a kid myself."

"Maybe it's instinctive, then. But you're sensitive and caring, and you have a way of getting inside people."

This last was a little close for comfort in light of the direction his thoughts had been taking. "Maybe we really are strangers. I'm none of those things. I'm a vicious, cutthroat news pirate, who won't stop at anything to get a story."

"You're a pussycat. And don't deny it . . ." Her voice trailed off until her words were nothing more than whispers.

Their gazes locked. His heart stopped beating; time seemed to stand still; the world stopped spinning. And even as he dipped his head, he told himself what a bad idea this was.

Other Avon Contemporary Romances by
Emilie Richards

EMILIE RICHARDS

TWICE UPON A TIME

AVON BOOKS  NEW YORK

AVON BOOKS
A division of
The Hearst Corporation
1350 Avenue of the Americas
New York, New York 10019

Copyright © 1997 by Emilie Richards McGee
Inside cover author photo by Best Photography
Published by arrangement with the author
Visit our website at http://www.AvonBooks.com
Library of Congress Catalog Card Number: 97-93176
ISBN: 0-380-78364-9

First Avon Books Printing: November 1997

AVON TRADEMARK REG. U.S. PAT. OFF. AND IN OTHER COUNTRIES, MARCA REGISTRADA, HECHO EN U.S.A.

Printed in the U.S.A.

WCD   10 9 8 7 6 5 4 3 2 1

ᦁ Prologue

THE WINTER AIR WAS FRIGID ENOUGH TO make Mary Kate McKenzie's teeth ache, but she forced herself to smile at the teenagers gathered in a semicircle in front of her. Thanks to the stern warnings of the judge who had sent them here, every one of them had arrived on time.

The girls—she quickly counted six of them—were dressed in stiff jeans and heavy jackets, the luckiest two with sturdy leather boots. The others wore high-top sneakers to seal out the worst of the snow that had fallen since early morning. All of them wore scowls, as if even a hint of Christmas spirit would doom them to eternal damnation with their peers.

The boys—eight of them—wore the same teenage uniforms and sullen expressions. Antoine, the tallest and most dangerous of the lot, chewed gum with lightning-swift efficiency, turning the wad over with his tongue and cracking it as loudly and as often as the laws of physics dictated. The others hung back, as if they had already determined that Antoine would be their leader.

Mary Kate scanned her list to be sure all the teens were here. From the corner of her eye she noted that the caseworker and the two college-student counselors who had brought the teens to Eden's Gate looked as cold and miserable as she felt. She supposed the bus drive from juvenile court hadn't been pleasant. The next hours probably wouldn't be, either.

Not for anyone.

"It's good to see you again," she told the kids, even though it wasn't. Not today, anyway.

"You think so?" Antoine said. "Well, we ain't glad to be here."

"Merry Christmas to you, too, Antoine." She met his eyes, hers benign and accepting, his so hostile they seemed to darken with rage.

Someone snickered, and Mary Kate realized she had made an error. Nothing was more unacceptable to these kids than to be laughed at. And Antoine would never forget that she had caused laughter at his expense.

"But enough good cheer," she continued, trying to defuse the situation. "I know you don't want to be here, at least not all of you. I'm glad you came anyway."

"You think we got a choice?" Antoine said.

She squelched the uncharacteristic sarcasm rising inside her. "You do," she said evenly. "You made your choice when you got on the bus today. I'm glad you did."

"Yeah? Well, coming here's one step better than jail! What kinda choice is that?"

She stared at him, thinking about the choices she had made of late.

Thinking *particularly* about the choice she had made only that morning.

As she continued to stare, Antoine took a step forward, and she snapped back to the present. "But it's not jail," she said. "And right now you're going to have a chance to do something a lot more fun than stamping out license plates. Is everybody ready?"

A general rumbling was the only answer, but it was enough to let her know what she was up against today.

She nodded to the program staff and social worker and started inside the large greenhouse which had once been attached to a nursery in Shandley Falls, the closest town. Grace and Samantha, two of the nuns who lived at Eden's Gate, were waiting inside the door to help divide the teens into groups and get them started on the day's activity.

Mary Kate had thought long and hard about what project to pursue this afternoon. The fourteen teenagers ranged from ages thirteen to seventeen, with differing levels of skills and intelligence. The only thing they truly had in common was that they were all juvenile offenders. Among them they had committed a range of misdemeanors and minor felonies that read like a sample page from a police blotter. Most of them had perfected and escalated their offenses over the past year, as if competing for the gold in a teen-crime Olympics.

The only other thing they shared was a judge's belief that they could still turn their lives around. The teenagers had been assigned to Eden's Gate Ecology Center on Saturdays throughout the school year to do community service and learn new skills. In the summer they would take up residence here. While they were at Eden's Gate, Mary Kate was one of the people in charge of their futures.

"Listen up, everybody," she said, once they'd all been herded inside. "We're going to pot bulbs to give as Christmas gifts to families who need the good cheer. I've been forcing them in buckets in the garden. We're going to tease them out of the buckets and into plastic pots to set in baskets. I'll show you how, and the sisters and I will help you get started. Sister Grace and I have collected moss and twigs in the woods to add to your arrangements. You can use your imagination, and everyone can take home his best effort."

This time the grumbling wasn't as intense, but Mary Kate hardly registered the change. She was on automatic pilot today, and she continued that way as she did her demonstration.

Afterwards the teenagers were separated into groups and as had been agreed previously, she was left with the most difficult to manage herself. Besides Antoine she had two other boys, Tyson and Pfeiffer, and a girl who was new to the program. She led them to a worktable and settled each of them at a station with the necessary supplies.

She found a place for herself at the middle of the table, purposely positioning herself between Antoine and Tyson. She knew from previous experience that the two young men disliked each other—her word, not theirs. She always separated them and paid close attention to their every move.

But today her attention wandered immediately.

She knew there were prayers she ought to repeat, forgiveness to plead for, promises to make. But none of the right words were on her lips or even forming in her mind. She had not set out to sin this morning, and even now, the sin in question didn't feel like a sin at all.

It felt like a secret and a pledge. It felt like the greatest gift imaginable.

She felt like her heart was breaking.

Mary Kate McKenzie knew better than to let her mind drift beyond her immediate environment. She knew better, but for once that didn't matter. As her hands performed the comforting ritual of repotting bulbs, her heart and mind fled somewhere else, far away from the teenagers surrounding her.

Lost in her thoughts, she missed the first signs of danger, and when she finally realized what was happening, her response was too slow.

She heard the angry words and saw the flash of movement. Precious seconds passed before she rallied to throw herself against Antoine to keep him from jumping Tyson. But she was too late, and the two boys were fighting before she could stop them. She grabbed Antoine anyway, hoping the small resistance she could offer would be enough to help Tyson free himself. But once again she was not prepared.

She wasn't prepared when Antoine turned on her, Tyson forgotten in the heat of his fury. She wasn't prepared when Antoine grabbed a shovel leaning against the table behind them, the same shovel she had used to fill containers with potting soil so the teenagers could learn the value of nurturing and creating in a world that had taught them to destroy.

She wasn't prepared when Antoine stepped back and slammed the shovel against the side of her head. But as she fell to the floor and her eyes closed, she *was* prepared for the darkness and the peace that eclipsed the pain and turmoil inside her.

Mary Kate McKenzie was prepared to die, and she did so with complete faith that something better waited for her in the distance.

1

"HEY MAN, YOU GOT A CIGARETTE?"

Charles Casey got out of his car and faced the boy who had asked the question. The teenager wore a Cavaliers Starter jacket and a sneer, one as well-worn as the other. "Nope," Casey said. "Not even a stub."

The kid shoved his thumbs in the pockets of his jeans in a stance Casey recognized from childhood street corners. "I bet."

"Sorry, but those things can kill you."

"Yeah? Something else'll get me first." The kid spat on the ground before he sauntered off.

Casey watched the kid for a moment before he realized he ought to lock the car. This was rural mid-America, where "delinquent" was a word the gas company stamped on an overdue bill. In the month since he had left the Big Apple, Casey's street smarts had already gotten rusty. "Welcome to Eden's Gate," he said under his breath.

He twisted his key in the lock and started toward the house where the Sisters of Redemption lived and administered the Eden's Gate Ecology Center. It was a hulking Victorian monstrosity—Second Empire, if his memory of old college lectures served him correctly. He didn't have to knock. Two more teenagers, a boy and a girl, came out the side door with a middle-aged woman between them. She smiled and held the door, and Casey entered the house through a warm, fragrant kitchen.

By the time someone showed him to the administrator's study, Casey had already gotten a feel for the house. The rooms were spacious, the furniture simple and comfortable. The atmosphere was serene, with a subtle character all its own.

As he waited for Sarah Bradshaw he went to the window to contemplate the winter-brown landscape stretching beyond the house. Contemplation was becoming Casey's closest friend. Every night when he was supposed to be sleeping, he questioned the events that had brought him so far from his home in New York. Every morning when he thought about the day stretching in front of him, he considered the decisions he had made.

In between he had plenty of time to ask himself if he had lost his mind.

"Mr. Casey? I'm sorry I've kept you waiting."

Casey turned to see an attractive woman somewhere in her late forties coming through the open door, her right hand extended. He had prepared himself to discover that the Sisters of Redemption were nothing like the nuns that had taught in the Hell's Kitchen parochial school he had attended as a boy. But Sarah Bradshaw was still a surprise. She was dressed in a dark-plum skirt with a blouse of palest lilac, and the colors perfectly complemented her ivory complexion and straight black hair with its wide silver streak.

He shook her hand. "I'm pleased to meet you, Sister." He paused at her grimace. "I'm sorry. Isn't that correct?"

"We're an informal bunch here. Just call me Sarah."

Casey stepped around a coffee table as she ushered him to a couch set at an angle from a massive rosewood desk.

The office had provided a number of clues to the woman, if he had cared to look for them. Despite the carved walnut paneling and twelve-foot ceiling with its ornate plaster frieze, the room had a no-nonsense appearance. The paired

triple-hung windows were unembellished, so that the countryside view seemed to come right into the room. Books and
photographs were the only adornments on the shelves, and
the desk was uncluttered.

Sarah seated herself beside him, which was another surprise, and fluffed the cushions behind her. "You know,
you're an answer to a prayer," she said as she settled back.

He barely suppressed a snort. "That has to be a first."

"Not a religious man, I take it?"

Since adolescence Casey had been much too busy and
much too guilty to risk crossing the threshold of a church.
"Not so that anyone would notice."

She lifted a brow. "But raised a Catholic."

His surprise must have been obvious, because she nodded.
"I can tell. No one knows what to do in the presence of a
nun. Catholics think we're judging them for every sin
they've committed, and non-Catholics remember the terrible
jokes they've heard. But you definitely look like a man hoping to escape a thousand Hail Marys."

He liked Sarah Bradshaw already. "A thousand might not
cover it. Anyway, I'm not here for confession. I want to find
out if we can come to an agreement about a feature article
for the paper."

"And that's the prayer that was answered," she said, going back to her first statement. "Some decent publicity for
Eden's Gate."

"How do you know it'll be decent?"

"Do you mean considering the publicity we've already
had? Or your background?"

He whistled softly. "Not pulling any punches, are we?"

"Sorry, but I never seem to have time for tact. Someday
I'm going to resurrect my social skills, but for now, I have
to cut to the chase. Keeping the center going is a big job."

"Some would say a big *futile* job."

"Oh, absolutely. Most of the town of Shandley Falls
would say so."

A knock sounded, followed closely by the same woman he'd seen coming out of the house. "I have tea and coffee, Sarah, and some of my shortbread."

"Wonderful." Sarah leaned forward and made a place for the tray on a table between symmetrical stacks of *Sierra* and *Utne Reader*. "Marie Bennett, this is Charles Casey."

As he murmured a polite greeting, Marie, a sandy-haired blonde, peered at Casey through thick glasses of a trendy oval design. "Better in person," she said calmly.

"Nicer, too," Sarah agreed.

"Glad to meet you, Mr. Casey." Marie turned her gaze back to Sarah. "If you want anything else, let me know. I'm on patrol this morning."

Sarah glanced at her watch. "Any problems yet?"

"Nothing worth noting."

Casey wondered if Marie meant that there was nothing worth noting in front of *him*. He listened with interest.

"No more destruction by the pond?" Sarah said.

"Everything looks peaceful. Most of the kids are washing windows in the greenhouse now." The door closed behind Marie, and Sarah bent to peek inside a white china teapot. "Coffee or tea, Mr. Casey?"

"Just Casey, please. And coffee." He didn't pause. "Tell me about the kids."

"During the school year we have a dozen or so teenagers assigned here for weekends by the juvenile court. In the summer they live and work here full-time. But I bet you knew that already." Sarah poured a cup from a taller pot and held it out to him. "I'll bet this coffee beats anything you had when you were working on *The Whole Truth*."

"The coffee at the paper's not much better." He took the cup and then a sip. "This is excellent."

"Well, we believe in quality." Sarah poured herself tea. "I hope you do, too."

"My reputation has preceded me." He tried not to smile. He was dark-haired and dark-eyed. He had been told by the only woman he'd ever loved that he had the black-hearted grin of a pirate.

"Your reputation would be hard to hide, wouldn't it? Until just a few months ago I could turn on my television five nights a week and watch you *making* your reputation."

"Or destroying it."

She watched him intently, as if trying to read his thoughts. "It all depends on perspective, doesn't it? You were very good at what you did."

"I don't do it anymore. I left *The Whole Truth* forever."

"And moved well down the career ladder to a weekly paper in Ohio where the most exciting story you'll ever encounter will be the one about this center."

Casey, who didn't want to talk about his reasons for leaving New York, realized they were back at the beginning of their conversation. "Let's talk about that."

She didn't probe any further. "We've had more than our share of bad publicity since our center was established. No, it goes even further back than that. It began when the Sisters of Redemption inherited Eden's Gate. Right from the beginning, people in Shandley Falls felt our presence could only detract from progress in the community. I'm not sure what they expected, but they did seem to feel we would change the character of the town, and they were right, of course. Because we have."

He pulled a notebook from the inside pocket of his sports coat. "You've been here one year?"

"One and a half. We spent the first six months assessing the property, improving the buildings, and working with the local zoning board, the city council." She shrugged to show that the list went on and on.

She didn't seem at all perturbed by the experience. "And then?"

"We began to put together our programs. We made arrangements to work with the local hospice. We built dormitories and opened our program for juvenile offenders during our first summer. We spent that summer fine-tuning it and publicizing our goals. And this year we've doubled the number of teens we're working with.''

''As I understand it, that means you've gone from nine kids to eighteen, which is still surprisingly few considering how many troubled kids roam the streets of Ohio. Just from glancing around the estate and the facilities, you appear to have room for many more than that.''

''Oh, we do. We hope to have up to sixty kids in the next two years, maybe more after we build new dormitories and renovate the barn as a meeting center.''

''Has that program remained small because you're still feeling your way?''

''We've remained small because we haven't yet proven ourselves.''

Casey's instincts were still intact, despite his career change. He leaned in for the kill. ''In fact, haven't you proven that there are good reasons to be concerned about safety here?''

''I suppose if we were on television, this is where you'd zoom in to find me sweating and shaking.''

Casey set down his cup, surprised to see that he'd already finished the contents. ''Are you?''

''No.'' She looked absolutely calm. ''We've had our share of trouble at Eden's Gate. That's a matter of record.''

He opened the notebook. ''Let's see. Last summer while camp was in session you had a fire in the girls' dormitory—''

''Which was immediately extinguished.''

He continued. ''A boy found with a knife on a field trip to the Cleveland zoo, a girl who accused a male counselor of attempted rape—''

''A charge she dropped immediately because it wasn't true.''

''And finally, on a Saturday in December you had a nearly fatal attack on one of your sisters which resulted in permanent brain damage.'' He flipped through his notebook until he found a fresh page and pulled out a pen. ''Am I wrong?''

''Not about the things that really matter, although some of your assumptions are incorrect.'' Sarah sipped her tea a moment, then she set down her cup. ''First, Mary Kate, the woman who was injured, was—and is—on staff, but she's not one of the sisters.''

''Really? I was told the teenagers called her Sister Sunshine.''

''Their name. Not ours. Mary Kate had been working with us for some time before she was attacked, but she'd never taken vows. As for the brain damage . . .'' Sarah looked up. ''Her recovery has been astonishing. There was a time, at the very beginning, when we were told she would never walk, talk, laugh, pray. Her heart stopped on the trip to the hospital.''

She shook her head. ''It was a very difficult time for all of us. We were advised to put her in a nursing home, but no one was willing. So we undertook her rehabilitation here, following instructions and working with her constantly. No one in the medical community was hopeful, but one day . . .'' Her voice trailed off.

''She's better, then?''

''Better?'' Her eyes widened. ''No, Casey. Nothing that mundane. Quite simply, Mary Kate is a miracle.''

Mary Kate McKenzie was not a woman to ponder the infinite. In the long months of her rehabilitation she had thought very little about things religious, and only then when she couldn't avoid them. She supposed she believed in God, or at least she had until the moment earlier that afternoon when she'd dug her first scoop of clotted brown soil and found that deep inside the earth was a kingdom of slimy, wiggling worms.

And what kind of a God wasted time making worms? Whose idea of a joke was that, anyway?

The woman pulling weeds at her side looked up and cocked her head in question at the expression on Mary Kate's face.

Mary Kate immediately forced a smile, but the woman shook her head in warning. "Don't overdo, now. I'm sure you're glad to be back in the garden, but we don't want any relapses."

Mary Kate had learned a million things in the last three months, a million things she had painfully sorted from vital to downright inconsequential. And at the top of her list was the one that told her not to argue. She wasn't glad to be back in the garden. As far as she knew she'd never been in a garden in her entire life. But she had learned by trial and error that those kinds of revelations were not productive. Or welcome.

Mary Kate drove her shovel deeper into the earth, but only so that she could lean against it. "I *am* feeling a little . . ." She searched for the right word.

"Tired?" Sister Grace Mullens got slowly to her feet. She was a thin woman, with short graying hair and a strong sense of style that could turn even denim jeans and a plaid shirt into a fashion statement.

"Well, that's to be expected." Grace put her hands on the small of her back and leaned against them. "We'll work for a little longer, then we can go inside."

Mary Kate thought about what was waiting for her inside. Simple, mind-numbing chores. More time to think. More time to remember that she didn't remember anything . . . "Not tired," she said quickly. "Excited."

"Well, we don't want you to get overexcited. There will be other pretty spring days and lots of help to get the garden ready."

"Your back's bothering you. Why don't you go in?"

Temptation flicked across Grace's tranquil face. "I don't think—"

"Really. I'd like to stay here by myself."

"Oh."

Mary Kate watched as Grace tried not to give in to her aching back, but coupled with a deeply rooted belief that solitude was a fine thing indeed, the desire to go inside was too strong to fight.

The nun tried on a tentative smile. "Okay. But you're sure you'll be all right? You're still recovering."

"I'll be fine. Go on. I'll be in later."

"If any of the teens try to bother you . . ."

"I'm not worried. This time *I'm* the one with the shovel."

Grace jerked to attention, and Mary Kate realized her own error. Two errors, actually. The statement *and* the sudden snarl in her voice. "Not that I'd use it," she added before Grace could respond.

"Mary Kate, maybe I'd better—"

"Please. I'll be fine." Mary Kate gripped the shovel handle until her knuckles were the color of the snow that hadn't yet melted at the edge of the garden pathway. "I'm almost well again. Even the doctor says my recovery is remarkable. You have to learn to trust me, Grace."

Grace looked contrite. "It's not a question of trust."

"Good. Then I'll see you later."

Mary Kate watched as a defeated Grace picked up her basket of gardening tools and wound her way through the precisely laid garden rows crusted with decomposing leaves and windblown winter trash. Fast-food wrappers hung from dried-up cornstalks and two empty cigarette packs mulched the remains of a row of asparagus, but Grace looked straight ahead and passed them by.

Mary Kate waited until the other woman had disappeared before she exhaled forcefully. "Yeeeee . . . ssss!"

Somewhere inside her there was an Irish jig, a tribal victory dance, a frenzied forties jitterbug, but Mary Kate stood perfectly still. She knew better than to tempt fate. Her body was not yet totally at her command. She still suffered bouts of dizziness and an occasional queasy stomach to go with them. Besides, the sight of her dancing in the school garden might be just the excuse the sisters needed to make her go inside.

And she never wanted to go inside again.

Against her will her eyes were drawn to the building in question, or rather the buildings. Because there was more than one building that she wished she never had to reenter. A complex stood waiting to draw her through its doors and submerge her in a life that seemed so alien, so impossible, that if she could run—and if she had a place to run to—she would race there now, screaming all the way.

The field where she stood was situated between a wide gravel driveway and a folk-art barn stenciled a generation ago with the Mail Pouch Tobacco logo. Mary Kate would bet a million dollars she had never been inside that barn before her "accident." She was absolutely certain she had never been inside *any* barn. If she had, wouldn't she be used to the rank smell? The rustle of mice running marathons in mountains of decomposing hay?

She didn't remember any of those things. Worse, she found them all disgusting and unnatural. Like earthworms. Or the huge compost pile behind the barn where the sisters faithfully took their vegetable scraps and buried them every night after the evening meal.

Then there was the Victorian nightmare that housed the center staff. Wouldn't something in the house seem familiar to her if, as the sisters claimed, she had lived there for years? If she really had been raised in that house before the sisters took it over, wouldn't she remember something? A room? A stairwell? A gable or an arch?

Beyond small stands of oaks and sycamores and out of sight of the public road stood the new dormitories that held the center's summer campers. These, too, were unfamiliar.

Yet the sisters claimed that she had nailed siding and finished drywall.

She was trapped in a life she didn't remember, in a body that was as foreign to her as the view from Mt. Everest or the smell of the Ganges on a hot summer day.

Her gaze moved slowly from the buildings to those parts of her she could see. She started at the ground, wishing she would find that something had changed in the last few minutes. She had a child's feet, probably size five on a hot day, wide little feet with stubby toes. Right now they were encased in red high-top tennis shoes and wool socks that tormented every cell of skin they touched.

Her ankles, like the denim-clad legs connected to them, were sturdy and dependable, but certainly not what she had expected to see when she examined them the first time. Her legs were short; her thighs were solid—and to her eyes, massive—and they melted into hips that were appallingly perfect for childbearing.

The news didn't get any better as she moved up the line. Her waist seemed narrow enough—but what wouldn't, compared to those hips? Unfortunately the waist was easy to evaluate since there was nothing much jutting out below her collarbone to hide it. If she ever planned to nurse a baby—and that was unlikely considering her choice of career—she had better hope the baby had a small appetite and a large supply of patience.

Her eyelids drifted shut in defeat. She knew her body without looking at it, of course. She had been looking at it for weeks, memorizing every detail. Unfortunately she also knew her face, her rust-colored hair, the relentless splotches of freckles that covered otherwise pale skin. The face belonged to a leprechaun: tilted nose, wide mouth, shamrock-green eyes. The hair was a mass of Little Orphan Annie curls.

The woman might as well be a nun, considering how little she had to offer the male of the species.

Mary Kate didn't know how long she stood that way, eyes closed, the cool spring sun seeking new patches of skin to freckle. When she opened her eyes nothing had changed, except that a crow had landed on a fence post in her line of sight, and as she watched, he flapped his wings and issued a long, raucous stream of crow curses.

She waved a fist in his direction. "Up yours!" But the crow merely preened his feathers and settled himself more firmly on the post.

She hadn't noticed the post before. Now she noticed more of them, four posts marking the corners of a huge rectangle that adjoined the center's garden. As she squinted into the sun, she noted smaller posts, little more than stakes, in between. Curious, she dragged the shovel beside her as she went to investigate.

The crow observed her approach, but didn't fly away. She wondered if they were friends, that if in addition to all the other virtues she had been told she possessed, she was a female St. Francis of Assisi who communed with wild animals. Perhaps even the barn mice were friends that shared in regular philosophical discourses about the meaning of life.

"Like hell," she muttered.

When she was only a few feet away the crow finally flapped his wings and made a graceful takeoff. As he drew closer and soared higher, something unmistakable plopped to the ground just in front of her.

Mary Kate leaned against the vacated post and tried to imagine the purpose of marking this plot of land. During the months of her recovery she had paid scant attention to the inner workings of Eden's Gate. She knew the land had been consecrated as an "eco-spirituality" center, a healing place where the earth would be respected and cared for while it nurtured those in the community who were in need.

Four sisters were in residence, and more lived in nearby Cleveland and sometimes helped with programs. The Sisters of Redemption funded Eden's Gate in the hope that one day the center would be self-sufficient. In the meantime, and in addition to their weekend and summer programs with the juvenile offenders, the sisters did outreach work in the community by visiting terminally ill patients and donating vegetables to the local food bank. In the future, they hoped Eden's Gate would become a retreat center where people in need of a closer connection to the land could live for months at a time.

They hoped for many things, apparently at least one of which had to do with the area staked out in front of her.

Mary Kate's interest waned. She couldn't rid herself of the feeling that none of this had anything to do with her. Everything she knew about Eden's Gate had been explained to her during her recovery. She had no memories and no sense of connection.

She turned away to head back to the garden when her shovel clanged against something jutting from the earth. She stooped to investigate and found a metal marker planted firmly beside the post. Squatting on the ground beside it to look more closely, she read the words inscribed in rounded script.

The Eden's Gate Community Garden, dedicated in memory of Kathleen and Patrick McKenzie by their loving daughter Mary Kate.

Mary Kate felt something rising inside her, something all too familiar and frightening. She understood the term "claustrophobia." She might not remember her short legs, her red hair, or any detail of her past life, but she did remember concepts. She didn't remember even one story about a woman who had felt trapped in her own body. Yet the panic rapidly expanding and clawing for release could only be explained that way. She was like a child locked in a dark closet, pounding on the door and pleading for someone to let her out.

"Damn it to hell! Holy shit!"

She broke out in a sweat and the cold air nearly turned it to ice on her skin. She was trembling, and if she had been standing, her legs would not have held her. The world began to spin, and a roaring filled her ears.

She struggled to control her breathing, commanding herself not to hyperventilate. She concentrated with difficulty, forcing the air in and out of her lungs in measured, even breaths, but she was still swamped with dizziness.

Her name was Mary Kate McKenzie. She was twenty-five years old. After the death of her parents she had lived in the old Victorian mansion for most of her life with an aunt and cousin. She had always been a good girl, a religious girl. No one could remember a single sin she'd ever committed. Apparently she had been born to the religious life.

The air wheezed in and out of her lungs, but she still felt as if she were falling through a black chasm, endlessly tumbling head over heels through space.

In high school she had declared her intention to be a nun. No one was surprised. By then she'd already racked up hundreds of hours as an altar girl. In college she had begun to search for the congregation where she could best use her talents. And then, just as she was starting graduate school, her cousin died, followed later by her aunt.

She clutched the ground beneath her, digging her fingernails into the dirt, worms or not. She closed her eyes and tried to envision a peaceful place, a place where she was anchored firmly to the earth and the sun was shining brightly. Someplace where she wasn't tumbling, tumbling . . .

Her aunt had left her a sizable amount of money in her will, but Eden's Gate had gone to the Sisters of Redemption, a tiny, publicity-shy congregation of nuns who were committed to changing the world. She had seen her aunt's choice as a sign from God and decided then to join the sisters in their crusade to protect the environment and pro-

vide a safe haven for teenagers who needed a second chance.

Mary Kate's heart began to slow and the world began to level. She could feel the dirt against her fingertips and the spring sunshine trying to warm her.

For some reason she didn't yet understand, she had never taken her vows. She had lived here, worked here, but never joined in fully. Then one day, in the greenhouse just down the path, she had been savagely beaten by one of the teens. For days everyone had been afraid she would never recover, but she had surprised them. She had climbed out of a coma and begun to live again.

And that's who she was.

That's who she was.

Minutes passed before the panic receded completely, leaving her with shaking hands and icy skin. She opened her eyes and took in the earth-tone canvas of an Ohio spring. Only then did she register that she was no longer alone.

"Well, if it ain't Sister Sunshine, alone in the garden."

Mary Kate's eyes followed the baggy khakis up to the Cavaliers' Starter jacket that hung from the young man's shoulders. She tilted her chin to stare at his face. White teeth gleamed against tawny brown skin, and darker brown eyes assessed her, as if scanning for any sign of weakness.

She felt for the shovel, which had fallen to the ground beside her, and wrapped her fingers around the handle before she spoke. "What are you doing here?" Her voice trembled.

"I come here on weekends during the school year. You don't remember me?"

She didn't, of course. If she couldn't remember herself, plans for this garden, or the parents to whom it had been dedicated, if she could only parrot what she'd been told over and over again, she certainly couldn't remember anyone else.

"You're not supposed to be *here*, are you?" she countered, looking around for a nun or one of the college students who worked with the teenagers to fulfill course requirements.

"Sure I am. I'm a scarecrow, come to scare *you*."

Mary Kate considered her legs and decided they were strong enough that she could stand again. She rose awkwardly to her feet. Her coordination was improving every day, but she still had a distance to go. Funny thing, but when your head got smashed with a shovel blade, it took a while to recover.

"You don't scare me." She thrust the shovel out in front of her and leaned on it the way she had before.

"No? You looked pretty scared last time I saw you."

Mary Kate tried to remember if she'd seen this student, obviously one of the court system's finest, during her recovery. Even though the sisters had tried to keep her away from the offender program during her rehabilitation, it had been impossible to keep her away from all of it. She had been reintroduced to the teens gradually.

They were a pretty pitiful bunch, but apparently next to this kid, the others were shining examples of adolescence.

"When was the last time you saw me?" Mary Kate knew there was no point in trying to pretend her memory was intact.

"Me? I was right there when Antoine hit you over the head."

"Were you?" Mary Kate looked past the boy, where a girl in a black biker's jacket was coming toward them. Behind her, another girl without a coat was struggling to catch up.

"You don't remember, do you?" the boy taunted.

"Apparently enough of you kids stood by and watched to fill in every detail." Mary Kate pulled her gaze back to the boy and saw he was smirking. Smirking because she had nearly died.

Rage exploded inside her, a powerful, cleansing rage that

made her heart pump faster again. But this time, the feeling was a heady one.

The boy nodded. ''Yeah, I stood there and watched. Stood right there.''

Rage was like life surging through Mary Kate's veins. It was so good to feel something besides confusion and panic that she reveled in it. She gripped the handle tighter and lifted the shovel off the ground to rest it against her hip. ''And you didn't do anything?''

''Sure didn't.''

Everything she'd been through flashed across her mind, at least everything she could remember. The months of recovery. The day she had first become aware of her surroundings. Her first steps. The first time she had fed herself again. And just a few moments ago, when once again—as it had far too often—the reality of her situation had overwhelmed her.

''You little prick! Why didn't you try to stop the kid before he hit me?''

''What'd you call me?''

Mary Kate heard the new menace in the boy's voice, but she didn't care. ''You heard me right!''

The first girl, a blonde with a buzz cut and a six-inch gold cross dangling from one earlobe, reached them and grabbed the boy's arm. ''Tyson, come on . . .''

''Where you think you get off calling *me* names?'' Tyson stepped forward, shaking off the girl's hand.

Mary Kate felt fury filling in the empty spaces left by the panic attack. Her breathing sped up, and this time she didn't struggle with it.

She lifted the shovel higher. ''I call it like I see it. You're not a man. A man would have stepped in and tried to stop the kid who attacked me.''

''Sister, don't talk to him like that—'' The blonde tugged at Tyson's arm again.

Mary Kate moved forward. ''No? And why not? Is Tyson

here the only one who gets to say what he wants?''

Tyson moved closer, too, but she stood her ground. ''Out!'' she ordered. ''Unless you're here to work, get out, and do it right now.''

''Or what?''

The other girl finally caught up to them. Her braided hair was as long as the other girl's was short, and her skin was darker than Tyson's. ''Tyson, come on,'' she said, grabbing his other arm. ''Break's just about over with. We don't get back, we're gonna be in trouble.''

''He's already in trouble,'' Mary Kate said, without taking her eyes off the boy. ''He's in trouble with *me*. This time I'm going to remember your name, kid, and I'll never forget it. Tyson the coward. Tyson the prick!''

''Jeez . . .'' The blonde rolled her eyes and tugged in tandem with the other girl. ''Oh, jeez! Tyson, come on. You come on right now. Remember, Sister's not right in the head. That's all. Everybody knows it.''

Mary Kate drew herself up to her full five foot one and raised the shovel in warning. ''Well, you can just tell everybody they're wrong, honey. I am not crazy. I'm royally pissed!''

''And royally dangerous.''

Mary Kate whirled at the sound of a man's voice directly behind her, and the shovel whirled with her.

He jumped back, but not in time to avoid contact. Mary Kate stumbled forward and didn't have the reflexes to catch herself. The shovel slammed into his thigh, and she fell into his arms.

ᖋ 2

AFTER CASEY HAD ASKED SARAH FOR PER-
mission to wander the grounds, she had offered him a guide,
but he had declined. From experience he knew he might
discover more alone.

*Like the feel of a shovel smacking his thigh, and the solid
weight of a young nun in his arms.*

"Let go of me!"

The nun in question splayed her hands against his chest
and shoved. Their balance had been precarious at best. Now
he completed his graceless sprawl to the cold ground and
took her with him.

"Let go of me!" She pounded his chest again, this time
from a vantage point on top of him.

He felt her squirming against him, trying to find her way
out of the tangle of arms and legs. "Drop the weapon," he
commanded, when it seemed she might hit him with it again.

She sat up, painfully pinning one of his thighs with her
rump. "What do you mean coming up behind me like
that?"

"Get . . . off . . . me . . . now!"

She scrambled to her feet, but he could have sworn the
parting bounce that drove his thigh farther into the ground
was deliberate. He rolled to his side and ran his hand down
his hip. "If this is the way you ladies deal with kids, no
wonder no one wants to send them here."

"So what's your point?"

He massaged his thigh while he contemplated her red basketball sneakers, which hadn't been in fashion for years. "I used to get my knuckles rapped with a ruler. You've escalated."

His gaze traveled up her denim-clad legs. The shovel-wielder wore shapeless overalls over a man's wool shirt and a scowl squashing a face best suited to a County Cork calendar.

"You won't like the next stage." She slowly folded her arms across her chest, as if the movement had to be carefully planned before execution.

"Let me guess. Public floggings." Wincing, he sat up and looked around. The teenagers had fled—which said something about their good sense.

"Listen, who are you, and why were you sneaking up on me?"

Despite the way she bit off her words, Casey thought she really might be shaken up. "I was exploring the grounds, and I thought I'd see what you were doing. I got here just in time to hear you threaten that boy. I talked to him earlier."

"Yeah? If I was feeling stronger, I'd have swatted him."

"Why?"

"To give him a taste of his own medicine."

He had a sudden, impossible thought. He had heard the blonde call her *Sister*, but . . . "You're not—"

"Sane?" She pushed a hand through a riot of auburn curls. "God, no. The kids were right. I'm probably as nutty as a fruitcake."

"You're Mary Kate?"

Her frown deepened. "So they tell me."

"Well." Casey got to his feet and dusted off his pants. "Mary Kate."

"How do you know me?"

"Not by your halo, that's for sure."

"What's that supposed to mean?"

Casey thought about his conversation with Sarah Bradshaw. This was Mary Kate McKenzie. In the flesh. Very much in the flesh, as a matter of fact, since this woman seemed to have nothing remotely spiritual about her.

"I was just talking to Sarah about you," he said. "She seems to think you're something of a miracle. I was expecting someone who could turn water into wine."

She had never stopped frowning. Now he was afraid if she frowned any harder the lines would be permanent. "You look familiar. Have we met before?"

Casey knew why he looked familiar. Sarah had told him a lot about Mary Kate, including the fact that she had watched hours of television every day during her recovery. Apparently Mary Kate had been drawn to news shows, *The Whole Truth* among them.

The best part of Casey knew he ought to tell this woman who he was immediately, but the best part of him had never gotten much exercise. "We haven't met," he said.

She didn't look convinced. "What are you doing here?"

"I'm the managing editor of the local newspaper, *The Cricket*." He still couldn't believe his name was on a masthead with an insect. "We're planning to do a feature on the center. I was just taking a look around."

"Since when do editors write their own stories?"

"Since this one took a job at a one-horse weekly with more part-time than full-time staff." Casey knew he was about to lose her. The frown was disappearing, but the suspicious gleam in her eyes was not. "Sarah supports the idea of a little good publicity," he said.

She didn't respond.

"The center's had its share of bad public relations," he continued. "She's hoping I'll turn that around."

"What's your lead? Staff member goes after delinquent with shovel?"

"Unless I find something better."

She looked suddenly tired and pale, as if all the spirit he'd witnessed was draining away. "I've caused them enough trouble."

Mary Kate McKenzie was not pretty. She was, at best, cute, something Casey despised in a woman. She had a small athletic body best suited for turning flips and cartwheels to international applause. Her skin was pale, and her eyes were wide and childlike. Only her Kewpie-doll mouth hinted at thoughts and feelings unbecoming to a nun. But even though he didn't find Mary Kate one bit attractive, with her temper fading, the vacant look in her clear green eyes was disturbing, as if the woman herself was disappearing.

Luckily Casey was both adept and experienced at pushing down his better instincts. "Look, why were you going after that boy? You said he needed a taste of his own medicine. He's not the one who attacked you, is he?"

"No. They tell me that kid's locked up somewhere and won't be back. This one watched me get clobbered and didn't lift a finger to help."

"They tell you?" Casey picked up the shovel. He tossed it from hand to hand, then, after weighing the perils, presented it to her.

She reached for it with a hand that wasn't quite steady. "Apparently Sarah forgot to mention that I'm a miracle with a flaw. Yes sirree, folks, she walks, she talks, she crawls on her belly like a reptile. She just doesn't remember anything from before the attack. She's a one-hundred-percent gen-u-ine sideshow freak."

"Bummer."

Mary Kate shrugged. "I suppose. But how would I know? Since I can't remember anything, this feels perfectly normal."

He was more intrigued by the moment and surprised Sarah hadn't warned him. "Nothing?"

"Forget it. I'm not an interview waiting to happen."

He did his best to look sympathetic. "Too bad. I'm sure

a lot of our readers would be touched, maybe even changed by your story."

A spark of spirit returned. "You're pretty good. Is that from a textbook on how to con the brain-dead?"

He tried a slightly different tactic. "I can't even imagine what it must be like not to remember the simplest things."

"Well . . . I do remember some things."

"Do you?"

"Like how to tell when someone's trying to screw around with my head."

Beneath the perky exterior dwelled a woman with a certain amount of savvy. Casey acknowledged defeat. "I'll quit for now."

"What did you say your name was?"

"Casey."

"And a last name?"

"Casey."

"Casey Casey." She shook her head. "A mother with no imagination."

"Just call me Casey. Everyone does."

She frowned again, as if her muddled brain was trying to make a vital connection. He pressed his advantage—while he still could. "Sarah promised me a guide, but I decided to take off alone. Look where it got me."

"I'm sure you usually have better luck."

He grinned. If wheedling hadn't gotten him anywhere, the grin might. "Why don't you be my guide? Unless . . ."

She raised an eyebrow that was one shade darker than her hair.

"Unless you still don't know enough about this place to be helpful," he finished.

"Challenges, challenges."

"Will you show me around? I promise not to dig for information. Just show me whatever you feel like. I'll behave."

"I'm sure that'll be a first." She thrust the shovel into

the ground hard enough to make him glad he wasn't standing any closer. "Do you know there are worms living under
here?"

He stared at her.

She shook her head, as if to clear it. "All right, Casey
Casey. You're on. Where would you like to start?"

If Mary Kate had little religion left in her soul, she had
even less poetry. But though her own peculiar situation consumed almost every thought, the beauty of Eden's Gate still
managed to touch her. The estate embraced an assortment
of landscapes and environments, one hundred and thirty
acres of meadows and fields, forests, orchards, and wetland.
She was sure her ancestors must have chosen the location
for its variety. Best of all, they had preserved it with care.

Casey stayed beside her as she trudged along a path
through the center of the estate. From time to time as she
pointed out landmarks she glanced at him to see if he was
growing impatient with her slow progress, but he seemed
reconciled.

Their path was bordered on both sides by a meadow
which dipped lower and turned marshy with cattails and flag
iris as they approached the pond. She had been told the
meadow was beautiful in the summer when it was ablaze
with native wildflowers, and the pond was a birdwatcher's
paradise. Sarah was fond of saying that the house was the
mind of Eden's Gate, but the pond was surely its heart.

By the time they stopped she was so exhausted she leaned
against a tree to catch her breath.

Casey stood beside her. "Tell me about Eden's Gate.
Who owned it?"

Mary Kate only knew what she'd been told, but by now
that had been committed to memory. "My mother's family.
My great-great-grandfather was a railroad tycoon in Cleveland. This was his summer home. He entertained lavishly,
which is why the house is so large. Over the decades it

deteriorated, but the family saw to the biggest concerns, so by the time the sisters inherited it, it was still structurally sound.''

"Your family?"

She heard his surprise. She'd been surprised to discover it herself. "I grew up here. I lived with an aunt and cousin. They're both dead now."

"And your parents?"

"They died when I was little."

"I'm sorry."

She thought about the garden marker. *In memory of Kathleen and Patrick McKenzie by their loving daughter Mary Kate.* She felt nothing but an increased sense of alienation. No sadness. No longing. "I guess *I* should be sorry, too. Only I can't remember any of them, so at this point my life's just a story about strangers."

"One of the unheralded benefits of memory loss."

She appreciated his casual attitude. She hated to be treated like a freak. "My aunt inherited Eden's Gate from her parents. And when she died she left it to the sisters."

Mary Kate could almost hear Casey's brain turning that one around. "No story there," she assured him. "Apparently when my grandparents died my aunt got the estate and my mother inherited their investments, which now belong to me. My aunt left me money as well. I'll never starve."

"Do you know why your aunt left the estate to the Sisters of Redemption?"

"My cousin Tim was a troubled kid. He ran away from home when he was sixteen, and the next time my aunt saw him was at the morgue. She never really recovered. She was a religious woman, so when she died she left Eden's Gate to the sisters with the condition that they find a way to use it that would benefit troubled kids like Tim. She wanted this to be a place where kids could have a second chance to make a new life for themselves. The Sisters of Redemption are known for taking on lost causes."

"Lost causes?"

"You saw those kids in the garden."

"You're not saying they're lost, are you?"

She heard the reporter at work, but she didn't care. "I wish that kid Tyson would *get* lost. Preferably somewhere on another planet."

"Very unchristian of you, Sister Sunshine."

"Don't call me that. Not if you want me to guide you back."

"A real zinger, huh?"

She gazed up at him through narrowed eyes and saw he was struggling not to smile. "In case you haven't noticed, I'm not exactly the Singing Nun. The sunshine beaming in my soul must have gone under a cloud during my recovery."

"I'm sorry."

"Right. I can see that." She cocked her head. "You're pretty darned sure of yourself, aren't you? You know what? I can't help feeling I was that way once upon a time. Even though I can't remember. But try getting your brain reorganized, then see how confident you are."

He was no longer struggling with a smile. "I know. But maybe you really are something of a miracle, because I forgot how tough this must be for you. I just find it interesting, and you . . ."

Mary Kate pushed her hair back from her forehead. "What do you find me?"

"Funny. Brave. Cocky."

"Was that multiple choice?"

"Try all of the above."

Her bluster seeped away. "Sorry, but you've got 'cocky' sewed up."

"I'll share."

"I'll bet you don't share often. I'll bet under that charming smile you're as ruthless as a pirate."

He looked surprised, more surprised than the casual comment warranted. "A pirate?"

"If the peg leg fits . . ."

He seemed to be considering that. "Maybe I was ruthless. Once upon a time."

"And now?"

His lips twisted into something even more cynical. "Just burned out."

"You'll burn in again."

"Is that a sisterly pep talk?"

"You've got the wrong girl. I've got no pep worth talking about."

Mary Kate had forgotten more than she remembered, but she hadn't forgotten what made a man good-looking. This man had it all. Thick dark hair with just the suggestion of a wave. Penetrating coal-black eyes. A lean face and rock-hard jaw. He had just the hint of a cleft in his chin, and when he smiled he could probably induce most women to commit any number of sins.

But he wasn't smiling when he turned away to examine the view.

"Not too bad, is it?" she said.

"Not exactly Central Park, but it'll do."

"City boy, huh?"

"Born and raised. But this really is beautiful." He was quiet a moment. "Of course not everybody likes what you've done with the place."

She wanted to sink to the ground. She had overdone it, just as Grace had warned her she might. "You don't give up, do you?"

"Why don't you tell me what you know about the problems the sisters are having with the community."

"I'm sure you already know what they are. We've found a few small trees toppled. Signs of displeasure more than anything else. Obviously not everyone is happy with the way we're using the property. This is a conservative area, and preaching environmental awareness and bringing troubled kids into the community aren't going to win popularity contests.''

"You seem to know a lot about it."

"I'm like a computer after a power surge. I've been relentlessly reprogrammed. Everything's up and running, except that even the sisters can't make me remember the things they never knew in the first place." She hesitated. "Or what I thought and felt."

He turned back to smile at her. "You'd better be careful. This is sounding like an interview."

"*You'd* better be careful. I've got easy access to a bunch of juvenile delinquents who'd do anything I ask for a little pocket change."

He laughed, and she liked the sound of it. His laugh was as deep as his voice, a rumble with a dark velvet edge. She found herself almost smiling. The panic attack seemed far behind her, even though a touch of dizziness still lingered.

"We can walk a little farther around the pond if you'd like, then head back toward the garden," she said.

"You know, I hate to say this, but you're looking pale. Are you all right?"

She was determined not to coddle herself. "I'm still recovering. I just put one foot in front of the other and keep going. That's the only way I'm going to outdistance this thing."

"Are you sure you aren't pushing yourself too hard?"

"I'm okay. I—" She frowned and looked beyond Casey. "Damn it, look at that."

He turned to see what she was pointing at. "Not your handiwork, I take it?"

In the water at the pond's edge, nearly hidden by fallen logs, were half a dozen plastic garbage bags. "That's one of the ways the locals show their displeasure," Mary Kate said. "They use the pond as a garbage dump."

"What are you doing about it?"

"Turning the other cheek. Cleaning up after them." She ground out the words.

"Not your personal solution, I take it."

"The only reason I'd ever turn my cheek is to find out who's sneaking up behind me."

"You were right. You're not the Singing Nun."

"I'd better get those bags out of there before one of them bursts. If it hasn't already."

"You're not in any shape to be hauling trash."

"No? I'm not in any shape to watch the pond turned into a sewer by a bunch of rednecks, either."

"You rest. I'll do it."

"We'll both do it." She picked her way down to the shore, and after a few seconds, Casey started after her.

"Have you made any attempt to discover who's doing this?"

She searched her memory, which was not the lengthy process it should have been. "I don't know I . . ." Finally she shrugged. "Can't help you."

"I might be able to help *you*."

"What do you mean?"

He was silent so long she knew he was turning over something in his mind. "Just that I'm a good investigator, that's all. I can probably find out who dumped this here."

"Go get 'em, tiger. We've got better things to do than clean up somebody else's garbage."

"Can I get my car down here?"

"No problem." She pointed to the other side of the pond. "You can come in over there and follow the road around to this side. I'm sure that's how the garbage arrives."

"Then we'll pull the bags out and set them up on the bank. I'll be back for them."

"You're going to sort through them?"

"Yeah. After I've had a few stiff drinks."

"Better you than me."

The bags were just far enough out into the water that they

couldn't be reached by leaning over and hauling them to shore. Mary Kate looked at the murky shallows which were still ice-encrusted in patches. She was in overalls, and Casey wore dress slacks.

With a sigh she balanced on one foot and untied a sneaker.

"You're not going in?" he said.

"What choice do I have?" Actually she did have a choice, and she knew it. She didn't have to go in after the bags. She wasn't even sure what compelled her to. But from everything she'd been told about herself, she was that kind of gal. A regular Girl Scout.

She removed the second shoe and both her socks, then began to roll her overalls to her knees. "I'll be in and out in a flash."

He didn't argue, but he looked skeptical as she waded into the water, skeptical and worried. She had prepared herself for the worst, but even so the water temperature was a shock. She gasped as her feet sank into the mud just below the surface. Three feet out the water was halfway up her calf, but she was able to reach the first bag. She lifted it, struggling as the water and mud sucked at it, then she slung it toward the shore. Casey grabbed it and carried it up the bank.

She was sure her feet were turning blue, but she continued tossing the bags to Casey until only one was left. Mary Kate reached for it triumphantly, but when she lifted it from the water, the bag split open and a week's worth of rotten kitchen scraps spilled into the water. The air filled with a smell like fermenting cabbage. Mary Kate got one big whiff before she ordered herself not to breathe, but it was too late.

Nausea welled inside her, followed by a wave of dizziness so strong that for a moment, she thought she might just pass out. She bent her head and the world twirled around her.

"Don't move, I'm coming."

She opened her eyes and saw Casey kicking off his shoes.

Before he could launch himself and ruin his pants, she turned and scrambled back up to the bank and away from the smell. Then, mindless of where she was and who she was with, she plopped down on the ground and rested her head on her knees.

In the shadow of the barn Casey shot Mary Kate a concerned glance. "You're sure you're okay?"

Mary Kate sucked in cold air and followed it with more. Both the dizziness and nausea had passed, and the only thing wrong with her now was frozen feet. "I've been told to expect these kinds of episodes once in a while. Head injuries are unpredictable."

"It must be hard to forgive the kid who hit you."

She heard the reporter at work again. "I'm not sorry he's in jail. From what I can tell, jail is the next logical step for most of our boys."

"Not a fan of young men, I take it?"

Strangely Mary Kate suspected she was a big fan of men in general. She wasn't sure when she had first noticed her fascination. At the beginning of her recovery it had seemed perfectly normal to her. The male doctors and physical therapists had been entertaining and energizing, much more so than the women who cared for her. But several weeks had passed before she realized that none of the men she'd met during her recovery made her feel like a nun. Not even the parish priest, who badly needed a hair transplant and cataract surgery. Her own reaction was a great source of mystification. How could a woman who thrived so completely on male attention ever have considered living her life without them?

She looked up and realized Casey was still waiting for an answer. "Not these young men."

"When I was their age I was in trouble so deep I could hardly see over it."

"When I was their age I was apparently plotting to become the next Mother Teresa."

"Sarah says there's been a conscientious attempt to admit anyone here, regardless of religion or background, if the sisters think they can help. Do they help, do you think?"

"Is that a trick question?"

"It's an honest question. I won't quote you."

"I'm afraid I'm the wrong person to ask. But I can tell you they've helped me."

"How?"

"They brought me back to life. They worked with me, prayed over me, fed me, bathed me." She flashed him a smile. "Put up with me . . ."

He frowned at her, his brows drawn together so tightly they looked like a woolly worm.

"Something wrong?" she said.

He seemed to realize why she'd asked. His brow smoothed. "Uh, no."

"Come on. I can spot a liar a mile away."

"It's just that you reminded me of somebody then."

"Oh?"

"An old friend."

"Better than an old enemy."

"Those dimples. When you smiled . . ."

She doubted she would remind him of the friend again, since smiling was something she only did at great intervals. "I guess we're done. You've already seen the garden area."

"Sarah told me that before the attack you were in charge of it."

"She's told me the same thing."

"I gather it's not your idea of a good time?"

"You gather correctly."

"What are your plans for spring?"

Now that Mary Kate had seen a marker dedicating an entirely new garden, she wondered the same thing. "Last year I helped the campers raise most of the center's produce.''

''And that's why you were working outside today? You're planning to do the same thing this year?''

''If I stay.''

''If?''

She wished she hadn't been so honest. ''They tell me I was quite the little entrepreneur before I got broadsided. We sold our excess produce at the Saturday market in town, and I turned the garden into a lesson on the capitalist system. I'm sure my fans among the teens were legion.''

''*If* you stay?''

She stopped and folded her arms. Somehow she had known that he wouldn't let that go by. ''That's right.''

''Where would you go?''

That was the problem, of course. She wasn't fully recovered. She still had problems with her coordination. She had panic attacks, tremors, nausea and headaches, erratic fits of temper, and the granddaddy of all memory losses. She had an entire lifetime to reclaim.

And who was to say that leaving was what she really wanted, anyway? Years ago she had committed herself to the sisters, even though she hadn't yet taken any vows. Apparently she had dreamed of being a nun since she was a little girl, even if she couldn't remember it. She was alone in the world except for these women. How could she walk out on the life she had known before to a life outside this estate that would surely be strange and frightening and terribly, terribly lonely?

''I don't know.'' She looked up at Casey, who was nearly a head taller than she was. ''I don't know anything. I'm an empty shell. Nothing feels right.''

She saw compassion in his eyes, and for just the briefest moment she felt a real connection to him. But it was the connection of one old friend to another. Mary Kate realized she had finally found a man who didn't twist her insides into knots. She wasn't sure about the rest of this day, but that much, at least, was positive.

She looked away. ''Don't you dare put that in your paper.''

''You can count on it.''

''I suppose I'm not going anywhere. I suppose this *is* my life, whether I remember it or not.''

''Don't you think you should take all of this one step at a time?'' He rested his hand on her shoulder.

She looked up again, her eyes narrowed. She was sick of being someone other people felt sorry for.

He lifted his hand, as if he'd realized his mistake. ''Why don't you show me the inside of the barn? It looks like a real classic. Then I'll let you go.''

''The barn?''

''Sarah says it's your headquarters. We'll just walk through. I might do a feature on historic structures in the county.''

''Can you stand the excitement?'' She started toward the door, grimly putting one leg in front of the other. As they passed the garden area she retrieved the shovel to put it away.

The barn really was quite spectacular, a huge hardwood structure of deteriorating red, capped with a gambrel roof of slate shingles. The Mail Pouch logo—*Chew Mail Pouch Tobacco. Treat Yourself to the Best*—which was fading slowly into obscurity, adorned the side closest to the road.

''This is a barn,'' she said, waving her arm to encompass the whole structure.

''That much I can see.''

''I'll tell you what I know about it. It smells. It's filled with rotting hay, and there are so many mice they've put up 'No Vacancy' signs. If we could just market cobwebs, the sisters would live in relative splendor. And we keep it locked up tight because one kid with a grudge and a cigarette lighter could turn it to ashes.''

"It's not locked now." Casey pointed to an open padlock hanging from a safety hasp.

"I was probably supposed to fasten it after I put away the shovel." She made her way to the large door and pushed it open. Light streamed inside and she heard an inevitable rustling. "The world is just filled with nasty little creatures, isn't it?"

Something too close to a chuckle sounded from Casey's throat. She ignored him, peering into the interior until her eyes adjusted. Casey moved past her, stepping inside to gaze around. Stalls lined the walls, ten of them on each side. Above them, parallel hay lofts jutted toward the wide aisle running down the middle.

"Seen enough?" she asked. "We keep the tools over there. And Mary Kate had her office—" She stopped, hoping he wouldn't notice what she'd just said. But, of course, he did.

"Do you usually talk about yourself in the third person?"

"No." She often thought about herself that way, though. "*I* had an office over there. Somebody said it used to be a tack room in the days when my forebears kept horses here."

"An office?"

"Incredible, huh? It sounds like I was hoping the kids would come here and confide in me. A country counseling center, maybe. I drew up elaborate plans for the future, kept books on gardens and animal husbandry. I have an agricultural degree." She couldn't help the next remark. "Do you believe it?"

"Apparently you don't."

She remembered so many things that were part of the everyday world, but nothing that was particular to the world of Mary Kate McKenzie. Her vocabulary was good. Her math skills were adequate. She had a general knowledge of the way the world worked and, to some extent, why. She knew what behavior was appropriate and what behavior wasn't—even when she was engaging in it. She remembered songs and movie plots. She recognized political leaders, entertainment figures—

Entertainment figures. She stepped closer to Casey and squinted up at him.

"Something wrong?" he asked.

"You never did tell me your first name."

He hesitated just long enough to confirm her suspicion. "My God, you're *Charles* Casey, aren't you? Of *The Whole Truth*? *That's* why you looked familiar. I've seen you on television."

"Frequently, I'm told."

"Charles Casey . . ." She moved even closer. "Here? You lied about being on the newspaper? What's going on?"

"I didn't lie. I quit television."

"Oh, come on! No chance. No one quits television to take over a stupid little weekly paper like *The Cricket*."

He forced a smile, but his tension showed. "Watch it, you're attacking my livelihood."

"I don't believe you."

"Look, maybe it sounds impossible to you, but it happened."

"Why?"

"I wanted a change."

"Well, boy, did you ever get one."

"Can we talk about the barn?"

"Why didn't you tell me who you were?" She watched him roll answers around in his head. "Did you think I'd faint with admiration?"

"If I did I'd say I was dead wrong."

"I don't like people hiding things from me. My whole life's one big fu—" She caught herself. She was working on cleaning up a vocabulary that astonished the sisters with its color and variety. She couldn't remember one detail about her life, but she could put a rapper to shame.

"My life's one big puzzle I have to unravel. I don't need more secrets," she finished.

"Look, some people can't seem to get past who I used to be. Okay? I'm sorry. I should have realized it wasn't fair not to set you straight at the beginning."

"You're right about that."

"It's just that Sarah said you used to watch *The Whole Truth* a lot."

In the weeks of Mary Kate's recovery she had hardly missed an episode. She had found it mesmerizing, more so than any other show, but she wasn't going to tell him. She cocked her head, her eyes narrowed into slits. "That doesn't have anything to do with this—"

"Mary Kate, I'm not with *The Whole Truth* anymore. I quit. I wasn't fired. I quit, and I'm not going back. I have no interest in helping them with future stories. I'm finished with that kind of show. Done. Fed up."

She wanted to ask him more. This was information she couldn't quite process. Charles Casey had had a wonderful job, an important job, and he'd given it up to come to out-back Ohio and write about barns and nuns and kindergarten registration.

She opened her mouth to say more when she heard a giggle.

Casey went still at exactly the same moment.

The tension between them evaporated. She put a finger to her lips, and they stood silently, listening.

Something rustled in the hay loft to their left. Something larger than a mouse, larger than an owl.

"All right," she shouted into the space above her. "Get down here now, or I'm coming up after you."

"Your counseling technique leaves a little bit to be desired, don't you think?" Casey said softly.

"I mean it," she shouted, ignoring him. "Right now this is between you and me, but in one minute I'm going to call for help."

"You have a phone in here?" Casey said.

She pulled a compact walkie-talkie from the pocket of

her overalls and waved it in his face. "This is not Boy Scout camp. If there were any questions about that before, the sisters got their answer when I almost died."

The rustling grew louder, then two hay-dusted forms rose from the farthest haystack.

"Tyson. I should have known." Out of nowhere the girl's name came to her, as it hadn't in the garden. "And Lola."

"Definitely better without the black leather," Casey said.

"Hey, what's happening?" Tyson called down to them. "You and the man looking for a place to do the nasty, Sister Sunshine? More than one stack of hay here."

Casey stuck his hands in his pocket and craned his neck to see better. "If you have a walkie-talkie, why were you about to take a shovel to this kid?" he asked Mary Kate.

"Because hitting him with the walkie-talkie wouldn't have been nearly as satisfying." She stepped forward and pointed to the ground in front of her. "Come down here, you two."

"We're not done talking," Tyson said. "You're interrupting a conversation. Nobody ever told you that's rude?"

"That's all we were doing," Lola said. "Really, Sister. We just needed to find a place where we could talk. Then we hid when we heard you coming."

Casey was right, the girl *had* taken off her black leather jacket. But that did appear to be all she had taken off. Still, anyone truly adept at the art of stripping for a quickie would also be adept at dressing in record time.

"Why don't you come down here," Casey said. "So we can talk."

"Why should we?" Tyson said.

Mary Kate felt her temper rising again, but before she could answer, Casey took another step forward. "How would you like to be in the newspaper?"

Tyson put his fists against his chest, Tarzan style. "Why? You need a centerfold stud?"

"I'm doing an article about the center. I need some kids I can talk to."

"You won't like nothing we've got to say."

Casey gave an artless grin. "You're talking to a journalist here. We thrive on the things no one else likes to hear."

Mary Kate waited for Tyson to throw back the next rejoinder, but for a second he seemed stumped. Just long enough for Lola to cut in.

"You're going to kick us out of the program, aren't you?" Obviously she was addressing the question to Mary Kate. "You're just looking for an excuse to get Tyson now, aren't you? Because of what happened to you."

Mary Kate tossed that around in her battered head for a moment. Most of her thought that revenge was a perfectly acceptable motive for going after Tyson, but some tiny, better part of her wasn't quite in tune. "You're not supposed to be in the barn," she said, compromising.

"There's no place anybody can be alone when we're here! It's like a prison. We don't get any free time at all."

"No, it's not," Tyson said. "In prison, you get to play basketball."

"So free time is an issue," Casey said, as if he was really going to put that in his article.

"Shut up, man!" Tyson shouted. "You don't care. Don't pretend like you do."

Mary Kate opened her mouth to respond, but Casey beat her. "Did I say I gave a damn? No, I said I work for a newspaper and I'm looking for a story."

"I'll give you a story." Tyson started for the ladder. "I'm being brainwashed by a bunch of prissy-ass nuns who think they know what it's like where I come from. Like they know who I am."

"And they don't?" Casey said.

Tyson turned his back to them and took the rungs two at a time. Mary Kate's fingers wrapped around the walkie-talkie. She was sorry she'd left her shovel at the door.

"Nobody here knows nothing. Place I come from's like a war zone. And back on my street, I'm the general," Tyson said as he descended.

"Got any good battle scars?" Casey asked.

"You want to see scars?" Tyson strode toward them and pulled open his shirt, nearly taking off the buttons in his haste. A ten-inch trophy zigzagged from one shoulder to his breastbone, the product of a knife and murderous intent. "That answer your question?"

Casey's hand went to his tie, and he pulled it loose. Then, as Tyson watched, he unfastened the top six buttons of his shirt and spread it wide. "Hell's Kitchen, summer of 1980. I was fourteen."

Mary Kate turned to stare at Casey's chest. The scar wasn't as long as Tyson's, but it was even more jagged and carved closer to the heart. The chest itself—and she couldn't help noticing—was hard as a rock.

"There were a few times when I wished a bunch of prissy-assed nuns would brainwash me, even if I'd ended up in a place like this," Casey said. "This place might feel like prison, but I don't see anybody trying to kill you. Except maybe Mary Kate here. I'd stay out of her way."

Tyson was silent. Lola, who had maneuvered her way down the ladder in a skirt that was inches shorter than it ought to be, joined them.

"I meant what I said. I'd like to talk to you about the program," Casey said. "Both of you."

A woman's voice sounded from the barn doorway. "I think that can be arranged."

Mary Kate turned and saw Sarah coming toward them.

"We've been searching all over for you two," Sarah said to Tyson and Lola. "Your counselors are frantic. You're not supposed to be in here, and you're not doing your jobs."

"Barn door wasn't locked. That looked like an invitation to me," Tyson said.

Sarah folded her arms. "Mary Kate?"

"I didn't think to lock the door before I left the area," Mary Kate said. She weighed her next comment while she battled with herself. Then she grimaced. "I don't think anything was going on except conversation."

"You can't skip your work assignments without some consequences," Sarah told the two teenagers. "Go back to the greenhouse right now and apologize to your counselors. We'll talk at the end of the day."

Mary Kate waited for Tyson to refuse. Lola took his arm, and though he hesitated, he finally turned and started for the open doorway.

The kids were gone before Sarah spoke again. "You handled that with skill, Mr. Casey. He was spoiling for a fight."

Casey buttoned his shirt. "I've been where he's been. Only the streets are a lot meaner now than they were fifteen years ago."

"You understood what he was feeling."

Casey shrugged as he pulled his tie back into place.

"Tyson has an extraordinary IQ, and he's a talented artist. His caseworker tells me he wrote an entire screenplay for his last English assignment and illustrated it with his own drawings. And he did it in a week's time."

"Why do I think something's coming?" Casey said.

"You developed great instincts on the streets of Hell's Kitchen. I'll get right to the point. We've decided to put together a newsletter, and we want the teenagers to write it. We want you to come to Eden's Gate and teach them how. That's part of the reason I was so enthusiastic about your article. I was hoping you'd live up to my expectations. You're a celebrity, and the kids will relate to you. You're exactly what we need to get their attention."

"I'm not a celebrity anymore, and I'm not a teacher."

"You don't fool me. I was raised on the streets of Grosse Pointe." She smiled, and her attractive face lit up. "Casey, we need you here, and you need us."

"What on earth does that mean?" Mary Kate said. As far

as she could tell the only thing this self-confident man needed was to run the other way.

"It means for Casey what it means for you, Mary Kate."

"And that is?" Casey said.

"Let's just say I have you pegged. Like Mary Kate you're at a crossroads in your life. You need what we can give you. A chance to make a difference. A chance to pass on everything you've had to learn the hard way."

"All that?" Casey said, a smile twisting his hard mouth into something much softer.

"All that and something more."

"And what would that be?"

"This center is an answer to a prayer you haven't even prayed. Come here, work with us, and find yourself again. I promise, you don't have anything to lose except your heart."

$\backsim 3$

THE SISTERS OF REDEMPTION WERE RENE-
gades among the many congregations of nuns who taught
and healed and prayed for the sins of the world. They had
never been a high-profile community. From their conception
they had preferred to stay out of sight, doing good in the
world in their own way and according to their unique and
ever-changing talents. They lived in the inner city, in tiny
third-world villages or refugee camps, and always in
communion with leaders of other faiths.

The sisters adhered faithfully to the basic tenets of Ca-
tholicism, taking the standard vows of chastity, poverty, and
obedience, but even before Vatican II their interpretations
of those vows had been slightly unconventional. They were
encouraged to give their opinions, to educate themselves on
important issues, and to stand up for what they believed in,
even when they were in the minority.

Mary Kate had given her opinion with great volume when
Sister Grace had come to her on Monday with the suggestion that she see a new doctor about her continuing dizzy
spells. She was still giving her opinion on Tuesday afternoon, even as she donned a skirt and blouse for the trip into
Shandley Falls.

"I really don't want to do this, Grace. I've been poked
and prodded enough for one lifetime, don't you think?"
Mary Kate held the skirt away from her thighs. "Didn't I

have any taste at all? Why didn't you take me in hand?" The two-piece outfit was a moldy-colored paisley print, shapeless and a foot too long.

"You never had even the slightest interest in clothes. I have a belt that might help. Want me to get it?"

Mary Kate bunched the fabric and grimaced. "Nothing's going to help. But thanks anyway."

"The doctor's just another precaution. Another opinion. We want you to recover everything. Your balance. Your memory—"

"My temper?"

Grace wandered to the window. "We're hoping."

Mary Kate's room was in the attic, with a slanted roof and a gabled window that looked out over the greenhouse and fields that were slowly turning green as the earth warmed and the spring rains fell. The boys' dorm was visible through a thicket of trees; the road to the east was visible beyond another.

The view was lovely but the rest of the room was plain. She owned very little. A small outdated tape player, an impressive selection of antique overalls and jeans, a dozen hardbound volumes on organic gardening and horticultural therapy.

She had three photographs in narrow metal frames which were displayed on her dresser. One of her cousin Tim in the happy days before he discovered drugs. One of her mother and father on their wedding day, and another of herself in her mother's arms, taken some years before her parents were killed in a plane crash. As she had recovered she had searched in vain for more photographs and memorabilia, but apparently the pre-battered Mary Kate had believed that ties to her past weren't important and had disposed of them. The clues to the woman she had been were few and far between. In too many ways it was as if she had no past at all.

The room itself was painted a soft violet-gray with warm ivory trim, and a circular rag rug covered most of the maple floor. She supposed the room had once housed a maid or housekeeper. It was cold when the wind blew and promised to be hot in the summer. The distance to the closest bathroom was far enough to make planning essential.

The day she had been able to climb the stairs by herself and move back into the room had been a momentous one. She had spent her recovery on the first floor, close to the room the sisters used as a chapel. Someone had always been with her, and as she had slowly gotten better she had longed for privacy. She'd had precious little solitude to try to put her thoughts back together. Someone had always been there to explain things, to help teach her what to do next, what to think, and what to say. The shadowy memories that still lived in her head had faded farther and farther away as the good-hearted nuns tried desperately to give her a life again.

Only she could swear it wasn't her own life they'd given her.

"You've got the best scenery and the chilliest room in the house . . ." Grace turned away from admiring the countryside and picked up the photograph of Mary Kate as a child. "You look a little like your mother. Same hair. Same dimples."

"Dimples?" Casey had mentioned her dimples, too. Mary Kate couldn't remember ever smiling at herself in a mirror.

"They're as deep as a well when you smile, which isn't often these days." Grace set down the photograph. "You used to smile all the time."

Since the room was too small for a chair, Mary Kate had plopped down on her bed to pull on sensible leather shoes. "Good old Sister Sunshine."

"Actually the kids are calling you Sister Tornado now."

"Creative little bas—" Mary Kate stopped herself. "Tell me, did I ever like teenagers, Grace? Because I can't remember having one warm thought about them since I . . ." She shrugged. "Woke up."

"Before the beating you were the most caring, most accessible, most positive person here." A heartbeat passed, then another. Grace finished with a sigh. "The kids hated you for it."

For once Mary Kate couldn't think of a response.

Grace folded her hands. "They couldn't believe you were real. They couldn't connect. They did everything they could to get a rise out of you. You were much more successful in your other work."

"Why are you telling me this?"

"Well, I've been thinking. You remember so little—"

"I remember *nothing*."

"All right. Nothing. And I think if I were in your situation, I'd long for all the things I'd had before. I'd build up a story in my head about how wonderful life was and how terrible it is now. And I think we've been encouraging that by not telling you the whole truth about your life here."

"What you are about to hear is the truth, the whole truth and nothing but . . ." Mary Kate intoned the opening to the show she had nearly been addicted to during her recovery, the show Charles Casey had been such a big part of. Even now, whenever she caught *The Whole Truth* she experienced the warm glow of familiarity.

Grace sat down on the bed beside her. "No one can tell you the whole truth, because no one knows it, of course. But I think it's time we started telling you something other than the positives."

Mary Kate was intrigued. "Was I unhappy about the way the kids treated me?"

"No, I don't recall ever seeing you unhappy. You were always convinced that something good was going to happen, and that it just took time. You had more than your share of faith."

"But apparently, it didn't move any mountains."

"Well, you were working very hard at it."

"It sounds like I watched too many Disney movies."

Mary Kate jiggled her foot even as she struggled with the shoe. With her energy returning she found it hard to sit still. "I don't like the kids, and they know it. They're always trying to antagonize me."

"And these days they're usually successful."

On the weekend after she had threatened Tyson with the shovel, Mary Kate had been thrown together with the teenagers repeatedly. None of those times had been good. "I can't help myself, Grace. I wasn't cut out for this life."

"No?"

Mary Kate knew Grace was a trained psychologist, which was why she had been assigned by the congregation to Eden's Gate. She worked hard with the teenagers both in groups and one on one to help with whatever problems had brought them here. In the days after Mary Kate had regained consciousness, Grace had worked with her, too, to help reestablish her life. Even now she would listen for hours if that's what she thought Mary Kate needed.

But Mary Kate needed something more. "Look, if you're suddenly going to start telling me the truth, why not go all the way? I don't belong here, do I?"

"What do you mean?"

"I mean that since I was smacked in the head, I'm nothing but a drag. I don't contribute anything. I take up your valuable time. I make things worse for the kids . . ."

"Your recovery's been miracle enough for us. We're not expecting you to walk on water, too."

Mary Kate felt frustration fill her, as it often did. Most of the time she was nothing but frustration, with a side order of outrage and a dollop of paradox. "I want my life back." She wedged her foot into the shoe with such force that the leather caved in under her heel.

"Maybe not," Grace said calmly.

Mary Kate glanced at her. Grace looked wonderful in a black turtleneck and sweater which complemented her silvering hair. "What do you mean?"

"*That* life is over. I always had the oddest feeling that you'd reached your potential so early, there was almost no reason for you to be alive."

"I don't understand."

"You'd learned all your lessons. You were so far above everyone else that all the vital connections were missing."

"You mean I was arrogant?"

"Oh, absolutely not. You were so humble it put you that much farther away from the rest of us."

"You're making me sick. *I'm* making me sick. What a prig."

"Oh, never a prig. Just not quite in step with the rest of the world."

Mary Kate lifted her heel and smoothed the shoe into place. "If I was such a saint, why didn't I join you?"

"I wish I could help you, but I don't know. I'm not sure you were certain this was the right place for you. Whatever your reasons, they were personal and you kept them between yourself and God."

"God and I don't have much to say to each other anymore."

Grace looked at her watch and stood. "Look, I know sometimes you feel like your own evil twin, but frankly it's nice to see you struggling a little. That's how people learn."

"Puh . . . lease!" Mary Kate stood, too. "I don't want to learn anything. I just want to feel good again. Have fun. Forget about everything that's happened. I just want to be somebody else."

"I don't think that's an option. I think you're stuck with Mary Kate McKenzie."

Mary Kate looked down at her unfamiliar body, clothed in baggy paisley. She shook her head and closed her eyes.

Shandley Falls called itself a city, but that was wishful thinking. The business district was three blocks wide and four blocks long, and the shops that lined its streets couldn't hold their own against the chain stores at the nearest mall. A village green sat squarely in the center of town with the requisite statue of a long-forgotten war hero and a wooden gazebo that in its prime had probably sheltered summer band concerts and trysting lovers. Now the gazebo needed paint, and local teenagers had filled in the gaps with the spray-can variety. The city fathers seemed to be on permanent paternity leave.

Grace parked the sisters' van in a narrow lot beside a two-story house with pale-green siding, then turned to Mary Kate. "I've got errands to run for Sarah. I'll make sure you get settled, then I'll be back to pick you up. If you're done first and want to wander a little, just plan to meet me here at two."

Mary Kate squinted at the discreet wooden sign in the front yard advertising Doctors Kane and Wood. "Grace, this is a gynecologists' office."

"I told you that. Remember?"

Mary Kate didn't, but some portion of everything that was said to her seemed to get lost in the information shuffle. "What are we doing here?"

"Dr. Wilkins talked to Dr. Kane, and he agreed you ought to have a checkup. You told me yourself that your menstrual periods haven't returned since the injury. Dr. Wilkins is afraid it might be a hormone imbalance."

Mary Kate had forgotten a lot, but not basic biology. "Good God, he's afraid I'm pregnant, isn't he?"

"Not at all. When you were admitted to the hospital they did a pregnancy test as a precaution. It's standard procedure, and it was negative."

Mary Kate felt such a flood of relief she was nearly limp by the time the last drops trickled away. "That would be terrific, wouldn't it? The virgin Mary Kate and the Second Coming."

Grace smiled. "You're making quite an assumption about yourself."

"From everything I've been told, it seems logical."

Grace got out of the van, and Mary Kate joined her. They said good-bye in the waiting room, and Mary Kate settled in a corner with the only available fashion magazine.

The room was crowded, and most of the women were in different but obvious stages of pregnancy. One, a blonde slumped on a comfortable sofa, looked as if she were going to deliver momentarily.

"Is this your first baby?" the woman beside Mary Kate asked. She was dark-haired and plain, but her face glowed with unmistakable radiance.

"I'm not pregnant," Mary Kate said.

The dark-haired woman widened her eyes. "Really? I'm sorry. I just thought . . ."

Mary Kate wasn't in the mood to chat. "I'm going to be a nun."

"Oh! Oh, I'm so sorry. I just thought . . . You know, you have that look . . ."

"What look?"

"I don't know. The look. The pregnant look."

"It's these clothes."

"No, I mean your face. It must be . . . like . . . uh, a nun look, too." The woman searched for help, and it arrived in the form of a nurse who came to the door and called out her name. She jumped to her feet. "Whoops, that's me. Good luck, Sister."

Mary Kate didn't correct her, but she knew she was still frowning after the woman disappeared into the hallway. What was a pregnant look, and why did she have it? If she were pregnant she wouldn't be glowing. She'd look like a doe caught in the crosshairs of a high-powered rifle.

Some of the women had small children with them, and the room grew progressively noisier. One child, a toddler dressed in a navy sailor suit, came to visit her, babbling and slobbering on her skirt before his mother, visibly pregnant with his brother or sister, retrieved him.

"He's such a handful," the woman said. "All I do is run all day." She made the pronouncement with a certain amount of glee.

"What will you do with two?" Mary Kate asked, before she could stop herself.

The young woman grinned. "Easy, I'll teach them to run after each other."

With the toddler safely whisked away, Mary Kate tried to concentrate on fashion tips, but the advice seemed like old news to her. She knew what she ought to wear. Instinctively she knew what colors would look good with her hair and complexion, what styles would flatter her petite figure. What she didn't know was why she had never used that information when she shopped.

She closed the magazine and was grateful when the nurse arrived again, this time to call her name.

In the examining room she undressed and slipped into a gown that looked better on her than her own clothes. Someone came in to take her blood pressure and temperature and gave her a plastic cup to take into the bathroom for a urine sample, then a different nurse arrived to take a preliminary medical history. Mary Kate had to tell her the truth.

"I don't know anything," she explained. "I got knocked on the head back in December and I've lost my memory."

The nurse, middle-aged and chirpy, was fascinated and asked questions until the doctor arrived.

Dr. Kane was middle-aged, too, and decidedly unchirpy. He wore thick glasses that he removed as often as possible to rub the bridge of his nose. "You don't remember anything?" he asked after he read her chart.

"Not a thing. Except I seem to remember that I don't like doctors' offices."

He gave a weary smile. "Well, you were never a patient here, but I do have your records from the hospital. That's a start. Got pretty badly banged up, didn't you?"

"So they tell me."

He called the nurse, who got Mary Kate into position for a pelvic exam. She counted dots in the acoustic tile as he poked and prodded.

"I'll be back to talk once you're dressed," he said, after he'd finished.

Clad again in baggy green she waited for fifteen minutes before the chirper bustled in. "I can't tell you how sorry we are about this, but the doctor's been called to the hospital for an emergency caesarean. Dr. Wood's out of town for two weeks, and it's a madhouse today. Can you come in tomorrow morning to finish up?"

Mary Kate could come in any time. She had no life. She had no plans. She had no memory of ever having a life *or* plans. Mary Kate slid off the examining table, wishing as she did that her legs were longer. "Just tell me when."

Outside in the sunshine she contemplated what to do in the half hour before she had to meet Grace. She was only a block from the main part of the business district, so she made careful note of where she was and started into town.

The March day had very little to recommend it, except that it wasn't snowing. The sky was gray, and even the few brave crocuses poking their heads out of the earth wilted sadly, as if they wished they had waited awhile.

She strolled past a pet groomer, a hardware store, and a shop that promised greeting cards for every occasion before she saw a small, nondescript restaurant on the corner. She didn't have time for a real look around town, and she doubted she'd find much of interest, anyway. She headed for the restaurant more for someplace to sit than for anything else.

Inside, a tall man behind the counter showed her to a table as he chatted about the weather. He left her with a menu and the impression she'd been here before.

"Oh, Mary Kate! How you doing? Too long since we seen you."

Mary Kate looked up into yet another unfamiliar face surrounded by brassy blonde hair. Her eyes flicked to the woman's name badge, a red heart worn on a bright-pink nylon uniform. "Millie" looked to be in her early fifties, as well as fifty pounds plump to boot, and she grinned when Mary Kate echoed her greeting.

"We heard you were out of the hospital. We were all so worried."

"I appreciate it." Mary Kate would have appreciated it more if she could remember who "we all" were.

"Want the usual?"

Mary Kate closed the coffee-stained menu. "Sure."

"I told you to be careful out there, Mary Kate. Them kids don't belong at Eden's Gate. They ought to be in jail."

Mary Kate could hardly argue, considering what "them kids" had done to her life. "Is there a newspaper lying around somewhere?"

"You bet. I'll get you one." She leaned closer. "I haven't forgotten what you and the other sisters did for my Robby, Mary Kate. You were the only ones who'd come and see him at the end. You're a regular saint." She straightened, and Mary Kate saw the unmistakable sheen of tears in her eyes.

Guilt shot through her. She wanted to tell Millie she had the wrong woman. She didn't remember anyone named Robby, but she suspected that news flash would upset Millie more. "I'm not a saint, just a . . . um . . . friend."

"I know what I'm talking about." Millie nodded, and her double chins wobbled in emphasis.

She returned with an unfamiliar newspaper and placed it in front of Mary Kate. "You take it with you when you go. I'll be right back with your pie and coffee."

Mary Kate perused the headlines and made a silent bet that apple pie was on the way. Apple pie went with her girl-next-door reputation. She probably liked Mickey Mouse and fireworks and spareribs burned black on a backyard barbe-cue. She probably cried at G-rated movies and read poetry that rhymed—when she wasn't reading theology or horticultural magazines. She had probably never kissed a boy on the first date, and if one's hands had wandered into forbidden territory, she had almost certainly quoted Bible verses to still them.

"Hello, Mary Kate."

She looked up, prepared for yet another unfamiliar face. The man staring down at her *was* a stranger, but one of the best-looking she'd seen. "Hello." The next sentence was the truth. "It's good to see you."

"You look wonderful. I've been so—" He shook his head. "I'm sorry I didn't come to see you in the hospital. I just thought . . ."

She had no idea what he thought, but she was sure it was going to be fun to find out. "Why don't you have a seat." She gestured to the chair beside her.

"You're sure? It won't . . ."

The man had a bad habit of not finishing sentences. But watching him purse his perfect lips in contemplation made up for a lot. As he seated himself she did a quick survey of his face. His blond hair was conservatively cut, which went with his pinstripe suit and prudent tie. He had sharply chiseled features and eyes the purple-blue of Concord grapes, sad eyes, which grew sadder as he gazed at her.

"You must think I'm a jerk," he said.

That wasn't exactly the sentiment that had been going through Mary Kate's mind. She dimpled. "Why? Because you didn't come to see me?"

"I should have, I know." He sat very still, but he scanned the room, nevertheless, as if to be sure no one was listening. "Carol wouldn't have understood."

She nodded, as if she knew exactly what he was saying. "I'm sure you're right."

"She thinks . . . she's jealous . . ." He sighed, as if he was in great need of comfort.

"Is she?"

"She doesn't . . . There's so much she doesn't understand."

There was so much Mary Kate didn't understand. But this was still the most fun she'd had in a while. "What wouldn't she understand?"

"Our history." He shrugged.

Mary Kate considered that. She had already discovered the man was married. The wide gold band on his left hand was proof enough. She discovered his name when Millie returned to the table with a tray.

"Pete," Millie said. "How's Carol? And Little Pete?"

"Just fine. Little Pete's in preschool now."

"Bright little thing. Just like his mommy."

Mary Kate tried not to smile. Millie's tone had dropped twenty degrees since Pete had joined her at the table. Mary Kate watched as Millie set chocolate meringue pie in front of her—a sign that she might be wrong in some assumptions about herself—and a steaming cup of coffee.

"I'll get the cream," Millie said.

"Oh, don't bother," Mary Kate said. "I don't use it."

"Since when?" Millie frowned. "Never saw anyone use as much as you do. Sugar, too."

"I drink it black now. I guess that hit on the head was good for something."

"Not good enough," Millie said, looking pointedly at Pete.

"I'll have some pie, too," he said. "Make mine blueberry."

"All out of it." Millie didn't stay to find out what he'd prefer instead. She sauntered off, leaving them alone once more.

"She doesn't think I should be sitting here with you," Pete said. "Carol will know by the time I get home tonight."

"Quite a grapevine, huh?"

"Always was. When we were teenagers, if I kissed you

good night, my parents knew about it before I'd gotten back in my car.''

She was delighted to find that her life had been more exciting than she'd feared. She wondered if she ought to confess the truth to Pete, and ask him to fill her in on her adolescence. But something stopped her. She had a strange feeling that if she told Pete the facts and asked for his help, he would rewrite their history. He was already concerned about something. What better way to fix the problem than by erasing it?

''Small-town life,'' she said, shaking her head.

''I never thought I'd end up staying in Shandley Falls. Never thought you would, either.''

''Where did you think I'd end up?''

''For a while, I thought you'd end up with me,'' he said bitterly.

She pondered that, wondering if the bitterness was aimed at her or at a decision he had made. She mouthed yet another platitude. ''Well, things don't always work out the way we plan.''

''You were always more philosophical than I was. I guess that's how you ended up . . .''

''With the sisters?''

''Are you happy, Mary Kate? Because if you aren't . . .''

She wanted him to finish this sentence. She would settle for just this one, because she suspected the end of it would be truly enlightening. But Pete sat back and toyed with a spoon on the paper placemat in front of him.

Mary Kate realized it was almost time to meet Grace. She dove into her pie, only intending to sample it. But after one bite she realized she wasn't going to stop until it was finished.

She pushed away the plate when there was nothing left on it except a scrap of crust. ''Amazing pie,'' she said. ''Scrumptious. Sorry you didn't get any.''

''You always did like to eat. Not like Carol. She picks.''

"Carol's probably skinny as a rail." The moment she said the words she realized she'd made an error.

His frown broadened. "Carol's a tub. You know she is."

"I'm sorry. I thought you were saying that she'd gone on a diet."

"Carol? On a diet?" He laughed humorlessly. "She picks all day. A little of this, a little of that, and complains about all of it. She's bigger than she was when she was carrying Little Pete."

Mary Kate stood before she could make any more blunders. "I have to go, Pete, but I'm really glad I got to see you."

He got to his feet. "You don't have to pretend."

"No, really." And she *was* glad to have seen him, because now she knew a little more about herself. Enough to whet her appetite.

"Mary Kate . . ."

She waited, leaning forward to encourage him.

"That last night we were together . . ."

She didn't even breathe, afraid she'd scare him five words short of a period.

"I behaved badly."

She realized he was finished. Curiosity tore at her. "I understand."

"I just . . . I don't know what I was . . ."

"Thinking?" she prompted. "What were you thinking, Pete?"

"It's just that you were the only one . . ."

She wondered what this man did for a living. He dressed like an attorney trying to make partner, but if so, she pitied the plaintiffs he defended. *Your honor, my client* . . .

"What exactly are you sorry for?" she said. "So I'll know which part to forgive."

For a moment she thought she might get her answer. Then he shook his head. "Don't make me say it. You know."

She didn't, of course, but before she could find a way to

wheedle it out of him, Millie approached with her check. "Did you like the pie, Mary Kate?"

"Best ever."

"You come back now. Don't be a stranger." Millie aimed the words at Mary Kate and stressed the "you."

"I'll take care of the bill," Pete said, plucking it from Mary Kate's fingers. "It's the least . . ."

"Carol's daddy usually comes in for coffee about now," Millie said, narrowing her eyes at Pete. "Bet he'll be surprised to find you here."

Mary Kate said her good-byes and made for the door. Outside, the day didn't look nearly as gloomy as it had. She still didn't know the details, but apparently her former life had been a lot more interesting than she'd thought. Somehow that perked her up considerably.

4

CASEY DIDN'T KNOW HOW HE HAD LET SARAH Bradshaw persuade him to help a bunch of juvenile delinquents put together a newsletter. But he had been too slow on his feet, and Sarah had bested him. Casey had pointed out that he had absolutely no teaching experience, but Sarah had seen that as a positive. Without preconceived notions, Casey could approach the experience with a fresh new outlook. He had mentioned his lack of time; she had agreed that he should work at his own convenience. He had mentioned both his brown thumb and his indifference to all things spiritual; she had promised he would not be responsible for content, just mechanics.

Casey had not remembered that nuns were such wily creatures.

During his exchange with Sarah, Mary Kate had stood beside him, a faint smile realigning her freckles. He interpreted that to mean that she knew what he was experiencing, and she had some sympathy for him. He supposed she did. After all, she lived with the sisters. In the past months she had probably been convinced to do any number of things that felt alien to her.

Of course, probably everything felt alien to Mary Kate McKenzie. Even something as mundane as doing supper dishes.

On Tuesday night Casey made himself comfortable in the

doorway of Eden Gate's kitchen and watched Mary Kate and an older woman pile plates in a stainless-steel dishwasher and pots and pans in the sink. When Mary Kate turned and saw him, her eyes lit up, but he wasn't sure if it was his presence or the excuse to stop working.

"Hi," she said. "How long have you been there?"

"Just a minute. Sarah let me in and told me where to find you."

"You go on," the other woman told Mary Kate. "We're almost done here. I'll finish up."

"You're sure?"

"I really don't mind."

Mary Kate followed Casey into the hallway, drying her hands on a dish towel. "What gives?"

"What? You don't think I came for the pleasure of your company?"

She slung the dish towel over her shoulder. "The first and only time we've been in each other's presence I slapped you with a shovel, forced you to haul garbage from the pond, and trapped you in the barn while Sarah talked you into a volunteer job. I can't believe I'm one of your favorite people."

Actually, he had thought about Mary Kate frequently since their first and only meeting. Her situation fueled his imagination. It was nothing more than that, of course, but he had found his time with her intriguing. Every day since then he had tried to envision the world through her eyes.

"It was high drama," he said. "Even better than sitting through the Women's Club annual luncheon."

"Do you want me to arrange something for tonight? We could study the nocturnal habits of groundhogs, sand butterfly boxes—"

"I have a project in mind."

She lifted a brow in question.

"Remember the garbage?"

"How could I forget? My feet were blue for a week."

"I know where it came from."

"Do you?" She considered for a moment. "Casey, did you really sort through those bags?" She paused. "Wait a minute, that's probably second nature to you, isn't it? You've probably sorted through a thousand bags in your time."

"Celebrity garbage was a lot more entertaining."

"Tell me. What did Michael Jackson eat for breakfast the morning Lisa Marie told him she wanted a divorce?"

"You're still mad I didn't tell you the whole truth about who I used to be, aren't you?"

"The truth, the whole truth, and nothing but the truth. Remember?"

"You have no idea how much I hated being on a show that started that way, then distorted facts to make them sell."

She pondered him for a moment, then shrugged. "So, whose garbage bags were in the pond?"

"A guy named Jake Holloway. He lives down the road. I thought we could pay him a visit tonight, if you'd like."

"Have you told Sarah?"

"No. Does she know about the bags?"

"She has enough on her mind. I thought I'd tell her if you discovered who was doing it."

"I don't think Sarah's solution and mine would be the same."

Mary Kate lowered her voice, although nobody was nearby. "So, what's yours?"

"I just thought Mr. Holloway and I could discuss a story I'm considering for *The Cricket*."

"A story about trespassing and illegal dumping?"

"That would be the one."

"I'll get my jacket."

She returned, sliding her arms into the sleeves while he watched. The jacket in question looked like it had once belonged to someone's kid brother. Mud-brown and overstuffed, the jacket's cuffs almost buried Mary Kate's tiny hands. Casey was sure that nuns and nearly-nuns didn't worry a lot about fashion, but he wished that Mary Kate hadn't shut her eyes when she'd shopped. He was curious—just curious, nothing more—how she might look in different clothes.

As if she'd read his expression she grimaced. "I know. Awful, isn't it? But I'm going into town tomorrow morning, and I thought I'd do a little shopping while I'm at it."

"Get some advice."

She dimpled. "Maybe I should take you along."

"If that's what it takes."

They left the house quietly so that they wouldn't have to explain where they were going and went straight to his car. "Did you find out anything about this Holloway character?" she said along the way. "Anything we could use against him?"

"I didn't run him through the FBI computer, if that's what you mean."

"Sorry, I guess I'm getting carried away."

He helped her into the passenger seat, then got into his own. "You're enjoying this, aren't you?"

"My life's one big investigation. I'm getting into the spirit."

She seemed to think about her own words because she continued once they were out on the road. "I was in town today, and I met some people who knew me. It was the strangest thing, Casey. I didn't recognize even one of them. Not a bit. And Shandley Falls looked completely unfamiliar. Like somebody's nightmare of small-town America. You're the only person I've run into who seemed familiar to me."

"Because you saw me on television."

"Right." She stared out the window. The sun had set, but the sky was still light. The days were getting longer, and when spring truly arrived, Casey thought her opinion of the town might change. But he wondered if she would ever remember her life, and if she did, if she would want to resume it.

"Let me do the talking after we get there," he said, slowing to check addresses painted on mailbox posts. The road was rural here, and the mailboxes were few and far between.

"Why you? I'm representing the sisters."

"Which is why you need to be quiet. This Holloway's already shown what he thinks of Eden's Gate and the people running it."

She dissented low in her throat, but he suspected she would do what he asked, at least for a while.

"What did you find that convinced you?" she said. "Envelopes? Bills?"

"Newsletters from two different gun lobbies. A cover from *Soldier of Fortune* magazine with his address label. A form-letter solicitation from a paramilitary group."

"Stop the car."

He laughed. "I did check around, Mary Kate. But everyone says Holloway's harmless. His weapon of choice is hot air."

"Why is he so unhappy with Eden's Gate? A guy like that couldn't possibly want developers in the area. He sounds like somebody who'd be happiest in the wilds of Idaho."

"Probably because Eden's Gate is bringing people into the area. People of different colors and cultures than he's used to."

"Oh . . ."

"Having trouble with that?"

"I guess I am."

"Apparently you've forgotten a whole lot more than a town and some old friends." He slowed at the next mailbox, an old nail barrel mounted on a tree trunk. Tacked below it was a hand-lettered sign that read: *Keep Out. Killer Attack Dogs.*

"Looks like we're here," Casey said.

"This should be fun."

She didn't sound scared. In fact she sounded as if she could hardly wait for the confrontation. "You know, you ought to reconsider your choice of occupation," he said. "I know a television show in New York that would love to have you working for them."

She flashed him a smile, and those dimples stabbed him straight through the heart.

He knew his reaction had been obvious when she frowned. "Casey? Something wrong?"

He told himself Mary Kate McKenzie did not have a smile like another woman he had known. No two women could be less alike. "Not a thing." Silently he reassured himself as he turned into Jake Holloway's wooded drive.

The architectural style of the Holloway residence was Early Prison Complex. Constructed from unadorned concrete blocks, the tiny house was closely surrounded by an eight-foot chain-link fence topped with a slack length of barbed wire. Two peephole-style windows looked out over a pair of graying Dobermans who didn't even rise as Mary Kate and Casey approached.

"Killer attack dogs." Mary Kate shook her head. "Hey boys," she called. "Scarfed up any mail carriers lately?"

One dog thumped his stumpy tail on the ground, then closed his eyes and joined his partner for a nap.

"What happens if we open that gate?" Mary Kate said.

"It's probably locked."

"Guess we ought to shout for Mr. Holloway to come out. One of the dogs might gum us to death."

They didn't have to shout. An old man opened the door and stepped out on the porch. Despite her bravado Mary Kate was relieved to see that he wasn't armed.

"Mr. Holloway?" Casey said.

"Who wants to know?"

"My name is Charles Casey."

"Sure it is."

"I have my driver's license, if you'd like to see it."

The old man started toward them, climbing stiffly down the steps. He hobbled to the gate and peered through the wire mesh. He was bent with age, and he had a permanent scowl that would have made smiling a heroic effort. "What d'ya want?" he said with a snarl that was more impressive than anything his dogs had produced.

"We have something we need to discuss with you, and we'd rather not do it through a fence," Casey said.

"No? That's too bad."

"Mr. Holloway, I found something that belongs to you."

He narrowed his eyes and squinted at Casey. "You *are* Charles Casey from that television show."

"Not anymore. I'm with *The Cricket* now. And if you don't come out here and talk to me I'm going to be writing a story about you tomorrow. Without your cooperation."

"You can't do that!"

"Watch me."

Mary Kate observed the two men trying to out-macho each other. Although she admired Casey's technique, she also felt sorry for the old man. This ridiculous prison might be of his own making, but it was still a prison.

Before she realized what she was doing, she was standing right in front of him. "Hi, Mr. Holloway. My name's Mary Kate McKenzie."

"I know who you are!"

She supposed he would at that, since she had grown up right down the road. "It's been awhile since I've seen you."

"Not long enough."

She demonstrated her brightest smile, the one that seemed to make Casey uncomfortable. "You always were a kidder." She went on before he could respond. "Look, we've got a teeny, weeny problem. Somebody, and I can't imagine who it could be, has been dumping *your* garbage in Eden

Gate's pond. Stealing your garbage and dumping it. Can you believe it?"

"How do you know it's mine?"

"I'm afraid your name was all over the contents. Of course I told everybody that Jake Holloway would *never* do something like that. He's a law-and-order kind of guy who believes in everybody minding his own business. I vouched for you."

He looked surprised, surprised enough not to know what to say. Mary Kate stepped back. "You're the only one who can help us figure out who's doing this awful thing. Why don't you come out here so we can talk about what to do."

"I'm not going to open this gate!"

"Please, Jake. We aren't going to hurt you."

He barked a laugh. "Always were a persistent little thing."

"I haven't changed a bit." Which was a lie of some consequence.

"You really want me to come out there?"

"I really do."

"Mary Kate . . ."

Mary Kate heard Casey's warning, but she was sure she knew what she was doing.

Jake opened the gate, but he didn't step through. He stood still while his eyes brightened considerably. Mary Kate heard something that sounded like a freight train roaring around the side of the house. Then as she lifted her eyes in horror, a dog the size of a sports car came tearing through the yard.

Jake lifted his hands toward the heavens. "Told you I didn't want to open it."

"Mary Kate!"

Mary Kate heard footsteps running toward her, but she knew the dog was going to be out the gate before either she or Casey could slam it shut. She didn't even think about what to do next. As the dog leapt into the air she threw herself to the ground, directly in its path. The dog squealed and tumbled over her back like a gymnast performing a prizewinning vault.

Mary Kate picked herself up off the ground. The dog picked himself up off the ground. They stared at each other, one as surprised as the other.

"Mary Kate, back away slowly," Casey said. "I've got a stick."

"Oh, good Lord," Jake said. "Godzilla wouldn't hurt a flea." He raised his voice. "Godzilla, get back in here!"

Godzilla, part Great Dane, part Newfoundland, a dog who would have struck terror in the heart of Dr. Dolittle, sank down to his belly and slunk back through the gate.

"You trying to kill my dog, Mary Kate?" Jake demanded.

She dusted off her jeans and jacket as outrage filled her. "That's it, you old bastard! Here's the deal. You have problems with what we're doing at Eden's Gate, you come and talk to me. No more garbage in the pond, or there *will* be a story. I'll write it myself."

She glared at him, not a dimple in sight.

He glared back at her, then he dipped his head. It wasn't exactly a nod, but it passed for one.

"And slap some paint on this house and plant some flowers," she shouted, as she marched back to the car. "Or I'll bring a bunch of my juvenile offenders over to do it for you!"

Back at Eden's Gate Casey opened Mary Kate's door and held out his hand to help her from the car. He hadn't said a word on the drive, but now he spoke as if there hadn't been a gap. "You know, that took split-second timing."

Mary Kate took a moment just to admire him. She liked the way Casey dressed. Nubby wool sports coat, collarless shirt, and worn jeans. She also liked his pirate smile and the stubble on his cheeks, assuring his status as dark and dangerous.

"I'm impressed," he finished. "I thought you were a goner."

"I'm exhausted." Every muscle in Mary Kate's body hurt from throwing herself on the ground. But something inside her had rebelled at the sight of the dog racing toward her. She was tired of being a pawn of fate. She wanted a life, and she wanted it right now. She hadn't been about to let some stupid mongrel interfere.

"Well, it was spectacular to see. I don't know if I could have done it. Or would have. You were pretty foolhardy."

She let him help her out, then she wiped her forehead on the sleeve of her flannel shirt. She had taken off her jacket in the car and now she tied it around her waist. It probably wasn't much above forty outside, but it was going to take her a long time to cool down.

"Walk you to the house?" Casey said.

"Why? Afraid I'm going to collapse?"

"Why would I want to prevent a story from unfolding?"

"I have to go out to the barn and see if the leaf mold arrived while we were gone."

"Leaf mold?"

She grimaced. "Disgusting, huh? The county turns leaves into compost and sells it in bulk. I ordered some last week and they were supposed to deliver tonight."

"How do you know what to order if you don't remember anything?"

"The sisters help, and Mary Kate—" She sighed. "*I* kept a gardening journal. I'm using it as a crutch until I remember or at least learn what I'm supposed to do next. I ordered leaf mold last year at this time."

"Then you're going ahead with the garden? You're going to work with the kids?"

"What other purpose do I have on this earth?" She started toward the barn. She was actually checking on the leaf mold because she was hoping to miss the sisters' evening devotionals. She was not required to attend; the sisters exerted no pressure on her to join them. But she felt obligated to be there when she was in the house. And when she did join them, she knew more clearly than at any other time how little she was cut out for this life.

But what life was she cut out for?

"What have you done so far?" Casey said.

Her mind had wandered so far afield that she didn't know what he was referring to. "Done?"

"About the garden . . ."

"Oh. Not much. I'm reading the journal, the textbooks I kept, back issues of magazines. I had a comprehensive filing system. What a self-righteous little do-gooder I must have been."

"Because you kept an organized filing system?"

"No, it's just that I was so perfect. Grace says I didn't seem to have enough to learn from being here. Now I have everything."

They crossed a field spongy with melted snow and spring rain. She was aware of him beside her. She suspected that few women found Casey's presence comforting, but for some reason she did. Already he seemed like an old friend, someone she could talk to without lengthy preliminary explanations, someone she would never have to primp or preen for. He seemed as oblivious to her as a woman as she was oblivious to him as a man.

They followed the road to the barn. The night had turned dark, but a moon was rising to light their way. One bright star shone overhead; soon the sky would be filled with them.

"I lived in the city so long I forgot about stars," Casey said.

"You were busy with the other kind of stars. I envy you. Famous people, glamour, intrigue. I can't understand . . ."

"Why I gave it up?"

She saw a dark pile in front of the barn and knew the

leaf mold had arrived. Her excuse for continuing the walk had ended. She stopped. "Why did you? You have a nothing job in a nothing little town. They tell me there's a guy in Shandley Falls who can whistle Beethoven's symphonies through the gap between his front teeth, but he's all the celebrity we've got."

He didn't face her. He looked toward the barn. "It's a long story."

"I've got the time. The longer you talk the less chance I have of making evening devotionals."

He rewarded what he probably thought was a joke with his rich, dark laugh. "I thought we were going to check out the leaf mold."

"Yeah. All right." She started toward the pile, slowing her steps. She wasn't sure what to expect, but she was sure anything called mold was going to stink to high heaven.

"There wasn't much glamour in what I was doing," Casey said. "I was on the road most of the time, trying to make stories out of nothing but lies and innuendos. I knew some celebrities, sure, but I knew their housemaids, their dry cleaners, the clerks in their attorneys' offices a lot better. My specialty was cultivating people who would expose their own mothers."

"You were just doing your job."

"That was the problem."

"I can't imagine giving up that life for this one."

"This life is only temporary. I knew the managing editor of *The Cricket*. He's on a leave of absence for most of this year, taking some time off to see the world. When he heard I was leaving *The Whole Truth* he asked me to fill in here while he was gone. *The Cricket's* not a big-city daily, but it has a surprisingly wide circulation and there are a number of people who would like his job. He was afraid to give the position to a local because he might have had trouble getting it back when he returned. The paper's owner agreed."

"Why did you agree?"

"I needed time to decide what to do next."

"You must have plenty of options." She wondered what that would be like. Her own options seemed so limited.

"I don't know. Most of the options I have seem to be the kind I ditched. Dubious news shows that want to cash in on my contacts. The *Enquirer* invited me to write for them. The FBI offered me a job at the academy teaching classes on the authentication of Elvis sightings."

She punched him in the arm, a companionable punch that stopped her in her tracks in sudden agony.

"Lord . . ."

"What's wrong?" Casey stopped, too.

She bent forward and grabbed her right arm. "My . . . shoulders." Actually, it wasn't exactly her shoulders. It was every related muscle and every muscle related to those muscles.

"Muscle spasm?"

She managed a nod.

"You overdid it tonight. Come here."

They were nearly at the barn. One remaining section of an old pole fence jutted at an angle from one side. As he led her there, she stumbled and bit her lips to repress her moans.

Casey hefted himself to the top railing and pulled her to stand between his legs. "Turn around."

She was in no shape to argue. She settled her bottom against the fence and leaned forward.

He rested his hands on her shoulders, then whistled softly. "You're as hard as a rock. This must hurt like the dickens."

"Worse . . ."

Casey dug his thumbs along the edges of her spine and pushed. She yelped, but the pain he was inflicting was better than the cramps. "Take it easy there!"

"Sorry." He eased up just a little. "Better?"

She grunted, the best she could do under the circumstances.

He began to rotate his thumbs, moving them slowly as he dug his fingers into her shoulders in a strong, steady rhythm. "I used to do this for—" He paused. "I had a friend who got cramps like this when she was under stress. And she was under stress most of the time, so I had practice."

She imagined this man had had practice in myriad uses of his hands. Even if he didn't jumpstart her libido, she was sure he'd jumpstarted a thousand other women's.

She gasped as he moved to a particularly sore spot, but as he worked on it, the pain began to ease. She rotated her head with something akin to pleasure. "Bet she misses you."

His fingers stilled, then began their slow massage again. "She died."

Her head jerked, and the pain returned. "Oh." She gasped again, trying to catch her breath. "I'm sorry."

"So am I. Now, stop talking and relax."

She tried to obey. But as she stood there and let him work the kinks from her muscles, she mulled over what little she knew about him. And suddenly she knew who the woman must have been.

"Gypsy Dugan."

"I told you to be quiet."

"Like that would shut me up." She thought about this new revelation. Until December Gypsy Dugan had been *The Whole Truth*'s anchor, a sexy, intriguing woman with a spectacular smile and the ability to make love to a camera and read news simultaneously.

Sometime in December, about the time Mary Kate had been injured, Gypsy had been killed. During Mary Kate's recovery she had witnessed bits of the actual footage of Gypsy's death, which had been caught on camera during the secret filming of a story. At the time, Mary Kate had been stunned and shaken. Grace had come into the room to find her nearly in tears. Grace had promptly turned off the television set, but the damage had already been done. Mary Kate had been haunted for weeks, even though Gypsy Dugan was nothing to her. Her reaction to Gypsy's death was probably related to her own brush with it. But what must it have been like for Casey?

She tried rotating her head again. "I saw the footage on television. The show got a lot of play out of her murder. They still do."

"Yeah. Gypsy would have loved it. More famous in death than in life."

"Was she the woman you were talking about? Were you close?"

"Close?" He seemed to ponder that. "We were lovers, but not friends. Then we were friends, but not lovers. She was in a car accident months before she died, and afterwards she changed. She had some memory problems, too. It was like getting to know a brand-new woman."

Mary Kate couldn't follow that exactly, but she heard something close to sadness in his voice. "Did you like her better afterwards?"

"I don't know how to answer that."

She suspected he saw no point in answering it. "Well, no wonder you seem to understand what I'm going through. Been there, done that with somebody else."

"*Do* I understand it?"

"Nobody really understands it, me in particular. But at least you've had experience with another woman who couldn't remember exactly who she was."

"Exactly?"

"Okay, who can't remember anything at all. At least in my case."

"No memory flashes, huh? No new revelations?"

"I've been told not to count on anything. I'm supposed to try to build a new life because the old one may be gone for good."

"You could be in a worse situation, you know. I imagine you can stay here forever, if you choose."

She closed her eyes. His words were like the screech of jail cell doors sliding shut. She stood in silence, allowing his hands to work their magic. He took that moment to reach under her shirt, pulling it low against her neck so that he had better access to her shoulders. His hands against her bare flesh were warm and firm.

She had disturbing dreams about men's hands. She was certain her actual experience with men must be microscopic, but the dreams, at least, were full-blown, erotic blockbusters. How could a woman with those kinds of dreams have committed—or nearly committed—her life to the church?

She rolled her head forward, giving him wider access. She was surprised at how comforting his touch was. Not only was he soothing away the cramps, she felt reassured and cared for. She told herself that was ridiculous, that she hardly knew this man, but the feeling wouldn't go away.

He reached lower, and the shirt was so loose that it didn't prevent him. He dragged his fingertips along her spine, and surges of heat seemed to pulsate along her nerve endings.

"Delicious." The word came out as a purr.

"Better, huh?"

She made a sound of pleasure low in her throat. "You're a miracle worker. Maybe you should become a masseur."

"The hours would be better, and maybe the pay."

"You'll go back to television."

"Will I?"

"It's in your blood."

"You know that? After such a short time?"

"You miss it, don't you?"

His sigh stirred the curls at her nape. "Immensely."

"See? I knew I was right."

"I don't know what I'll do. I was working my way up the legitimate news ladder when I got the offer from *The Whole Truth*. I saw stars and dollar signs, and the temptation was too great. Now I don't even know if I can start over with the networks. Or if I want to.''

"Is there really such a difference between what you were doing and what they are? It seems to me the major network news shows are becoming more like the tabloid shows every day. Maybe you'd have an edge.''

"You know a lot about this.''

She shrugged—and discovered the pain had vanished. "I watched a lot of television. I'm told it was the only thing I wanted to do at the beginning of my recovery.''

"I think I'm finished here.'' His hands lingered a moment. She could feel each separate finger, and then the absence of them as he withdrew his hands. He straightened her collar as she rotated her head one last time.

She turned, still cradled by his knees, and rested her elbows on his thighs. "That was a nice thing to do, Charles Casey. Were you always a nice person? Or is that something that's just developing?''

"I've never placed much value on being nice.''

"Then it must be instinctive.''

"You were something tonight. I don't know which surprised me more, the canine acrobatics or the lecture you gave Holloway.''

"I don't know what possessed me. But I think he's sad, don't you? He really needs people, but he shuts them out.''

He tilted her chin so that she was gazing into his eyes. "Maybe there's more do-gooder left inside you than you think.''

She smiled, something she found easier to do when she was with him. "Don't bet on it.''

He didn't smile back. "You're doing it again.''

"Doing what?''

"Flashing those dimples.''

"Dimples. Right.''

"It's the oddest thing, but when you do that, you remind me of Gypsy.''

Her smile deepened, but only in disbelief. "Gypsy Dugan? Come on. Tell me more lies."

"You're absolutely nothing like her, but there's something about your smile. The mouth isn't even the same . . ."

"No?" She thought about the woman she'd seen on television. "Not the mouth, not the hair." She grimaced. "Not the boobs."

He laughed his darker-than-sin laugh. "The boobs are fine, Mary Kate. Bigger's not always better."

"At least bigger is visible."

The laugh tapered into a surprisingly warm smile. "I'd think that after everything, you'd have the right to question yourself as a woman. But you don't have to worry. I know a dozen men who would find you absolutely charming."

"On the off chance I ever want a dozen men in my life, I'll file that away."

"Are you going to want even one man in your life?"

"Are you asking if I'm going to leave the sisters and become a wicked, worldly woman?"

"Something like that."

"It's too soon to say. I wanted this life before the accident. Doesn't it seem like I ought to give it a chance now?"

"You're asking me? The guy who was known as Callous Casey on his nicest days?"

"I thought all those years of trying to worm secrets from other people might have made an amateur therapist out of you."

He touched her hair, just a light, reassuring touch. "If I was going to give you advice it might be something like take your time. Things will work out, if you let them. You'll know what to do when you have to know."

She didn't feel shy, and she didn't feel strange. She smiled at him again. He didn't move his hand. And for the first time since the beating, the world didn't seem like such a strange place after all.

ᴄᴏ 5

"**I**'M WHAT?"

Dr. Kane folded his hands and rested them on the desk. "Pregnant, Mary Kate. I'm sorry, but there's no way we can ignore the evidence. I was sure after your examination, but we did a pregnancy test just to confirm it. You're very definitely going to have a baby. In September, if all my calculations are correct, but we'll confirm that, too, with a sonogram."

"They did a pregnancy test when I was admitted to the hospital. It was negative!"

"The pregnancy must have been very recent at that point. Frankly, after the trauma you endured, I'm surprised you didn't abort spontaneously, but apparently this is one baby who is determined to be born."

Mary Kate was too stunned to ask questions. Dr. Kane took off his glasses and rubbed the bridge of his nose. "Do you know who the father is?"

Under most circumstances that would have seemed a tactless question. But Mary Kate knew the doctor wasn't referring to a life of promiscuity. She slumped in her chair. "I don't have a clue. I can't even believe it's true."

"Why not? Because you were considering joining the sisters? Surely you don't think that means you can't have a baby?"

She was beginning to like Dr. Kane, which was a good

82

thing since apparently they were going to be seeing a lot of each other. "I've been told all these things about myself. How perfect I was. How committed to the church. Things that have been pretty hard to believe considering the impulses I have now."

He smiled. "Normal human impulses."

"What am I going to do?"

He hesitated, then leaned over his desk. "What do you *want* to do? You have alternatives."

Abortion. Perhaps there were other solutions, too, but Mary Kate knew from the expression on the doctor's face that this was the one they were discussing first.

She sat quietly and considered it. If she decided to terminate this pregnancy, no one would ever have to know. She could drive to Cleveland and have the procedure without anyone but Dr. Kane being the wiser. Under the circumstances, abortion made perfect sense. She was pregnant, with no idea who the baby's father might be and no sure way of finding out. For all she knew, she might even be carrying the child of a stranger, a rapist, or a sleazy one-night stand. She really knew nothing about her own life except what other people had related.

But even as she considered abortion, the image of an abortion clinic and what she would experience there seemed surprisingly clear to her. Not a memory, exactly. Perhaps nothing more than propaganda that had been forced on her or the recollections of a friend. But whatever the answer, she was not uneducated about what would occur if she chose that alternative.

On the heels of that image came another question. "Dr. Kane, I don't know who the father is. I don't even know if I consented to having sex. Did you test for sexually transmitted diseases? HIV?"

"They did a routine blood screen in the hospital."

"Right. And they did a pregnancy test, too."

"We'll check again and do some cultures, but I don't

think you have any reason for alarm. Make an appointment on your way out for early next week. I'll have the nurse give you a vitamin prescription and our booklet on prenatal care. Until you decide what you're going to do, you should take care of yourself. No drinking or smoking. And cut down on regular coffee and tea. In fact, cut them out entirely if you can."

She got to her feet. "I have a lot of thinking to do."

"I hope so." Dr. Kane stood, too. "Abortion isn't the only alternative, you know. You can have the baby and keep it. You can give it up for adoption. You can even choose an open adoption situation where you have contact with the child and its new parents. Considering your background, Mary Kate, and the plans you had, I would recommend counseling before you make a decision. You'll have to live with your choice for the rest of your life."

Casey sat bleary-eyed at his desk, even though he'd single-handedly consumed half a pot of the sludge the staff fondly called coffee. He rested his face in his hands and hoped that he wouldn't fall asleep right then and there. Although maybe he needed to, since he wasn't getting any sleep in his own bed.

He tried to remember when the dreams about Gypsy had begun. He'd had a few just after her death, nightmares where she pleaded with him to help her. Each time he had awakened in a cold sweat, his eyes brimming with tears. He, who hadn't shed a tear since his childhood.

Those dreams had disappeared after a week or two, and insomnia had taken their place. When he had slept, it had been so lightly that he hadn't seemed to dream at all. Not until two weeks ago, anyway, just after he started work on the Eden's Gate story. Then the insomnia had disappeared and new dreams had begun.

He was in a car, searching for something, although he couldn't remember what. He only knew he had to find it, because if he didn't, someone was going to die. A clock ticked loudly on the dashboard of his car, speeding up with the miles until he could hardly distinguish one tick from another. He sped faster and faster until he was thrown from the car by sheer force of velocity, hurtling for seconds through space. And when he landed he was in a silent house, some place he had never been. He ran through the house, and as he slammed doors in a fruitless search he heard a woman screaming. He followed the sound, running faster and faster, flinging open a door at last to see Gypsy standing across the room. Then, as he watched, she crumpled to the floor . . .

And he awoke.

Casey massaged his forehead with his fingertips and realized he was sweating.

"God . . ."

The dream was as real to him as if Gypsy's death had happened just that way.

"Chuck?"

Most of the *Cricket* staff worked part-time and were seldom in the office. Casey whirled in his chair to see Jim Fagen, his one and only full-time reporter, standing in his office doorway. "Two things. The name's Casey. And next time knock, damn it!"

Jim, a chinless young man with little confidence and less backbone, blushed visibly. "I'm . . . I'm s-sorry."

Casey sighed and silently rebuked himself. He was no knight in shining armor, but from the moment he had been introduced to Jim, he had tried his best to pump him up, praising his work—which was generally excellent—and treating him like a valued employee. Now he'd undone it all. "Look, I'm sorry, Jim. I didn't get much sleep last night. I didn't mean to take it out on you."

"That's all . . . right. I . . . I sh-should have knocked."

"It's not all right. But the Chuck thing has to go." Casey forced a smile. "What's going on?"

"This Eden's Gate story. I just wondered if you . . . well, if you w-wanted me to proof it for you?"

"I'd like that. I'm all finished with it."

"I read it."

Casey leaned back in his chair and closed his eyes so he didn't have to see the anxiety in Jim's. "What did you think?"

"Great. It's gr . . . great."

Casey knew Jim wasn't trying to sound like Tony the Tiger in an old Frosted Flakes commercial. Most of the time he had few problems with his speech at all, usually only when his small store of self-esteem was shaken. He kicked himself again. "Is there anything you'd like to change?"

"No. I . . . I thought the part about Mary Kate McKenzie was gr . . . fine."

"Do you know her by any chance? I suppose she went to school here."

When Jim didn't answer Casey opened his eyes and sat up. Jim was blushing again. "I did. We . . . we went to high school together."

"What was she like?"

"Mary Kate?" Jim shifted his weight from one foot to the other. "She was . . . the best."

"The best what?"

"Just . . . the best."

Casey nodded encouragingly, but Jim vacated the doorway without elaborating.

Casey wondered if Mary Kate had realized that she'd made a conquest all those years ago. Perhaps she had been so focused on her growing commitment to the church that no young men had impressed her. But no matter whether she had realized it or not, with her memory loss she certainly didn't know it now.

Jim and Mary Kate. The picture just wouldn't form in Casey's mind. The Mary Kate he knew, despite her life choices, was a spunky, cut-to-the-chase kind of woman. He wondered if she'd been that way in adolescence, or even if she'd been that way before the accident.

Or was the Mary Kate Casey knew simply a product of a vicious blow to the head? If so, he almost had to thank the kid who had beaned her.

Mary Kate had wandered the streets of Shandley Falls for an hour, but she couldn't have answered one question about what she'd seen.

There's no way we can ignore the evidence.

Well, *she* had ignored it. She had attributed her nausea and dizziness to her head injury. The same had been true for her mood swings. To her knowledge no one had ever pointed out that getting smashed in the head and getting pregnant had so many delightful similarities. Perhaps if they had . . .

"Pregnant." Even now muttering that word sent a shiver down her spine. But how would she have known? Her body seemed unfamiliar, so any changes in it had gone unnoticed. Her life seemed unfamiliar, too, so any changes in it . . .

She'd had sex with a man, a man she didn't remember. He could be anyone. A friend, a colleague, an old boyfriend or a new one. He could be a stranger who had thrown her to the ground in some isolated field or an acquaintance who hadn't taken no for an answer.

He could be anyone. Anyone with a viable sperm count.

She shuddered and wrapped her arms around her waist. If the sex had been consensual, why hadn't she taken precautions? Surely she'd been smart enough to know that it could lead to pregnancy. If she'd made love to a man of her own free will, hadn't she considered the consequences? Or had the act been so spontaneous, so surprising, that she had been swept away by her own emotions?

Gusts of wind skipped along the street and she shuddered again. She had left her jacket at the doctor's office, and she

supposed she should go back for it. But she didn't even
know how far she'd walked.

She had been standing at a shop window, staring blindly
for longer than she cared to remember. Now she forced herself to focus, only to realize that she was looking at a model
of a nursery. A wicker bassinet stood in the foreground,
draped in white lace and lined with yellow-and-white ging-
ham. A brown teddy bear with a red bow tie resided where
a baby should have been sleeping. A changing table and
rocker of the same wicker flanked the bassinet.

"No . . ." She turned away, and perhaps she turned too
fast, because dizziness overwhelmed her. She stumbled into
a stranger, an older man who steadied her, asked if she was
all right, then took off the moment she said yes.

She wasn't all right. She needed to talk to somebody, but
who? How did she tell Sarah or Grace that she was carrying
a child? Perhaps she was no longer the woman they had
known, that she *had* been when this child was conceived.
Grace had said that she'd seemed almost too perfect to need
the lessons of this world.

Grace had been sadly mistaken.

She ran through the list of people she knew—or at least
remembered—a list with so little potential she might as well
be completely alone in the world. She couldn't talk to the
sisters, not until she had decided what to do. And if she
chose abortion, not even then. She certainly couldn't talk to
any of the kids who came to the center. She had no family,
no friends that she knew of. She couldn't spill this to Millie
at the coffee shop, or to Pete of the unfinished sentences—
although for all she knew he could be the baby's father. She
couldn't see herself hiking to Jake Holloway's house to discuss her condition with him or Godzilla.

She only knew one person who might listen and understand.

She found a newspaper stand a block away, and she
dropped in her thirty-five cents to retrieve the most recent

Cricket. She searched the masthead for the paper's address, then she set off to retrieve her jacket and find Casey.

The Cricket's office was just out of the main business district, sandwiched between a pierogi palace and a practice of cardiologists. One neighbor was great for lunch, the other for post-lunch cholesterol checks. After a couple of weeks and a couple of pounds, Casey had sworn off Polish cooking and now preferred to eat across town where he could have a less tasty meal that didn't turn his blood to Jell-O.

Today he broke with tradition and decided to head for Warsaw's instead. He was still so sapped from his lack of sleep that he didn't want to drive. At noon he slipped out of the office and crossed the alley as a cold wind tossed milk cartons and old newspapers in his path.

Warsaw's was tiny, dark, and smoke-filled, with a counter perpetually inhabited by the local cops and six wooden booths lining the wall. He slid into the closest booth facing the sidewalk and rested his head in his hands until the waitress came to take his order.

He settled on the daily special, an assortment of six pierogis and a side order of kielbasa and sauerkraut. "Whatever's on tap, too," he added.

He wondered if he could drink his way out of the nightmares. If he started now, would he be so sloshed by bedtime that he could go to sleep and not dream at all? Maybe after a few nights of that, he'd have the whole thing out of his system.

Unfortunately, he wasn't really a drinking man.

Outside the wind was picking up and more trash sailed through the air. Somewhere somebody's garbage can had blown over.

Casey hadn't smiled spontaneously all day, but now, he thought of Mary Kate lecturing Jake Holloway about *his* garbage, and the corners of his lips turned up in response. She was adorable when she was angry—which meant she was adorable much of the time. Adorable women ranked right up there with cute women in his estimation, but Mary Kate was a cut above most of them. Last night with her eyes glowing like a spitting cat's and her curls bouncing in indignation, she had reminded him of—

"Gypsy . . ."

Suddenly Casey understood where his nightmare had come from. Unaccountably Mary Kate had reminded him of Gypsy Dugan. He'd already noticed a resemblance in their smiles. But last night he'd noticed a resemblance in the way Mary Kate expressed her anger. The similarities were subtle, but definitely there. And subtle or not, they had been enough to trigger last night's dream.

Almost as if he'd conjured her from some deeper part of himself, Casey looked up just in time to see Mary Kate fling open Warsaw's front door and march inside, straight to his table.

"Tell me I'm welcome to sit down," she said.

"By all means." He gestured to the bench across from him, and she slid into the booth. "What are you doing here?"

"I was looking for you. I was on my way to your office. Then I saw you sitting here."

"You were lucky you caught me. I try to avoid Warsaw's when I can. The food's too good."

"It smells wonderful."

"Have you had lunch?"

"No. I . . ."

He signaled the old woman behind the counter who only needed a babushka to complete the image of a nineteenth-century peasant. "Do you like pierogi? Or do you remember?"

"Sure, I like them. But—"

"Another order for my friend here," he told the woman. "I'm having a beer," he told Mary Kate. "Would you like one?"

"Damn right I—" She stopped and her eyes widened. "Uh, no. No beer."

"Coffee?"

"Yes, I—" She stopped again. "No, no coffee either. I'll have . . . milk."

"One milk for the lady." He grinned at her. "On a sudden health kick? Or just feeling uncommonly nun-like?"

She didn't answer. Instead she began to toy with the napkin dispenser at the table's edge.

"Are you okay, Mary Kate?"

"Yes." She folded her hands in her lap, as if she'd just realized she was fidgeting. "I'm fine."

"Well, I'm not."

"No?"

"I was just thinking about you."

"What? I'm the reason you're not okay?"

"No. Gypsy's the reason I'm not okay. I dreamed about her last night." He lifted his gaze to hers. "Not good dreams."

"I'm sorry. I—" She looked as if she wanted to say more, then she shook her head. "Do you want to talk about it?"

"I don't know. Why were you looking for me? You never said."

She appeared to consider her answer. "Oh, I don't know. I was in town. I thought I'd see where you worked. That's all."

"Are you sure? Nothing's wrong?"

"Nothing I want to talk about here. It'll keep. Tell me about your dreams."

"Look, if you're having a problem yourself, you don't want to hear all this."

"Trust me." There was a definite edge to her voice. "I'll enjoy thinking about somebody else for a change."

"Have you remembered something?"

She grimaced. "You couldn't be further off course."

He wondered what was wrong with her, but he was too exhausted and too self-absorbed at the moment to probe any further. "You said you saw the film of Gypsy's death."

"I saw bits and pieces of it. I'm sure you know how the producers tantalized the viewers. A little here, a little there. It was pretty close to home after what I'd gone though. Whenever they could the sisters changed the channel."

"Maybe we shouldn't talk about this."

"I'm not going to fall apart. I was just beginning my recovery when I saw the footage. Tell me exactly what happened to her."

It was a long story, but he wanted to tell it all. He hoped it would be therapeutic.

"The December before last, Gypsy and our newest director, a guy named Mark Santini, were off having a business lunch together. On the way back to the studio, Mark was shot at point-blank range by a man who turned the gun on Gypsy. For some reason he took off before he fired. The guy was never caught, but Mark died immediately. Gypsy was sure she was supposed to be a target, too, but because there were too many people around or the gun misfired, she was spared."

Mary Kate sat forward, but she didn't say a word.

"After that the studio provided round-the-clock protection for Gyps, but no one seriously thought she was in danger. The theory was that Mark's family had ties to organized crime, and he had been murdered as retaliation for someone else's sins. Not a good theory, as it turns out."

"That wasn't the reason?"

Casey waited until his beer was served, and Mary Kate got her milk. He toasted her and took a sip. "Gypsy was the only one who thought there was more to this. Everyone else thought she was just overreacting. After all, she was the one who had to watch Mark take a bullet. One day she was on her way to give a speech on Long Island and her bodyguard, who was driving the limo, thought they were being followed. When they reached the campus where she was to speak, the bodyguard got out of the limo and collapsed on the sidewalk. Gypsy apparently thought he was the victim of foul play. She took off in the limo alone, and that's when she was in the crash I told you about before.''

"So she was running for her life . . .''

"No. The guy was a diabetic who had gone into insulin shock. But after the accident Gypsy almost died. In fact, she was pronounced dead in the emergency room before she revived.''

"I died on the way to the emergency room,'' Mary Kate said.

Casey frowned. "How long were you . . .''

"Just moments, I think. Enough to scare the pants off the paramedics.''

"Gypsy didn't have *her* memory when she recovered, either.''

"That's what you said before.''

"But there was a big difference, Mary Kate. When Gypsy finally regained consciousness, she swore she was somebody else. She thought she was the woman driving the car that she'd hit.''

Mary Kate sat up straighter. "What?''

"Yeah. When she could talk again Gypsy swore she was this other woman, Elisabeth something-or-other. Apparently while she was still out of it she heard us talking about this Elisabeth, who was in a coma down the hall. Gypsy thought she'd actually *become* her. The mind's an amazing thing.''

"How long did this . . . delusion—is that what you call it? How long did it last?''

"She stopped talking about it as soon as she realized how crazy she sounded. And she got on with her life. She went back to work, and she was still good. Damned good. The only thing is that her memory never really returned. And she'd changed. She was kinder, and she wasn't as self-centered anymore. I told you, we became friends after that, something we'd never been before.''

"Maybe she really *did* become somebody else. Maybe she *was* this Elisabeth person.''

Mary Kate sounded as incredulous as Casey felt. He allowed himself a cynical grin. "Right. Only I hear Elisabeth finally came out of her coma and resumed her life. Somebody told me the story just before I left New York. And Elisabeth's not claiming to be Gypsy Dugan.''

"I guess when someone has a near-death experience, you can't expect them to remain the same. It probably changes everybody, whether they wake up with their memories intact or not. What happened then?''

"After a while, when there was no evidence that Gypsy was in danger, the show canceled the extra security. Right afterwards Gypsy witnessed a mugging. The guy turned around and tried to shoot her. She was sure that incident was related to Mark's death, too, so the studio rehired her bodyguards. But by then, Gypsy was determined to find out who was responsible, because she was afraid that if she didn't, she would never be safe. Some people thought she was the Chia Pet of serious journalism, but Gypsy had the instincts of a top investigative reporter.''

"She found out the hard way, didn't she?''

"As it turns out, the whole thing had to do with a story that Gypsy had never even been part of. But Mark had made some discoveries about a scandal involving a former senator, Richard Adamson. Adamson wanted to be the next governor of New York, and he fixed things so his toughest opponent was caught in a compromising position. When Adamson discovered that Mark was nosing around and getting close to the truth, Adamson had him killed. We think he intended to have Gypsy killed, too, in case Mark had told her his suspicions. But something happened, the gun didn't go off, the crowds made it impossible. We'll never know. Whatever happened, Adamson's timing was bad because watching

Mark die made everything personal for Gypsy. And whatever else you could say about Gypsy, she knew how to get answers.''

Casey picked up his glass again and drained half the contents. The old woman arrived with their pierogi, and he waited until she was gone before he spoke again.

''I could get maudlin here.''

''I can see that.'' Mary Kate stared at her plate. The pierogi, filled with potatoes and cheese, were swimming in melted butter and sour cream. As she watched in obvious fascination, juice and fat from the kielbasa leaked slowly into the surrounding sauerkraut. ''Is it possible to live through this lunch?''

''If not, you die happy.''

''That's good enough for me.''

He watched her lift her fork, and he realized that she was trembling. He kicked himself for having burdened her with his problems when she obviously had some of her own. ''Mary Kate, eat. I'll tell you the rest later.''

''No. I want you to go on.''

''I'm upsetting you.''

''You're not the first today.'' She bit her lip, then she managed a smile. ''Look, I want to hear the rest of it. Please?''

He ate for a while, wishing he had never started it. ''Gypsy asked me to help her find the truth. She had a lot of enemies. People at work, people she'd done stories about, people on the far right who thought she was a tramp.''

''Was she?''

''Not really. She wasn't nearly as wild as her reputation. But she had her own way of doing things, and she didn't usually consider what trouble she might be causing for other people. If she wanted something or someone, she went after it, no holds barred.''

''Did she want you?'' Mary Kate looked up, as if she'd surprised herself. But she didn't retract the question.

"I don't know. She was as manipulative as hell. I never knew where I stood." He set down his fork and picked up his beer. "When we finally narrowed this to Richard Adamson, we decided to go after him on film. Or rather Gypsy decided. We could have presented what we'd learned to the authorities, but Gypsy said that Adamson had friends in high places and would use them. She claimed we needed direct proof. And of course, she wanted a story. So she approached a society friend who was giving a Christmas party and asked her to let us set up a camera. Gypsy was supposed to wear a microphone, maneuver Adamson into the appropriate room, and get his confession on tape."

"That sounds enormously foolhardy."

"Yeah. Doesn't it? But I was supposed to be there, right outside the door in case of trouble. She insisted Adamson wouldn't hurt her, that if he tried, she'd tell him he was being taped and that would stop him. We had our crew right on the scene. She swore she'd be all right."

"But she wasn't."

He changed the beer for a fork again and tapped it against his plate in an accelerating rhythm. "I think Gypsy knew somehow that this was going to be the end for her. I don't know how she knew, but she did. She purposely gave me the wrong directions to the party. I think she didn't want me there because she didn't want me in danger or she didn't want me to witness her death. But I did anyway, as it turns out. She confronted Adamson the way she'd planned. When he realized he was on tape, he went berserk. He picked up a paperweight and crashed it into her skull." Casey looked away. "I got there too late. She died in my arms."

Mary Kate was as pale as his napkin. Casey, who had been lost in his own story, felt a thrill of alarm. "Mary Kate?"

"I'm . . . I'm okay."

"I knew I shouldn't have told you this."

"No. I wanted to hear it. You said you dream about it. What do you dream?"

"That I'm trying to get to Gypsy. The party was in Connecticut. I drove like a maniac that night trying to find the right location. She'd sent me on a wild-goose chase all the way to the other side of the county. In my dream I'm still trying to get to her. I know she's in danger. And when I get there, she collapses." He swallowed once, then again. His voice was husky. "I guess it doesn't take a psychiatrist to figure it out, does it?"

"I guess not. You blame yourself."

"I should have known she wasn't playing straight. When a story was involved, Gypsy wasn't above lying and cheating to get her way."

"You said before that you think she was trying to protect you . . ."

"Yeah."

"If it's true, she must have cared about you."

"By then we were friends. She cared. I cared. But we'd fallen out of love."

"You loved her?"

His own words had surprised him. "It's a figure of speech."

"Not for some people." Mary Kate toyed with a pierogi, sliding the plump little turnover back and forth in its pool of butter. "Some people make the strangest decisions when they think they're in love. They . . . do things they wouldn't normally. They take chances. And then they pay the price."

"Well, she paid it big-time, didn't she? And I guess I'm paying it, too. Because I miss her." He cleared his throat. "A lot."

"Which one, Casey? The Gypsy you loved, or the woman she turned into after the accident? The lover or the friend?"

"I miss them both."

"I can understand that. If I disappeared, maybe people would miss the person I was before the beating, *and* the person I am now.'' She smiled humorlessly. ''Then again, maybe not.''

''You aren't going to disappear, Mary Kate.''

When she didn't reassure him, he narrowed his eyes. ''Unless you do something stupid.''

''Something *else* stupid.''

''What do you mean?''

She shook her head. ''I'm glad you told me, Casey.''

''Want to tell me your story now?''

''I just want to finish lunch. Then I have to get back to the center. Do you suppose you could give me a ride? I can call Grace, but—''

''I'll take you back.''

''Thanks.'' She looked up. ''I hope you don't have the dream anymore.''

''I'm having the dream because of you.''

She cocked her head in question.

''You remind me of Gypsy sometimes. Last night when you yelled at old man Holloway—well, that's exactly what she would have done.''

''Have you been friends with a woman since Gypsy died?''

''No.''

''Maybe that's the reason, then. Maybe we're becoming friends.''

''Could be . . .'' Impulsively he reached across the table and pushed a curl behind her ear, brushing her cheek with his finger as he did. ''I don't know. Maybe your friendship is even worth a nightmare or two.''

LEAF MOLD DIDN'T SMELL LIKE MOLD AT ALL, Sister Samantha was telling Mary Kate. The smell was rich and dark, the innermost reaches of a primeval forest, the fragrant elements from which life must have evolved. Mary Kate counted the newly emerging buds on the closest oak tree as Samantha, the sister she least enjoyed, continued her rhapsodic—and unscientific—ode.

"Cut it short," Mary Kate said at last, when she had counted to thirty and couldn't stand another metaphor. "We crawled out of the ocean, not a pile of decomposed leaves. The stuff doesn't smell as bad as the horse sh . . . manure. I'm grateful, you're grateful. Let's just get to work."

Samantha, tall, blonde, and the youngest, at thirty-five, of all the sisters who lived at Eden's Gate, pulled her unfocused vision back to earth and Mary Kate. "You have a way of getting right to the point, don't you?"

"Life's too short, and I've already missed a whole bunch of it."

"You didn't miss it. You just don't remember it."

And one of the things she didn't remember was growing inside her. Mary Kate scowled. "Yeah, well, take it from me, it feels exactly the same."

"I guess I'll have to take it from you. No one seems inclined to take a shovel to *me*." Immediately Samantha

99

looked contrite. "Oh, I'm sorry. I really am. I don't know what I was thinking."

"I do." Mary Kate selected a rake for herself and one for Samantha. "Let's get going."

"I'm really sorry, Mary Kate. I guess I'm just having trouble adjusting to the new you."

Mary Kate didn't remember the "old you," but she did know that everyone was having trouble readjusting. Particularly her. And particularly now that she was carrying a little secret.

She had come back to the center on Wednesday after her lunch with Casey, her mind in turmoil. It was Saturday and nothing had changed. She was carrying the child of a stranger, but why should that surprise her? She was a stranger to herself. At best she felt like a surrogate mother. Not her egg, not her lover's sperm. Not her baby.

Not her life.

"Say you forgive me," Samantha said.

"I do. Forget it." Mary Kate glanced at her watch. "We'll have our first crew out here in a few minutes. So we'd better get ready to supervise them."

Samantha, who still looked as guilty as if she had just paid her last installment on a contract killer, tossed her rake inside a wheelbarrow and trundled it out of the barn.

Mary Kate released a pent-up breath, blowing her bangs out of her eyes for good measure. As part of her recovery she had begun to take on more responsibilities. She was strengthening her body and filling her head with the information she'd forgotten. To distract herself, she had waded into her impossibly perfect gardening files and textbooks from a college education she didn't remember. Physical labor had taken the place of her physical-therapy sessions. And hard work was already improving her coordination.

Unfortunately nothing was improving her state of mind.

She couldn't understand anything about her former life. The more she studied and probed, the less she understood.

What had enticed her into a career that revolved around dirt, animal waste, and juvenile delinquents? What had brought her to the Sisters of Redemption, or to a decision that now haunted every waking moment?

"Sister Sam told me to see you . . ."

Mary Kate turned and found herself face-to-face with Tyson. Since it was a Saturday, the kids from the offender program had arrived early that morning along with the college students who got credit for helping with the program. Some of the offenders were working in the greenhouse or clearing winter debris from the orchards. Some were preparing a meal under Marie's strict supervision. Some had been assigned to help ready the garden. This was the first time Mary Kate and Tyson had been face-to-face for a conversation since she'd threatened him with a shovel.

"Oh joy." She shook her head. "Since when did you get assigned to the garden? I thought you were working in the kitchen with Marie today."

"Since they kicked my ass out of the house ten minutes ago."

"Great. And to think all I had to worry about until now was what you were putting in our lunches."

For a moment she thought Tyson was going to smile. Instead he folded his arms and hunched his shoulders as if to tell her he didn't care what she thought.

She turned her back on him, despite a voice that told her that was probably a bad idea. "Look, I don't have time for a personal war, even if I'd enjoy it immensely. So let's call a truce, shall we? You've got muscles, and we need muscles. Let's just see if we can get the garden ready for spring planting."

"Don't eat nothing green myself. Why should I help? What's in it for me?"

She selected another rake and faced him again, holding it out. His question might have been facetious, but it also went straight to the heart of this project.

When he didn't take the rake she continued to hold it out, studying him as she did. Tyson, with his short-cropped hair and long, curling eyelashes, was better than good-looking. His features were irregular but more striking because of it, and his smile, on the rare occasions it was genuine, was charm itself. He was only average height, but he had large hands and feet, as if he hadn't stopped growing. Mary Kate suspected that someday he would top six feet to become a force to be reckoned with.

"What's in it for you?" she asked, after seconds had passed and his rake was still in her hand. "You know, I don't exactly have that figured out. I'm still trying to figure out what's in it for me."

He frowned, as if that was the last answer he'd expected. She took the opportunity to continue. "I'm trying to get stronger. Nobody's ever going to hit me again, not if I have anything to do about it. I could lift weights, but that seems stupid when I can work out here instead. And this gets me out of the house, which is good enough for me right now."

He mulled that over, then he grabbed the rake. "I should have told the judge I'd rather be in jail. This place makes me crazy."

"We have that in common."

"Something's making you crazy, that's for sure."

"Yeah? Well, Sister Sunshine's gone forever, so you're just going to have to get used to Sister Tornado."

"I killed somebody. Did you know that?"

Mary Kate's heart seemed to stop mid-beat. She froze.

"Nobody told you?" He rested the rake in the crook of his arm and used it to pantomime a shotgun, squeezing an imaginary trigger once he had her in his sight. "Now, that seems like a real shame. Seems like you ought to know what you're up against."

"If you killed somebody, why aren't you in a locked facility?"

"'Cause I did it a long time ago." He smirked.

She pulled herself together. He had to be lying, just to get a rise out of her. "Oh, that relieves my mind considerably. As long as you haven't killed anybody in the last week or so . . ."

The smirk disintegrated. "You think you're something, don't you?"

"Yeah, only I don't know *what*, exactly. But one thing I'm not is afraid of you. So let's get that out of the way right now."

Tyson was like a lot of the kids who came to the center. He had learned early and well how to cover up his emotions. But for a moment Mary Kate could swear she saw something in his eyes that wasn't hatred or even confusion. For one second she thought she had a crystal-clear glimpse of the man he was meant to be. The man she and the others were supposed to help him become.

The glimpse frightened her more than his declaration, more than his imaginary gunplay. She didn't even know who *she* was. How in the hell was she supposed to help a despicable kid?

The second ended, and the boy she knew returned. "Oughta be afraid." He jabbed the rake into the ground.

"Oughta be a lot of things, I guess." *And there was at least one thing she "oughten" to be.*

"Yeah, you ought to be smarter, that's for sure."

Mary Kate leaned toward him. "You know, that's something you and I have in common. We both have a long ways to go before we figure out life."

"You and me?" He spit on the ground to make his point.

"Not a pretty thought, is it?"

A scuffle at the barn door announced the advent of three more students who were assigned to help in the garden, Lola among them.

"Look," Mary Kate said to Tyson, as the others started toward them. "I'll talk to Marie. Maybe she'll take you back in the kitchen. But if you decide to stay out here with me,

I don't want any threats. We're going to have enough to do
without you making trouble. I've forgotten more than I remember about gardening. I'm going to be winging it as it
is.''

"She kicked me out for good."

"Then you'd better take that rake and get outside. If
you're not working, they'll kick you out of the program."

She really didn't expect him to obey. Clearly life with
Tyson was going to be one complex encounter after another.
But he threw the rake over his shoulder and started for the
door. Mary Kate watched him go, and despite herself, she
wondered what the center could do to turn him into the man
who had peeked out at her from those suspicious brown
eyes.

A neighbor had plowed the garden area in preparation for
the season, and now, after a long afternoon of work, the leaf
mold and composted horse manure had been spread and
worked into the section the sisters would use for their spring
crops. The area was only about twenty by twenty feet, a
small portion of the overall garden, but by the time they had
finished, Mary Kate felt as if she had personally cultivated
half of Mother Earth.

"What are we going to grow, Mary Kate?" Lola asked.

Mary Kate placed her hands against the small of her back
and leaned into them. She recited the list she'd prepared
from her research. "Peas, potatoes, lettuce, spinach,
greens . . ."

"Greens?" Tyson raised a skeptical brow. "How would
you know what to do with greens?"

"I grow them." Or at least it appeared that she had last
year. "I don't cook them. That's Marie's job. Why?"

"My grandma cooked greens. Turnip greens. Mustard
greens. Collard.''

She was surprised at the personal revelation. Coming on
top of some really good work on Tyson's part this afternoon,

she was particularly surprised. "How did she cook them?"

"With ham fat and onions, then we ate them with vinegar. She always put a hot pepper—" He stopped and scowled. "Don't matter anyway."

"If Marie cooked them that way, I'd eat them myself." Mary Kate closed her eyes and wished she was sitting in a Jacuzzi with a big slug of Irish whisky—and maybe, a big Irishman, too. But look where thoughts like that had gotten her.

"What else did your grandmother cook?" She halfway expected him to ignore her, but the question must have been too tempting.

"Yams, okra, crowder peas."

She remembered enough to realize the vegetables he'd named were all selections that flourished south of the Mason-Dixon line. "We could give that stuff a try, I guess. We've got lots of room."

"How about melons?" Lola said.

"You don't put that stuff in now." Tyson snorted to show his disdain. "That's hot-weather stuff."

Mary Kate had the sudden suspicion that she wasn't dealing with an amateur here. "How do you know?"

"Anybody knows that." He swaggered off and with a shrug, Lola followed behind him.

The students were due back on the bus in a few minutes, so Mary Kate let them go. If they didn't show up on time, somebody else would look for them.

Samantha came to her side. "I think it went well, don't you? It's so important for them to be part of nature, so affirming of life and its cycles—" She fell silent at the expression in Mary Kate's eyes.

"Come off it. It was nasty, dirty work," Mary Kate said. "Somebody had to do it and these kids got the short straw. I doubt they were thinking about life and its cycles."

"Don't underestimate the worth of this garden, Mary Kate. The kids also learn the joys of giving. Not only will they eat from the garden when they're in camp this summer, but they'll give away a big portion of what they grow to the needy.''

Mary Kate looked at the garden, which to her seemed as large as the whole state of Kansas, and could only see all the sweat—hers, in particular—that was going to go into it this year. "Well, if gardening's such a great thing, why don't we let the needy grow their own food? Then *they* could learn all about life and its cycles.''

For once Samantha was silent. She left without saying a word.

Mary Kate felt a twinge of conscience. She had been thinking about everything that had to be done and wishing that in her former life she had been interested in something, anything, that was more glamorous than this.

She gathered the tools and put them in the wheelbarrow to store inside the barn. Every muscle ached, but at least her muscles were working the way they were supposed to. In the barn she knocked the worst of the dirt from the tools and hung them in place.

Alone for the first time that day, she realized she had nowhere to go for the next hour, until the staff meeting she was required to attend. She was supposed to report on preparations for spring planting.

She leaned against the door to her "office" and closed her eyes. Who exactly was she kidding, anyway? She didn't know what she was doing. She didn't even know what she was doing *here*. Nothing felt right. Not the place, not the work, not the life, and most certainly not the fit. Because she had nothing in common with these women or their goals. Her dreams were not of universal salvation for mankind; her dreams were of mankind, period.

She could swear she had never known the camaraderie, the friendship these women experienced with each other. She had nothing to say to them. No small talk. No common topics to discuss. She didn't think she even liked women particularly. She missed men, their voices, their smell, their touch. Except for a bunch of hostile, unappealing adolescents she was cut off from the male of the species almost entirely. The sisters' doctor and their priest were three times her age. And under the circumstances she didn't think Dr. Kane was going to find her appealing.

Only Casey was young, single, and attractive. And he was simply a friend.

She fought down the sensation that she was a prisoner in her body. She hadn't had a panic attack for weeks, not even after she'd learned she was pregnant, and she didn't want to ruin her record. She told herself she didn't have to stay at Eden's Gate. Whatever she decided about the baby, she could move on. She was young; she had a college degree; she had a private income. She could go anywhere and try her hand at anything she wanted.

Only the things she wanted seemed so foreign, so out of her reach . . .

She stumbled outside, hoping the fresh air would nip her attack in the bud. She leaned against the barn wall and closed her eyes, forcing herself to breathe slowly. Little by little the panic subsided. When she opened her eyes at last the sound of a motor drew her gaze to the driveway.

She watched as a panel delivery truck burst out from under the leafless canopy of trees and grunted toward the field. The driver slowed, then stopped, although he left the engine running. He slung his long legs over the side of the seat and slid to the ground.

Her heart picked up an extra beat or two as she watched him saunter toward her, a package tucked carelessly under his arm. He was a tall man, and he walked as if he owned the world.

"Hey there," he called.

She didn't know what to say. She lifted a hand in greeting, then quickly dropped it.

He stopped just in front of her. "Well, it's been awhile

since I seen you. How you doing these days?" The delivery man was wearing a uniform that consisted of dark, tight-as-Spandex pants and a shirt with a pocket logo that matched the one on his truck. His brown hair was long and slick, combed back from a high forehead, and she had a clear view of a tattoo on the back of one hand, a bare-breasted woman in a grass skirt and lei who danced the hula as his hand flexed.

When she didn't answer he grinned at her and pulled a cigarette from a pack in his shirt pocket. Then he reconsidered and removed the whole pack and held it out to her. "Want one?"

Had she ever smoked? She had no idea. She shook her head, but when he shrugged and lit his own, tossing the burning match on the ground at his feet, she decided the smell was not unpleasant.

He smoked silently, examining her. Finally he spoke again. "Something wrong with you? You forget how to talk?"

She cleared her throat. Somewhere inside her befuddled head there was probably an entire library of casual banter. But for the moment she couldn't access much more than a sentence. "I can talk."

"Maybe you got nothing to say?"

She had nothing to say to *him*. She couldn't imagine that she ever had, but obviously this man wasn't a stranger. It was just that like everyone else in the world, he seemed like a stranger to her. "You said yourself it's been awhile," she said, settling for something general. "What should I say?"

"You could start by telling me you're glad to see me."

Mary Kate found that hard to believe. Yet the delivery man seemed perfectly certain she *was* glad, as if they'd been friends, perhaps even more, in her pre-shovel past and expected that to continue.

Something buzzed a warning inside her. Or was it a warning? Because right along with it came a surge of something all too familiar, some distant cousin of desire despite this man's overstated preening and nonexistent charms.

And then an impossible thought . . .

"Maybe I'm not welcome here anymore?" he said.

She pulled herself together as best she could. "Everyone's welcome here. It's just that I'm a little busy."

"That so?" He blew smoke out his nostrils and propelled one hip forward so his pants stretched even tighter and the telltale bulge between his legs became more apparent. "Seems like you'd get lonely out here, nothing but nuns and delinquents to keep you company."

Mary Kate's gaze flicked down, and he shifted again, a slow rotation of his pelvis that left nothing to the imagination.

He shoved a hand in his pocket, stretching the pants even tighter. "I seen you from a distance. That's why I came out here. You're hard to miss."

She forced her gaze to his face. "Why?"

"That hair."

"Oh."

He finished his cigarette and tossed it in the vicinity of the match. He straightened. "You want the package? Or should I take it up to the house?"

"It must be something for the garden." She swallowed and reached for the carton. A quick scan indicated it was from a garden supplier, perhaps part of an order Mary Kate . . . *she* had made in the fall.

He had big arms, and under the shirt she could see the play of his muscles as he pulled his arms back toward his chest.

Her surroundings seemed to dim and shimmer, and suddenly she had a vision of a man's naked chest and muscular arms. Worse yet, she had a vision of herself in those arms. And the woman's body she glimpsed was not small and sturdy. The panic began to build again, stronger this time.

"Not much for conversation anymore, are you?" He

shook his head. "You ever decide you want to . . . talk or *something* again, you just let me know. Just tell the dispatcher Cooper told you it was all right to call."

His lips curled back and nearly disappeared, showing crooked teeth and an oversized tongue, then with a wink he turned and sauntered back to his truck.

The tires squealed as he backed it into the field and turned toward the road, and in a moment he was out of sight again.

Mary Kate rested her head in her hands. "Or something? Damn it! Or *something? Again?*"

Her mouth had suddenly gone dry and her hands had compensated by sweating profusely. She was supposed to be a nun. Well, almost. She was a nun wannabe. Her heart's desire was to be a nun—or at least that's what she had been told.

The delivery man in the tight, tight pants hadn't treated her like a nun or a wannabe. But had he treated her the way a man treats a woman with whom he'd been intimate? Was this man, this caricature of masculinity, the father of her baby?

The barn seemed to dissolve behind her so that she was left floundering in space, and a buzzing began in her ears. She clutched the carton under her arm, as if it would keep her from falling, and her eyes squeezed shut as she tensed all her muscles.

Suddenly she was in another time and place again, both unfamiliar, and she had a cloudy vision of herself returning a man's wink. It seemed like the most natural thing in the world. She could see herself winking . . . Only the face, the eyelid snapping shut with sassy intent didn't seem to be her own.

And then, as if it had never happened, the vision was erased.

Her eyelids flew open. Panic began to build inside her. Mary Kate drew a shaky breath, then another, but neither was enough to prevent her from sinking to the ground.

*   *   *

"You're sure you're up to this, Mary Kate?" Sarah was one of the few women Casey knew who could combine compassion with a business-as-usual demeanor. "Someone can fill you in later, if you'd rather rest."

"I'm fine. Please. I just got dizzy for a few moments. I didn't even faint. I just stretched myself a little too thin today. I'm sorry I frightened Samantha."

"Well, we're all concerned about you."

Casey watched something, humiliation perhaps, flit across Mary Kate's perky little face. "There's no need to be," she said.

Sarah straightened a sheaf of papers on the table in front of her. "All right. We're hoping to make this brief, anyway."

Casey hoped that Sarah would live up to that promise. He hadn't wanted to attend this Saturday staff meeting. Sitting in a Victorian parlor with a handful of nuns and other assorted helpers was not his idea of a good way to spend an afternoon.

He still asked himself on a daily basis why he had agreed to help with the center's newsletter. But every time he thought about telling Sarah to find someone to take his place, he remembered a young man who had grown up with few adults to supervise him and none who had been willing to hold a simple conversation. As a teenager he had longed for someone to listen and care about him, and the more he had longed for it, the harder he had worked to drive away all possible candidates.

He understood these kids. And as much as he hated the thought, he owed them something.

He sat through a barrage of reports, professionally rendered and edited to the bone. He had come at Sarah's request just to get a feel for the way the center staff worked together. His own project didn't start for another month.

His mind wandered, and so did his eyes. Mary Kate

looked tired, and he supposed the sisters had reason to be worried about her. Her freckles stood out in sharp relief on skin as pale as buttermilk. Her hair was a freshly washed rebellion of curls that bounced against her forehead and ears with more energy than she seemed to have elsewhere in her body. She was dressed in a shapeless navy-blue sweatsuit, and not for the first time he wished he could see her in something more form-fitting.

Just to subdue his curiosity.

Sarah looked at her watch at last. "I think we're about finished here. Mary Kate, do you have anything to tell us before we go?"

Casey reined in his wandering attention to hear what she would say.

"We prepared a plot for a spring garden this afternoon. Everyone worked well together. Abraham's lazy, but the other kids kept him in line, especially Tyson." Mary Kate looked up from the spot on the floor where she'd been staring. "You know, Tyson told me that he killed somebody. How am I supposed to handle a lie like that one?"

The ticking of a grandfather clock filled the pause.

"It's not a lie," Sarah said at last. "So you handle it as his attempt to share something important with you."

Mary Kate's eyes widened. "He *killed* somebody?"

Casey was glad he'd already finished his article about the school. This was not something he wanted to add to it.

"Accidentally, yes. Tyson and his little brother were living with his grandmother at the time. Tyson found a revolver in his grandmother's dresser drawer and didn't know the gun was real. He aimed the gun at his brother and pulled the trigger, and his brother died."

Mary Kate looked stunned. Casey had reported too many handgun stories himself to be anything except saddened.

"Tyson was eight years old," Sarah said. "His grandmother had a heart attack at the funeral and died two days later. Tyson was sent back to live with his mother. Apparently every single day she reminds him of what he did. The result is exactly what you might expect. Tyson's been in almost every kind of trouble imaginable. And the story might end there except that he found his way to this program, and we're going to make sure he has another chance.''

"Why would he say it to me that way? He sounded proud of himself.''

"A kid like Tyson won't let you get next to him,'' Casey said, before he had realized that he was going to join the conversation. "He probably said it the only way he could.''

"I think he was hoping he could shock me.''

"It's interesting that he's chosen you to confide in,'' Sarah said. "This may be his way of establishing a relationship.''

"Bad choice. His brain must be as scrambled as mine.'' Mary Kate examined her nails as if none of this mattered, but Casey thought her hand was shaking. "Anyway, that's about it. If the weather remains dry, we'll plant the garden over the next two weeks. Then we'll prepare the rest of it for summer crops.''

"That's not quite all,'' one of the younger sisters said, a blonde with a beatific smile.

Sarah looked at her watch in warning. "Yes, Samantha?''

"I have an idea. May I present it quickly, then you can decide whether to discuss it now?''

"If it's a *short* presentation.''

"Mary Kate said something important to me today. She pointed out that if working in the garden is important to us, we have to find a way to let the needy do the same thing.''

As Casey watched, Mary Kate sat up straighter, her eyebrows drawing together in an unfocused frown.

Samantha continued. "I know we agreed to postpone the community garden until Mary Kate was better. But I think she *is* better. I think she's ready to tackle this, aren't you, Mary Kate?''

Mary Kate seemed stunned into silence. Casey was filled

with sympathy, and he bought her some time. "What community garden? I don't remember hearing about this."

"We have lots of land," Samantha said. "And most of it's not being used. The center's garden is well underway because of all the work Mary Kate's done in the past. Last fall we decided to begin a new garden this year, a community garden that we could open up to anyone in Shandley Falls who would like to participate."

Casey watched Mary Kate. The frown was deepening, the eyes were widening.

Samantha continued. "We need better relations in town, and we thought this might be one way to make that happen. The land we've set aside adjoins our own garden. We planned to plow it, divide it into beds, and let people have space to grow anything they want. We'll take surplus produce to local food banks or shelters, the way that we do with our garden. Only there will be more of it. We can even use it as a teaching garden for schoolchildren in town."

"This isn't the inner city," Casey said. "A lot of people in the area already have gardens."

"That's true, but we'll be drawing from three primary sources." Samantha continued as spokeswoman. "The public-housing project out on the highway. The Landsdowne Apartments for seniors down the road. And children from the day-care center just beyond the apartments. No one in public housing is allowed to garden there. The Landsdowne has no attached land and very formal landscaping, and the day-care center has taken up all their available space with playground equipment. The residents of the housing project and the Landsdowne can walk here, if they have to. The day-care center has a bus. The garden will bring together old people, young people, poor people, the teenagers in our offender program . . ." She beamed a radiant smile to all four corners of the room. "Think what we'll be able to do!"

"This is a very comprehensive plan . . ."

"Yes, I know. But we have Mary Kate, who will organize

it. We have the teenagers and the student counselors to help with the chores. We have—''

"What?" Mary Kate sat forward, her attention one hundred percent focused. Casey tried not to smile.

Samantha beamed a laser-intense smile right at Mary Kate. "Of course you'd have to be in charge. You're the only one who's had the experience and training, the only one who knows how to pull this off. How to prepare the soil. How to—''

"Why didn't you ask me? Maybe I don't want to pull it off. Maybe I don't remember how.''

"Oh, of course you want to do it. It was your idea. You dedicated the site to your parents in the fall.''

"I don't know anything about putting together a garden like this one. I don't know anything about anything!''

"You're not giving yourself much credit,'' Sarah said. "Look how far you've come already. Are you saying you can't do this or you won't?''

Mary Kate clamped her lips together, as if she was afraid something terrible might slip between them.

"Well, I think it's a good idea to reconsider this now,'' Sarah said. "We definitely need a project that will unite the community and prove our goodwill. And it's a perfect use of the land we were given by your aunt, Mary Kate. It's not as if you'd have to do the work alone. You'd just have to organize everyone. And I think you're up to the challenge.''

"Your faith is misplaced,'' Mary Kate said.

"It never has been before.'' Sarah got to her feet. "Let's adjourn for now. Mary Kate, you think about it. Samantha, I'm assuming that since you brought this to our attention again, you'll be willing to take on some of the work above and beyond what you're doing now?''

"Oh, absolutely.''

"Good. We'll consider it again at our Monday planning meeting.'' Sarah held out her arms. "Let's join hands for prayer.''

Casey hadn't expected this finale, although if he'd given even the slightest thought to it, he would have. He stood, unsure and uncomfortable, but the two women beside him nonchalantly grasped his hands and pulled him into the circle.

The prayer was short and to the point, very Sarah. He was struck by how comfortable these women were with each other and their God. For the most part they were practical and down-to-earth, secure in their faith and in their purpose in the world.

Before his discomfort could grow, the prayer was over and everyone was heading for the door.

Mary Kate was the only other person who wasn't moving. She looked much as she probably had at the beginning of her recovery. He didn't feel sorry for her. Not exactly, anyway. Mary Kate was much too feisty to elicit sympathy. But with a sizable dent in her bravado, she stirred something else inside him. Recognition, he supposed. A few times in his life he'd felt that life was out to get him, too. He knew the signs.

He strolled to her side and stood shoulder-to-shoulder with her, staring at the same spot on the carpet. "You can still say no. They'll understand."

"No one here ever says no, Casey. It's just not done. It's a benevolent dictatorship, only the guy in charge is invisible."

"Come on, what could happen if you refuse? They won't tell you to leave. You're still recovering, and they know it."

"Don't you see?" Life sparked in her eyes again. "They've been so good to me. They've held my hand every step of the way."

"And you're afraid of hurting them?"

"Not particularly." She laced her fingers behind her neck and rested her head against them. "I just don't want the hassle."

Casey thought she was lying to them both. "I see. It's just a bother to have to deal with it."

"That's right."

"Well, I bet you'll figure out a way to break the news to Sarah and Samantha. I'm sure they'll come up with someone else who can supervise this project."

She seemed to brighten a little more. "They could, couldn't they? Maybe they could get a grant and hire a professional—"

"Sure. But not for this summer, of course. Next year, or the year after. But what does it matter?"

"Right. I don't see why it does . . ."

"Absolutely not. The ground will still be there in a couple of years. People will still be hungry. Hungrier, even." He shot her his best pirate smile. "In a couple of years the sisters will be in even bigger need of good public relations. Hell, by then they might be in really serious trouble."

She faced him, eyes narrowed. "They've gotten to you already, haven't they? You're thinking like them."

"Oh, I doubt that. They're much kinder than I'll ever be."

"I'm not going to supervise a new garden. I don't know a pea from a potato! I'm not going to do it."

He laid his palm against her cheek, a cheek that was even softer than it looked. "Go get 'em, Katie girl. Tell them, the way you just told me. They'll be quaking in their Reeboks."

~ 7

OWNING NEXT TO NOTHING MADE PACKING easy. Mary Kate conducted one last search of her attic room and didn't turn up anything except two frugally sharpened pencil nubs and a 1994 calendar with a different sugary platitude for each day of the year.

She didn't have a suitcase, but she didn't have much she wanted to take with her, anyway. How many overalls would she need in her new life? How many gardening journals? Along with the world's most boring underwear she folded a Rock and Roll Hall of Fame sweatshirt, her best pair of jeans—which weren't going to fit much longer—two T-shirts, and a tent-style dress that was as outdated as the calendar. She stuffed them into an old leather briefcase along with the framed photographs of her family. She had changed into green stretch pants and a white sweater; now she slipped on her brown worn-at-the-cuffs ski jacket and discount-store hiking boots. Finally she rose, clutching the briefcase under her arm.

She wondered whether to leave a note. What would she say? *I'm pregnant, and I have to find out how it happened? Oh, and by the way I hate this life? I hate the garden, the kids? And most of all I don't understand the way you women think and feel about things?*

Mary Kate didn't think she was easily overcome by emotion, but her heart was pounding, and her breath was coming in rapid, shallow puffs. She fought for control, trying hard to regulate each lungful of air.

She had to leave this place. She had to get out tonight. She hadn't told anyone about the baby. In fact, she had lied about her visit to Dr. Kane, reporting that he had found no cause for alarm. How could she tell these women that she was pregnant and she didn't even know if she was going to carry the baby to term? She could just see the looks on their faces, the disappointment, the shattered trust.

Even if she went through with the pregnancy she didn't belong here. There were too many expectations at Eden's Gate, too many demands. The community garden was the worst example yet. She had seen the markers, but she hadn't understood. Despite the sisters' faith in her and Casey's jibes, she had no intention of slaving from sunrise to sunset for a project she couldn't remember suggesting in the first place.

She waited until she was calmer, then she stood again and picked up the briefcase. Since nothing she could say made her departure easier, she decided against a note. When she was settled somewhere and secure she would call Sarah. She owed her that much. But until then, the best she could do was to get out quickly.

The house was silent. The Sisters of Redemption might not conform to many traditions, but they did respect each other's privacy at night. Mary Kate guessed that even if she banged her briefcase on every stair rail and yodeled as she made her escape, no one would come to investigate.

She checked her wallet. She had forty dollars, a credit card, and checkbook plus the phone number of the attorney in Cleveland who was in charge of her estate. She had concentrated so hard on her recovery that she had paid little attention to his reports about her own financial situation. But she would find a motel, then call him tomorrow to find out how secure she really was. At that point she would decide what to do next.

And what to do about the baby and the baby's father.

She took one look around the attic room before she closed the door behind her. She had been raised in this house, but it still felt foreign to her. She experienced none of the nostalgia or regret she should have. She was simply glad to be leaving.

No one confronted her as she descended the steps or made her way through the first-floor rooms and let herself outside. The night was cold and damp, but she supposed by the time she made it into town, she would be warm enough. For just a moment she hesitated on the brick walkway leading to the road and freedom. Sarah, the warmhearted bureaucrat, would worry that she had asked for too much from Mary Kate too soon. Grace, the psychologist, would be afraid she hadn't listened well enough. She wondered what Tyson would say when he discovered she was gone. Who would he torment now? And what would Casey think?

She was glad none of them was her problem. She zipped up her coat and started the long walk to town.

Shandley Falls was exactly the kind of town that Casey had vowed to leave behind forever. He had started his career in a place much like this one, a shell-shocked city boy marooned in an Iowa farm town until the day he finally moved up to a "big city" paper in Cedar Rapids. He had gotten his start in television in Cedar Rapids, too, moving swiftly up the food chain to Santa Fe, Denver, and finally back to the east coast and an anchor position in Baltimore. From there he had gone on—and home—to New York and *The Whole Truth*.

Now he was back in the Midwest again. More specifically he was in a nondescript compact car, parked beside a building with a plate-glass window advertising carpet remnants, organic flea remedies, and the best doughnuts in Shandley Falls. Across the street a randomly blinking neon sign announced that the Dew Drop Inn, a run-down bar with iron grilles on the windows—and his real purpose for parking here—was famous for its chicken-wing specials and boycott of imported beer.

Casey had been told that the Inn's unadvertised special was the fistfights that broke out every other week when payday rolled around at the viscose factory. The fights were the stuff of legend. The local hospital routinely assigned extra staff to the emergency room that night, and once a year or so the cops staged a raid and used the brawls to sharpen their skills and train their rookies.

For the most part the raids, like the fights, were good-natured. The participants were led from the bar in handcuffs, booked, and fingerprinted while they chatted with the arresting officers about football and hunting. Bail was made, fines were paid, and two weeks later there was business as usual at the Inn.

Nearly a year had passed since the last raid. This morning Casey's source at the local police station had warned him that there were plans for one tonight.

He had kept watch all evening. So far the only thing that had passed for excitement was a teenage boy mooning a speeding car. The Dew Drop Inn was a male bastion, and a parade of jovial men had wandered in and out of it all evening. But the witching hour was approaching.

Bars all over the country heated up at ten o'clock. By ten-thirty they were swinging, and by eleven the fists were usually flying. Casey glanced at his watch and saw it was past ten. He had waited to go inside so that he wouldn't attract attention. He knew the police were on alert. The only provocation they needed was one balled fist, one customer hitting the floor. Casey planned to watch from the sidelines to cheer on his favorite and record the results.

There was a little bit of Hell's Kitchen in every city.

Casey flipped through several notepads before he found one that was inconspicuous enough to slide into his pocket. He was looking forward to getting out of the car, if not to the evening's entertainment. On the other hand, the last story he'd covered was a library slide show entitled "Traveling with Your Toddler." He had learned more about graham crackers and disposable diapers than he would ever need, even if he suddenly inherited an orphanage. At least this promised to keep him awake.

His hand was resting on the door handle when he glanced up to see a familiar figure strolling down the sidewalk. He took in the green pants, the familiar, shapeless ski jacket, the hiking boots. He didn't move; he didn't even breathe. He watched and waited.

And Mary Kate didn't disappoint him.

Mary Kate's feet were sore, and every inch that wasn't sore was numb. The center of town was farther than she'd remembered. On her search for a telephone she had passed a grocery store that was closed for the night, a service station with a telephone but no receiver and a telephone booth occupied by an old woman with quarters piled so high it might well have been her life savings.

Mary Kate had needed a phone to search for a motel. A motel itself would have been that much better, but so far nothing had materialized. Apparently Shandley Falls closed its doors at dark. She had discovered a video store that was still open, but the clerk—as young as the kids in the offender program and every bit as hostile—hadn't had any suggestions for a place to stay. Mary Kate had passed right by the police station, but on the odd chance that the sisters had reported her missing she had been afraid to stop there.

So she had continued her hike until she saw the blinking sign of the Dew Drop Inn. Since the invitation seemed particularly welcome to her tired feet, she decided she *would* drop in and see if anyone there might have a suggestion. She could have a soft drink, rest a little, and plan the remainder of her night.

She was inside the bar before she wondered if she had

made a mistake. Country music screeched from an oversized jukebox in the corner, and men shouted over a game of pool. Smoke from a dozen cigarettes was so thick that the bar which ran down the left side of the room seemed to hover in a cloud. With something approaching guilt, she wondered what Dr. Kane would think.

She stood blinking in the doorway, searching for another woman. She didn't want a friend. She didn't want a conversation. She just wanted a little reassurance that women had survived this experience.

A couple of men turned to watch her, and one by one the others fell into line. The song on the jukebox ended, and there was a lull. Just as she decided to turn and leave, someone opened the door behind her, shoving her farther into the room.

It was too late to turn back now. She squared her shoulders and headed for the only empty seat in the room, smackdab at the middle of the bar. The stool looked as if it had been used for every purpose except firewood, but she climbed on board, adjusting her fanny so that the ripped plastic seat cover didn't gouge her private parts, and stowed her briefcase on the floor at her feet.

"You're one of a kind in this place, doll," the man on her right said.

Mary Kate had already figured that out. She ignored him except for a glance and a raised brow.

"Not too many women brave enough to come in here."

The man was a giant with a blond beard and a bandanna. Mary Kate had seen enough to know he was not to be trifled with. She felt him move closer, felt the brush of his huge thigh against hers.

"I'm not brave," she improvised in a small, scared voice. "But when you've got . . ." She let her voice drift off. She sniffed. "Well, when you've got . . . my problem, there's no reason to worry about little things. Not anymore." She faced him so he could appreciate the full extent of her talent. "Do you know what I mean?"

He looked as if he ought to be scratching his head. But he didn't move any closer.

"I guess you don't know Bruno, then," she said in a breathy voice. "And what he's capable of when he's mad. And he'll be so mad when he finds I've left him."

"Bruno?"

"I thought everybody knew Bruno. But maybe it's just those sharks who work for him . . ."

He moved away, and they were no longer touching.

She gave him a shaky smile. "I can't blame you for not wanting to get involved."

He moved farther away and turned his head. In a moment he got up and vacated his seat.

Mary Kate searched for the bartender, but he was down at the other end of the bar engaged in a heated conversation. She tapped her nails on the counter and looked around.

Enough testosterone oozed through the room to coat the plywood paneling and peel the vinyl off the bar, but she wasn't afraid. She took a deep smoky breath and felt it fog her lungs. *This* was why she'd left. Maybe before the beating she had believed that the narrow confines of Eden's Gate were all she needed, but the woman who had come back to life afterwards knew better. She needed men and the world they lived in. She needed excitement.

She needed to figure out *what* man she had needed approximately three months ago and counting . . .

"Remember me?"

Ready to go through the same stupid story again, she glanced toward the stool that had only stayed empty for a moment, and found a familiar face grinning at her.

She remembered the delivery man's name from their brief conversation that afternoon. "Cooper . . ."

"What are you doing here?"

She considered telling him that she was running away.

But she didn't think that Cooper was really her friend. She knew nothing about him except that he had at least one tasteless tattoo and wore his pants too tight.

"I just came into town for the evening. Looks like I came to the right place. This seems to be where all the action is."

"Oh, I don't know. There's plenty of action at my place . . . or could be."

She might have escaped from a convent, but a nun cloistered for seventy years would not have mistaken his meaning.

She considered telling him to get lost. But wisdom prevailed. Cooper had intimated a number of things that afternoon. Everything he'd said could be taken for idle chitchat, but what if it wasn't? What if she had known him before her injury? What if she'd known him in the Biblical sense?

God forbid, what if he were the father of her child?

She tried to swallow her distaste so she could probe for information. "And where is your place?"

"By the tracks, over the auto-supply store."

She was relieved he hadn't expected her to know. "Traded comfort for scenery, huh?"

His expression remained blank, as if he wasn't quite sure what she'd meant.

She cut to the chase. "Are you married, Cooper?"

"Name only."

"You mean your wife lives somewhere else?"

"She and the kids live with her mother up in Michigan. I'd get rid of her for good, only it costs too much."

She wasn't sure if he was talking about a divorce or a hit man. "You'd better work on your line."

"Why? You looking for something more than a little excitement tonight?" He signaled the bartender, who finished his conversation and strolled over to stand in front of them. He was nearly as big as the blond she'd scared away, with a jagged scar distorting one cheek.

"Hey, Coop. Who's your friend?"

Cooper was silent, and Mary Kate realized he didn't remember her name and probably wouldn't have even if he was cold sober. She hoped he had never *known* her name. She hoped he had never known *her*.

"Jennifer," she said, choosing a name from thin air. "Jennifer . . ." Her eyes focused on a sign just beyond him. "Jennifer Miller." She considered hyphenating it to "Miller-Lite," but figured there was a slight chance the two men would catch on.

"I call her Jenny. What'll you have, Jenny?" Cooper put his hand on her knee and squeezed.

Mary Kate's breath caught, and for a moment she wasn't sure she could breathe again. "Um . . . a Coke. No, make it club soda."

"She's not much of a drinker," Cooper told the bartender. He squeezed her knee again.

Mary Kate gazed down at Cooper's hand, and the hula dancer did an extra little shimmy as his hand crept higher. When she looked back up at him, he was leering at her, his intentions clear.

"What do you say we drink up and get out of here?" he said, when the club soda arrived. "Bar's no place for a lady. Not on payday."

Apparently he thought his apartment was the appropriate place for a lady. Mary Kate supposed that if she asked Cooper to help her find a motel, he would make sure she got a room with a king-size bed.

"What happens on payday?" she asked, buying time.

"Things get a little noisy." He winked.

She wanted to tell him that winking was not a good idea. The resulting wrinkles were a preview of Cooper at sixty, and not a pretty sight. But she supposed if she told him that much, she'd have to tell him not to smile, too. And then, what was left?

"I like noise." She picked up her glass and toasted him. "I miss noise. Excitement." She knew better than to add "men." Right now she was reconsidering whether she missed them or not.

"I can give you all the excitement you need."

"You're a real philanthropist, Cooper."

"No need for name-calling."

"I mean you obviously like to do things for people."

He still looked confused. "Like it better when people do things for me."

She knew exactly what kinds of things he was talking about, and all the hormones in the world couldn't make any of them sound like fun to her. Not with him, anyway.

"Do you come here often?" she asked, shifting her leg in hopes that he would move his hand.

He held on as tight as a drowning man. "I'd come more often if I knew you were gonna be here."

"I seem to be the only woman in the room."

"Don't you worry. I'll take care of you."

She was afraid he might actually try. "That's okay. I like to be independent."

His hand crept higher until his fingertips were wedged where they really shouldn't be. She looked down, then back up at him as she sipped. "I also like friendly. But not that kind of friendly."

"Only kind I know . . ."

In that moment she realized how truly confused she must have been to think that she might ever have had a relationship with Cooper, how victimized by her odd situation. The guy was witless and slimy, a married man whose entire world revolved around the activity between his legs. He wasn't attractive or sexy. He was just a man, and a poor specimen at that. She didn't remember anything about who she had been, but she *knew* she had not been attracted to this man.

Only one approach was going to work to discourage him. "Move your hand. Right now." She scowled at him over her club soda.

"Now, don't go getting mad." He inched his hand to a safer place. "I was just letting you know I was here."

"Oh, I know you're here. You and your little hula-dancing friend and whatever diseases you're carrying. You might be here, but I'm not going to be in a minute."

She set the nearly full glass on the counter and pulled out her wallet, selecting a five-dollar bill and dropping it in front of her. She tried to get up, but he pressed down on her leg to keep her there.

"You think you're too good for me?"

"Truthfully?" She pretended to think for a moment. "I think almost anybody is."

"You got so many men beating down your door out there with them nuns you can afford to be picky?"

"I can afford to be picky even if nobody *ever* looks at me."

"Maybe it's true what they say about you ladies. Maybe you live out there with no men around 'cause—"

That was all Mary Kate needed to hear. She stood, despite his attempt to hold her in place, picked up what was left of her club soda, and dumped it in his lap.

He screeched and leapt off his stool. She grabbed her briefcase and backed away, moving steadily toward the door. "Don't follow me," she ground out between clenched teeth as he started toward her. "Or you'll get more than club soda between your legs!"

He sprang, and anticipating that, she threw herself to the side to evade him. She expected to see Cooper stretched out on the floor, but when she looked down there were two men where one should have been.

Cooper and Casey.

She didn't know *how* Casey had gotten there, or when. And she didn't have time to wonder. The men were rolling toward her, and she backed away. Casey was on top, then he wasn't. Cooper looked drunk enough to get a new tattoo, but he was punching and kicking with more expertise than she would have expected.

Someone shoved her from behind, and she realized that now fists were flying in that corner of the room, too. In fact, the whole bar had erupted in a fight, and she seemed to be the only one without an opponent.

"Casey!" She pounded on his back with the briefcase the moment he rolled on top of Cooper again. "Casey! Come on! We've got to get out of here. We're going to get killed!"

A new sound joined the ones of glass breaking and chairs splintering. A high-pitched screeching, like the wailing of someone in pain.

Or the siren of a police car.

"Casey!" She grabbed him by the shoulders and tried to haul him away from Cooper, who was still going strong. "Casey, the cops are coming!"

"I know! It's ... a raid!" He shrugged her off and shoved Cooper against the floor.

"Come on! We've got to get out of here."

For a moment she thought he might listen. Then Cooper landed a punch on Casey's chin, and the two men were at it again.

Mary Kate ducked her head as something whizzed through the air in her direction, then she made one last grab for Casey.

"Casey! We've got to get out of here!" This time she held tight to the shoulder of his shirt and tried to pull him away, but Cooper tugged him down for another roll, and she was left with a handful of good-quality cotton.

Mary Kate looked around for help, but everyone in the bar was already busy with other things. "The cops are coming!" she screamed. "Cops!"

But nobody was interested in a news report.

"Jeez!" Through the grimy window of the bar she saw the distant flashing of a red light that was moving closer.

"Casey!"

He was on top momentarily, at least, but Cooper had him by the hair. He couldn't, or wouldn't, look in her direction. She considered all her options, then took the only one that was really left to her.

The door slammed behind her, but she doubted that anyone slugging and dodging inside the Dew Drop Inn even knew that the cause of their battle had vanished into the night.

8

THE HOLDING TANK AT THE SHANDLEY FALLS jail was ten by ten and perfumed with equal parts of stale urine and Lysol. As if that wasn't bad enough, Casey was sharing his new quarters with twelve men who added top notes of vomit, sweat, and cigarette smoke. One of the most fragrant was sitting beside him on the bench that stretched along one wall.

"Shoulda hit him harder." Buddy, a Homer Simpson lookalike, was too drunk to successfully control any part of his body, which was the reason for the smell. On the last word his head lolled back against the wall with a resounding thump. "You shoulda hit Cooper—"

"I did hit him. He's snoozing the night away in that corner over there." Casey had judged that sitting beside Buddy was better than standing, but now he understood why no one else had grabbed this seat. He fanned the air with little effect. One of Shandley Falls' finest, the same potbellied cop who had arrested him, came to the cell door jangling a key ring that looked like it had been lifted from an old *Gunsmoke* rerun. "Who's next?"

Casey wasn't. Right at the beginning the men had drawn lots to decide the order in which to make their one telephone call. He was number nine. Worse, Buddy was number ten.

The door swung open and number two, a little man with a dried-apple face and tufts of hair springing from his ears, followed the cop with the keys down the hall.

Buddy thumped his head again. "Shoulda hit him."

"Shut up before I practice on you." Casey propped his elbows on his knees and rested his forehead in his hands. The threat was idle. He hadn't been in a barroom fight in years, not since he'd first started at *The Whole Truth* and one of the other reporters had accused him of stealing a story. He had no intention of hitting anyone again.

He couldn't imagine what had gotten into him tonight. He had followed Mary Kate inside, purely for protection. Well, that and a huge dose of curiosity. He didn't know why he felt responsible for her, except that she was new to the world in more ways than one. She had led the most innocent of lives, and she didn't even remember that.

So, all right, he had followed her because his heart wasn't as black as his reputation. He had been concerned and curious. But unfortunately the second had taken precedence over the first. He'd had the opportunity to let Mary Kate know he was there, to steer her out the door before violence erupted. But he had been so intrigued by what she might do and why she'd gone into the bar that he'd put his good sense on hold.

And now he was sitting in the Shandley Falls jail and Mary Kate had disappeared into the night.

She was a crazy woman.

"Casey? Charles Casey?"

Casey realized that the cop with the keys was back and calling his name. He lifted his head. "I'm not next."

"Somebody paid your bail."

Casey sat up straight. "What?"

"You can go."

He sat perfectly still, frowning at the cop.

"Shoulda hit him," Buddy mumbled.

That was all Casey needed to spur him to his feet. "Who paid it?" he asked as he crossed the cell, picking his way over two men who were sitting on the floor.

"Think I care?" the cop said.

Casey couldn't imagine who might know he was in jail. He had told Jim about his plans for the evening, but Jim lived on his family's farm outside of town and always went to bed early so he could get up with the roosters.

The cop took care of the final paperwork and made sure that Casey had the contents of his pockets and his nylon windbreaker returned to him. Then he opened the door and ushered him into the next room.

Mary Kate was waiting, thumbs hooked in the pockets of her beat-up ski jacket. "You shouldn't have hit him, Casey."

"Ah, the mystery lady."

She took her time closing the distance between them, then she reached up to touch a bruise on his cheek. "Whatever possessed you?"

He winced, although her touch was as light as a feather. "I could ask you the same." And he intended to.

"Let's get out of here."

"You're not driving, are you?"

"No, I've got a cab outside to take us back to your car." She slipped her hand through his arm as if he might need help balancing. "Come on."

He let her lead him outside. The cab probably qualified for heritage plates, but once they got in, the driver sped away from the curb and started toward the Dew Drop Inn.

"It's the only cab in town," Mary Kate said. "A one-cab town." She shook her head.

He watched her from his side of the backseat. "You've been a busy girl tonight. Bar-hopping. Trips to the bail bondsman, the jail. Rides in a Model T . . ."

She fingered his torn shirt collar. "What were you trying to do in there? I was doing all right by myself. I didn't need a knight in shining armor."

"Sure, you were doing great. Where did you dig up that guy? Derelicts-R-Us?"

"He delivers packages to the center."

"And you arranged to meet him at the bar tonight?"

"No! I was trying to find a telephone."

"I see. You walked into town from Eden's Gate. That's what, two miles? Three? Just to use a telephone? The phones at the center weren't working?"

"I left Eden's Gate. Period." She lifted a battered leather briefcase from the floor at her feet. "I've got everything I own in here."

"You were running away?"

"Not running away. I was . . ." She was silent a moment. "I was running away."

"Why? What happened?"

The cab driver interrupted. "Where do you want me to drop you, lady?"

"In the lot across the street from the bar," Casey told him.

Mary Kate sat back. "I'm not sure *what* happened. I just thought . . . I just didn't think . . ."

"You sure didn't think before you went into the Dew Drop Inn."

"Yeah? Well, you didn't think too hard before you punched Cooper either."

"I was protecting your virtue."

"That's rich. Sorry, but you wasted your time."

He opened his mouth to ask her what she meant but decided against it. He was silent for the minute it took to turn the corner and screech to a halt in front of the Inn.

He held up his hand when Mary Kate reached in her pocket, and paid for the cab ride himself. Then he got out and waited for her to join him.

The cab roared away and they were left to contemplate each other on the dark street. Not surprisingly the Dew Drop Inn had closed for the night.

"How much did they hold you up for at the bondsman?" he asked.

"A couple of hundred. Luckily he took credit."

"I'll pay you back tomorrow." Casey hesitated. "If I can find you."

"I can't tell you where I'll be. I . . . I haven't had time to find a motel."

"Yeah. It's been a busy night. Running away. Starting a riot. Visiting jail to see how the locals live . . ."

"I thought . . . maybe you'd give me a ride somewhere? I guess I should have asked the driver . . ."

"Why didn't you?"

She sighed. "Because you need somebody to help you get cleaned up, you big oaf. And I feel responsible."

"I see. You want to go back to my place and pour alcohol on my wounds?"

"That's not the first invitation I've had tonight."

"The best one?"

"You don't live over the auto-supply store, do you?"

He shook his head.

"You don't have any stupid tattoos, do you?"

"Not that you'll ever see."

She dimpled. "Then it's the best one."

He couldn't help himself. He smiled, too, even though his face felt like a raw sirloin. He slung his arm over her shoulders and propelled her toward his car.

Mary Kate hadn't had any expectations about Casey's accommodations. If she'd given them any thought she would have guessed a nondescript apartment in a singles complex, the kind with Friday-night getting-to-know-you parties beside a swimming pool with too much chlorine.

She certainly never would have envisioned the brick Colonial on the outskirts of Shandley Falls.

"Where's the wife and the one-point-eight kids?" she asked, when he pulled into a driveway lined with lilacs.

"She piled the kids and the dogs into the station wagon and took off for two weeks at the Grand Canyon."

The house was two-story and solid, in a neighborhood where stay-at-home moms kept an eye on each other's children when they weren't chairing PTA fund-raisers or volunteering at the library. It was the kind of neighborhood where a pregnancy would be celebrated with showers and gifts, where the baby was supposed to grow into a secure, well-rounded child and teenager and finally into an adult who would raise more of the same.

It was the kind of neighborhood and life a baby deserved.

Mary Kate clasped her hands over her belly. "Casey, this isn't you at all."

"I guess that's why I'm enjoying it. I feel like I'm living in a foreign country." Casey hit a garage-door opener attached to the sedan's sun visor and drove into a three-car garage. The remaining two spaces were taken by a motorboat and a worktable sporting enough power tools to construct a small city.

Casey parked and got out and Mary Kate joined him. "Actually, I was kidding about the dogs," he said. "They aren't at the Grand Canyon. They're inside."

"You have dogs?"

"The house, car, dogs, life, everything belongs to Watson Turnbull, the guy I'm replacing at *The Cricket*. It was all part of the package."

"He trusted all this to a guy who used to stalk celebrities for a living?"

"We've been friends for years. And I guess he thought there wasn't anyone worth stalking here, so I'd be on my good behavior."

"Was he right?"

"Until tonight. I guess Watson wasn't counting on my meeting you." Casey unlocked the door into the house. "The dogs are friendly. They're also bigger than a bread box, so brace yourself if they jump on you."

The moment he pushed open the door into the laundry room, the dogs appeared. There were three of them. A collie lookalike with a body like cast iron, a retriever-mix with chorus-girl legs, and a moving bale of wool without eyes.

"Okay, guys," Casey said, trying to pet them all at once. "I'm home. Everything's fine. Go away."

"Uh, Casey, I don't think they go away if you keep petting them."

Casey squatted on the floor and hugged the dogs, two under one arm, one—the collie—under the other. "Meet Floppsy, Moppsy, and Cottontail."

"Oh, puh-lease!"

"They're not my dogs. Don't blame me."

"They don't seem to know that they aren't your dogs." The dogs abandoned Casey one by one and came to sniff Mary Kate. It was the second time that night that her crotch had been inappropriately explored. "Call them off, Casey."

"Just push them away."

She tried, and ended up petting them instead. Apparently she had passed a dog test of some sort, because now they were all vying for her attention.

"Maybe we ought to get rid of the kids at Eden's Gate and turn it into a kennel." She bent over and scratched Cottontail—the bale of wool—to see if the dog had eyes under its frizzy bangs. "Dogs smell better than adolescent boys and they sure are cuter."

"Hey, I was an adolescent boy once upon a time, and most adolescent girls preferred me to a cocker spaniel."

"I was an adolescent girl once upon a time, and I know that particular species doesn't have a bit of sense."

"Do you remember your adolescence?"

"Sure. I was—" She stopped, then frowned. "Well, it seems like I remember it, even if I don't."

"Gotcha." Casey stood. "You remember feelings, not events."

She hadn't thought about it that way, but she supposed that was exactly right. "Let's get your face taken care of, then I need to get going. If I'm going to pay for a motel, I ought to get a few hours' use out of it.''

"Don't be an idiot. I'm not taking you to a motel. You can stay here. There are three bedrooms to choose from in addition to mine. Then you can get up tomorrow morning and make a sensible decision about your life.''

"Let me get this straight. I can choose from three bedrooms? Or I can choose from four, including yours?''

He managed his best pirate grin, made even more convincing by the swelling along his left cheekbone and the cut over his lip. "Hey, I know I'm nothing like Cooper, but you gotta take what you can get.''

"Good. Then I'll take the dogs. They look like they'd be fun to sleep with. Unlike the alternative.''

"Ouch.''

"You say that now, but wait till I turn into Florence Nightingale.''

He ushered her into the main part of the house, and the dogs came with them. The house itself was an advertisement for middle-class, middle-income mid-America. Neutral plush carpeting, easy-care wallpaper with country motifs, comfortable furniture, landscapes and framed family photographs on the walls.

She followed Casey into a pale-yellow kitchen lined with oak cabinets and crossed the room to fill a teakettle at the sink while he rummaged through drawers for a first-aid kit. "You know, Casey, we have something in common.''

"What's that?''

"We're both living somebody else's life.''

He stopped rummaging long enough to lift a brow in question.

"You're living Watson Turnbull's,'' she explained. "And I'm living Mary Kate's.''

"You *are* Mary Kate.''

"I know that, but I feel as much like Mary Kate as you feel like Watson.''

"That bad, huh?"

"Are you sorry you came here?"

"Not one bit." He pulled open the bottom drawer beside the sink. "Here it is." He held up what looked like a plastic fishing tackle box. "Watson's wife ought to be a general. She lives to organize. You ought to see the linen closet." He flipped open the top and whistled softly. "Look at this. You could do major surgery if you wanted."

"Oh, goody. A tonsillectomy, an appendectomy, hold the anesthesia."

"I *could* do this myself."

"Don't be a sissy. I've lived a lonely, barren life, and now I'm free. Let me have some fun."

He looked like he wanted to say more, but he let her lead him to the kitchen table. She stripped off her jacket and tossed it on a chair. Once he was seated she turned his face toward the light before she began to rummage through the box to see what was available.

Mary Kate knew Casey was going to interrogate her about her reasons for leaving Eden's Gate, and she wanted to stall him as long as possible. She hadn't told him about the pregnancy during their lunch at Warsaw's because of a simple failure of courage. She had wanted to talk to him; she desperately needed to share her secret with someone. But the closer she'd gotten to telling him, the harder it had been.

Now that days had passed, it was even harder.

"So you're not sorry you came to Shandley Falls?" She took a cotton ball and soaked it with peroxide, then she pushed his hair back from his forehead and held it there with her left hand as she began to dab a scrape just below his hairline.

"Trying to distract me? That's a pretty decent bedside manner, Doc." He rested his head against the back of the chair and closed his eyes. "You'd have to know more about me to understand."

"Like what?"

"Like where I came from and the road I traveled to get here."

"I bet you could give me a quick summary."

He was silent as she moved to the bruise on his cheekbone. She had finished with it and moved to another scrape beside his ear before he spoke.

"Okay. Here's the story in a nutshell. Broken home. Mother who drank too much and slept around. Father who didn't visit or pay child support. High-school dropout. Bad attitude. Dead-end life. Army and GED. Scholarship to NYU. Climb up career ladder. Fame and moderate fortune. Dead-end life. Climb back down. Rest stop here."

She whistled softly. "That's the Spanish-peanut version, not the Brazil nut." She started on the cut above his lip with a new cotton pad. "How'd you end up in the army?"

"A prosecutor gave me a choice between the army or jail. Ouch!"

"I'm sorry. What did you do to rate that?"

He waited until she'd moved on to his chin before he spoke. "I got caught."

She smiled. "I had that much figured out."

"I was eighteen and running a scam with a friend of mine. We sold Rolexes assembled in somebody's garage in Jersey."

"People actually bought them?"

"Yeah, including an undercover cop. The cops weren't really interested in me or my friend. They just wanted the guys who owned the garage, and we gave up every name we knew. So the DA had someone take us down to the recruiting center and that was the end of my days in Hell's Kitchen."

"Bad boy makes good, huh?"

"I guess that depends on how you look at it."

"You're pretty good at leaving one life behind and moving on to another. You're an inspiration."

"Don't kid yourself. If I knew where I was going and why, *then* I'd be an inspiration."

She straightened, eying her handiwork critically. "I don't think you'll even have the trace of a scar, but I'm going to put some ointment on the cut and a Band-Aid. Then you ought to be set." She started to rummage through the tackle box again, but he took her hand.

"I answered your questions. Now you answer mine. Why are you running away?"

He really had beautiful eyes. Dark, soulful, Latin eyes. Most of the time his feelings were well-hidden behind them. But not now. Maybe it was because she had convinced him to talk about his life. Or maybe it was because he really was a nice guy under the macho facade. But Casey's eyes signaled real concern. And compassion. Not pity, but something much warmer and more intimate.

"Katie?"

She shook her head, playing for time. "It's too hard to explain."

"Give it a try."

She decided to start with the easier part—which wasn't easy at all—and see where it led. "You'll think I'm crazy."

"What's new?"

"That life back at the center? It's not my life."

He didn't respond. She bit her lip, trying to come up with an explanation. "I can't imagine it ever was."

"What triggered this?"

"Well, this is the part where you'll call the men with the butterfly nets."

"They're all in bed asleep by now."

"I . . . I have these panic attacks sometimes. I feel like I'm trapped inside myself. I don't know how else to say it. Like I'm imprisoned in this body."

"You poor kid." Casey rested his hands on her shoulders. "But what can you expect? You may be a walking miracle, but that doesn't mean you're completely recovered yet. You'll have setbacks. That's natural.''

"There's no guarantee I'll ever be completely recovered, Casey. The doctors aren't sure I'll ever remember the past. But sometimes—'' She stopped, afraid to go on.

"Sometimes what?''

"Sometimes I *do* remember things. Only I'm not in the memories. It's someone else.''

"You're remembering other people?''

"No. It's like I'm there, but it's a different me. I tried to tell the doctor. He called it disassociation. He said I haven't integrated what's happened to me, and that's why it seems like I'm really somebody else. It's my mind's way of protecting me.''

"Do you remember what I told you about Gypsy? About her delusion that she had become the woman who was in the accident with her?''

"I remember.''

"That story isn't coloring what you're telling me, is it?''

"No. This has been going on since well before then. And besides, you said that Gypsy thought she knew exactly who she was. My experience is nothing like that.'' She grimaced. "At least Gypsy was *somebody*. I'm nobody at all.''

"But isn't it good you're remembering something, even if it's hazy?''

"I don't know. It's not like I've repressed the past. This isn't hysterical amnesia. My brain was injured and I've compensated well. But my memories are gone. What's left may well remain shadows.''

"What do you see when you remember? Who are you?''

"I don't know. The images are hazy. But I'm taller, thinner. I think my hair is different . . .'' She shrugged. "Maybe I'm just imagining myself the way I want to be.''

"There's nothing wrong with red hair.'' He lifted a hand to touch a curl springing over one ear. "I like your hair.''

Her breath caught and for a moment she couldn't restart

it. Casey's fingertips brushed against her earlobe, feather-light and calloused. He might look like Rocky Balboa after the big fight, but his touch was as sensitive as a sculptor's.

Her eyes met his and she saw awareness sparking there, followed quickly by denial. Self-preservation pushed oxygen through her lungs and attraction out the window. Casey was the only person in the world she could talk to. Her life was too complicated to risk his friendship. She couldn't, wouldn't, destroy her relationship with the one man she really knew and liked.

The teakettle chose that particular moment to whistle, support for clear thinking.

"I'm glad you like it," she said. "I tell myself there are women all over the world trying to get hair this color from a bottle." She stepped away from him, noting as she did that he seemed relieved. "Let me make us some tea."

"It's in the canister by the stove. Cups are in the cabinet above it. I'll fix the cut. You've done enough."

She busied herself selecting teabags—Earl Grey for him, Sleepytime for her—and pouring the water. She rummaged further and found a bag of Oreos and brought everything to the table on a tray. Casey had cleared away the first-aid kit to make room.

She sat across from him and worked on a cookie while the teabag steeped.

Casey, battered but still beautiful, folded his arms across his chest and leaned back in his chair. "Where is your life, if the one you're running away from isn't yours?"

She didn't know much about body language, but anyone could see he was simultaneously protecting himself and moving away to get some distance from her. And how could she blame him? So far she'd brought him nothing but trouble.

"I don't know." She paused, willing herself to tell him about the baby, but the words still weren't there. "I guess that's what I need to find out."

"Uh huh."

He didn't sound convinced. She tried again. "See, the thing is, if I don't fit in there, why should I stay? I don't like kids. I don't like gardening. I don't even seem to like religion very much. So what's the point of continuing the charade?"

"Right. What's the point?"

"I mean, I'm a failure already, but nobody there can see it." She latched on to an example, although it wasn't the one that would *really* make her case. "You know that community garden? Well, they all think it's a brilliant idea, *my* brilliant idea, but I was just being sarcastic, Casey. I said something about how the poor ought to have the joy of growing their own food and the next thing I knew . . ."

"So you're a failure, and they can't see it? That's why you're running away?"

She wasn't liking the sound of this, but she went on. "Then there are the kids. I don't know how to treat them." She paused and narrowed her eyes. "Not that I want to know. Don't misunderstand."

He shook his head. "I wouldn't."

"Good. I can only be me when I'm with them. Good old Sister Tornado. I can't be like Grace or Sarah or even Samantha."

"I think I see. The nuns want you to be exactly like them, but you can only be Mary Kate."

"No. Nobody's asking me to be like them. Nobody's criticizing."

"Oh . . ."

"But they should be. Don't you see? I'm not worth much, but nobody there can see it."

"I get it. The sisters lack insight. They're just not smart when it comes to human nature."

Mary Kate's temper flared. "Oh, come on! How can you say that? You know how intelligent Sarah is. And Grace is the most perceptive . . ." She stopped, realizing what he'd been trying to get her to see.

"They're only stupid when it comes to you, Katie? Is that what you're saying?"

"Now you're making *me* feel stupid."

"You're a lot of things, but stupid's not one of them. You're complex, smart, and remarkably savvy about some things. And you're authentic. The kids know exactly where they stand with you, and they find that comforting. But your expectations of yourself are outrageous. And you're impatient, given to rash actions, and a bit of a coward."

"You know what else I am, Casey?" She leaned forward, her eyes flashing. "Pregnant!"

For moments the only sound in the kitchen was the ticking of a clock.

"Did I hear you right?" he said at last.

"Yeah." She was surprised to realize her eyes were prickling. She might not know much about herself, but she had learned that she didn't cry.

"Would you like to tell me the details?"

"I'd love to, just as soon as I find out what they are."

"Katie . . ."

"I found out on Wednesday. That's why I came to see you. But I lost my nerve. I just couldn't tell you."

"Why not? Did you think I'd judge you?"

"Casey, I don't know what I'm going to do about the baby. I thought maybe it would be easiest if no one else knew so that if I decide . . ."

"Decide?"

"If I have an abortion."

His expression didn't change. "Is that an option?"

"I think I'll have to decide right away. I don't think I could live with myself if I wait much longer."

He nodded. "You said it would be easier if no one else knew. But the baby's father?"

"The baby's father is a mystery man. Apparently I got

pregnant just before I ended up in the hospital. That's the only thing I know for sure right now."

"You didn't keep a journal? Have a girlfriend you confided in?"

"I kept a journal, a gardening journal. But unless my lover was a tomato plant, the journal's not going to be any help."

"I think we can safely count that out."

"If I had a girlfriend, she's been invisible since I came out of the hospital. I didn't keep photographs, except a couple of my family and me. I don't have letters or scrapbooks. I don't even have a high-school or college yearbook, just some textbooks. I went through those looking for notes in margins. I shook out magazines to see if anything was caught between pages." She shook her head.

"It's sounds like you had relinquished all ties with the world."

She managed a humorless smile. "Not all, apparently."

"Then the baby's father isn't going to be any help with your decision."

"No. He can't exactly offer his hand in marriage, can he? Although if I carry the baby to term, maybe he'll be gallant enough to propose once he sees I'm as big as a house."

"Well, it's clearer why you left."

"I have an appointment with the doctor on Monday. I want to be able to tell him what I've decided."

"Don't rush this. You don't want to make a decision you'll regret."

"I've already *made* a decision I regret. I got pregnant."

He reached across the table and took her hand. At no point in their conversation had anything like disapproval showed in his expression. He threaded his fingers through hers. "Katie, you drank milk with your lunch the other day. I teased you about it."

"So?"

"And if I'm not mistaken that's herbal tea in your cup?"

"What's your point?"

"My point is that some part of you thinks you're going to have this baby. You're already taking care of it."

She pulled her hand from his. "I'm leaving my options open."

"Leave them open a little longer. You need to be sure you're doing the right thing, whatever it is."

"And what do I do in the meantime? I can't stay at Eden's Gate. I don't belong."

He reached for his mug. "No? You're needed at Eden's Gate. Who else needs you, Katie?"

"Who needs *you?* Tell me that, then maybe I'll understand."

"Nobody. I'm thirty, and nobody needs me. And you know what? I used to think that spelled freedom, and now I'm not so sure anymore. Now, I think it might just spell meaningless."

She sat back and picked up her mug, too, sipping the herbal tea which was indeed healthier for the baby inside her. "*You* ran away."

"I left a job that required at most a full head of hair, a sexy baritone, and the ability to think like a criminal. Maybe I left so I could find what you already have. But I didn't run away. I said my good-byes. I made my peace with who I'd been. And I made sure my replacement was waiting in the wings."

And she had done none of those things.

She finished her tea before she spoke again. She'd had enough time to think. "I guess if no one knows I left, no one will find it strange if I go back."

"Especially not if you go back tonight." His eyes flicked to the clock. "Make that this morning."

"I'll stay there for a while. Until I decide what I'm going to do."

"Good. That's a plan, not a reaction."

She got to her feet. "I don't know how you talked me into this, Casey."

The expression in his eyes was warm, and something more. He seemed proud of her for not taking the easiest way out. "You did most of the talking, Katie," he said. "For once in my life I just listened."

﹏9

ON MONDAY MORNING AFTER BREAKFAST
Mary Kate put on her best jeans and the least distasteful of
her sweaters and went to find Sarah. Sarah, in work clothes
and a bandanna, was scrubbing out the stainless-steel oven
that took up a sizable portion of the kitchen.

Mary Kate was always fascinated by the way each woman
in residence took on whatever job had to be done. No one
was too proud or important to get her hands dirty. And com-
plaints were rare enough to be conversation stoppers.

For a moment she considered telling Sarah about the baby
while Sarah's head was in the oven. That way Mary Kate
wouldn't have to witness her disappointment. She wasn't
sure why Sarah's good opinion mattered so much to her.
She didn't feel guilty about what had happened. How could
she feel guilty if she didn't remember the circumstances
behind the pregnancy? But the sisters had believed that
Mary Kate McKenzie was going to become one of them,
that her commitment to their way of life was strong and
sure.

And growing inside her was proof that their faith had
been misplaced.

"Sarah?"

Sarah peeked out just long enough to discover who was
speaking. "Yes, Mary Kate."

"If you don't mind I'd like to spend the day in town. I

149

have some shopping to do. You know." She didn't mention her appointment with Dr. Kane.

Sarah disappeared into the oven again. "You don't think you have to ask permission, do you?"

"I just wanted someone to know where I was."

"I appreciate it. We've cranked up the engine on your car now and then to keep the battery in condition, but the car itself needs a good spin on the road. Marie probably has your keys since she's the one who's been taking care of it."

Mary Kate didn't know what to say. She had a car? Apparently no one had thought to mention it to her. She had her own car, and she had walked into town on Saturday night?

"Well, um . . . thanks. I'll see you this evening."

Sarah mumbled something that sounded suspiciously like "damn oven."

Mary Kate went to find Marie and retrieved a set of keys on a Ford key chain. She was glad that she wouldn't be forced to swallow her pride and ask which car was hers. How many Fords could be parked in the old carriage house which had been converted to a garage and toolshed?

At the carriage house, she threw open the wide door to peer inside. The center's van stood beside a sober gray Chevy. She peeked inside the only other car in evidence, a sporty white Escort with a sunroof, red interior, and stereo system complete with a compact-disc player. In the automotive world it was a moderate player, but in the world of Eden's Gate, it was an extravagance beyond compare. She unlocked the door and climbed inside, resting her hands on the perky leather-bound steering wheel.

Something had simmered just under the pleasure she'd felt on learning she had her own car. She had been pushing it away as she'd walked toward the carriage house, but now it boiled over and she could no longer ignore it.

"What in the hell do I do next?"

She was sitting in her very own car, a car she had obviously chosen out of love. Not because it was an appropriate car for a woman who wanted to be a nun. Not because it was environmentally sound or even large enough to haul a load of horse manure. She had chosen it because she wanted it.

Now she just wanted to remember why she'd owned a car at all.

Because she was terrified to drive.

She leaned back against the seat, forcing herself to breathe slowly. She recognized a panic attack coming on, and she was determined to thwart it. She owned this car, and she knew from flipping through her wallet that she had a driver's license. She needed the freedom that driving brought.

The fear eclipsed all attempts to reason with it. She told herself she could do this, and a voice inside her vehemently disagreed.

"I *can* do it!" She tried to remember what she should do first. But even the fundamentals seemed hazy, clouded by apprehension and disuse.

She was sure the key went somewhere. She searched for a moment until she found an appropriate slot and stuck the key inside. She was sure she was supposed to turn the key, but what if there was something else she was supposed to do first? What if she turned the key and the car lunged forward, straight through the wall in front of her? She knew about brakes and accelerators, but she wasn't sure she remembered which was which. And what if this car wasn't automatic? Didn't some cars require more than just flooring a gas pedal?

She rummaged anxiously through the glove compartment until she found a booklet with a picture of the car on the front cover. She started with page one and began to read. By the time she had finished she knew every gadget on the car and exactly how to make them work. She could recirculate air or draw it in fresh from the outside. She could vary the speed on the windshield wipers, switch her lights to bright and back, and adjust her seat until it was comfortable enough to sleep in.

But she was still afraid to drive.

It was noon by the time Mary Kate made it to the outskirts of Shandley Falls. The trip thus far had been treacherous. She had stalled twice, flooded the engine, and run the one and only red light because she didn't find the brake pedal in time. For the most part she had driven well below the speed limit, thwarting more courageous drivers who had made sure she knew what they thought of her.

By the time she began to pass clusters of homes and the stores that served them her hands were welded to the steering wheel. She was heading right for the center of town, and she was almost sure her driving skills weren't up to it. She sat at the next stoplight for seconds after it turned green and ignored the honking behind her.

"Right foot off the brake and on the gas pedal," she said out loud. "Push slowly, gently." She followed her own instructions, moving surely, professionally even, into the intersection.

Unfortunately the driver in the car just behind her lost patience and decided to take the situation into his own hands. He started to pull around her just as she moved forward. He slammed on his brakes with nothing but inches to spare. The resulting screaming of tires so unnerved Mary Kate that she braked, too, coming to a halt in the middle of the intersection.

The engine died. She rested her forehead on the steering wheel and wondered why she had remembered how to eat, how to shower and dress herself, how to read, write, and add long columns of numbers, but she had *not* remembered the fine points of driving.

Someone rapped sharply on her window, shouting as he did. "What the hell do you think you're doing?"

She sat up and opened her window to confront a middle-aged man without one feature half as impressive as his scowl. "If you hadn't tried to pass me, we'd both be on our way, wouldn't we?" she said.

"What? You're going to try to make this my fault? Where'd you get your license, lady? A Cracker Jack box?"

She remembered Cracker Jack. She remembered licenses. She even remembered bad-tempered bullies. She just didn't remember why driving frightened her so.

"That's it," he shouted when she didn't answer. "You don't have a license, do you?"

Her temper flared and licked at her anxiety. "I've got a license, mister."

"Yeah? You expect me to believe that? I ought to—"

She leaned out the window. "Listen, you. Back away from this car before I shove my license up your—"

"Mary Kate, are you all right?"

From the corner of her eye she followed the progress of a young man coming around the car from the passenger side. A young man who had called her by name. He was tall, lanky, and not particularly good-looking. But he knew her.

She waited until he joined the bully at her window. "I'm . . ." She took a deep breath. "The car stalled. It's been giving me trouble all morning."

"That happens." The young man turned to the older one. "No . . . no one was hurt. Your car wasn't even scratched."

"So? She ought to be off the roads!"

"Sure. Go tell the cops she waited a few seconds to pull into the inter . . . intersection. I'm sure they'll have her arrested."

The bully slammed his palm against the side of the car, then stalked back to his own. In a moment he had zoomed around the Escort and continued his journey into town.

"Thanks." Mary Kate sent the young man a bright smile.

He looked as if he'd been struck by lightning. "We'd better get out of here before we cause an accident."

She forced herself to turn the key, and the car jumped forward, then died. Her hands were sweating. She turned the key again, giving the car more gas, and it did the same thing.

"Wait." The young man stuck his head through the open window. "You're going to flood it."

"I guess I'm nervous," she confessed.

"Do you want me . . . me to move it for you?"

She noted a Laundromat at the farthest corner. "Would you mind? Maybe into the parking lot over there? It'll give me a chance to calm down."

"Sure." He looked thrilled.

She got out and let him take the wheel while she walked around and got in on the other side. The ride was brief, but she spent it trying to figure out how to ask him who he was. He seemed so glad to be helping her, almost as if she were the one doing the favor.

He didn't park in front of the Laundromat. He parked along the edge of the lot, where Mary Kate wouldn't have to do anything except pull back on to the road once she was ready. He left the engine running and got out. "I've got to get my . . . my car out of the road."

"Sure. Look, I appreciate your help so much."

"Mary Kate, I was so sorry . . ." He took a deep breath. "About . . . you know."

"Thank you." She wondered exactly what he meant.

"You're . . . you're doing all right now? I saw the article Casey's doing about the cen . . . center."

"Really? It's not out yet, is it?"

"No . . . but since I work at the paper."

"Right." She shot him another of the smiles he had responded so favorably to. Now she had a clue. He worked at *The Cricket*. Casey could tell her his name.

"Better get your car tuned up," he said.

"I'll make an appointment right away."

With a wave of his hand he left to move his car.

She was left to wonder exactly what he was sorry about. Her accident? Or something she didn't remember?

She finished the trip into Shandley Falls without incident, and she was flushed with pleasure and pride by the time she climbed out of the car and locked her door. She had known better than to try to park the car against the curb. Instead she had chosen the parking lot of a grocery store near the center of town, pulling carefully between two cars and tapping the brake until she was satisfied.

She had a car, although she was still frightened of it. She even had a driver's license—although she had no idea how she'd conned anyone into giving her one. She was a free woman in charge of her own destiny.

She turned and saw a young mother pushing a grocery cart complete with toddler and two packages of disposable diapers, and her excitement vanished.

She was a pregnant woman who couldn't remember a thing about her past.

Chastened, she leaned against the car door and considered her plight. That morning she had awakened with a plan. She would spend the day in town refurbishing her wardrobe and looking for clues. The wardrobe wouldn't take long since her future was so uncertain she didn't know what kind of clothes she might need. She would buy just a few things, then move on to the second part of her plan.

She would find out who had fathered her baby.

She had given this a lot of thought. Yesterday she had gone to mass and considered her problem throughout the service. She had considered it that afternoon as she helped put Sunday dinner on the table and later that evening as she dodged vespers by taking the long way to check the pond.

She didn't know who she was or even the things she had liked to do, but other people knew. She had grown up here, interacted with Shandley Falls citizens, made friends and perhaps even enemies. The obvious place to start was with people who had known her. She had discovered she was good at covering up the truth about her memory loss. Already people seemed to believe she was a good listener. She would talk as little as possible and listen to everything that was said to her. Someone in Shandley Falls must know who had fathered her baby. If she searched for clues and followed leads, she could discover his identity, too.

She wasn't sure why she felt so compelled to discover her lover's identity. She wasn't even sure that his opinion about the pregnancy would matter in the long run. But somehow, knowing who he was and understanding the circumstances behind their relationship seemed imperative.

How could she make a decision about her baby without knowing how she had felt about the baby's father?

She started her search by finding her way to the Hometowner, the restaurant where she'd met Pete and Millie, hoping that one or both of them would be there. She was hungry anyway, and she was looking forward to another slice of pie. But neither Millie nor Pete were in today, just a dour old man who seated her in a corner where she couldn't see the door. When no one paid attention to her, she ordered the quickest thing on the menu and left without pie.

She struck out at the first dress shop she visited. Not only were the clothes designed for older women, the sales personnel were older, too, and acted as if they had never seen her before. At the next shop the woman behind the counter was friendly but didn't call her by name. After a few minutes of fruitless conversation, Mary Kate decided they were strangers.

The third shop was really a small department store, a slightly down-at-the-heels independent with limited stock and unlimited fashion no-nos. Mary Kate sorted through racks in the petite section looking for something to brighten her mood. So far, except for teaching herself to drive again, her day had been a complete waste of time.

"You know, this would look great with your hair."

Mary Kate turned to find a woman about her age and size holding out a saffron-colored rayon dress. She was a pretty brunette with a heart-shaped face and huge gray eyes, and she returned Mary Kate's hopeful smile with one of her own. "I don't remember seeing you in this color, but I bet it'll be terrific."

Mary Kate had struck out all day. Now she felt like she'd struck gold—and not the color of the dress. "I like it." She took a risk. "You've always had such good taste."

"And you always find something nice to say. I used to look for you in high school if I was having a bad day, just to hear you say something positive."

Mary Kate made another calculation. "How many bad days did you have? You were always so pretty and easy to talk to."

"See? You're still being nice." The woman's cheeks flushed with pleasure. "How have you been? I knew you'd been hurt. I hope you got my card."

Mary Kate wondered if there was anyone in town who hadn't heard. "I'm fine. I'm . . ." She decided to take another risk. "Absolutely recovered except that I still have occasional memory lapses. Mostly names, I'm afraid."

"I'm Joanna Kennedy."

"Oh, I remembered the Joanna part," Mary Kate lied. "The Kennedy part was taking longer."

"I bet that's because it's my married name."

"I'm sure."

"Pete told me he saw you the other day. He and Carol are in a bridge group with Don and me. It's a chance to get out once in a while. You know?"

"It sounds like fun." Actually, it sounded like small-town hell, but Mary Kate hadn't forgotten what a statement like that could do to a conversation. "Pete's looking good. He says that Carol and their little boy are doing well."

Joanna raised a brow. "Oh, does he? That doesn't sound like Pete. He likes to play the martyr." The other brow shot up, too. "Oh, I'm sorry. I know you were close. I didn't mean to criticize—"

"Don't worry. I know his bad points, too." Or wanted to, at least.

"Really? Because I always thought . . ."

Mary Kate wished there was a local ordinance against unfinished sentences. "What did you think?"

"Well, I was never sure you saw his bad points. You always defended him, no matter what he did. Even after . . . well, you know."

"I'm not sure I do."

"Well, after he got Carol pregnant in college. When everybody thought you two . . ."

"I guess Pete and I just weren't destined to spend our lives together. He's married now, and I'm—" She stopped herself. What had she been about to say? *I'm pregnant? I'm about to become a nun?* Both seemed to be true, although they were opposite ends of the 'life's little choices' continuum.

Joanna picked the better-known of the two extremes. "Are you really going to be a nun, Mary Kate?"

"I still have a lot of thinking to do."

Joanna leaned forward earnestly. "Not because of Pete, I hope. He's not worth it. If that's why you're doing this."

Mary Kate knew little about herself, but she felt almost sure she hadn't planned to give her life to God just because she couldn't give it to Pete. Even after one brief encounter, she thought Pete would come up short if he were placed side-by-side with the big enchilada.

"That doesn't enter into it," she said firmly.

"I guess you think this is none of my business, but I just about idolized you. We all did. I want you to be happy."

Mary Kate knew the conversation had come full circle. Unless she confessed to total memory loss and threw herself on Joanna's mercy, she wasn't going to get more information out of her. And she wasn't ready to do that yet.

"I think I'll be happy trying on that dress. Shall I?"

"Let me show you a couple of other things, too." Joanna lowered her voice. "Between you and me we don't have much worth looking at here, but we do have a few good buys. And I always wanted to help you pick out your clothes. Style was never your strong point." Joanna put her arm around Mary Kate and guided her into the dressing room.

Mary Kate felt like a hot dog in a gilded bun wearing the gold dress, so she passed on it. But Joanna found a jumper in a subtle plaid with a high waist that was surprisingly flattering as well as useful, since she could wear it with a turtleneck or as a sundress when the weather warmed.

She bought a new jacket in a muted turquoise color and two cotton sweaters as well as a couple of oversized T-shirts and leggings to match. She wasn't Cindy Crawford, but at least she no longer looked as if she'd been shopping in a mission barrel.

She had discovered just enough about her relationship with Pete to be even more suspicious, but not enough to draw any conclusions. As she'd rung up the sale Joanna had mentioned that Pete worked for Shandley, Rose and Kowalick, the town's most prestigious law firm. Fred Shandley, of the Shandleys for whom the town was named, was the senior partner and Carol's father.

Mary Kate decided she needed some legal advice.

She found the address with the help of a drugstore phone book. The office was in the tallest building on the main street, a five-story brick edifice that was as solid as the firm's reputation.

She still didn't know Pete's last name because it hadn't yet come up in conversation. But that turned out to be easy, too, since there was a roster in the foyer and Peter Watkins was the only possibility. She took the elevator to the top floor and wandered down the carpeted hallway looking for the right office. But her search was simple because there was only one. The entire floor belonged to the Shandley firm.

The matronly receptionist looked strong enough to act as a bouncer if someone without an appointment showed up, but Mary Kate tried her biggest smile. "I'd like to see Pete Watkins if he's not busy."

They traded the ritual responses. Did she have an appointment? What was this in regards to? Mary Kate stood her ground until the woman buzzed Pete's office.

"He'll see you," the receptionist said after she hung up. "But he has an appointment in fifteen minutes."

"I won't take up more than that."

The woman rose to guide her through the warren of offices, but Pete arrived to do it himself.

"Mary Kate." He held out his hand. His eyes flicked once to the receptionist, who was watching them as if she would tuck one of them under each arm and drag them into the hall if Mary Kate held Pete's hand longer than required.

Not feeling up to a judo match, Mary Kate dropped Pete's hand immediately and kept her tone as businesslike as possible. "Are you sure you have time to see me?"

"Of course. Let's go back to my office."

"Mr. Shandley expects you in his office at three," the receptionist told Pete in frostbitten tones.

"I'll be there," he promised.

Mary Kate covertly examined him as they walked along the hall to a tiny office in the very back. Today Pete was wearing a charcoal-colored suit and a black-and-red figured tie. She had nearly forgotten how good-looking he was in a Beach Boy, California surfer sort of way. Something purely female stirred inside her. She had already learned she was anything but immune to men. Had this one sneaked past her defenses right straight to her womb?

It seemed possible.

"You're looking good," Pete said, after he shut the door

to his office. They were alone, but not really. A wide panel of glass flanked either side of the door. She doubted she and Pete could be heard, but they could be seen by anyone walking by.

"Thanks." She favored him with the smile that Casey claimed reminded him of Gypsy Dugan. "You, too."

He seemed surprised. "Do you like the suit? I have to pick out my own clothes. Carol's taste . . ." He shrugged.

"Wonderful. Italian, right? Armani?"

His eyes widened. "How did you know?"

She heard the way he stressed "you." Actually, it was an excellent question. How *did* she know? "I have all sorts of interesting talents," she said, nearly purring the words. She wasn't sure what response she was trying to evoke, but she knew that she wasn't going to get anywhere pretending to be a counterfeit Julie Andrews. She didn't think Pete was really the type to respond to goodness.

"How come I didn't know about your . . ."

"Talents?" she said to prompt him. "I suppose I kept my light hidden under a barrel."

"Well . . ." He looked up nervously as someone passed in the hall. "Maybe you were always too busy listening to me. I used you . . ."

She wondered just *how* he had used her. "No you didn't. I was always crazy about you."

"Not after . . ."

She wanted to rip out his indecisive tongue. "After what?"

He lowered his voice. "It's not like you to throw this in my face, Mary Kate."

A buzzer sounded on his desk. She sat back as he answered it. When he'd finished she leaned forward again. "I'm not trying to throw anything in your face, Pete. I just need to understand what you feel so guilty about."

The buzzer sounded again. She wanted to rip the buzzer out, too.

"Why did you come here today?" he asked after he finished with the receptionist again. "Do you really want to talk about this?"

Yes, she screamed silently. But she was going on instinct here, and instinct told her that approaching Pete directly wouldn't lead anywhere. He was obviously uncomfortable. He was not going to give up the information she wanted if he felt threatened.

"I didn't come for a confrontation," she said. "I came to see if you'd make a will for me. After everything that's happened, I'd feel better if I had all my legal work in order. You know."

"You want me to do it?"

"Yes. Unless there's a problem."

"But your family always used Plainfield, Rhodes and Sampson in Cleveland. Don't you already have a will?"

She probably did. She didn't know. "I want you to look over everything I have. I thought another opinion might be helpful. And if I need something more, then I'd like your advice."

"I don't understand. After everything . . ."

She clamped her lips shut, hoping the force of gravity would pull the rest of the sentence from his lips. But nothing more was forthcoming. "If you don't want to do it . . ." she said at last.

"Of course I do!" He stood as she got to her feet. "It will give us a chance . . ."

She waited with no real hope that he'd continue, and he didn't disappoint her. "Yes, well, I appreciate your help, Pete."

"You always used to call me Peter."

She filed that away. "What does Carol call you?"

"Nothing. We hardly speak. My marriage is a nightmare."

"I'm sorry. Is there anything I can do to help?"

"I'm surprised you'd want to."

She resisted asking why. She knew it wouldn't get her anywhere. "You underestimate me."

He came around the desk as his buzzer sounded once more. But this time he ignored it. "I never underestimated you, Mary Kate. I knew what a warm, caring woman you were. Better than anyone else. That's why . . ."

"Why . . ." The word came out on a squeak.

The buzzer rumbled insistently again. "Damn, this is no place to talk," Pete said. "We have to get together . . ."

This time the receptionist was obviously leaning on the button. There was no cessation of sound. If anything, it seemed to grow in volume.

Mary Kate covered her ears. "Call me, Pete. We'll set up a time to go over this."

She made her escape as he circled the desk to answer his summons.

Mary Kate's appointment with Dr. Kane was late in the afternoon since it was mainly for discussion. She spent the time after her talk with Pete walking the streets of Shandley Falls. She visited the library and the post office, where no one acted as if they knew her, and four hair salons.

The first three yielded no helpful information. No one on duty at any of them seemed to recognize her. At each she gave the same story to the man or woman sitting behind the reception desk. She'd had a really terrific cut there but couldn't remember the name of the stylist who had done it. Would they mind looking through their records to see who she had seen the last time so that she could make an appointment?

Her name wasn't on file at any of them. She promised that she would go home and see if she could find her last appointment card, and went on to the next salon where she told the same story.

At the fourth salon the owner informed her that her stylist, a woman named Jan, had moved to Cincinnati six months ago. Since she'd already noted the finished products of the remaining stylists, she'd refused an appointment with any of them and left to continue her detective work.

By three-thirty she was tired and ready to call her search quits for the day. She was on her way to the doctor's office when she passed an old man who stopped to stare, as if he expected her to say hello.

Willing to give her investigation one last try, she strolled back to speak to him, face-to-face. "How are you?"

"I wondered if you'd stop. You mean I got so old you don't recognize me anymore?"

Mary Kate tried not to frown. Of course the man was completely unfamiliar. "I'm sorry." She told him what she'd told Joanna. "Sure I recognize you, but I was injured months ago and I'm having a bit of a problem with names."

He didn't give his. "Yeah. Heard you got whacked over the head. Been wondering how you were."

She played the game like a pro. "You're probably a pretty good judge. How do I look to you?"

"Okay. But I bet you're every bit as snooty."

Her eyes widened. "What?"

"Snooty, that's what you were. A different kind of snooty, but snooty all the same. You were better'n anybody else. Knew more. Worked harder. Thought you were just like this with the Almighty." He crossed his fingers.

"Boy, have I changed." She shifted her shopping bag to her other arm. "I'm sorry, but you didn't tell me your name."

"Sergeant Gorse."

"Sergeant? I really have forgotten a lot. Was I in the military?"

He was a small man, bent and twisted and compacted into something as tough as a tree trunk. He grinned and his teeth looked strong enough to gnaw through steel. "First name's Sergeant. Whack on the head gave you a sense of humor. That's an improvement."

She grinned at him, liking him more each moment. "Was I really such a little know-it-all?"

"Only kid I ever hated on sight. First day at Eden's Gate I took one look at you and knew you'd be trouble."

"I sure don't remember that."

"Being the head gardener over there was the best job I ever had."

"Really?" Her mind clicked into overdrive. "Head gardener?"

"Until you got me fired."

"Whoops." She concentrated on his face, willing even a wisp of memory to return, but he was a complete stranger to her.

"Just because you caught me taking a swig out of my hip flask," he said. "You were just a little sprout, not more than four foot high, but you lectured me good. Next thing I knew, I was out on my ear."

An idea formed. "You know, Sergeant, I definitely owe you something for that. Definitely."

Sergeant had little round eyes that sparkled like a teen-ager's. "Oh?"

"We're starting this garden . . ."

"That so?"

"Right. A community garden. We thought there might be some people around town without land of their own who'd like a spot to grow vegetables and flowers. So we're plowing up the field over by the barn and dividing it into plots. We're going to start work on it a week from this coming Saturday. Maybe you'd be interested in helping? Do you have a garden of your own?"

"I'm over at the Landsdowne. Got no space to garden over there."

Mary Kate watched him turn over the idea in his mind. She was reminded of the day she had watched a neighboring farmer plow his fields with a tractor. Weeds disappearing.

Rich dark earth sifting through the tractor tines. Finally, Sergeant smiled. "I'll do it."

She was genuinely thrilled. Here was a man who not only knew what he was doing, he knew Eden's Gate. He could give her advice, explain the things she didn't understand. She shot him her best dimpled grin. "That's great!"

"Yep, I'll do it. 'Cause this garden idea of yours will never work, missy. Not in a million years. Nobody who does it'll get along. Nobody'll know what they're doing. You're going to make a mess out of this, and that's something I prayed I'd live long enough to see. Yep, I'll do it, all right. Just to watch you squirm. Every day. Squirm, squirm, squirm!"

She remained in the same place after he sauntered off. She thought she could still hear him cackling when he was long out of sight.

By the time she reached Dr. Kane's office, she was completely exhausted. Except for her, the waiting room was empty. Most of the doctor's other patients were already home fixing supper for the fathers of their babies or back at work at the jobs that would support them.

This time she didn't even bother with a magazine, restlessly shifting from side to side as she waited to be called. Despite her conversation with Sergeant she had still gotten to the appointment early, and she was sorry that she had. With nothing to do, she had too much time to think about the decision she had made.

When the door to the office opened, she didn't even look up. Only when someone took the chair beside her did she glance at the newcomer.

"Casey . . ."

Casey's dark eyes were bleary, as if he hadn't been getting much sleep. But his smile was focused and warm. "I thought you might need a friend."

She didn't know what to say. She suspected that she had never felt the lack of a friend so strongly.

He took her hand and squeezed it. "Look, whatever you decide, I'm here. Okay? I'll help any way I can."

Saturday night she hadn't asked for his advice, and he hadn't given it. Now it seemed important, imperative even, to know his opinion. "What do you think I should do?"

"I think you should do whatever's right for you."

"And what about what's right for the baby?"

"I'm not going to make the mistake of telling you what you should do with your own body, Katie."

She released a long, slow breath. "I've been giving this a lot of thought. I'm pregnant with a stranger's child, so he doesn't count. I don't feel like I belong in my own body, so I don't feel like *I* count. When it comes right down to it, the only person who seems to count is this baby."

"You're going to keep it, aren't you?"

She supposed the die had been cast the moment she'd heard the doctor's diagnosis. She had told herself she had choices, and she still believed a woman should have the right to make the choice that was best for her own situation. But the choice that was in some ways most logical had never sounded right for her.

"I'm going to *have* the baby," she said. "But I think it deserves a better home than I could give it. When the time comes, I'm going to be sure it has that home."

"You're nothing if not brave."

She saw compassion in his eyes and it was almost her undoing. Her voice wobbled. "Not that brave. I still haven't told the sisters. I guess I need some time to live with my decision first, to get used to it."

He linked his fingers through hers. "You still have time. And they're a fine group of women. They won't judge you."

She looked down at their hands, his tanned and strong, hers smaller, but square and capable. "Why did you come today? This baby doesn't have anything to do with you. You don't have to get involved."

"I don't know. I'm a lot better at demanding answers than I am at offering support. But maybe I need to develop my talents a little. I just wanted you to know I'm here."

Dr. Kane's chirpy assistant stepped into the room, carrying her chart. "Mary Kate, we're ready for you. Come on back. And you can bring your friend if you'd like."

"Oh, I don't think—"

Casey squeezed her hand. "I'd like to come, if you'd like to have me."

She met his eyes and saw nothing in them except warmth. "Really?"

"Why not? Just be sure you tell the doctor I'm not the baby's father, so he won't give me a lecture on living up to my responsibilities."

All the things that had been tied in a knot inside her began to dissolve, the doubt that she was doing the right thing for everybody, the fear that she would screw this up somehow. Casey smiled at her, and for the first time since she'd discovered she was pregnant, the world didn't seem like a lonely place.

10

E VEN THOUGH SHE HAD PERSONALLY INVITED him, Mary Kate was surprised to see Casey and two of the Turnbull dogs at Eden's Gate on the morning of the community-garden launch nearly two weeks later. He had moved his life to Shandley Falls so that he would have a year to unwind and contemplate his future. Instead, every time she turned around he seemed to be taking on more responsibilities at the center.

The full-page feature on Eden's Gate and the Sisters of Redemption had come out the previous Wednesday, with appropriate history and photographs. Despite a fair assessment of the problems the center had experienced, for the most part the article had been positive, stressing the ways that the center could enrich community life if Shandley Falls gave it a chance. A sidebar about the community garden had generated several telephone calls from people who were interested in reserving a space.

Mary Kate hadn't seen Casey since the day at Dr. Kane's office, but he had called once just to see how she was. She suspected he really wanted to know if she had told the sisters about the baby yet.

She hadn't.

"So, what do you think?" She leaned on a hoe and searched Casey's expression. She made a point of not needing anyone, but today she needed approval. His.

169

Casey was dragging Floppsy on one leash and Moppsy on another. Now he turned them loose to roam as he scanned the community-garden area. From his expression she suspected that he had envisioned something much smaller, something reasonable. Instead the garden spread nearly to the woods that bordered the estate. ''I think it's going to be a big job,'' he said.

Despite herself, despite everything that was wrong in her life, Mary Kate was beginning to feel a stirring of interest in this project. She had laid out all the information she'd acquired, comparing the way similar gardens were organized, and she had come up with a tentative plan for the center's garden that combined a number of features. She didn't enjoy the digging, the forking, the hoeing, but the planning wasn't too bad. She had found that she liked to organize, and that she learned quickly. She was rapidly acquiring knowledge about plants and pests and soil preparation, even if she didn't remember growing so much as a philodendron.

At the last staff meeting her final plan had been greeted with instant approval. She had decided to keep the basic structure the way she had laid it out in the fall. The garden would be divided into two long sections with a wide pathway down the center. Each side would be divided into ten plots twenty by twenty feet. Plots could be subdivided for anyone who wanted a smaller garden, and if all the plots weren't taken, anyone who wanted an extra one could have it. At the far end of the garden they would build ten four-by-eight raised beds on either side of the path for use by the day-care children. And at the end closest to the barn, they would leave vacant land for future projects. This year they would use that land for picnic tables so that gardeners could bring their lunches and enjoy the view.

She and Samantha had already recruited five people from the Landsdowne Apartments who wanted plots, and the day-care center had agreed to let their school-age children plant and tend small raised beds. By the end of the week, six families from the public-housing complex on the highway had asked for space, and the manager thought he could round up another two or three in time for planting in May.

Mary Kate had felt surprisingly vulnerable as she outlined her vision. She had told herself the project was silly and unimportant, but halfway through her presentation she had realized that it was important to these women. She was not one of them. She doubted she ever would be, particularly now that she was about to become a mother. But in a moment of revelation she had realized that she cared what they thought of the project and of her. And after they had praised her for her contribution, she had glowed.

Now she looked at the garden through Casey's eyes and saw yet again what a task she had undertaken. The glow diminished. "I know, it is big, isn't it? It didn't seem this large on paper."

"Under the circumstances, will you be able to keep up with it?"

She knew he was referring to her pregnancy. "I hope I won't have to. I hope everyone will do their share."

"Is that realistic?"

"From what I remember about people? Probably not."

"Remember?"

"A figure of speech."

The brief spate of optimism she'd felt on waking that morning continued to dissolve. Most people hadn't even arrived to help with the preparation. The sisters had decided to make a party out of this first workday. Sarah had spoken directly to the manager of the local pizza joint, who had agreed—undoubtedly under pressure—to supply a dozen giant pizzas at lunchtime. The closest grocery store had donated cases of soft drinks. The Dairy Creme out on the highway had promised to deliver five gallons of ice cream and cones to go with it. Even the kids in the offenders' program had gotten into the spirit and were setting up a face-painting table.

Mary Kate was impressed that so much had been done in so little time. The Sisters of Redemption were tireless *and* shameless when it came to standing up for their beliefs or their projects. She hoped she was never on the opposite side in an argument.

"How many people do you expect to come and help today?" Casey asked.

"I don't know. Everyone who wants a garden is supposed to come. A work group from St. Anthony's promised to be here. We have the teenagers and their counselors, all the sisters. Invitations went out to all the teenagers' parents, but most of them live too far away."

"Sounds like you'll have enough help without them."

"The weather was supposed to be good today. But look at that sky."

Casey obediently turned his eyes to the heavens. The sun had yet to come out. It was a chilly, gray April morning that promised to grow colder and darker as the day progressed. By mid-morning Mary Kate expected rain.

"We planted spring crops a week ago in the center's garden. Not one thing's come up," she said.

She knew she sounded as if she was taking it personally. She watched Casey struggling not to smile. "Maybe everything's waiting for the sun," he said.

"Well, I don't care. I did what I was supposed to. If the seeds don't do their part, it's not my fault."

"You know, I'm not sure why you wanted me to come today." Casey shoved his hands in his pockets. "I've done an article about the school. And I made sure there was a piece about the workday in our last issue. I can't do much more in the way of publicity."

"Publicity?" She dimpled. "Sorry, buster, but it's your sturdy back I need today, not your myriad creative talents. You're here to move dirt."

He looked like a man who'd just had his worst fears confirmed. "I used to uncover dirt at my old job. Are you sure that's not what you want?"

"Sorry, Casey, but except for me, this place is squeaky-clean. You'll have to settle for the crumbly brown kind, and move it right along with the rest of us."

Her smile turned slowly to something less pleasant as she saw trouble approaching. Casey moved to watch the group of teens coming toward them. The kids stopped halfway to play with the dogs. "Problem?" he asked.

"Recognize the kid in the middle?"

"Tyson?"

"He's still giving me trouble every chance he gets. I seem to be his favorite target. And he's been assigned full-time to the community garden."

"Why?"

"I don't know. He bombed out everywhere else. We seem to be his last chance."

"I'm not sure I understand the point of having the offenders working on this project. If they create too many problems, nobody's going to feel comfortable working in their plots. People in the community are scared of them as it is."

For some reason she found herself defending the sisters' decision. "Antoine was an exception. None of the kids who come here are supposed to be dangerous. You know that. They've shoplifted or skipped too much school or run away from home. For the most part they're kids who've been working their way through the school of hard knocks since the day they were born. They aren't a threat. They're poised somewhere between becoming worthwhile citizens and criminals. And we're supposed to nudge them away from jail. What better way to do it? For a change they get the chance to help other people, learn new skills, interact with decent, hardworking families who can serve as good role models—"

She realized what she was saying and wondered where the lecture had come from.

He grinned. "Sounds like you're beginning to like working with the kids. Even Tyson?"

"I don't even like to be around them. They make me—" Mary Kate stopped herself, then shrugged as an after-thought. She made a face, as if she was no longer interested.

"What? What do they make you?"

"Crazy. We get out here in the garden and for some reason they talk to me. I don't know why. I'm not much of a listener. I had the sympathy beat out of me right along with my memories."

"But not the lies."

She narrowed her eyes. "I'm going to assign you to the manure pile."

"You're the one who specializes in horseshit, Mary Kate. For some reason you understand exactly what these kids are going through and you feel for them. Why fight it?"

"Despite popular opinion, I'm not that kind of person."

"So you tell yourself."

"You're just like everyone else, aren't you? Can't anybody around here see the truth when it's right in their faces? I'm not the person everyone believes I am. And as soon as things are running smoothly and there's time to find a replacement, I'm out of here!" She set off for the manure pile, preferring it for the moment to more insights she didn't want to hear.

Mary Kate did not take defeat well. She saw it as a personal affront. "I'd sure like to know where everybody is." At ten-thirty she stood in the middle of the drive looking toward the road and hoping to see a line of cars turn in. But the road and the driveway were empty.

Samantha had followed her, and now she put her hand on Mary Kate's shoulder. "It's the weather. It's just too cold. And with rain threatening—"

"We're here, aren't we? It's the same weather for us as it would be for them."

"Mary Kate, get real, please. Volunteers are volunteers. They don't have the same connection or commitment to this project that we do."

"Okay. That accounts for the folks from St. Anthony's. But what about the ones who've signed up for gardens?"

So far only Sergeant, a woman named Elvira Cecil from Landsdowne, and one family from the housing project had arrived. Sergeant had been here an hour, gleefully exclaiming about how little had been done and how unlikely it was that anything would ever grow in the newly turned ground. Elvira, who had grown prizewinning African violets but never a garden, had spent most of her time clucking about whether to plant pansies along the border of her plot or parsley. The family, Glenn and Gladys Manning and their six small children, had spent most of their time trying to keep the two-year-old twins from eating dirt.

No one was working with enthusiasm. There was a consistent grumbling that was as loud as the sound of hoes, pitchforks, and shovels. The teenagers had never been enthused, but they had showed some energy in their preparations for face-painting. They were obviously disappointed that their efforts had gone for nothing. A suspicious Gladys Manning had refused to let them come near her children.

"I'd better get back to work," Mary Kate said. "It looks like I'm going to be slaving dawn to dusk by myself from now on."

"You know that's not true." But even Samantha didn't sound convinced. Of all of them, she had been the most optimistic.

Mary Kate had covered several yards when Sam called her name. She turned and followed Sam's finger with her eyes. A battered minivan had turned onto the property. Then, as Mary Kate stared, another car followed it and then another.

" 'Faith is the substance of things hoped for, the evidence of things not seen,' " Sam quoted.

"We'll talk again after we find out who's in those cars."

"You won't be disappointed."

For once Mary Kate hoped that Sam knew what she was talking about.

An hour later even she was beginning to have some faith. The minivan had held a crew of six from St. Anthony's. Four of them had been young and strong enough to really lend a hand. The other two had taken charge of setting out lunch. The two cars had held more families from the project. A pretty young single mother named Josephine Turner had even agreed to let her two lively little boys have their faces painted. Tyson, of all people, had crafted an exotic peacock on one boy's cheek that was nothing short of a masterpiece, and Gladys was rethinking her decision not to let her children participate.

Rain hadn't yet fallen, although it still threatened. Half of the plots were beginning to take shape. Sergeant was working on his while he gleefully forecast gloom and doom, and Elvira, with the help of two young men from St. Anthony's, had settled down to hoe her plot into sections.

"Feeling cheerier?"

Mary Kate turned around to find Casey beside her. Along with two students and Floppsy and Moppsy, he had spent the morning working on a plot that didn't yet have a taker.

She started to make one of her standby flippant responses, but something stopped her. Casey was looking at her differently, as if he was assessing her and liked what he saw.

"I know you must have been glad to see the volunteers pull in," he said.

She nodded. "How's your plot coming along?"

"It's more fun than I expected."

"You're kidding."

"No." He hunched his shoulders in something close to

nonchalance, but not quite close enough. "It's surprisingly therapeutic."

"Therapeutic?"

He didn't elaborate. "Whose plot is it, anyway?"

"Nobod—" She stopped, and suddenly she was grinning, her dimples inches deep. "I thought you'd never ask."

"Why? Is this one a secret?"

"More a surprise. It's *your* garden, Casey."

He laughed, and the dark, rich chuckle vibrated deep inside her. "Come on, Katie. Whose is it?"

"I mean it. It belongs to you and anyone else at the paper who wants to participate. It's a weekly column waiting to happen. Great publicity for us, a cute come-on for you. *The Cricket* in the garden."

A new idea occurred to her. "No. Get this. 'The Cricket in the Garden at Eden.' That's what we'll call this project. All your extra produce can go to the food bank, and your staff will come off as humanitarians. You said yourself the work was therapeutic. We ought to charge you for the privilege."

"You're nuts."

"It's a good idea. A great one."

"I've already been roped into working on the newsletter. Why don't I just move out here?"

"Sure. Why don't you? I'll trade my single bed for a double, and you can bunk with me."

She'd meant her response as a joke, but the moment the words were out, she regretted them. Something sparked in his eyes, and the very same thing sparked along her nerve endings.

Their gazes locked, and for a moment neither of them moved or even breathed. She was aware of him and nothing else, not the shouts of the teenagers, the laughter of the Turner children, the grinding roar of a rototiller.

He was the first to recover. "Sorry," he said in a gravelly voice, "but I think the sisters might notice."

She forced another smile. "I guess you're kind of hard to ignore." She cursed herself the moment the words were out. She needed a censor, someone like the sour-faced old nun, Sister John the Baptist, who had once told her that every word she uttered ought to be washed clean before it left her lips.

Sister John the Baptist. For a moment the earth twirled a little faster. Her knees grew weak, and her head felt as light as a balloon.

"Katie?" Casey grabbed her elbow. "You're as white as a sheet."

"I expect better of a journalist." Her own voice sounded very far away.

"You're going to sit down."

She let him lead her to a chair that had been set up for their lunch break. He didn't have to force her to sit. Her knees gave way at the proper moment. He squatted beside her, and she closed her eyes.

"What's going on?" he asked.

"Nothing. I just . . ." She tried to hold on to the memory, but it was fading. Still, unlike the brief flashes she'd had before, this one hadn't totally disappeared. She could still see Sister John, a prune-faced old woman in wire spectacles and a traditional black habit with a wimple starched so heavily it could have passed for a mainsail.

"Should I call someone?"

"No." She opened her eyes. She wasn't going to remember more. She was sure of that. "I just remembered something. That's all."

"That's good."

"Is it?" She searched his eyes, his dark chocolate eyes that now held nothing except concern.

"What did you remember? Or don't you want to talk about it?"

"Nothing important. Just the face of a nun I used to know. A teacher, I think."

"Maybe you're going to recover even more."

"Maybe."

"Did you see yourself this time?"

She remembered admitting that she sometimes saw a different Mary Kate in her memory flashes. "No, I just remembered her face and something she used to tell me." Now that the dizziness was passing she felt her lips curve into a smile. "I don't think I was as perfect a teenager as everyone's led me to believe. Sister John the Baptist surely didn't think so."

The worst of the work was finished by two. With rain threatening, no one took a real lunch break. They washed hands under hoses and grabbed pizza slices or ice-cream cones but got right back to work the moment the last bite was swallowed.

By two-thirty most people had packed up and gone home. The sisters and most of the teenagers drifted away to other projects, and Mary Kate was finally left with Casey for company. Tyson and a few others were off beside the barn taking a break.

"None of the parents came, did they?" Casey said.

"No, but a couple of them promised to come another time."

"Tyson's?"

She shook her head. "I don't know where his father is. He lives with his mother, but apparently she has no use for him. She refuses to take part in counseling. According to her, trying to help him is a waste of time."

Casey whistled softly.

"How is Tyson going to know he's okay if his own mother can't see it?" Mary Kate said.

"My mother never had a good word to say about me, either. She was so caught up in her own problems, her eyes were never open to mine." He smiled. "And look how well I turned out anyway."

She punched him in the arm. "But how many people get to your level with that kind of background, Casey?"

"Actually, Gypsy's mother should never have had kids, either. That was one of the reasons I understood her so well. We both knew what it was like to have to look for your self-esteem anywhere except inside your own four walls. It explained a lot about Gyps."

She heard wistfulness in his voice and something much too close to longing for her taste. "Is anyone ever going to replace Gypsy Dugan in your heart, Casey? Because every time you talk about her, you get this certain sound in your voice."

"Oh?"

"Yeah, like you wish you could turn back the clock."

"I guess I do sometimes. But I don't know what I'd do differently. Nothing between us was ever simple."

"You want simple? Go pet your dogs."

"What do you know about it? Are you remembering something you haven't shared with me?"

She knew he was referring to her baby's father. "No, but I know love's not supposed to be simple. It's complicated and painful and it ties you into a million nasty little knots."

"Don't plan on writing romance novels for a living, Katie."

She had been staring after Tyson. Now she turned and puckered her brow. "Do you believe something different? You seem way too cynical to buy this love stuff."

"I know what I believe. And I know what I feel."

She wanted to know more. She really did. But before she could ask, she felt the first splash of raindrops on her skin.

"I'll help you get everything into the barn," Casey offered. The teenagers had already taken off toward the dorms. Casey whistled for the dogs, then took off for a pile of tools that one of the students had neglected to put away. Mary Kate started for the wheelbarrow as the heavens opened.

They met inside where the sound of rain pelting the roof

was as loud as a drumroll. Mary Kate knew her hair was plastered to her scalp and forehead and her turtleneck to her breasts.

"Well, either we can brave the rain or wait it out," she said, running her fingers through her curls.

"I'm beat. How about you?"

He didn't look beat. He looked masculine and rumpled and altogether sexy in soft faded jeans and a Cleveland Indians sweatshirt pushed up above his elbows. Her heart sped a little faster, and she was even more aware of just how bedraggled she probably looked in comparison.

"I suppose we can make ourselves comfortable while we wait," she said, looking around for some way to do just that. "Somehow."

He pointed to the dogs, who had already snuggled into a clean pile of hay. "Ever made yourself at home on a bale of straw?"

"Can't say I have. But then I can't say a lot of things."

"This could be the high point of your day." He started for the straw bales, piled against one of the stalls to use as mulch later in the summer.

"I'll help." She joined him, interested to see what he had in mind and happy to stay by his side.

"You get the coffee."

"Coffee?"

"There's a Thermos with the tools I brought in."

The afternoon seemed to be shaping up. In what passed for her office she had a tin of cookies that Marie had baked yesterday. She told herself she was just tired and needed to rest. That was the only reason she was suddenly feeling so expectant, so warm and fuzzy inside. But no matter how many excuses she made, she found herself hoping that the rain would just keep falling.

Casey didn't know how he'd let himself get suckered into spending more time with Mary Kate. He had to be worse than bored with Shandley Falls and his life here.

His gaze followed her as she went to get the coffee, watching the way she rolled her sassy behind in the faded jeans, and the way her bright curls bounced against her neck.

Something stirred inside him, and then suddenly, something more obvious stirred between his legs. For a moment he couldn't believe what was happening. Surely he was imagining his reaction. He hadn't felt anything more than passing attraction to a woman since Gypsy's death. He had almost forgotten what desire felt like. But as he watched Mary Kate disappear around the corner, his body remembered.

Casey's taste in women had always run to the exotic. Gypsy Dugan had been striking, one hundred pounds of sexual energy in a long-legged package complete with firm, high breasts and a tiny waist. The first time he had seen her he had known she would be trouble. But he had been drawn to her anyway, pathetic male moth to a flame so hot his wings had been scorched at first contact.

He had known better than to pursue their relationship. Gypsy's sights had been on the high life. She had fought her way up the career ladder with a single-mindedness that had intimidated even those on the rungs above her. She hadn't been a cruel woman, just a self-centered one. Casey had known at first glance that she would step on him if he ever got in her way, even if it pained her to do it.

And still, that powerful revelation hadn't stopped him.

Now he leaned back in the warm nest of straw bales he'd created and watched his newest mistake striding toward him. Mary Kate wasn't exotic or striking. She was athletic and cuddly and cute, nothing like the women who had attracted him in the past, and not one bit like Gypsy.

Except sometimes she reminded him of Gypsy anyway. She had the same inability to see herself clearly, the same apparent disregard for the feelings of others, and sometimes the same little-girl-lost expression in her eyes when she thought no one would notice. He wondered sometimes if he was the only man with whom Gypsy had ever let down her guard, even for those briefest of moments.

Or perhaps he had been the only man who had cared enough to see what was buried under the surface.

"Chocolate-chip cookies." Mary Kate, her cheeks flushed with the cold and still dewed with raindrops, held out a tin. The Thermos was wedged under her arm. "And I couldn't find a cup for the coffee, but we can use the one with the Thermos and share."

"It's a regular party."

"Well, if we're stuck here, we might as well make the best of it."

Casey thought she looked surprisingly pretty today. Her jeans hugged her hips and highlighted a waist which, now that it had been released from layers of baggy clothing, was still smaller—considering everything—than he'd imagined. Her turtleneck was a rusty-red that set off her hair to perfection. And she was wearing makeup, just a little that had nearly worn off, but enough to play up the sparkling green of her eyes and the cherub bow of her lips.

He listened to the rain beating harder on the old barn roof. The straw beneath him smelled as if it had just been brought in from the fields, as clean and sweet as a spring day. Since Mary Kate had gotten back to work, the old mouse-infested hay had been removed to a compost pile. Now the barn seemed almost like a haven.

He watched her perch on the edge of the bale across from him. "How are we going to share coffee if you sit over there?" he asked.

She didn't answer. She shivered as a gust of wind blew through cracks in the siding.

He lifted an arm in invitation. "Come on over here, Katie, and get warm. There's no point in catching cold."

"There's a blanket in my office. Let me get it."

She disappeared again, and he waited, wondering what

she would do when she came back. She returned with the blanket, then to his surprise, settled herself next to him and tucked the blanket around them both.

For long moments he didn't know what to say. Of the two of them he had thought he was the one with experience. Now he wondered. There had never been a moment quite like this one. The woman snuggled beside him was someone he had no right and no reason to pursue. Not so long ago she had planned to give her life to God. Since then she had gone through hell both to recover and to rediscover herself. And most recently she had discovered that she was pregnant. Somehow they had become friends, of sorts. He would be a fool to want anything else.

As if on cue, that traitorous part of himself with a strong mind of its own stirred again as Mary Kate settled herself more firmly against him.

She unscrewed the top of the Thermos and poured coffee in the lid, which doubled as a cup. "Mmm . . . this smells heavenly."

"Fresh-brewed this morning."

She sipped some then offered it to him. "French roast. It's yummy. But I'm not supposed to have caffeine."

"It's my own blend. Half Colombian, half Italian roast. And decaf. That's why I brought my own. I was on a six-cup-a-day habit. I'm trying to wean myself."

"Wait a minute. You brought your own coffee with you? You knew I was going to ask you to work in the garden, didn't you? You came prepared."

He smiled. "Trapped."

"You deserve a reward. Want a cookie?"

"Two."

She pried off the lid and held out the tin for him to make his selection. They munched in silence, sharing the coffee cup like old friends. She poured more once they'd emptied it and they finished a second cup.

"The rain sounds nice in here, doesn't it?" She rested

her head against his shoulder after they'd finished and punctuated her question with something between a purr and a sigh. "Simple pleasures."

Casey thought there was nothing simple about Mary Kate McKenzie. At least not anymore. She was as complex and difficult as a three-dimensional jigsaw puzzle. But not all pleasures were meant to be simple.

He felt her turn her head, and he knew she was looking at him. It would take the slightest movement, the merest dip of his chin to put his lips against hers to find out how simple and pleasurable it would be to kiss her.

He restrained himself with difficulty, keeping his eyes firmly trained on the door beyond them. "I think you're beginning to come to terms with this life."

"Am I?"

"You enjoyed what you did today—the people, the organization, maybe even the work itself."

"How can you tell?"

"Because I know you so well."

"Casey, you hardly know me at all. We're practically strangers."

He supposed if one measured intimacy in terms of hours spent together, she was right. But she didn't feel like a stranger to him. In fact, in all the ways that mattered, she was the most familiar person in his life.

"If we're strangers," he said, "why are we sitting this way? Isn't this the way friends sit?" His heart beat once, twice. "Or lovers?"

Laughter bubbled in her throat. "Are you trying to prepare me for something? Like an announcement that we knew each other before my accident, and I'd better change the story I gave Dr. Kane?"

"We were complete strangers. And I was merely making a statement."

"I wish you *were* the father of my baby."

This time his self-control failed and he looked down at her, his lips just inches from hers. "What?"

"Don't be so surprised. You'd make a terrific father. I watched you with the Turner kids today. Don't think I didn't see you giving them piggyback rides between rows."

"I'm a journalist, not Mr. Rogers. I don't know anything about kids. I was never a kid myself."

"Maybe it's instinctive, then. But you're sensitive and caring, and you have a way of getting inside people."

The last was a little too close for comfort in light of the direction his thoughts had been taking. "Maybe we really are strangers. I'm none of those things. I'm a vicious, cut-throat news pirate, who won't stop at anything to get a story."

"You're a pussycat." She rested one finger against his lips after brushing away a cookie crumb. "Don't deny it."

He wondered if she had any idea what she was doing. The ordinary lemony scent of her hair was as provocative as Giorgio or Chanel and the sparkle in her green eyes as priceless as emeralds. He told himself it was just the situation. Right from the beginning their relationship had been fun, special even, precisely because of the lack of sexual attraction. Just because they were cuddled under a blanket like june bugs didn't mean that had changed.

He had gone too long without a lover.

"Don't tell me I hurt your feelings." She drew the tip of her finger along the edge of his lips. "Maybe not a pussycat. Maybe a tiger . . ."

"What? An old, toothless tiger in a cage?"

"Of course not. A young, virile tiger, who just happens to be less ferocious than he looks."

He kissed her fingertip. He did it before he knew he was going to. She smiled lazily and cupped her hand along his jaw. "I'm so glad I met you. I don't know what I'd do if I hadn't."

Her voice trailed off until the last words were nothing

more than whispers. Their gazes locked. For a moment he could have sworn he heard the hackneyed crescendo of violins. His heart stopped beating; time seemed to halt; the world stopped spinning.

Even as he dipped his head, he told himself what a bad idea this was. Unfortunately his own good advice had lost all power to influence him.

Her lips were as soft as he had suspected, lush, sweet, and warm. They molded to the shape of his, and for a moment, they held him captive.

It was not too late to make less of this than it really was. Casey knew if he retreated now, he could make light of what had happened, smile warmly, and tell her he was glad to have made a good friend.

But somehow, the words wouldn't come. And the kiss continued.

A crash startled them both, and they drew apart instantly. Casey looked up to find the door had blown open on a gust of wind. No one was there.

But they had been warned.

He knew it was too late to pretend, yet he tried it, anyway. He struggled for a friendly smile. "You know, you're a find, Katie. I'm glad our paths crossed. This year wouldn't be nearly as exciting without you." He cursed the word "exciting," but it was too late to take it back.

"Yes . . . well." She dimpled, but the expression in her eyes wasn't an exact match. She looked confused.

Stunned might be more accurate.

"How about more coffee?" he said.

She moved away, a subtle shift of her body that still left him feeling lonely, even though there were only inches between them. "You know, I think the rain may have stopped."

"Really?"

"Look . . ." She moved even farther away and pointed. "Maybe we ought to head out while we can."

"That might not be a bad idea." Although it certainly felt like one.

She threw off the blanket and stood. "Race you back to the house."

"I think I'll go directly to my car. I don't have any reason to stop."

"Oh, sure. That makes sense." She was already moving toward the door.

He called the dogs, then caught up with her, and they exited together. She stopped long enough to fasten the padlock, then they walked along the garden plot.

The sky was still dark, and Casey knew that the rain had only stopped temporarily. He stepped up his pace, but Mary Kate began to lag behind. He stopped at last to let her catch up. This was no way to end the day. He didn't want her to feel that anything significant had changed or that they could no longer be friends. He didn't know what had happened inside the barn, but he was damned sure he wasn't going to let it happen again.

Mary Kate didn't catch up with him. She stood glued to the path, staring at the center's plot. Somewhere in the distance thunder boomed, and immediately afterwards Casey felt raindrops splash against his cheeks and forehead.

"Katie, come on. You have enough going on without catching cold."

"Casey . . ."

"Look, I'm sorry about what happened in there. But you don't have to start avoiding me. I promise it—"

"Casey, look." She pointed toward the end of the row where she was standing.

He was miffed that she'd ignored him. "What?"

"Look." She started down the wide aisle in the middle of the plot. "Oh, look!"

He had no idea what fascinated her so, but he knew she was about to get soaked to the skin. He debated following or ignoring her to run for cover. Grumbling, he started after her. "You know, it's probably not more than fifty-five degrees out here, and it's going to be miserably cold if you let yourself get—"

She knelt in the dirt, ignoring him, ignoring the fact that the ground was already wet enough to make mud pies. "Look! They're up!"

For a moment he didn't know what she was talking about, then he drew closer and saw the pale-green shoots in a wide flat row in front of her. "What is it?"

"Lettuce, I think. Yes, it is. I marked it. I learned how from myself." She laughed. "Apparently I mark everything. I hated to spoil the tradition. Buttercrunch, and black-seeded Simpson, and . . ." She nearly put her nose to the ground. "Oak leaf. Regular and bronze. Casey, the seeds came up! The rain uncovered them."

He didn't know what to say. For a few moments after he'd kissed her, he had almost believed his own lies. He had kissed her because of the rain. It was the coziness of having her soft little body cuddled up to his. It was the friendship, the compassion he felt for her.

But now, watching Mary Kate kneel in the mud with rain splashing the ground around her, he knew his lies for what they were. Staring at the lettuce patch Mary Kate looked like a kid on Christmas morning.

Casey was afraid that he did, too. And not because of anything he had planted.

ॐ 11

USUALLY BREAKFAST WAS MARY KATE'S FA-
vorite meal. The sisters rose early for prayer, something she
had managed to avoid. Most of the time she showered and
dressed while they worshiped, then joined them for whatever gourmet surprise Marie had produced that morning.
Whether breakfast consisted of whole-grain waffles or fresh
omelets with herbs from the greenhouse, there was always
a bowl of cinnamon-rich applesauce or spicy peaches from
their own orchard to go with it.

On Friday morning nearly a week after the community-
garden workday, Mary Kate came down late to find the sisters finishing breakfast without her. She hadn't meant to
sleep in. But even though she had plenty of energy during
the day, she was also finding that like most pregnant women
she needed extra rest. The last time she'd been late for a
meal she had apologized to Sarah, blaming her recovery.
But she didn't know how much longer that excuse would
work.

This morning Marie had fixed oatmeal, rich with bits of
dried fruit, and bran muffins laced with molasses and raisins.
Mary Kate was over the worst of her morning queasiness,
but the moment she sat down she realized that she wasn't
going to be able to handle the muffins. Even the smell of
them made her stomach turn.

She shook her head when Marie passed the basket to her, but Marie refused to take no for an answer.

"You're sure, Mary Kate? They've always been one of your favorites."

Mary Kate didn't trust herself to speak. She knew she would be fine if she could just get something else in her stomach. The nausea would pass. She shook her head, managing a thin smile, and reached for the oatmeal, splashing milk on it before she took her first bite.

"Applesauce, Mary Kate?" Sarah asked in a brusque voice. Obviously she had a thousand things to do that day.

Mary Kate weighed that menu possibility and shook her head again, silently exhorting her roiling stomach.

"Coffee?" Grace asked, her concern audible.

"I'm . . . fine." She took another bite and wished it was true.

One by one the others got up and took care of their dishes. Mary Kate forced herself to eat slowly, taking deep breaths between bites until finally, her stomach had settled enough that she knew she was past the danger point.

At last only Sarah remained at the table, despite her full schedule, sipping a fresh cup of coffee and watching Mary Kate finish her oatmeal.

"Mary Kate," she said at last, "do you trust me?"

Mary Kate raised her eyes and knew the jig was up. Sarah more than suspected the truth. She was merely waiting for Mary Kate to confirm it.

Mary Kate was in no mood for revelations. She considered her words carefully. "Of course. But I hope you trust me, too."

"I do."

"Then maybe we need to talk. But not right now."

Sarah rose, coffee cup in hand. "All right. Whenever you're ready."

Mary Kate knew that she'd better be ready soon. She had pulled on her Levi's that morning to find them almost impossible to snap. She supposed she was lucky. For whatever reason her taste had apparently run to baggy clothing and although her body was changing, the pregnancy wasn't yet visible. But that would change quickly.

She hated to have the evidence right out in front of her for everyone to see. The moment her former lover realized what he'd done, his motivation to keep their relationship a secret would be tripled.

Particularly if he was a married man.

As always, when she thought about the mystery man, she thought of Pete. Right now all roads seemed to lead in his direction. She and Pete had dated in high school. People had expected them to marry, until Carol had gotten pregnant. Pete obviously felt guilty about something that had happened during their last encounter before she was injured.

Pete could very well be the father of the child she carried.

"Do you have plans today?" Sarah asked from the sink, where she was taking care of her dishes.

"I'm going into town this morning to pick up some plants the extension service is contributing. We can give them out tomorrow if anyone comes to work in the garden."

"They'll come. While you're in town, would you run some errands if I give you a list? You can take the van if you need the room."

Mary Kate tried to imagine herself driving something the size of a small bus. "I'll have plenty of room in my car," she assured Sarah.

She finished cleaning the kitchen after Sarah left, then she went upstairs for her purse and jacket. She stopped for Sarah's list on the way out before she headed toward the carriage house.

Her driving skills hadn't returned miraculously, but she made her exit without incident and started for town. She supposed it was a sign of some improvement that her mind kept drifting to other things rather than locking shut in abject terror.

Of course the other things had to do with Casey.

Nearly a week had passed since Casey had kissed her in the barn, but every chance she got she still replayed the kiss. She hadn't seen him since that afternoon. She hadn't even spoken to him. Something substantial had changed between them, and for no other reason than that their lips had touched. They had left the safety, the nonchalance of friendship and moved toward something infinitely more complicated.

Why in the hell had Casey kissed her? Sure, the two of them had been snuggled up like lovers in the barn, but they weren't lovers. Never had been and never would be. Surely he could see how difficult their relationship might become if it moved beyond friendship. She liked him. She trusted him. Right from the beginning she had been proud that she hadn't fallen prey to his Latin-lover looks and his heart-stopping smile. She saw her reaction—or lack of one—as a sign of good mental health.

So what was this new reaction a sign of? And what did it say about her that she couldn't forget the taste of his lips, the rock-hard breadth of his chest pressing against her non-existent breasts? That now she imagined what it might be like to dig her fingertips into his hair and kiss him back, baring teeth and tongue and soul to him?

This was Casey, for God's sake!

Love didn't happen this way. It was a raging fire, not a slow, steady simmer. Lovers didn't talk for hours like old friends. They didn't share their every thought and feeling. She doubted a lover would support a woman through a pregnancy with another man's child. A lover wouldn't hold a woman's hand through a difficult doctor's appointment or jump another man simply because that man had been rude to her.

She wanted things the way they had been.

She wanted him to kiss her again.

A car slowed on the road ahead of her, and a second

passed before Mary Kate remembered what to do. She gripped the steering wheel harder and told herself to forget Casey.

Fifteen minutes later, exhausted and nearly boneless from anxiety she parked at the nursery where she was supposed to pick up her plants. As before her hands were locked on the steering wheel and she had to jerk them loose to turn off the engine.

The nursery sat on an acre of ground just outside the city limits. The man Mary Kate was supposed to see hadn't arrived yet, so she wandered through aisles of trees and shrubs, plotting her detective work for the day. Pete had not called to set up another appointment. Apparently the lure of another client he could bill by the minute hadn't been strong enough. She needed to find a quiet place to talk to him, somewhere without a nosy waitress or receptionist, and somewhere out from under the thumb of his powerful father-in-law.

Somewhere cozy enough to see if he made a pass at her.

Maybe the barn. It had worked for Casey.

She wandered through the greenhouse, vaguely admiring flats of colorful annuals as she thought about all the mysteries of her life. Magenta petunias waved in a soft breeze stirred by a ceiling fan, and pale-pink impatiens preened in the filtered sunlight.

A woman wearing a navy blazer and flowered skirt stood at the end of her row, assessing flats of snapdragons and pansies. Because she fit in so perfectly with the surroundings she caught Mary Kate's attention. She had the dewy, pink-tinged complexion of an English rose and long flaxen hair to go with it. Although she weighed enough to resemble Camilla more than Princess Di, she held herself like an aristocrat. Mary Kate expected a uniformed chauffeur to appear at any moment to whisk away her selections for the castle gardens.

The woman raised her gaze from the flowers, and as she

took in Mary Kate, her eyes widened. Mary Kate had seen that look before. Apparently she was not gazing at a stranger.

"What are you doing here?" the woman demanded.

Mary Kate frowned. She certainly owed the woman no explanations, but Mary Kate was intrigued by the hostility in her voice. "The same thing you are, most likely," she said, expending considerable effort to keep her own voice pleasant. "I'm here to pick up some plants."

"Why were you staring?"

"I wasn't." Mary Kate moved closer, although not close enough to seem threatening. "They have a nice selection, don't they? Are you planning a garden?"

"Pete expects flowers in the front beds. As always, I'm elected to do the work."

With a start Mary Kate realized that this must be Carol, the Carol who had stolen her boyfriend, married him in a shotgun wedding, and produced the Watkins heir in record time. Yet Carol was angry at her.

"You don't sound very enthused," Mary Kate said.

"Should I be?"

Mary Kate smiled benignly, an idea forming. If she couldn't get to Pete, maybe she could find out some information from Carol. "If I'd married Pete, I would have made him put in the flowers himself."

Carol stepped closer. "But you didn't marry him, did you?"

"We both know why."

"What? Are you finally admitting that you care? After all those years of trying to make me think you didn't want him anyway?"

This was a new piece of information. If Mary Kate had indeed been sorry to lose Pete, apparently she had never let on. "You're putting words in my mouth, Carol. Would you mind telling me why you sound so angry?"

"I'm tired of this act, this everybody's-friend charade.

I'm on to you, Mary Kate. I've always been on to you.''

"Exactly what are you on to?''

"You still want Pete, no matter what you tell everybody else. Well, as far as I'm concerned, you can have him. I wish I'd never—'' She clamped her lips shut.

"Married him?''

"No! I wish I'd never gotten pregnant. That's what I wish! I trapped him into marrying me, and now I'm stuck with him. And you could sit back and laugh at me if you wanted, only you're not smart enough to see the joke!''

"I'm smart enough to see you're pretty upset.''

Carol kept her voice low, but her tone was venomous. "Daddy's receptionist told me you've been to the office to see Pete. What did he do? Cry on your shoulder? Tell you how bad things are at home, then tell you he can't leave me because he loves our son too much to divorce me? Did he tell you that?''

Carol stepped closer, as if she was moving in for the kill. "Well, listen up, Mary Kate. Pete doesn't know Little Pete's around most of the time. He doesn't even want Petey to eat meals with us because his talking annoys him. He doesn't read him bedtime stories. He doesn't play ball or take him to the movies. He's a failure as a husband and a failure as a father, and if you really want him, then I say take him!''

"Why would you think I want him? I went to see him for some legal advice.''

"You want anybody who needs you. That's why! You're this perfect paragon, stronger than the rest of us, wiser, kinder, closer to God. You name it. You always saw Pete as a work in progress. You didn't love him. You wanted to save him from himself. I loved him!''

"And you still do,'' Mary Kate said, seeing clearly that it was true.

Carol turned her face away to hide her expression. Mary Kate had just borne the brunt of Carol's wrath, but despite that she almost felt sorry for the woman. Pete was no prize, but Carol wanted him anyway.

Mary Kate tried to ease Carol's misery. "Look, I don't want Pete." That much, at least, was absolutely true.

"No?" Carol faced her again. "Oh, I know you're not out to get him in your bed. You don't seem to have those kind of inclinations. Maybe there's something wrong with you in that department. But you won't let go of him. You're the path not taken. Every time he looks at you, every time he thinks about you, he wonders what life would have been like if I hadn't gotten pregnant."

Mary Kate wondered what good old Pete was going to think when he looked at her in a few months or maybe even weeks and saw that *she* was pregnant. "Maybe this doesn't have anything to do with me. Maybe it's the other choices he's made, like living here and working in your father's firm."

"Has he told you that?"

"I was there, Carol. They watch him like a hawk."

"You want to know why? Because he had an affair last year, and my father knows it." She pinched her fingers together in demonstration. "Daddy came this close to firing him, only I refused to get a divorce, and Daddy couldn't fire his own son-in-law."

Mary Kate was silent. Despite herself she was disturbed by Carol's story.

Carol picked up a flat of pansies, as if she was about to leave, then she set it down again with a thump. "Pete blames me for forcing him to get married. He blames me for giving him a child he didn't want. He even blames me for having to give up dreams of having his own business."

Apparently she interpreted Mary Kate's confusion as something else. "Oh yes, he blames me for that, too," she continued. "He goes out in his workshop every chance he gets and works on that furniture of his. We don't have much time together as it is, and that's how he spends the few hours that should belong to Little Pete and me.''

Mary Kate took a chance. "Pete's furniture is beautiful, and it's very important to him.''

"Keep telling him that, Mary Kate. Who knows? You might get what you wanted all those years ago." Carol turned and swept down the aisle, her shoulders thrown back and her chin high. No one watching would have been able to tell she was upset.

But Mary Kate had seen the tears in Carol's eyes.

The visit to town didn't turn up any other new information. Mary Kate lingered until it was after one o'clock so that she wouldn't have to face Sarah over lunch. By the time she got back to Eden's Gate and stored the new plants, she was ravenous. Since it was a warm afternoon she made a sandwich and took it to the pond where she was sure to be alone.

She had to tell Sarah the truth. She had to discover the identity of her baby's father. She had to figure out what to do if Casey kissed her again. On the surface hers was the simplest of lives, but in reality it seemed to teem with intrigue and secrets. She munched Swiss cheese and tomatoes and wondered how she would survive in the real world if the complexities of her world at Eden's Gate were almost too much for her.

She was nearly finished with her sandwich when movement at the far edge of the pond caught her eye. She squinted and leaned forward. A man stood in a small clump of trees, trying for all the world to look like one of them.

A man who didn't belong here.

"Jake Holloway!" She stood, tossing her crust to the ground for the ducks to discover. "You bastard! Are you polluting our pond again?''

She stomped toward him, skirting the edge of the pond with vigilante determination. "If you've thrown anything else in this pond, I'm going to toss you in after it!"

He stepped out of his private little grove to meet her. His eyes snapped with emotion. "I got no trash. I was just taking a walk. A man's allowed to take a walk!"

"You're not a man, you're a weasel!" She stopped just inches from him, her hands on her hips. "What's the real reason for being here? Planning to carve a few swastikas on the tree trunks? Or maybe you're looking for just the right spot for the next Klan barbecue?"

"I was just looking around, I tell you! Walking and looking!" As if to prove his point he gave a shrill whistle. Godzilla came charging out of the underbrush on the other side of the pond. "Dog needed a walk!"

She braced herself, but at another whistled command Godzilla slid to a halt just inches from Mary Kate's feet.

Something about the defensive look in Jake's eyes convinced her he was telling the truth. If he'd been here for mischief he would have owned up to it proudly. As it was, he was embarrassed he'd been caught doing something normal.

"So you were just doing a little snooping," she said. "You're sure?"

"I ought to know what I was doing better'n anybody."

They were left with nothing to discuss. He turned and Godzilla leapt to his side. Something about the slump of Jake's shoulders nudged at Mary Kate's heart. She'd been feeling much that same sort of discouragement before he appeared.

"You want a tour?" she asked, before she could think about it. "I could show you around."

He faced her. "What makes you think I'd be interested?"

"Nothing. Except that you're here already. And Godzilla probably needs more exercise. You ought to buy that monster a treadmill."

"You give weasels tours?"

"If they want them."

"I don't care about anything you're doing here. Bringing in all sorts of undesirables, you are. I saw 'em coming up the road the other day."

"What's the deal here? Anybody who doesn't look just like you is an undesirable? You looked in the mirror lately, Jake?"

A muscle in the general region of his mouth jumped and twisted. He tightened his lips, as if he was trying not to smile.

Mary Kate was amazed. She would not have believed the man had a sense of humor. But after all he was the one who'd put up the warning sign at his house for two toothless Dobermans.

"Look, give us a chance," she said. "You might find some things to like. You really might. You'll never know if you don't take a good look around."

He didn't agree, he harrumphed. But when she started toward the greenhouse, Jake and Godzilla were tagging along behind her.

Half an hour later they ended up at the community garden.

Mary Kate walked with him along the center path, pointing out plots while Godzilla chased robins. During the workday Sergeant had marked his boundaries with wooden stakes. Now she saw that sometime over the last week he'd come back and pounded a sign in the center with his name on it.

"Sergeant Gorse's got a plot here?" Jake said.

It was the first thing he had said since leaving the pond area. Jake had spent most of their time together scanning the landscape like a paramilitary field scout searching for antinuke rallies or naked flower children cavorting in the orchard.

"You know Sergeant?" she said.

"Used to be friends, him and me. Before . . ."

"Before?"

He didn't explain. "I used to help him once in a while, when he was still the gardener here."

Mary Kate felt a pang of guilt, even though she couldn't remember having Sergeant fired. "So you like growing things?"

"Nah. Did once, that's all."

"You have a lot of land around your house you could put to good use."

"All trees and shade. I'd have to cut 'em all down, if I wanted a garden. Then people'd see my house."

He needed light and sunshine. If she remembered correctly a lot of the trees near Jake's home were dead or dying and needed to be culled.

"I don't suppose . . ." The idea was so preposterous she couldn't believe she'd come up with it.

"Suppose what?"

"No, maybe it's not a good idea for you to have a plot here. You'd be too busy watching everybody and judging them to get any work done yourself. Probably couldn't grow a thing."

"You're crazy! I was growing vegetables before you were born. Grew cabbages as big around as a beach ball. And string beans? Shoot, you lay all the string beans I grew in a line, they'd wrap all the way around the world and then some!"

She waited a moment, then another, hoping he would listen to his own words. "Talk's cheap." She shrugged.

"Don't want no garden."

She played another card. "Who could blame you? Nobody with a brain is going to want the garden right next to Sergeant's, anyway. Nobody'll be able to compete. That's why nobody's chosen it yet."

He glared at her. She knew he was perfectly aware of what she was doing. But he was like a rabbit who can't resist a carrot, even when it senses the snare.

Jake crossed his arms over his chest. "I have to grow

anything special? Or can I grow what I want?''

"Whatever you want. Long as it's legal."

"I don't want to share nothing. Not one lettuce leaf. People are hungry, let them grow their own.''

She nearly winced. It sounded too much like what she'd said to Samantha. "You don't have to share, if you don't have it in you to be generous, Jake.''

"Who's on the other side?'' He inclined his head toward the garden to the right of the one she was making the pitch for.

"If it matters, then we'd better rethink this. Because I don't have time to keep people away from you because you don't like their skin color or accents or the way they wear their hair. Or because they voted for Clinton instead of Dole or—''

"I get it. You don't have to go on and on. Jeesh!''

"Do you want the garden or not?'' She watched him sizing it up and played her final ace. "It's one way to keep track of what's going on here, Jake. You won't have to sneak around any more.''

"Put my name on it,'' he said.

"No, you can do that tomorrow. Come on over early. Sergeant will be here.''

He didn't answer. He just whistled for Godzilla and took off the way they had come. She followed him as far as the barn.

It was early afternoon, but already it had been a long day. She was determined to have at least one good experience. When Jake was safely on his way, Mary Kate strolled over to the salad patch to see if her newest row of lettuce had emerged.

For a moment she thought she'd wandered down the wrong row. Not only couldn't she find any signs of newly emerged seedlings, she couldn't find the old ones.

She fell to her hands and knees and put her nose to the ground. Up close she saw the chewed-off stumps of baby lettuces and scattered neatly among them, something that looked like buckshot. Only this buckshot had come from fluffy little behinds.

"Rabbits!"

She sat back on her heels. "Little fucking bunnies!"

The futility of the day nearly overwhelmed her. She closed her eyes. She didn't know who she was. And what she did know was as confusing as what she didn't. Now, to top it all off, the one thing that had been going well, the one thing she seemed to have some control over, had been destroyed by Peter Rabbit and his friends.

For a moment she reconsidered leaving Eden's Gate. She had spent time investigating her financial situation after her first escape attempt, and now she knew that she had enough money to live comfortably for the rest of her life. She could move anywhere and start over again. Even if her memory never returned she could have a new life. No one would have any expectations of her. No one would be disappointed that she was having a baby out of wedlock and giving it to strangers. And why did it matter who the baby's father was since obviously he wasn't a real part of her life anymore?

Why did it matter if Casey was ashamed of her for running away?

Her eyelids snapped open. She'd be damned if she'd admit defeat. Most of the time this didn't feel like her life, but it was the only life she had. She wasn't going to let anyone or anything take it away from her. When she left Eden's Gate, she wasn't going to do it like a coward. She would leave with her head high. She would leave with something to be proud of, something she *could* remember, even if she never remembered another thing.

She got to her feet and shook her fist toward the woods. "Listen up, bunnies!" she shouted. "We're not going hungry because of you!"

Mary Kate was declaring war.

ᥴᢙ 12

CASEY, HIS CAR LOADED WITH *CRICKET* STAFF members and one panting sheepdog, listened as they debated the merits of six or twelve tomato plants. Jim, who had agreed to supervise *The Cricket*'s garden plot, was leaning heavily toward the larger number.

For once Jim's soft voice rose above the others. "You can freeze them, can them, make spaghetti sauce, catsup, tomato paste, fried green tomatoes . . ."

"This is beginning to sound like a scene from *Forrest Gump*," Casey said from the driver's seat. "Do we have room for a dozen?"

"If we stake them they don't take up that much room. We'll still have room for anything else we want to grow."

Mary, the office manager, spoke up. "I want basil. Lots of basil. I'm planning to make pesto. I can't make pesto, I don't want to do this."

Phil, the classified salesman, turned to shout down the others. "Squash. All kinds. Butternut to store for the winter, zucchini for summer."

"I hate zucchini," Sandy, the graphic designer, said as soon as she could be heard. "You plant zucchini, don't get it near me."

"We'll have plenty of room to do whatever we want." Casey was grateful to see the Eden's Gate driveway. "Just don't forget we're doing a column about this. Each one of

204

you takes at least one turn over the summer. No excuses. So start collecting experiences.''

He drove directly to the barn where people had already gathered. He saw a group of the offenders with their college-student counselors off to one side and several families having picnics off to the other. Since the *Cricket* staff was late, people were already hard at work in the garden area. He thought he saw Mary Kate, although since she was bent over he was judging solely on the contours of her nicely rounded butt.

"Okay. Now everybody knows where the garden is. You get yourselves over here from now on," Casey said. "Come work any time you like, except when you're working for me. And pay attention!"

"Dictator." Sandy, an attractive blonde who was just a few years older than he was, gave him a ravishing grin. Sandy had been trying to get Casey into the sack since the day they'd met. But Casey had learned his lesson about mixing work and pleasure from Gypsy Dugan.

Staff and dog piled out with good-natured grumbling. Casey introduced them to Samantha, who promised a brief tour. He stood back with Cottontail as everyone else followed her, reluctant to make his own presence known to Mary Kate.

He hadn't seen or spoken to her since their rainy afternoon in the barn, but that didn't mean she hadn't been in his thoughts. Casey didn't know what had possessed him to kiss Mary Kate. At best she was a friend, a diversion in a life with few others. And despite her earthy, pragmatic view of the universe, she had led a sheltered life. He had no right to complicate it still further.

Unfortunately, he wanted to kiss her again.

"Looking for something to do?"

He turned to find Sarah at his elbow. He hadn't even heard her approach, but like the nuns in his parochial school, someone had taught her to glide soundlessly, even though she was wearing jeans. "I think I'll find plenty."

"We appreciate your staff agreeing to take a plot. The publicity will be wonderful. We may have to expand next year." She hesitated. "If Mary Kate's still here to oversee it."

Casey had gotten to know Sarah fairly well while he worked on the article about the center. He knew her to be capable of great subtlety as well as great compassion. He also knew when she was fishing for information.

"I don't know what Mary Kate will be doing next year," he said, coming straight to the point. "I don't think she knows."

"You've become friends, haven't you?"

"She needs friends."

"Do I sound critical?"

"I don't know. Do you mean to be?"

Sarah was watching Mary Kate, who was talking to two old men in the garden, her hands on her hips. "I don't know her anymore."

"Not surprising. She doesn't know herself."

"The woman I'm coming to know will never become one of us." Sarah shifted her gaze to Casey's face. "But the woman I used to know might not have joined us, either. She sensed she was intended for a different path. And now?" She shrugged.

"I didn't know her before."

"If you had, you'd understand my concerns."

Casey wondered if Mary Kate had told Sarah about the baby. The time was growing short. Soon, whether she admitted it or not, everyone would know she was pregnant. "Concern or sadness? Are you unhappy that she seems to be moving away from becoming a sister?"

Sarah smiled. "If I'm unhappy it's only because she has to struggle so hard. But it's not my job to make things easy for people, is it?"

*　　*　　*

As the afternoon wore on, Mary Kate realized she was exhausted. Much of the backbreaking work of putting in a garden had already been finished, but today the job of keeping the new gardeners happy had been almost worse.

Everyone had wanted the cabbage and broccoli plants she had brought from the nursery, but unfortunately she hadn't gotten enough to go around. The seeds disappeared almost as quickly. Since it was still too early in the season to plant warm-weather crops, everyone was vying for the same limited resources. She'd emptied her pockets and sent Marie into town at lunchtime to buy whatever she could lay her hands on, but even those flats and seeds were gone now.

As she had hoped, Sergeant and Jake had hit it off immediately, but then, between the two of them, they had managed to discourage everyone who came in contact with them. The Mannings had threatened to quit if they weren't given a plot farther away from Sergeant, who had told them over and over that nothing they were doing was going to work. And Jo Turner, a shapely brunette, had been roundly insulted by Jake, who had insisted that her jeans were too tight and might well lead to the moral decay of Shandley Falls.

"Can . . . can I get you something to drink, Mary Kate?"

Mary Kate pushed away from the barn, which graciously had propped her up for the past five minutes, and gave Jim a wan smile. She had heard Casey call him by name earlier before he and Cottontail disappeared into the newspaper's plot. She had recognized Jim immediately as the young man who had assisted her when she'd stalled in the intersection. Since then he had danced attendance on her.

"I'm fine. How's your plot coming?"

"Casey's dog is dig-digging more holes than we are. Look, I . . . I don't mean to argue, but you look tired. You're . . . you're sure about that drink?"

"What do you have?"

"We brought Coke and Seven Up and juice."

She would have killed somebody, anybody, for a Coke, or better yet a Coke spiked with something that was forbidden to expectant mothers, but she nodded at the last choice. "Juice it is."

She watched him head back into the garden where the *Cricket* staff had a cooler of drinks they'd been sharing.

"That boy seems mighty fond of you."

She realized Sergeant had come up beside her. "Does he?" She hadn't thought about it, but Jim obviously knew her. And he did seem taken with her.

"I wonder why?" Sergeant said. "Kid's got no taste."

"You know, I'm out here in the garden practically twenty-four hours a day. And I'm perfectly capable of pulling all your plants out by their itty-bitty roots when you're not around to see me. So you'd better be nice, Sergeant, or I'll destroy your reputation."

He cackled. "You won't have to pull out anything, missy. Nothing's going to survive the deer in them woods, not to mention the groundhogs, the coons, the chipmunks . . ."

Her last remnant of energy drained away. "Don't forget the rabbits."

"They won't forget *you*, that's for sure. You're going down, down, down . . ." He was still cackling as he sauntered off.

Jim returned. "We had apple juice. I hope that . . . that's all right."

"Just fine." She took it and sipped, careful not to make a face. "So, how's the garden plot going?"

"Fine. Everyone's working hard. But we're so close to the woods . . ."

"You get sun most of the day. It should be all right."

"I live on a farm. I . . . I was thinking about pests."

"You and me both."

"We need a fence."

"I know we do, but there's no money in our budget. I've been over and over the figures."

"You just need something sturdy. It wouldn't have to be fancy."

"I priced chicken wire. That's cheap, but if we really do attract deer, they'd trample it in a minute."

"What . . . what did you do last year?"

Of course she couldn't remember what she had done. She had read every entry in her journal, but unfortunately in much of it her entries were so abbreviated she couldn't make heads or tails of them. After all, she'd never dreamed she'd lose her memory and with it the keys to deciphering her own code. She told Jim what little she'd learned from Samantha and the others. "We used organic controls. Blood meal, which the rabbits don't like. Dog hair from the groomer in town. Lifebuoy soap."

"Soap?"

"The deer don't like the smell of it. Don't use it before you go hunting."

"You know I don't hunt."

She didn't know what Jim did or didn't do, but she kept that to herself. As far as she was concerned every male over twelve was under suspicion, since she was no candidate for an immaculate conception.

"Do you have any other ideas?" she said. "Something we can try that's not as expensive as a fence?"

He smiled, and his thin face was transformed into something more appealing. "I don't hunt, but maybe you . . . you should."

"A gun-toting nun wannabe? Sister Mary Katherine of Justice for Carrots?"

He laughed. "Maybe you ought to start smaller. Take a clue from David. He . . . he did his work with a slingshot."

"Maybe I should think that over."

"Mary Kate . . . I don't think I've ever . . . ever said thank you. Then you almost . . . died." He cleared his throat. "And I . . . I never told you what you meant . . ."

Her exhaustion vanished and her body went on alert. She

waited, hoping he'd elaborate. When he didn't, she scrambled for a way to answer him and still leave the door open for revelations. "You could tell me now."

His face was turning red. "I . . . that is, I . . . um . . . I think of you as my most . . ."

She leaned forward, hoping that she had stumbled onto at least one answer to the mysteries of her life.

"Treasured friend," he finished.

"Oh." She realized belatedly how disappointed she had sounded. "Oh." She manufactured a little more sparkle in her voice. "That's so nice of you, Jim. I always thought of you as a treasured friend, too."

"You've always . . . always listened to me."

She had been a regular Donna Reed. Apparently *all* she had done was listen to men. Mary Kate's eyes flicked to her belly. Well, maybe not quite all.

Jim finished. "When others . . . you know . . . didn't want to take the . . . the time."

"Their loss." She patted his shoulder. "I'm glad I'll be seeing you more often now."

"Really?" His face brightened immeasurably. "You . . . you're not dis . . . disappointed in me?"

She cocked her head. What on earth had this shy young man ever done that could disappoint her? She made a half-hearted attempt to absolve him of whatever it might be. "How could you think that?"

"I'm . . . so . . . so . . . glad."

Mary Kate realized someone had joined them. She had been so absorbed in the nuances of their conversation she hadn't noticed. Now she looked up to find Casey watching her.

Mary Kate had managed to stay clear of Casey all afternoon, but she'd kept an eye on him. Or rather she hadn't been able to keep her eyes off of him, even from a distance. Today he was dressed more casually than usual. Ripped jeans rode low on his narrow hips, and a faded black T-shirt clung to his chest. He needed a haircut, and the wave that made his hair unruly was settling into curls against his nape. He also needed a shave.

She needed to stop noticing everything about him.

"Problems, Casey?" She forced a friendly smile, but it took some work.

"Just checking to see how things are going."

"I've . . . I've got to get . . . get back," Jim said.

Mary Kate extended her smile to Jim, too. "Nice talking to you, Jim."

Casey waited until Jim was gone before he spoke. "He doesn't usually stutter that much. Just when he's nervous."

She thought of Pete, master of the unfinished sentence. "I seem to bring out speech problems in men. I'm surprised you aren't lisping."

"I'm not head over heels in love with you."

"What?"

Casey folded his arms. "Have you forsaken the worldly life so long that you can't see the signs?"

She lowered her voice. "I don't even remember Jim. How can I recognize signs?"

"Let's just say he's usually at least a bit more self-possessed."

"He says we're friends. Treasured friends."

"Yeah, and I know where that can lead."

For a moment she was too stunned for a retort. Then she straightened. "What's that supposed to mean?"

"One minute a man thinks he's friends with a woman, the next minute they end up in bed together."

That image did the strangest things to Mary Kate. Her pulse quickened, and so did her breathing. "I hope you're not blaming that particular phenomenon on women. In my experience, most men will get into bed with any woman who's willing. Friendship has nothing to do with it."

"In your experience?"

"Right. My vast experience with men. Remember? After

all, I'm carrying proof I slept around, right here where everyone will be able to see it pretty soon. Hell, I probably slept with your friend Jim. That's probably why he's so flustered around me.''

"I'm just saying that being friends can lead to other things. A woman and a man have to be careful. And maybe you weren't.''

She inched closer. This was a conversation she didn't want anyone else to hear. "Oh really? And how would you know, Charles Casey? Have you been friends with that many women?''

She knew they were talking about the same thing, about a kiss that shouldn't have happened, a kiss that had confused her, excited her, made her long for new complications in an unbearably complicated life. But the only thing she had learned so far was that she wasn't the only one who had been upset by what had passed between them.

"If a friendship can be that easily destroyed, then it's not much of a friendship, is it?'' he said.

"Maybe it's not.''

"Maybe it would be better to let a friendship like that drop.''

She folded her arms over her chest. "Maybe it would be.''

"Mary Kate!''

At the sound of Samantha's shout, Mary Kate turned away. Her throat closed around an answer, but she waved at Sam, to let her know she'd heard her.

"We need you over here. Got a minute?'' Sam shouted.

Mary Kate nodded, then turned back to Casey and kept her voice low. "I have to go. But just so you know, I never threw myself at you. You were the one who kissed me.''

"You made it damned easy.''

Her voice shook with anger, but she didn't care. "I don't need you in my life. I'm not a charity case. I can get through this pregnancy without you. So don't worry about being my friend. Don't worry about anything as far as I'm concerned. I don't care if you were a tabloid-television star or a used-car salesman. I'm not now nor have I ever been one of your little groupies!''

She held her head high as she went to help Samantha. And she made sure she kept it high for the rest of the afternoon. Even after Casey and the *Cricket* staff went home.

Mary Kate had taken care of one of the problems in her life. When Casey left without a good-bye she knew she would never have to worry about him kissing her again. She wouldn't have to worry about him, period, because she doubted that he would ever come back to Eden's Gate. She felt hollow inside, as if she'd somehow shed a vital organ. But she knew she was better off without any man in her life, even as a friend. She didn't need anything anchoring her to Eden's Gate and Shandley Falls. Once the baby was born and gone to its new home, she was going to leave this place and this life. And the fewer encumbrances the better.

With that in mind, she went to find Sarah after dinner. It was time for their talk. Past time. After her afternoon shower she had folded her old jeans and put them away. Her overalls still fit, and leggings were comfortable. But soon everyone would know her secret.

Sarah was at her desk, her dark head bent over the center's books. As administrator, it fell to Sarah to find enough money for all their projects. When she wasn't raising funds she was robbing Peter to pay Paul—not to mention Matthew, Mark, and Luke.

Mary Kate knocked, then stepped inside when Sarah smiled a welcome. "Do you have a few minutes?" Mary Kate said.

Sarah got to her feet. "I suspect this might take longer than that."

Mary Kate launched right in. "I don't even know why

I'm here. You've already figured out that I'm pregnant, haven't you?''

"One by one the others have come to me and told me their suspicions.'' Sarah gestured to the sofa, then joined Mary Kate there. "Do you want to start at the beginning?''

"Sure, if I could. But unfortunately I don't remember how this happened.''

"Well, I may be a nun, but *I* can tell you how.''

Mary Kate was relieved at Sarah's casual tone. "I don't know who the father is, Sarah. I don't remember a man in my life.'' She hesitated, hoping against hope. "Do you?''

Sarah shook her head. "I'm sorry. I was hoping this was one thing you hadn't forgotten.''

"Do you think the others . . . ?''

"No one has mentioned any possibilities to me.''

"I didn't have any special friends? Any men I spent time with?''

"You had a legion of friends. But as time passed you saw less and less of them. I'm afraid no one stands out.''

"There's a possibility I was . . . well, that this wasn't my choice.''

"Do you think you might have been raped?''

"For some reason that just doesn't feel like the right answer.''

"What *does?*''

"I was hoping you could tell me. What was I like before I was injured? What did I do? What did I care about?''

Sarah sat back. "What do you know?''

"Well, Grace says I was very much above the rest of the world. Almost a saint.''

"I doubt she put it quite like that.''

"No. She also said the vital connections between me and the people around me were missing.'' Mary Kate grimaced. "At least one was still in place. Apparently I was connected quite intimately with at least one man.''

"I think I know you well enough to assure you there was

only one, Mary Kate. I can't even imagine that you slept around."

"No? Could you ever have imagined that I'd get myself pregnant?"

"It wasn't tops on my mind. But I think that possibility was there. You were—are—a giving young woman, a cuddler, a toucher. In the old days you wouldn't have lasted more than a day as a novice. But times have changed, and I always saw that physical part of you as an extension of the spiritual part. You wanted to take everyone right to your heart."

"And apparently, that's exactly what I did."

"Have you given any thought about what you're going to do?"

"I'm going to have the baby, and I'm going to give it to parents who are better equipped to raise it than I am."

"You've obviously thought this over carefully."

"Afterwards, I . . ." She met Sarah's eyes. "I won't be staying here, Sarah."

Sarah's expression didn't change. "If you're afraid we won't want you anymore because you had a baby—"

"No. I know you'd have to consider that in your decision, but that's beside the point. I know now that joining you isn't going to be right for me."

"And what will be?"

"I think I'll have to take that one step at a time." Mary Kate released a long breath. "Tell me you're not disappointed in me. Tell me you understand."

"How could you think I'd be disappointed? I've never had a plan for your life. I trust the process. I'm just glad you came to us when you did. I would have missed not knowing you."

Mary Kate had to look away. She had known that Sarah was fair and wise, but she hadn't expected this kind of unconditional support. "I'd like to stay here until after the baby's birth. But if you don't want me—"

"How could you believe that? Of course we want you."

Mary Kate hadn't realized how much relief she would feel. "Will you help me find a home for the baby, then? Through the church? I'd feel better if you made the arrangements. I know I can trust you."

"When the time comes I'll do whatever I can to make sure the baby has the very best parents."

Mary Kate stood, and Sarah stood, too. "Thank you, Sarah. I . . . well, I don't know what else to say."

Sarah rested her fingertips on Mary Kate's arm. "You'll get through this. We'll help you, but don't sell yourself short. You have all the strength you need, even if we weren't here to support you."

Casey didn't know why he had come back to Eden's Gate. He had left things with Mary Kate exactly where they ought to be. He didn't want her in his life. She was too needy, too exhausting.

Too appealing.

He fought that final adjective. But even in the short run he couldn't fool himself. Mary Kate had never asked for anything. Anything he had done for her, he'd done because he wanted to. She *was* needy, if that meant she was a woman who needed support. But she didn't invite it. In fact she was surprised when it was offered. She *was* exhausting, but only because lately he was fighting his own attraction to her whenever he was with her.

And God forgive him, but she was appealing. Immensely appealing. He had kissed her, and the ground had opened at his feet. The only mystery was why he had thought himself immune to her in the first place.

So now he was on his way to find her and ask forgiveness. He was going to have to tell her the truth. No fabricated excuse would be good enough. He had to admit what he was feeling and discuss it rationally with her. Perhaps between them they could explain it away. Loneliness. Compassion. Empathy. All seemed like possible candidates. Surely she'd had her own reasons for kissing him back, reasons she could explain away, too. They could work this out. They had to. He didn't want to lose her friendship.

But even as he went over this in his mind, he knew that the only place for this well-intentioned bullshit was on the center's compost pile.

He parked his car beside the house and waited a minute, trying to decide how best to approach her. Dinner would be over, and he knew the sisters held a worship service afterward. Mary Kate had told him that she tried to avoid vespers. Even if he knocked and disturbed the sisters at prayer, he probably wouldn't find Mary Kate among them.

He decided to try the garden. It would be like Mary Kate to retreat there, to make up excuses that she needed to do something outside, even though it was already dark. He knew he had upset her, and if she needed to think, she would prefer to do it away from the others.

Aware that he might just be delaying the inevitable, he started his engine again and drove toward the barn, parking beside it. Then he got out, thrust his hands in his pockets and began to search.

"Mary Kate?" He didn't want to shout and worry anyone inside the house. "Are you out here?"

He stood still and listened carefully for any noises. She might not want to talk to him, even if she was nearby.

"Mary Kate . . ."

He listened for a full minute. Warm weather was approaching, and the world seemed to be coming alive as he listened. Crickets chirped, not the full-scale symphony that would erupt in another month, but the tentative tuning up of the orchestra. Somewhere in the distance he thought he heard an owl. He hadn't heard that sound since he was a lonely young man, convinced that a small town in Iowa was prison.

"Mary Kate, I'm sorry. Let's talk. Please?"

He realized he could be talking to the night breeze. "Damn." Casey shoved his hands in his pockets. He wasn't sure what to do next. Should he go back to the house and find Mary Kate? Or apologize in a week or two when he had it down pat?

Or should he follow the clanking sound he'd just heard, which seemed to be coming from the direction of the center's own garden?

He followed the sound around to the other side of the barn. At first he saw nothing. Then, as his gaze dropped to the ground, he saw a lump in the farthest corner that was suspiciously woman-sized.

He made his way between rows. Mary Kate, wrapped in a sleeping bag, was sitting cross-legged against the side of the barn. Her hand was resting on a small pile of stones to her right.

"Just out of curiosity," Casey said, "what are you doing here?"

She didn't seem surprised he was there, although she didn't turn to look at him. "I've declared war."

"On who?"

"Whom. You're the journalist. On whom. On Bugs Bunny and his friends. My new row of lettuce is up. I noticed it late this afternoon. The battles start tonight. I've been practicing."

"I see." He didn't, of course.

"They chewed my last row right to the ground. Gone." She snapped her fingers. "Like that. But they won't get this one."

"Have you considered an easier solution? Something that doesn't involve a four-month camp-out?"

"We need a fence. We can't afford one. And I'll be damned before I let bunnies destroy everything I've worked for. Maybe once the grass greens up and all the weeds come up, too, they'll have enough to eat, and they'll leave our stuff alone. But until then, I'm not taking any chances."

"I see."

She wasn't looking at him. She was staring into the distance, as if her bunny radar was performing at peak. "I can't do much about my life, but I can do something about this. I can make sure nothing disturbs this garden."

Casey considered his alternatives and decided the only one that made sense was to drop to the ground, even though he had changed into good trousers before coming back to find her. He sat, ignoring the chill and the realization that his pants would probably need a talented dry cleaner.

"What are the rocks for?"

"You know the story of David and Goliath?"

"Where's your slingshot?"

"I don't need one. I've been practicing. Name a target."

He frowned. The garden was bare of possibilities. "I'll take your word for it."

"Name a target!"

He scanned the area and settled on a tuft of grass at the end of their row. He pointed. "That."

"No contest." With a flick of her wrist she lobbed a stone through the air to land exactly on the tuft with the same clank he had heard earlier.

"How are you at moving targets? Hopping targets, if I have to be precise," he said.

"Samantha says the bunnies are so tame they'll just stand still and stare at me."

"You're going to bean a trusting little bunny?"

"Watch me."

"Maybe I will." Casey leaned back against the barn, pillowing his head against his interlaced fingers. "Maybe I'll just stay here and see what happens."

"Nobody invited you."

"Oh, I know."

"I thought you'd decided that I was beneath contempt because I let you kiss me, Casey."

He was silent, trying to formulate just the right answer. "Look, I'm a jackass, okay? I'm sorry."

"Exactly what are you sorry for?"

"Do you want a list?"

"No. I don't think I care that much."

He looked sideways at her. Her pert little nose was stuck straight up in the air. If she wasn't careful, her view of the bunnies was going to be seriously compromised.

Something that had been frozen solid was melting in the region of Casey's heart. He didn't know how he could ever have believed that Mary Kate was anything but what she was. She was adorable, sassy, endearing. And she was courageous in the face of a life that was both unfamiliar and disturbing. How could he have believed that those qualities, qualities of the heart and spirit, were nothing? In years past he had lulled himself into believing that the size of a woman's breasts, the color of her hair, the length of her legs were what attracted him, when all along, the things inside a woman counted most of all.

Of course, this woman was carrying more inside her than fortitude and sass. She was carrying another man's child.

"You know, *I* care," he said. "And that's what scared me. Everything I said earlier was fear talking."

"What do you have to be afraid of? I'm not asking for anything. I don't want ties to Shandley Falls. I want to have this baby and get out. Maybe I can't remember a thing about my old life, but I have a new one stretching in front of me."

"That's one way to look at things."

"It's the way I'm looking at them."

"You're absolutely sure about everything, then? You're going to give away the baby, kiss off the sisters, and stick out your thumb?"

"No, I don't have to hitchhike. I have a car."

"Which Jim tells me you can't drive worth a damn."

"Jim has a big mouth."

She still hadn't looked at him. Casey watched the way

she clamped her lips together after every sentence, as if she was afraid any change in her expression might give her away. "Katie." He put his hand on her shoulder. "I know you weren't asking for anything. This isn't about you. It's about me. I like you. And I was afraid kissing you had ruined a good thing, so I overreacted. I've ruined some of the finest things in my life. And I almost ruined this."

"What makes you think you didn't?"

"Because I know you've forgiven me. Haven't you?"

She finally turned to stare him straight in the eye. "You must have me confused with the woman I used to be."

"Fat chance of that."

For a moment her expression didn't alter. Then, almost against her will, her eyes widened, her lips tweaked into something more vulnerable. "Damn you, Casey."

"Katie . . ." He hadn't known what to say to her, but he had been absolutely sure what not to do. He knew better than to kiss her again. He was smarter than this, much too smart to take his own apology and twist it into something else.

He kissed her anyway.

She didn't respond at first. She was stiff as he turned her to face him, and anything but pliant in his arms. Her lips were cold, and they didn't soften as he nibbled at them, planting soft, teasing kisses where they pressed firmly together. "I don't apologize often," he whispered. "Make it worth my while, okay?"

She rested her palms against his chest, but she didn't push. She kept them there as a defense, but for a woman who claimed she was mean enough to plug a baby bunny, she was surprisingly noncombative.

"This is what got me into trouble, isn't it?" He slanted his lips over hers, kissing, tasting, tempting. Her skin was as sweet and soft as whipped cream. Her lips warmed against his and gradually, tentatively, moved in delicious response.

"Does this mean I'm forgiven?" He pulled away at last, just far enough to ask.

"I think it depends," she said, opening her eyes, which had drifted shut.

"On what?"

"On whether you do that again."

"Damned if I do? Or damned if I don't?"

"Make your best guess."

He pulled her closer, and her arms circled his neck. He could feel her breasts against his chest, small, perfect breasts that felt exactly right against him. He wondered what they would feel like against his bare skin. The thought sent his sexual barometer soaring to a new and dangerous level.

If she noted the increased intensity in his kiss, it didn't seem to frighten her. For a woman who had planned to give her life to God, she was a surprisingly physical creature. She sighed and twisted her fingers in his hair, doing amazing things to his scalp with her fingertips. Her lips parted and her tongue touched his.

He hadn't planned to kiss her again, but he had. He hadn't planned to inch down the sleeping bag and smooth his hands under her sweater, either. He only realized what he was doing when he felt his palms gliding against her skin. She was so warm, so undeniably alive and aware of his touch. Her flesh seemed to throb against his palms, and when he realized she wasn't wearing a bra, his own flesh throbbed in answer.

"Katie, what are we doing?" He groaned the words, but he didn't stop kissing her, and he didn't stop his exploration. Her body was not familiar to him. He had never touched her this way, but just the same, he felt as if he'd come home.

He wasn't sure what would have happened next if he hadn't noticed movement in the row just beyond them. He closed his eyes, but the spell was broken. And well it should have been.

Mary Kate, too, seemed to come to her senses. She moved away, pulling her sweater down as she did.

He took a deep breath and tried to remember when he had denied himself anything he truly wanted. His life in New York had been a series of wishes fulfilled. He'd had money, recognition, his pick of women. He had almost forgotten how to think of anyone besides himself.

But he was thinking about Mary Kate.

"You have a friend," he said, before she could speak. "Someone's come to visit."

"What are you talking about?" She sounded dazed.

"Did you forget what you came here for?"

"No."

"Well, your first victim's arrived, and you're standing between him and his main course."

"A rabbit? Where?"

He inclined his head toward the rabbit, who was not more than eight feet away. "He's scared to death," Casey said. "Shaking in his boots."

She leaned forward and squinted into the darkness. The moon was nearly full, and it silvered the rabbit's soft fur. The rabbit sat contemplating them, almost as if he were about to offer a gracious invitation to his dinner party.

"Samantha was right," she whispered. "The little scoundrel trusts me. Completely."

"Now's your chance."

She felt beside her. He could hear her palm rustling against leaves. Then she lifted it and bent her wrist back over her shoulder. She remained poised in that position long enough to cut off the circulation in her hand. Then she let fly with the stone.

It missed the rabbit by a full three feet. The rabbit twitched its tiny nose, turned and slowly hopped down the row away from them.

"Scared to death," Casey said. "Mortally wounded."

"Shut up, Casey."

"Wasn't your aim just the tiniest bit off?"

"I've decided to train them instead."

"Train them?"

"You're the managing editor of a newspaper, such as it is. Imagine the publicity for Eden's Gate if anyone found out I was killing rabbits. So I'll train them. A little conditioning. They get near the lettuce, I throw rocks in their direction."

"I'm sure that's all it will take."

She laughed, low in her throat. "You think I'm a fraud, don't you?"

"The biggest." He put his arm around her. "And you're cold. Give it up, Katie, and go to bed."

"I'm not cold when you have your arm around me."

He rested his head on top of hers and pulled her closer. "There's got to be something in the barn that we can put around the lettuce. Something that will guarantee it survives through the night. I know I saw some wire cages. We can put them end to end temporarily."

"That's not going to work for long."

"One night at a time, okay?"

"Maybe that should be our theme song."

He wondered. He was very much afraid that their theme song was going to be more passionate and emotional. Chopin at his most poignant. Casey pulled her closer yet.

He felt her stiffen, and for a moment he thought she was resisting his touch. Then she made a noise, a sound that was half strangle, half gulp. "Oh . . ."

"What is it?"

"I think . . ."

"What?"

"It couldn't be. I don't even look pregnant, at least not very. How could I . . ."

"How could you what?" He rested his hands on her shoulders and turned her to face him. "Are you all right? Is something happening?"

"Yes. Well, yes." She covered one of his hands and guided it to her belly. "Can you feel that?"

What he felt was a slightly rounded mound under elastic leggings. Her waist was still shapely enough, but her belly was a different story. He rested his hand against it, and found it hard to believe that a baby was growing there.

"There. Again. Did you feel that?"

He pressed his fingertips harder against her. "I . . ." Her flesh moved under the soft knit of her leggings. Just a ripple. If she hadn't jumped in response, he might have missed it. "Is that . . . ?"

"You tell me. Is it?"

He waited for a repeat. He didn't wait long. "Uh huh. Katie, that's your kid."

"Not mine. Mary . . ." She stopped.

"You are Mary Kate."

She pretended she hadn't said a thing out of the ordinary. "So, is this what I have to look forward to for the next five months?"

He heard the emotion in her voice and her attempt to suppress it. "Or some version thereof. Are you all right?"

"Of course. Why shouldn't I be? It's perfectly natural. Women do this all the time. Right?"

He pulled her against his chest. Somewhere in between them the baby still fluttered. But for the moment he held the baby's mother, his lips against her hair, and his heart beating close to hers.

ᔥ 13

"**T**HIS MARY KATE AND THE OFFENDERS stuff has to stop. We sound like a punk-rock band." Mary Kate had been trying to derail Samantha and Grace, who were waxing enthusiastic about their newest idea. But even though they both smiled dutifully, clearly they weren't going to be talked out of this.

Someone had donated five hundred peat pellets to the center. Someone else had decided that Mary Kate and the offenders should use them to plant sunflower seeds to raise in the greenhouse until the plants were tall enough to set out.

"Last year every attempt to grow sunflowers failed," Samantha said. "The chipmunks dug up the seeds the moment we turned our backs. It was your idea to put them in peat pots this time."

"Why? Whatever the chipmunks don't get the bunnies will mow down. Why play favorites?"

"Will you give it a try?" Samantha said, encouraging her with a big smile. "It's raining too hard today for anyone to come and garden. And the kids need a project."

"Sure, it'll be swell fun," Mary Kate said. "I can hardly wait to get back into the greenhouse. Maybe somebody'll hit me over the head again, and this time when I wake up I'll remember how I got knocked up."

There was a silence. Mary Kate shook her head in apology. "Sorry about that."

"I know this is a strain," Grace said, like the psychologist she was.

Actually, the pregnancy wasn't the strain everyone seemed to think it should be. Two weeks had passed since Mary Kate had admitted the truth to Sarah. Her waist was definitely thicker and her breasts were larger. In loose T-shirts or the new high-waisted jumper, the pregnancy wasn't detectable. But when she was alone and stripped down to nothing, the evidence was irrefutable.

And it was irrefutable several times a day when the baby made itself known.

"Look, I'm fine," Mary Kate said. And she was. The baby was an alien creature. Despite everyone's fears she felt no connection to it. She couldn't remember its conception. She couldn't remember its father. She didn't even like babies, or what they turned into. In a way the remaining months of the pregnancy were a reprieve. She had an excuse to stay on at the center and get her bearings. Then she could start a new life. In the meantime she was growing a child for a couple who couldn't have their own. In a sense it was no different than growing vegetables in the garden.

Except that it was a little harder to forget.

"I'll do the sunflowers. But it will only take an hour or so," Mary Kate said. "Then what do we do with the kids?"

"Samantha has a project." Grace looked at her watch, then at Samantha, as if to prompt her.

"Right. I'm going to have them transplant their herb seedlings into bigger pots," Samantha said. "I have the college students. I won't need you for that. Then Mr. Casey is coming this afternoon to start work on the newsletter."

"I'll need you," Grace said. "I'm visiting several hospice patients today. I thought you might come along."

Like the daily worship services, Mary Kate had managed to find excuses not to accompany Grace or Sarah when they visited patients in the community. She knew about their work. The sisters had nearly a dozen seriously ill patients in the surrounding area whom they saw twice a week. They brought plants or flowers from the greenhouse, baked goods, or jams and jellies, but most of all they brought themselves. They stayed at bedsides to give family members a respite, cooked or cleaned if needed, wrote letters or read aloud to supplement the minimal help most of the families could afford. They considered the visits an extension of their work at the center. If they could not bring these dying patients to Eden's Gate, then they would bring what they could of Eden's Gate to the patients.

"You don't want to come, do you?" Grace said, when Mary Kate didn't answer.

Mary Kate didn't know why she was apprehensive about helping Grace. This was Grace's special project, but she had been told that before the accident she had helped often.

"Maybe it seems a little close to home," Grace said. "After what you've been through."

"No, I'll come." Mary Kate hated to think her own experience had had that kind of effect on her. "I just don't see what I have to offer."

"Let's find out, shall we?"

"The kids should be getting here any minute," Samantha said. "Let's get over to the greenhouse and set up."

An hour later Mary Kate was up to her elbows in muddy water. The peat pellets had arrived as flat disks the size of small cookies. But after they had soaked for half an hour, they had magically turned into miniature planting pots. The offenders had been surprisingly enthusiastic about watching every phase of the transformation.

"Okay. They're ready." Mary Kate pulled a pot out of the bucket where it had been soaking and held it up for all to see. "Now we push the seed down like so . . ." Although she didn't remember doing this before, she demonstrated with a large striped sunflower seed. "Until it disappears.

Then we set it in this tray. We'll keep them wet, then hope-fully when you come back next week, the seeds will be sprouts, and the plants will be ready to set in the garden.''

"Where are we going to put them?" Tyson said.

"I think they should go along the—" Samantha stopped. "Along the border," she said. "And I think you kids should be the ones to plant and tend them. This should be your project, since you're doing all the work."

There was a murmured assent. For once the offenders had forgotten how tough they were supposed to be. They almost sounded like kids.

Mary Kate *almost* felt a surge of warmth for them. "We have ten different kinds of sunflowers. Some are tall, some short. Some branch, some don't. Group them in flats ac-cording to type and mark the flats. Then when we plant them, we'll be sure the short ones can be seen."

She watched the kids fishing through their buckets for peat pots and playfully wrestling each other for the seeds. She didn't realize Tyson had come up to stand beside her until he spoke.

"I saw this thing on television."

She jumped, startled. She was always surprised when he sought her out. She tried her most encouraging smile. In return he favored her with his usual sneer, as if to be sure she knew he wasn't trying to be friendly.

Her smile died. "What did you see?" she said. "An after-school special on how to make sure adults hate you?"

"No. It was a garden show." His expression dared her to make fun of him.

"Oh . . ." She didn't know what else to say. "Anything useful?"

He shifted his weight from foot to foot. She could almost see his struggle. He was cursing his own impulsiveness. Ob-viously he wished he hadn't started this conversation.

Despite herself Mary Kate felt sorry for him. Sometimes it really seemed as if Tyson wanted to be someone else, but he just didn't know how. To make him more comfortable she lowered her voice, hoping the others would think they were discussing the best way to rob a bank. "I've got to tell you, Tyson, I get a lot of my information from those shows." It was true. In the last month she'd sat through every garden show she could find a listing for. "I don't remember a darned thing about this stuff, but the shows help. Which one did you see?"

"*Victory Garden.*" He shifted again. The sneer had long since disappeared. Now he just looked pained, as if he couldn't believe they were having this conversation. "They had a big sunflower patch, and they had pumpkins growing under them."

"Pumpkins?"

"They grow on vines."

She had a dim memory of reading that somewhere. "Do you think we could do the same thing?"

He shrugged, like he couldn't care less.

"Until yesterday I didn't know there were different kinds of sunflowers," she said. "I bet there are different kinds of pumpkins, too."

"Shit, yeah."

She didn't even blink. "Look, will you sort through the seeds over there and see if we have pumpkins? Check out the growing season, how far apart to plant them and stuff? I think this is a good idea."

"If I have time." He strolled back to his bucket. But he hadn't sneered at her again.

At the end of the hour the peat pellets had all been planted, tucked into their respective flats, and neatly labeled. Samantha appeared to start the next project, and Mary Kate went back to the house to change.

By the time she met Grace outside by the carriage house, her apprehension about what was to come had taken firm root. Once they were in the center's van she voiced her fear.

"Grace, what do you say to somebody who's probably dying?"

"No probably about it, Mary Kate. We've had a few of our patients go into remission, but most of the time we aren't referred to these cases unless the patients are terminal."

"Oh . . ."

"This bothers you, doesn't it?"

Mary Kate had no desire to talk about secret fears, or to have a conversation about theology and life after death. She knew what Grace believed. She knew what she had probably once believed herself. But now dying seemed just a little too familiar.

"I'd just like to know how I'm supposed to act," she said.

"Like yourself, of course."

"Come on, that could scare them right into the next world."

At the first stop light, Grace adjusted the dark scarf folded attractively around her collar. "You've always been a favorite among our hospice patients. People have been asking for you." She hesitated. "Of course, not all of the patients you knew are still alive."

"I know I should be sorry, but I don't remember any of them, living or dead."

"I know. I'll brief you before we go in. I don't think it's necessary to explain your memory loss. I'll steer the conversations until you're comfortable."

The next hours passed a lot quicker than Mary Kate had expected. Their first patient was an old woman who had lived a full, productive life. She was dying at home, surrounded by her family, and although no one was looking forward to the inevitable, everyone seemed reasonably well prepared. If Mary Kate had ever learned to cook, her injury had wiped away all her skills. But while the woman's daughter fixed lunch, Mary Kate cleaned up the kitchen and put away the black raspberry jam Grace had brought as a gift.

The daughter, middle-aged and much too busy, seemed grateful for their help and company. And later when Mary Kate reluctantly sat beside the dying woman's bedside, she found she didn't need to say anything at all. Her presence seemed to be enough.

Their next visit was much the same. This patient was an old woman, too, but her illness wasn't as advanced. She was still mobile, and she greeted them at the door. They cleaned her tiny apartment and heated soup for her lunch, remaining until the woman's neighbor came to spend the afternoon. Again, Mary Kate found that nothing was expected of her except the most basic kindness.

The third and last patient was the hardest of all. Gary Conway was in his early forties, with two children who were still living at home. He had been fighting cancer for three years but everyone had finally admitted he wasn't going to beat it. His wife Anne, an attractive woman who looked much older than her years, was stretched to the limit between the needs of her children and husband. Mary Kate took one look at her and knew what she had to do.

On the drive over she had noticed a bookstore that advertised its own coffee bar just a few blocks away. And the rain had stopped so that they could walk. "Anne and I are going out for coffee," she told Grace.

Anne protested, but Mary Kate refused to take no for an answer. In a few minutes they were strolling down the sidewalk while Grace and the nurse who was with Gary took care of things at home.

"When was the last time you were outside?" Mary Kate said.

Anne pushed lank blonde hair behind her ears. "Besides driving the children places? I don't remember."

"Have you done anything for yourself in the past two weeks?"

Anne shook her head.

"Well, I have an idea."

They visited the bookstore and ordered cappuccino. Then, after a dazed Anne began to revive a little, they left to walk farther into town.

"Here," Mary Kate said. They were standing in front of the nicest hair salon in Shandley Falls, where Mary Kate had skillfully guided her. "They take walk-ins. When was the last time you had your hair cut?"

"Ages ago."

"We have time. Let's go."

Anne protested, but without much energy. By the time she had finished voicing her concerns about getting back to Gary, she was already in the stylist's chair looking at photographs.

She left the shop forty minutes later with a shorter cut that took years off her face and needed nothing but shampoo and a comb for maintenance.

Anne opened up a little as they walked back home. "The hardest part is that I love him so much. I can't imagine what it's going to be like to live without him."

Mary Kate tried to imagine what Anne was experiencing. Had she felt that way about her baby's father? Apparently the feeling hadn't been mutual.

Anne stopped, momentarily galvanized by anger. "I know you're going to tell me I'll see Gary in heaven, but I don't care. I don't want to lose him now."

"Of course you don't."

"I pray, but I don't have any faith."

Mary Kate knew she was way over her head here. This was something Grace, with her innate warmth and wisdom, should handle. She could buy coffee and help choose hairstyles, but what did she know about faith?

They started walking again, and Mary Kate knew she had to say something. "You know, while you've been talking all I could think about was what it must be like to love somebody that much. It's a gift, isn't it? A talent Gary helped you develop. And when Gary dies, it's a gift you'll be able to use in other ways, with other people. Your children. Other people who come into your life. It's a very precious thing, Anne. I don't know how many people have that ability.''

They started back down the sidewalk, and Anne was silent. Mary Kate had rarely wished she could be deeper than she was. Now she wished she could be someone else for Anne, someone with the right answers. But she was a woman who didn't even spend time asking the right questions.

''You know,'' Anne said, when they were standing in front of her house, ''everybody else has told me this is God's will or that Gary's going to heaven so I should be happy for him. I'm so tired of hearing that. But I never thought about what you said, that being able to love him is a gift I can use again after he's gone.''

Mary Kate didn't know what to say.

Anne reached for her hand and squeezed it. ''Thanks. That helped.'' She started up the steps.

Grace met Anne at the door, kissed her cheek, then came to join Mary Kate on the sidewalk. ''I knew you had a talent for this,'' she told Mary Kate. ''She looks fortified. And she'll need to be. I don't think Gary's going to be with us much longer.''

Mary Kate choked back a lump in her throat.

Thanks. That helped.

She was silent all the way back to the center.

Casey was a loner, or at least he'd always thought so. Sometimes he suspected he'd become a journalist because he liked going his own way, researching stories, and putting them together by himself. At *The Whole Truth* he had worked with film crews, directors, and producers, but still much of what he'd done he had done alone. Only in his job as managing editor of *The Cricket* had he been forced to supervise, to practice the arts of compromise and encouragement.

Today, he was glad he'd learned all those skills.

"Okay, Pfeiffer, you help the guy with the posthole digger. He'll show you what to do. Lola, you look strong. Help with the unloading, will you? Tyson, go with Sister Samantha and help her work out the boundary lines."

Casey didn't recognize most of the other teenagers by name. He'd met them all, and he'd made a point of talking to each of them at the garden. But until he started working with them on the newsletter, their faces and names would probably remain a blur. He assigned the rest of the jobs by pointing. With the exception of a few grumbles, everyone cooperated.

Sarah joined him, handing him a coffee cup. "Mary Kate's going to be amazed."

"So are her pet bunnies."

"And the deer, and the groundhogs. I still want to know how you did this. I might learn something I can use in my fund-raising."

So far Casey had managed to keep the whys and wherefores of obtaining the fencing to himself. He shot Sarah his best grin to divert her. She smiled back, a smile as friendly as any he'd ever seen. Accompanying it was enough patience to tell him she would dig all the details out of him eventually.

"All right. I'll tell you," he conceded. "But you can't send it back."

"Let's have the story."

"A few years ago I did an investigation into a guy in western Pennsylvania, a wealthy businessman who was said to have connections he shouldn't have. I never got enough proof one way or the other to say if that information was correct."

"I'm listening."

He examined her from the corner of his eye. She was dressed informally, but she still exuded the watchful intensity of a CEO. "Don't cross yourself, okay? I don't think I could stand it."

"I'm listening."

"Well, I did dig up some other stuff. Nothing earthshaking, but enough for a story, something short but juicy. The thing is, I never went ahead with it. His daughter and wife were in an accident just before I started my investigation, and both of them were badly injured. The guy was facing months of heartbreak. I decided not to add to it. The police were already watching him. It wasn't as if I needed to expose him to get their interest."

"What happened?"

"He found out what I'd been up to, and with it the reason that I'd decided to let the story die. The law caught up with him, but he was able to keep it pretty quiet. He was fined and put on probation, but no real fuss was made. Afterwards he called to tell me that he was in my debt, and that if I ever needed anything, he was there. He owned half a dozen businesses . . ."

"One of them's a lumberyard?"

"Uh huh. By the way, he's a good Catholic. He was glad to do this."

"How are his wife and daughter?"

"They both recovered."

She smiled over her coffee cup. "I love a happy ending."

After Sarah wandered off Casey sipped his coffee and watched the fence posts being dug. The donor had sent his best men, along with enough lumber for a traditional paddock fence. They would set and mark the posts today, then one evening next week the *Cricket* staff would come back and nail the rails across them. Next weekend they could staple fine mesh along the bottom railing to keep out the rabbits.

He wondered what Mary Kate was going to say. He had

asked the sisters to lure her away in the late morning because he wanted to surprise her. He had surprised women with gifts before. Once he had even given Gypsy diamond earrings. But he had never given anyone a fence.

Of course there had never been anyone in his life like Mary Kate.

Nearly half an hour later he spotted the center's van. He knew it would be a matter of minutes between the time they parked and the time Mary Kate arrived at the garden. He was as excited as a little kid who'd just spent a month's allowance on a bottle of cheap perfume for his first girlfriend.

"She know what you're doing?"

Casey discovered that Tyson had come up beside him. Tyson had been working hard to clear away debris and help site the fence line.

"No. What do you think she'll say?"

Tyson folded his arms and glared. "She'll be dogging at somebody. Never does say what she means."

Casey was intrigued. "Really? I thought she was pretty outspoken."

"She's always fighting with herself. Like she's got stuff inside her she don't want no one else to see."

"She's been through a lot." More than this boy knew yet. Casey wondered what Tyson would think when he realized that Mary Kate was going to have a baby.

"I was there when Antoine hit her," Tyson said.

"A lot of you kids were there, weren't you?"

"Yeah, but I was *right* there."

Casey watched the boy walk away. He was still thinking about what Tyson had said when Mary Kate came loping across the field to the garden.

She was winded when she arrived, but her eyes shone. "Casey! What have you done?"

He strolled to meet her. She looked up expectantly, her lips softly parted.

"Nothing much. I just found somebody who wanted to give you a fence."

"Somebody just gave it to us? Just like that?"

"Miracles happen, Katie."

She clasped her hands in front of her, then she lifted on tiptoe and kissed his cheek. One of the kids applauded.

He remembered the day he had given Gypsy the earrings. She had received her share of gifts from men. She had been pleased, but almost immediately her attention had turned to something else. He wondered if he had tried harder to know the real Gypsy Dugan and searched for a gift that had real meaning in her life, if she might have looked at him the way Mary Kate was looking now.

Mary Kate smiled the deep-dimpled smile that startled him sometimes, the smile he still saw in his all-too-frequent dreams of Gypsy. "This is so wonderful." She stepped back, obviously flustered by what she had done. "*You're* wonderful. Thank you. Thank you so much."

He felt the strangest desire to cry. He put his arms around her and hugged her for all to see.

⟶ 14

IN THE MONTH FOLLOWING THE INSTALLATION of the fence, the center exploded with new life. Roses bloomed on an arbor beside the house; trillium and trout lily had bloomed in the woods, followed by violets and Virginia bluebells. In the garden lettuce and peas seemed to grow inches with each passing day, and potatoes had to be buried under mounds of dirt to give them room to expand. With the warmer weather, peppers, tomatoes, and eggplants had been moved to their permanent homes outside, and the sun-flower seedlings flourished in a thick border along the fence, interlaced with pumpkin hills.

Mary Kate bloomed, too. Dr. Kane had told her that women in their second trimesters often felt a spurt of energy. She was no exception. She felt healthy and looked it. Her hair shone and her cheeks glowed. She had gained weight and would soon need to move into real maternity clothes. But for the time being she could still manage in blousy styles and the ever-useful jumper.

The search for the baby's father had come to a halt be-cause of a lack of time to pursue it. She'd had no idea how much work the garden would be or she might have kept right on running after her adventure at the Dew Drop Inn. The teenagers had moved into Eden's Gate's dormitories for their summer program, and although their college-student counselors had moved in right along with them, Mary Kate still supervised their community-garden activities.

All the plots were taken now, and gardeners came and went, often with questions or requests she had to address. She coordinated activities with the local extension service, retrieved plants and supplies, and created new projects to keep the offenders busy. Additionally the day-care children arrived twice a week to tend their small plots, and she had to provide entertaining programs to keep their interest.

In what should have been free time, she was forced to research. She had a wealth of resources. Web sites and newsletters from similar groups and organizations she'd discovered she belonged to, the local extension agent—who was fast becoming a friend—books from her own as well as the public library, and most important, her journal. But the struggle to keep up with all the information and remember it was intimidating.

On the third Wednesday in June something even more intimidating was required of her.

"Mary Kate, can I talk to you?"

Mary Kate was weeding the lettuce bed in the center's garden as Godzilla stared longingly from the other side of the fence. She had heard footsteps, but she had expected to see one of the sisters. Instead Lola was standing over her. Mary Kate rose—a more difficult feat than it would have been several months before—and wiped her hands on her overalls. "What's going on?"

"I . . . like, um, skipped my period this month."

Mary Kate didn't need this now. She didn't know why the kids liked to confess their problems to her. They were a savvy bunch, and she hadn't yet figured out why they were dim-witted about their choice of role models. Unfortunately these days she was no longer Sister Sunshine or Tornado. She was simply Mary Kate, and they sought her out often.

"You're sure?" she said. "When was your last period?"

"Six weeks ago."

"Then you're two weeks late?"

"Well, maybe I am. I don't know. Sometimes I go six or seven weeks in between. It depends."

"Then why are you worried now?" She held up her hand as the obvious answer hung between them. "What I mean is, haven't you been practicing safe sex?"

"I've been careful. Real careful."

"Good. Then you're probably all right. But let me know . . ." She suddenly realized the truth. Lola didn't have a problem at all.

"You're not here to talk about you, are you?" Mary Kate frowned. She had been wondering how she was going to tell the kids the truth about her blessed event. Obviously she had waited too long.

"I just thought . . ."

"It's okay, I know what you thought. And you're right, I'm pregnant. So, of the two of us, obviously I'm the one who *wasn't* practicing safe sex."

"We thought . . . I mean, we noticed . . ."

Mary Kate was glad the pregnancy had gone undetected for so long. She was a small woman, but she had good muscle tone, and she was carrying the baby high.

"I guess everyone will be noticing soon," she said. "Lola, you know that I lost my memory after Antoine hit me."

Lola nodded.

"Well, I don't remember a man in my life either. I know that sounds far-fetched, but it's true. And I may never remember."

"You mean the father hasn't—the father doesn't . . ."

"Doesn't know? Well, I guess he might. But if he does, he hasn't made himself known to me."

"Radical . . ."

Mary Kate grimaced. "That's one way of putting it."

"Do you want me to tell everybody? I mean, I could do it for you."

For the past two weeks Mary Kate had considered calling

the kids together to explain the pregnancy to them, but it had seemed so awkward for everyone concerned. She felt no shame. How could she, under the circumstances? But now she was glad she had waited. This seemed like the ideal way to get the information to them without embarrassing anyone.

"Sure, go ahead. But tell everybody I'll be happy to talk about it if they want to."

"I guess . . . like, this means you aren't going to be a nun or something."

"I guess not."

"What's it like to be pregnant? Everybody I know got pregnant 'cause they thought it would be fun, you know? But afterwards, they never want to take care of it."

Mary Kate knew that many teenage girls got pregnant because they wanted something that belonged to them, but often when they discovered how difficult raising a baby really was, they felt trapped. She hated to tell Lola that *she* didn't want to raise this baby, either. Babies were supposed to be bundles of joy, cherished and nurtured and welcomed with open arms. What kind of world did Lola see when she looked around? How could the girl ever have the maternal feelings she'd need to raise her own children if she had no one to imitate?

Mary Kate chose her words carefully. "It feels very natural to be pregnant. Mother Nature worked the whole thing out nicely."

"Can you feel the baby move?"

Mary Kate did feel the baby move more every day. But most of the time she tried to ignore it. The baby's movements made it seem more real. It was harder to deny the truth, and harder to think about the inevitable parting.

As if on cue, the baby fluttered inside her. "Come here." Mary Kate took Lola's hand and placed it on her abdomen. "There, can you feel it?"

"Wow. Fucking fantastic!"

Mary Kate realized a warning was called for. "You know, it *is* neat. But like you said yourself, it's no reason to have a baby."

"But you'll be a good mother. You won't feel that way, the way my friends do, you know? You're good at taking care of things and stuff."

Mary Kate closed her eyes for a moment. "It's hard to raise a baby alone, Lola."

Lola didn't understand. "Yeah, it's a good thing you're strong, like you believe in things and shit like that. You really don't mind if I tell the others?"

"Go ahead." Mary Kate watched the girl head back to the community garden. She wondered what Jake and Sergeant would say. She supposed that in less than fifteen minutes no one on the grounds would be in the dark about this baby.

At least no more in the dark than she was.

"Hey, Katie."

Mary Kate turned to find Casey on the other side of the fence. She had to stop herself from finger-combing her curls. For weeks she had only seen him in passing. He was always friendly, always attentive, but they hadn't had any private moments. They had never discussed their relationship, but as if they had, both of them had backed away. She couldn't speak for Casey, but she had been frightened by their growing intimacy. She had come to depend on him too much. And she had yearned too often for his arms around her.

"What are you doing here?" She wiped her hands on her overalls again and started toward him. "No one else has showed up yet. Don't tell me you've come to pull weeds all by your lonesome."

"I'm supposed to be at the paper this morning, but I'm playing hooky."

"Are you? What a place to do it."

"Actually, I came by to see if you'd like to take in an

Indians game this afternoon. I've got two tickets. A friend in Cleveland gave them to me."

A baseball game sounded like a real date. For a moment Mary Kate was tempted to say no. But as the season had geared up she'd discovered one more thing about herself. She was wildly enthusiastic about baseball. In fact, it was one of the things she and the kids discussed at length while they planted and weeded.

She couldn't help herself. "Tickets? For a real game?"

"We're playing the Yankees." He hesitated, as if he saw the problem. "We'll be going with a crowd. You'll enjoy the company."

She couldn't resist. "I'd love to go. I really would. And Samantha's going to be in the garden all day, so she can handle things."

He told her when to be ready. "We'll get something to eat there, so don't bother with lunch."

"Peanuts and Cracker Jack?"

"Sure, and we'll root, root, root for the home team."

"Considering where you grew up, I'd expect you to be a Yankees fan."

"I guess I can work up some enthusiasm for the underdogs."

She leaned over the fence. "You'd better get this straight, Casey. The Indians are not underdogs. They're the finest team in baseball history. Do we have an understanding?"

It took him a moment to smile. "You know, Gypsy was a big Indians fan. I guess everybody from this part of Ohio has it in their blood."

She jabbed his chest with her index finger. "You'd better get a transfusion, buster. Or don't sit with me."

They were going to be friends. Pals. Mary Kate saw the handwriting on the wall, and that's what it spelled out. They were going to attend baseball games and movies, share popcorn and funny stories and never, ever touch each other again. Casey had set the tone of this phase of their relationship from the moment he had picked her up for the drive to Cleveland. He had been big-brother friendly, as if he had set out to prove that there was a comfortable middle ground for them between fighting and kissing. She had almost expected him to ruffle her curls or pull a frog out of his back pocket to wave in her face.

She tried to ignore how wonderful he looked in dark jeans and a brick-red shirt. He still hadn't cut his hair, and he only needed a parrot on his shoulder and a patch over his eye to complete the picture. She tried not to gaze at his long-fingered hands and imagine the way they had felt against her bare skin.

They talked about the kids and the garden, and he told her about the newsletter. He was surprised how badly the kids spelled and wrote but how wonderful their ideas were. She told him about her visits to the hospice patients.

"Don't you find it depressing?" Casey said. "Particularly now?" His eyes flicked to her belly.

"I feel like I'm part of a cycle, somehow. It's sad, but ... I don't know, it makes me feel connected." She shrugged. "It's hard to explain. Maybe it's because I don't seem to have any family of my own."

"You do now."

For a moment she didn't know what he meant. Then she realized he was talking about the baby. "Not for long."

He changed the subject. "You've been feeling all right?"

"Sure. Dr. Kane's going to order another sonogram." She looked out the window and remembered the first one which had been performed several weeks after she had discovered she was pregnant. She had tuned out the sounds of her baby's heartbeat and refused to look at the screen. But she hadn't slept well that night.

"Can they tell if the baby's a boy or a girl?"

"I don't know. Last time I asked them not to tell me anything except whether it was all right."

"When are you going in?"

"Soon."

Casey parked several blocks from Jacobs Field and locked the car. Out on the sidewalk the atmosphere was already festive. Vendors hawked Indians merchandise, and scalpers begged for tickets. Since all the games for the season had been sold out for months, the crowd was enormous. Casey took her hand, and they edged their way through it until he pulled her to a halt.

"Sun's shining pretty hard." He touched the tip of her nose. "I don't think there's room for another freckle."

"I'm hoping they all run together in something resembling a tan."

"Let me buy you a cap."

"Really? Didn't you buy me a fence?"

"I negotiated the fence. I'm buying the cap with my own money."

She pretended to sigh. "Darn. Some women get diamonds, and I get Chief Wahoo."

"Diamonds?"

"Sure. Don't they?" She grinned at his look of discomfort. "Don't worry, I've never liked them particularly. You're safe with me."

"Never?"

"I guess my 'never' doesn't go back too far, does it?"

"Maybe it does. Diamonds and vows of poverty don't go that well together."

"Can I pick out my own cap?"

"The sky's the limit."

She settled for one from the vendor closest to the ball-field. Despite what she'd said, she wasn't overly fond of leering Chief Wahoo, the Indians logo, so she chose the only hat without him, a blue-and-white-striped design with "Cleveland" emblazoned across the front. She formed the bill into a curve as they walked, then set the hat low over her eyes.

"What do you think?"

He gazed at her longer than necessary. "You'll do."

At the look in his eyes excitement tingled down her spine. "Good thing. You're stuck with me for the rest of the game."

He slung his arm over her shoulders, and she didn't imagine the way he squeezed her closer. "I guess I'll survive."

Jacobs Field was relatively new, an attractive stadium at the edge of the business district with comfortable seats and spectacular views of the skyline. Casey guided her through the crowds and up an escalator. Casey's friends were already in their seats, and Casey introduced her as the two of them wiggled past.

Howard Larkin, the station manager for a local network affiliate, was in his early sixties. His wife Rae, an attractive blonde about ten years younger than Howard, worked as a producer, and the others in the party, Barbara and Clark Jenkins, also worked at the station.

Mary Kate sat next to Howard, with Casey at her right. He was a robust man with thick silver hair, a florid complexion, and booming voice. As the ballplayers came out on the field he asked her what she did, and she explained about Eden's Gate and the community garden.

They rose to sing "The Star Spangled Banner," but Casey didn't sit when it was over. "Are you hungry?"

"I'm always hungry."

"What do you want?"

"One of everything." She got back to her feet. "I'll help."

"No, I don't want you pushing through these crowds again. I'll surprise you." He made his way down the aisle again.

"I'm glad to see Casey's got a . . . friend," Howard said. "He's had a rough year."

Mary Kate wanted to deny being Casey's "friend," but she didn't want to call attention to their relationship or lack of one. She settled for something safer. "It sounds like you've known him for a while."

"He came to Cleveland last year to film a segment for *The Whole Truth*. I got to know him then. I was surprised when he quit the show. Even more surprised when he turned up here."

"He's a talented guy. He can do anything he sets his mind to."

"I hope he's setting his mind for television. He's too good to lose."

"Why don't you offer him a job? I don't want to lose him, either."

Howard laughed, but Mary Kate hardly noticed. She didn't know where *that* sentiment had come from. After the baby was born she was leaving Ohio. There was a whole world out there, a world she had never explored. She craved excitement and glamour, a chance to reach for the stars. She didn't know what she was good at, certainly not at growing things or nurturing kids, hers or someone's troubled teenagers. And she knew she wasn't good at the things she'd need to be a nun.

Besides, she'd proved she wasn't good at keeping men in her life. Casey was treating her like a kid sister; the father of her baby remained a mystery. She had no reason to stay here.

"I might offer *you* a job."

For a moment Mary Kate was so deep in thought she didn't even hear Howard. Then his words registered. "Why? Do you need someone to grow tomatoes in your parking lot?"

He laughed again, something he seemed to do regularly.

The game started, and the Indians came up to bat after three quick outs. She jumped to her feet to cheer when Marquis Grissom, the Indians' first batter, hit a line-drive double.

"A real fan," Howard said when she was seated again.

"Good girl. That's the kind of enthusiasm I like to see."

"Vizquel's going to do the same thing. Just watch."

By the time Casey returned, the Indians had scored their first run. Mary Kate was so busy watching the game that she didn't even notice him until she had to stand to let him by. Her eyes widened when she saw the armload of food he'd brought back with him.

"Casey, I was kidding when I told you to buy one of everything!"

"I thought if the game got boring I could watch you eat."

"You'd better do your share."

She started with a hot dog dripping with stadium mustard. By the third inning, she'd had nachos, a soft pretzel, a slice of pizza, and a chocolate-chip cookie. She had also pounded Casey on the arm so many times that he was probably black-and-blue.

"You're a danger to yourself and everyone around you," he told her at the end of the fourth inning. "You don't really want peanuts, do you?"

"Watch me." She whistled for the guy selling them and passed her money down the aisle, catching the bag with no trouble when he tossed it in her direction. "Howard will help me eat them if you don't."

"Watch your fingers. Don't get in her way," Casey warned Howard.

By the seventh-inning stretch the Yankees and the Indians were tied, three to three. Mary Kate jumped to her feet and sang "Take Me Out to the Ballgame" in her off-key soprano, her arms linked with Howard and Casey.

They sat, but Mary Kate was still bouncing with energy. She wondered if she had ever had this much fun. She was animated by the crowds, the game, and Casey's presence beside her. She liked Howard and Rae, and although Barbara and Clark Jenkins were farther down the row and harder to talk to, they seemed nice, too.

"Want to make a trip to the ladies' room? It might be

our last chance before the game heats up," Rae said.

They plowed their way through the crowds, and Mary Kate was grateful for the escort since it was easy to get lost. She finished first and waited for Rae outside the door, idly people-watching to pass the time. The smokers congregated here since they weren't allowed to smoke in their seats, and others hurried by carrying food and beer.

A man at the far edge of the foot traffic caught her eye. He was probably about Rae's age, pale, thin, and stooped. What hair he had was nearly all white. He looked like a million other men, some not-so-small portion of which had come to watch this game.

But Mary Kate couldn't take her eyes off of him.

She had seen this man before. She was as sure of that as of her own name. The man seemed as familiar to her as her own face in the mirror.

No, much more familiar than that. And much more dear.

Before she'd had a chance to think, she was pushing through the crowd to reach his side, fumbling for an excuse as she went. She was hoping she wouldn't need one, that the man would look at her, throw his arms around her, and identify himself as an old friend. She could almost feel his arms around her.

Halfway there she was filled with elation. She recognized the man, even if she couldn't remember his name. Her memory was coming back.

"Excuse me." She caught up to him and touched his arm.

He turned and smiled politely. Not one trace of recognition shone in his dark eyes.

"Um . . . I think you dropped something back there." She pointed behind her.

"I did?"

"Uh huh. I thought I saw something fall." She glanced over her shoulder. Nothing littered the floor behind them except napkins and straw wrappers. "I'm sorry. I was sure I saw something drop. I guess I was mistaken."

He cocked his head. "Are you all right, miss?"

She knew she must look pale. She felt suddenly dizzy, and panic was welling inside her. She had been sure she knew this man, but obviously she had been wrong. He certainly didn't know her. No one was that good an actor.

For the first time in weeks she felt trapped in her body, a prisoner clawing for release. The loss of her past and everything that went with it, a loss that now seemed hopeless and permanent, nearly overwhelmed her.

"I . . . I just feel a little faint." She could barely choke out the words.

He took her arm and guided her farther out of the traffic. "What can I do to help? Can I get someone?"

She decided to tell him the truth. "I'm sorry, it's just that for a moment I was *sure* I knew you."

Of course he didn't understand. "You thought I was someone else? I'm sorry. That happens. I have a very ordinary face."

Obviously he had never seen her before in his life. This was all some strange product of her injury. "I . . . I'll be fine."

"Mary Kate?"

Mary Kate turned to see Rae coming toward them. She joined them against the wall, but it wasn't Mary Kate who interested her. Instead she held out her hand to the man, her face wreathed in a smile. "John?"

He looked perplexed, then he smiled, too. "Yes. You're Rae, from the television station, aren't you?"

"Yes. I'm glad you remembered. How are you?"

"Doing better. This young lady's not feeling too well, though. I was just trying to see if she needed any help."

"Mary Kate?" Rae looked concerned.

"I'm okay now," Mary Kate said. "I just felt a little light-headed for a minute." She paused. "You two know each other?"

Rae nodded. "It's quite a coincidence, since you're here

with Casey. But this is John Dugan, Gypsy Dugan's father. Since she was a hometown girl we did a tribute to her a few weeks after her death, and we interviewed John and some other family members. John, why don't you come back to our seats for a minute and say hi to Charles Casey? He and your daughter were close friends, and he's working in Shandley Falls now. I'm sure he'd like to meet you.''

"Have you ever been on television?" Howard asked during a pitching change in the ninth inning. The Indians were at bat and the game was threatening to go into extra innings.

"I have no idea.'' Belatedly Mary Kate realized how strange that sounded. Rather than recount the story of her recent life she made up an explanation. "What I mean is that I was interviewed once, but I don't know if it ever aired.'' She stopped embroidering her tall tale and shot Casey a warning glance. He was smiling at the way she'd gotten herself out of a tight predicament.

"You have a Katie Couric quality,'' Howard said, still watching the field. "All that bounce and enthusiasm. I think you'd photograph well.''

"Would I? I have no idea.''

"I'm sure you would. That hair's extraordinary, and you have nice bones.''

"Thanks.''

The game started again. Mary Kate sat forward. She was feeling better after convincing—or nearly convincing—herself that episodes like the one in the corridor were bound to happen. John Dugan had declined to accompany them back to their seats, but he had given Rae his phone number. Casey had said he intended to call him, and that the coincidence of meeting him had been extraordinary.

Twice now the Indians had loaded the bases but failed to make the run they needed to take the lead.

"I hate to tell you, but they aren't going to let you go out on the field to help,'' Casey said, pulling her back into her seat. He didn't let go of her arm. He tucked it under his and threaded his fingers through hers.

Suddenly the game seemed as if it were being played in another dimension. She didn't turn her head, but she was much more aware of Casey beside her. The sights and sounds of the ballfield seemed to diminish.

The crack of a bat startled her out of her romantic daydream. Casey leaped to his feet and pulled her along. Side by side they watched Jim Thome's home run soar over the fence into the bleachers. Fireworks exploded over the flagpole and the crowd roared.

"Hey, that's it! We won!" She fell against him. Casey wrapped her tightly in his arms. She smiled at him, but the smile wobbled a little as he bent his head to hers.

She knew it was meant to be a simple victory kiss. Instead, like the fireworks that preceded it, it was a razzle-dazzle explosion.

"Casey, let me show you the rose arbor before you go." Mary Kate still wore the ridiculous hat she'd selected from the vendor. Casey had never seen anything cuter than the baseball cap—brim carefully adjusted so that it looked like something one of the offenders might wear—sitting on top of Mary Kate's fiery curls. She hadn't even taken off the cap at dinner, where she'd continued to charm his friends.

As a matter of fact, he'd never seen anything cuter than Mary Kate today. Period. She wore denim leggings and a long kelly-green shirt that disguised her growing bulk and deepened the green of her eyes. He wasn't surprised that Howard Larkin had been so taken with her. Howard was a happily married man, but Mary Kate, with her girl-next-door freckles and sparkling dimpled smile, could rattle any man, without threatening destruction.

"Well?"

Casey realized he had been staring at her, and she was waiting for an answer.

He knew better than to stroll anywhere with Mary Kate on a warm summer evening. He had managed to check his downward spiral into infatuation. And if he hadn't, today's surprising reminder of Gypsy was enough of a warning.

In the past year he had learned something alarming about himself. He chose impossible women. Gypsy had been impetuous, self-centered, and so programmed to succeed that she would have mowed down the pope and the president if they'd stood in her way.

Then there was Mary Kate. He was undeniably drawn to her, but two people had never been less suited for each other. If he had somehow moved beyond his first estimation of Mary Kate into something far more flattering—all right, damn it, stunned—he still hadn't moved to the next plateau, where he started thinking about things like mortgages and private schools.

His warning system was still intact, and it issued buzzes and beeps every time he got near Mary Kate. Her life was as complicated as a Gordian knot, as confusing as a subtitled art film, as heartrending as a tabloid headline. Right now she needed his support and friendship, but what would she need when the baby was born? And what could he ask from her? He had taken a good look at himself, at the career choices he would soon be forced to make and the life he wanted for himself. He wasn't sure it was a life Mary Kate would want as well. And she damned sure didn't need to make that kind of decision now.

"I guess you're not in the mood," she said. "It's been a long night. Thanks for thinking of me when you got the tickets, Casey. I can't remember having so much fun. Of course I can't remember anything, can I?"

Her disappointment registered, although she had tried hard to disguise it. "Hey, wait." He put his hand on her arm to hold her back. "I'm sorry, Katie. I'm a million miles away. I'd love to see the roses."

"Really? There's a place we can sit. Last night we had

fireflies, but I guess it's a little early in the evening for that."

He tapped her chin. "You're a country girl at heart."

"Perish the thought."

He circled the car to help her out. By the time he made the trip he was already regretting his decision, remembering the kiss at the ballfield and the way he hadn't wanted to let her go. "I can't stay long. I've got to get up early tomorrow."

"No problem. We have mass first thing in the morning, then the kids decided to build planters in front of the dorms with rocks we cleared from the garden area. I'm supposed to help them design it."

"Supervise, don't do any of the lifting yourself."

"Well, they all know I'm pregnant now, so I guess my excuse is ironclad."

"They know?"

"Lola figured it out and quizzed me indirectly, so I told her. By now everyone who set foot on the property today is making lists of baby names."

"You're not embarrassed, are you?"

"No. It's just that . . ." She shrugged. "I was hoping I'd figure out who the father is before the pregnancy became common knowledge. Now he'll never show himself."

"Or he'll show himself the minute he hears."

"Think there's a chance?"

"If he's got an ounce of decency."

"I've got one lead, and I don't think he's the kind of guy who would expose himself that way."

"Why not?"

"For one thing, he's married."

"Rule him out then."

"Why?"

"Because you're not that kind of woman. I can't imagine you having an affair with a married man."

"You have no idea what I'm like inside."

They reached the arbor, a graceful arch of scarlet roses

with a subtle intoxicating scent that poured into the twilight air like champagne into crystal. Casey had half-hoped to find someone else there, but they were alone. Mary Kate took a seat on a wooden bench, and he joined her, careful to leave a space between them.

"What do you mean, Katie?" he asked once they were settled. "Do you really think you're capable of wrecking someone's marriage?"

She seemed to debate with herself before she spoke. "You know, I think I must have had a secret life. Not just because of this pregnancy." She rested her hand on her abdomen. "But because of what's here." She touched her chest. "And here." She touched her forehead.

"I don't get it."

"Okay. I'll make it easy. How could a whack on the head change me from the Goody-Two-shoes, saintly creature that everyone says I used to be to what I am now? I have the temper of a shrew, the patience of a gnat, the libido of a—"

"I'm all ears. Finish that sentence."

She didn't. "There's only one answer, and it's not brain damage."

"Let's back up . . ."

She swatted his arm. "Are you listening?"

He was listening, but with more of his anatomy than his ears. He was listening with every part of him. Her words, the soft ebb and flow of her breathing, the rustle of her shirt against the bench—everything seemed to move in waves across his flesh. The lemon scent of her hair entwined with that of the roses; the warmth of her body filled the slight space between them and beckoned . . .

He adjusted his position so they were farther apart. "All right. What's the answer?"

"It's staring you right in the face." She paused, then the answer exploded from the deepest part of her. "I was *never* the person everyone thought I was. Never. I was just a better actress. Don't you see? I might have been capable of anything. For all I know I had a dozen married lovers, and none of them is the kind of man who might come forward.''

''I doubt you had that much free time.''

''Fine. Go ahead and laugh. Just explain one thing.'' She placed a fist against her chest. ''Why do I have all these feelings inside?''

He knew better than to ask again, but he couldn't help himself. ''What kind of feelings?''

She shook her head, obviously seething with frustration.

The time had come to leave. That was absolutely clear. He even got to his feet to do it, but he found himself pulling her to stand in front of him. ''Let's walk.'' He dropped her hands immediately, because if he hadn't dropped them then, he would have lost the chance. ''I've never seen the garden at twilight.''

''I doubt that there's much to see.''

He had to walk, or he had to leave. ''There'll be enough. Come on.''

As they walked he chose his words carefully. ''Katie, I think you're wrong about something. All of us have a wide range of feelings. All of us get angry, impatient, scared. But we learn to control ourselves.'' He certainly hoped that last part was true.

''I don't think you understand.'' She didn't sound angry; she sounded as if she was completely alone in the world.

He tried to help. ''You have every reason to feel frustrated and out of control sometimes. Your whole life has changed. You can't remember anything about your past, you don't know about your future. Don't assume you were a fraud just because that woman you were seems alien to you now.''

''You've forgotten one teensy-weensy little thing. I'm carrying proof that I *wasn't* the woman everyone thought I was.''

''You're carrying proof you were human, and that you loved a man enough to sleep with him. That's all.''

"What does love have to do with it? Is that a prerequisite?"

It never had been for him, sad to say. He didn't want to attempt a mental nubile-body count of the women he'd made love to without loving them. "I think it was a prerequisite for you."

"Cripes, Casey, you have me on the same pedestal everyone else does."

"Katie, I don't care if you slept with one man or twenty. I'm not worried about who you were. I like who you are."

She released a long breath. "Do you?" She sounded young and unsure of herself. "Are you just saying that?"

He nearly groaned. She was tough as nails in some ways and so vulnerable in others that she practically oozed self-doubt. Out of the ashes of the former Mary Kate this one had risen like a phoenix with a broken wing. But he knew she was going to soar, and soon.

"I'm not saying anything I don't mean," he said. "You're not an easy woman to know, but I guess that's one of the things that attracts me most about you."

She didn't pretend to be coy. She would have to be a fool not to know he was attracted to her. "Well, I guess all this turmoil inside me is good for something," she said.

The drive came to the end at the barn. They circled it to stand side by side without touching, looking over the burgeoning plots in front of them. "It's strange to see it deserted this way," Casey said. "It's so still you can almost hear the plants grow."

"It's not really still. Hear the crickets? In another hour or so, the air will vibrate. And sometimes I hear owls . . ."

"It sounds like you come here often in the evenings."

"I come here to think." She sounded embarrassed. "And to see what's happening. It's always changing. I've found the sisters out here from time to time, just sitting quietly while the sun sets. Sarah and Grace have seen humming-birds."

"Hummingbirds?"

"They visit. We've encouraged the gardeners to put in some flowers to tempt them, and butterflies, too. It's Sarah's pet project. In her own efficient way she researched their habits. Now she sets out sugar-water feeders."

"You haven't seen them?"

"No, but Sarah says this is the time of day to spot them."

"Ask me anything about hummingbirds."

She faced him. "You?"

"Guilty as charged."

"How'd you become an expert?"

"I lived in New Mexico for a while and we had several different species that migrated there. I did a story once for my station. A three-parter. Big news."

"I have absolutely no questions. I—"

She stopped so abruptly he knew she'd spotted something.

She pointed. The sun had nearly set, and the light was substantially dimmer than it had been. He narrowed his eyes and stared into the rows of plants and flowers that a multitude of gardeners had planted.

"In Elvira's plot," she whispered, pointing at a spot not far from them.

At first he didn't see anything. He was the self-appointed expert, and Mary Kate admitted to having no experience with hummingbirds, but after a long, careful search of the lengthening shadows, Casey saw she was right.

A green hummingbird darted among spiking scarlet blooms in Elvira's carefully crafted bed.

He took his eyes off the bird just long enough to steal a glance at Mary Kate. She was obviously enthralled, as if she had never seen a hummingbird before in her life. He supposed that this, too, was something she had forgotten.

"Amazing little creatures, aren't they?" he whispered.

"It's so tiny. I mean, I know they're supposed to be, but look at that."

They stood side by side watching the hummingbird, which seemed not to know they were there.

"Their metabolisms are so high, they have to feed about every ten minutes," Casey said. "At night their heartbeats slow to nearly nothing."

"Look." She grabbed his arm and pointed again. "It's another one."

The other hummingbird was higher than their heads now, but as Casey watched, it zoomed toward the ground just in front of the other bird, pulling into an upward arc just before it would have crash-landed. At the lowest point of its flight the air was filled with a buzzing sound.

"What on earth?" she said softly.

Casey was silent, and as he watched intently the tiny bird repeated its odd behavior.

"Look, she's watching him," Mary Kate said.

"How do you know it's a him or a she?"

"She's playing hard to get. He's throwing himself at her, the way men always do. It's a mating ritual, isn't it? He shows off, she ignores him. He shows off some more, pretty soon . . ."

"Pretty soon more hummingbirds."

They watched until the male tired of his mating dance. He darted closer to the female who was still sipping nectar deep in the flowers. Their wings fanned the air just inches apart. Then, as suddenly as they had appeared, they were gone.

"Oh . . ." Mary Kate sounded disappointed.

"That was a special performance for our benefit. You may never see anything like it again."

She gave him a half-smile. "Will they build a nest together, do you think? Raise little tiny eggs until they turn into little tiny hummingbirds? Do they mate for life?"

From the story Casey had done he remembered all too well what *did* happen next. The male, after his extravagant courting behavior, mated with the female, then deserted her.

She was left to build the nest, lay the eggs, and launch the baby birds alone.

But Casey didn't want to tell Mary Kate the truth. It sounded much too much like another story that was closer to home. The story of her life.

He rested the back of his hand against her petal-soft cheek. Her skin seemed to heat at his touch. "Yeah. They mate for life. He'll help her build the nest and raise the baby hummers. Next year he'll find her again and dance for her, just the way he did tonight."

"Really?" She sounded skeptical.

"I promise." He forced himself to drop his hand.

"And they say humans are the most advanced of the species."

"Katie, there are men who stand by their women, who don't leave them alone and don't expect them to make a home and raise a family by themselves. There are more men like that than the other kind."

"You'll be one of them someday. You'll find a woman you love, one you want to raise a family with, and you'll be a good husband and father."

"You look at me and see all that? When others see a guy who just looks good on camera and knows how to sort other people's garbage and dirty laundry?"

"I look at you and see a lot of things. Maybe when it comes to each other, we're blind as bats."

"Or maybe we see things no one else ever cared enough to look for." He took her hand and raised it to his lips, kissing her fingertips, one at a time. It was all he could allow himself tonight, and it was not enough.

He started back toward his car, but she didn't follow him. He turned just before he was swallowed by the trees lining the driveway. Mary Kate was standing where he had left her, staring at the place where the hummingbird had danced.

ᥱᥲ 15

By MID-JULY MARIE WAS UP TO HER ELBOWS in fresh produce, and Mary Kate was up to her elbows in weeds.

She was also in real maternity clothes, visibly, indisputably, and for the most part placidly pregnant. By now the baby seemed like a natural extension of her own body. She could no longer ignore her rapidly expanding girth. She was in her seventh month, and although she had been able to keep her secret for longer than most women, now that the secret was out, the baby was making up for lost time. Dr. Kane had warned her that at the rate the baby was growing, she might not have an easy delivery. She was in excellent physical condition, but she was a small woman carrying what promised to be a large baby.

Mary Kate knew she was the talk of the Garden at Eden, and probably the community in general. She wondered if Pete and Carol discussed her blessed event over family dinners with Little Pete. Had Pete confessed fathering the baby to his wife, if not to Mary Kate? Had the sumo receptionist at Shandley, Rose and Kowalick been told to toss Mary Kate into the elevator if she ever darkened the law firm's doors again?

Now there wasn't much chance she would darken any door in Shandley Falls, except the one at Dr. Kane's office. She drove as little as possible. She fit behind the steering wheel, but not easily, and when she moved the seat back to accommodate her belly, her legs were too short to comfortably rest on the pedals. At least that's what she told herself.

Instead, to keep busy, she focused on the garden. She wasn't as adept as she had been at doing the hardest work. She tired easily, and bending strained her back. But she still managed her share of the load by supervising the teenagers and running interference between gardeners.

Even though she hated to admit it, she was sinfully proud of what all of them had accomplished. She looked forward to her hours in the garden. She relished the feel and smell of the soil and often found herself sifting it between her callused fingers for no reason at all. She had developed an amazing soft spot for carrots and broccoli. The first ripe tomato had sent her into ecstasy, and even now a salad from the lettuce she had defended against bunny incisors could make her coo with delight.

Actually, she reacted to almost everything these days. Her emotions were so close to the surface that she couldn't pretend them away anymore. Like the baby inside her, they couldn't be hidden. Not even from herself.

On the third Wednesday of the month her emotions were closer to the surface than ever. She'd had a poor night's sleep. The baby had kicked and squirmed, demanding her attention. She had longed for a man to snuggle up to, someone to rub her back and whisper reassurances.

More specifically she had longed for Casey. But in the past month Casey had performed another disappearing act. She saw him occasionally, chatted casually with him in passing, but since the evening they had watched the hummingbird dance, they hadn't exchanged a personal word.

This morning she had escaped the worst of the garden intrigues by weeding one of the raised beds that the child-care center had planted. It was a chore she could still do since she could sit on the wooden frame without bending or squatting. Best of all she was partially out of view, but still close enough to avert gardening disasters.

Unfortunately she wasn't far enough out of view to stop Jake Holloway from stalking her. Mary Kate had avoided Jake and Sergeant all morning. Alone, either of the men was enough to dampen a sunny day, but together they were a huge black cloud.

Surprisingly both men had stopped picking on the other gardeners, although certainly not on her. In fact, Sergeant had offered to help the offenders with the plot they had adopted as their own. The teenagers had decided to grow cutting flowers, particularly gladioli, purchasing the corms in bulk with their combined pocket money. With Grace and Samantha's guidance they had set up a stand on the road to sell bouquets. Some of the profit was earmarked for a blow-out party at the end of the season, some for supplies for next year's garden. Everyone was pleased with their initiative.

Sergeant had volunteered to show the teenagers how to stagger planting the corms to lengthen their harvest, how to mulch the plants and stake the flowers. He was down-to-earth and direct, and the kids seemed to like working with him.

But Jake was another matter.

"You ought to be ashamed of yourself, Mary Kate McKenzie!"

Mary Kate got awkwardly to her feet and rested her hands against her back, which thrust her swollen belly farther into the space between them. She no longer cared. There was nothing to hide.

She faced Jake, who was glowering at her, one finger extended to point directly at the evidence of her sin. She pretended not to understand. "What have I done this time, Jake? Brought down a plague of locusts?"

He narrowed his eyes, turning up the facial heat as she continued. "I know, it was that last interview with the FBI, wasn't it? The one where I gave them a detailed map of the land mines around your house?"

"Funny."

"Not funny enough. You're not laughing." She released a long breath, more a hiss than a sigh. "Come on, lighten up, okay? What do I have to be ashamed of?"

"Look at you."

Mary Kate looked at herself every morning in the small bathroom mirror. She knew she was huge and unwieldy; she didn't need an update. Jake was always surly and uncommunicative, but for weeks she'd wondered why he hadn't lectured her on the evils of fornication.

"I know. I'm pregnant." She managed a shrug with difficulty, considering the position of her hands. "And I'm not married. I ought to be stoned. At the very least I ought to wear a big scarlet 'A'. What else is new?"

He looked taken aback. "Is that what you think I'm talking about?"

"That's what I think."

"I'm talking about the way you're working, girl. You're not taking good enough care of yourself or that baby. Look at you grubbing in the dirt. You ought to be out of this sun at the very least. You ought to be taking naps! I know!"

For a moment she couldn't speak. In the interlude, Sergeant, his eyes snapping gleefully, left his plot to move in for the kill. "Always trying to prove you're better than anybody else, aren't you? Stronger, smarter, just plain better. You going to run yourself into the ground now just to show how virtuous you are?"

"Virtuous?" The word came out on a squeak before Mary Kate could squelch it. "Virtuous? I'm pregnant, you old fools! I'm not married. I don't even know who the father of this kid is! Does that sound like virtue to you? Not that I care one damned bit what you think!"

Sergeant frowned and so did Jake. They looked at each other, then back at her. "I'll tell you about virtue," Jake said. "It's staying where you don't want to be, doing what you don't want to do. It's doing the best you can with the hand you've been dealt."

He stomped back to his plot.

Mary Kate didn't know what to say. "I'm sorry," she told Sergeant, when she'd mastered the lump in her throat. "I guess I thought the worst."

"You don't remember much about Jake, do you?"

"I don't remember a thing," she said with feeling. "All I know is what I see every day."

"He lost his wife and son about ten years ago. He's a different man from the one he was back then."

Mary Kate didn't want to care. She really didn't. She didn't want to care about Jake or Sergeant, about Tyson and the other offenders or the families who, with such wonder, were harvesting gardens from soil she had dedicated to parents she didn't remember. She didn't want to care about the hospice patients she visited with Grace, about Anne who had buried her husband two weeks ago, about the sisters who supported Mary Kate without question, or the baby inside her.

She didn't want to care. She wasn't that kind of person. She still couldn't stop herself from asking the inevitable question. "How did he lose his family?"

"He and Hilda were visiting their son in Cleveland. The kid had just gotten a job, and he was taking them out to dinner somewhere to celebrate. They were walking back to their car afterwards when two men held them up. Jake's son tried to grab the gun. They shot him. Hilda got in the way." Sergeant lowered his voice. "You wonder why Jake's the way he is? He claims he blames what happened on those men, so he protects himself from anybody who's different or new to him. He tore down the little frame house he and Hilda had lived in and built that concrete-block dungeon. He's walling himself in because he blames himself for not taking that bullet."

She swallowed hard. For someone who didn't want to care, she was an abysmal failure.

Sergeant's expression softened, and so did his tone. "You've done a good thing there, Mary Kate. First time Jake's come out from behind those walls in years. I gave up on him a long time ago. You didn't know any better. I guess all these years I been judging you wrong."

He paused, then he shook his head. "You know back a long time ago, after you got me fired? I was furious, just like Jake. You know what? I stopped drinking just to show everybody you were wrong about me. Haven't had a drink in years and years." He gave a dry laugh and moved off.

Mary Kate sank to her seat on the garden frame. The ground at her feet seemed to be shaking again, just the way it had nearly every day since she had awakened from an injury she didn't remember, into a body she didn't remember, into a life she didn't remember.

She closed her eyes and gasped. Her head began to spin, and she felt as if she were tumbling through the air . . .

Rain was falling, not a gentle summer rain, but a rain that stung her bare skin and chilled her bones. She knew it was raining, but she didn't care. She wanted to die. But the rain wouldn't claim her, and she didn't have the courage to throw herself in front of a car. Her life as she knew it had ended that day. No one would help her. No one would comfort her. She had been alone for as long as she remembered, alone without anyone who really understood her. This problem, like every problem in her life, was hers alone to solve. She lifted her eyes to the sky above her, to the place where God was supposed to dwell, and she knew that He didn't understand her, either, and never would.

"Oh, God!" Mary Kate opened her eyes and tilted her face to the sky. The sun was shining brightly enough to momentarily blind her. She began to tremble uncontrollably.

"Katie?"

She heard Casey's voice, but she couldn't respond. She

was so locked in anguish and terror that she couldn't move or speak.

She felt him squat in front of her, felt his hands on her knees. "Katie, are you all right?"

She took a deep ragged breath, then another. "Where . . . where did you come from?"

"I came by to give you some news. And I'm supposed to proof the newsletter one last time before it goes out on Monday. I made the kids do some rewriting."

She heard concern behind the ordinary explanation. When she didn't speak he continued. "Katie, tell me you're not having contractions. It's too early."

"No . . . I . . . it doesn't have anything to do with the baby." She folded her arms over her abdomen protectively, only half-aware of what she was doing. "What do you mean news?"

"Remember Howard Larkin?"

She nodded.

"He approached me this morning about doing a program on your garden. They have a community-spotlight show on Sunday mornings called *Ohio Moments*, and he wanted to know if I'd put something together about Eden's Gate."

"Oh."

"And he wants you to help. He wants you on camera."

"Me?"

"Right. I told him about the baby. He already suspected. But we can film it so the pregnancy doesn't show."

She didn't say anything. Her mind was still reeling.

"Katie, if it's not the baby, what *is* wrong?"

"I had . . . I remembered something again."

"Did you? That's good, isn't it?"

"This wasn't good." She raised her gaze to his. "It was just a fragment. It doesn't make any sense. I was alone, walking in the rain. I felt terrible about something and I wanted to die. Casey, I was wrong. This *does* have something to do with the baby. I know it does. Maybe something's wrong. Maybe it was a premonition.''

"You said it was a memory.''

"It *felt* like one. But nothing anybody's told me about my past adds up to what I was feeling.''

"You know very little. Nobody can tell you everything.''

She forced herself to breathe deeply. He was looking at her with such concern that her first breath caught. She held it, then it exploded in a rush of words. "Where have you been?''

He tried to pretend he didn't understand. "I have a job, remember? And I've been here a lot to work with the teenagers. I've seen you.''

She lowered her voice. "I've had it with you, Casey. You're here, then you're not. You kiss me, then you can't even bear to get within ten feet of me. I haven't asked you for anything, but you're still running away. I don't need this.''

She knew the memory fragment was talking. She was still chilled to the bone by the blizzard of feelings she'd experienced. She felt so alone in the world that she couldn't believe anyone else lived in it with her. She had felt much that way since waking up after the beating. Only when she was with Casey had she really felt connected to this life. But for the past month Casey had deserted her.

"You know why I haven't been around,'' he said, dropping the pretense. "You have so much going on, you don't need more.''

"That's it? You're making my choices?''

"No, I made that choice for myself. I don't know what to do about you.''

"So you decided not to do anything.''

"Tell me what I should do.''

"I'm not a charity case, buster.'' She got to her feet, even though her legs were still trembling. The sun was shining, but she felt as if rain was still falling. "If you can't figure out what to do on your own, then it's not worth doing, is it? Forget the television show and just stay out of my way! Something tells me I've always been alone, so I'm pretty good at it, and I'm doing just fine.'' She pushed past him and started toward the house. She wasn't surprised when he didn't try to stop her.

Embarrassed at her own explosion, Mary Kate stayed out of Casey's way until she was sure he was gone. She was still shaken by the memory fragment, but even more so by her reaction. She had missed Casey; she had thought of him more than was good for her, but she hadn't realized until that moment just how devastated she had been by his absence. She had come to depend on him, but there was more to it than that. More than she wanted to examine now or ever.

Since she had an appointment for her second ultrasound late that afternoon, she got ready before she went back to the garden for one final check. She knew most of the gardeners had probably gone home, and she was hoping to wander the plots without having another conversation.

She tried to forget Casey by concentrating on what was in front of her. She was no judge of these things, but she thought the Garden at Eden was an impressive sight. Ringed by the thick golden border of sunflowers in glorious bloom, it was a little wedge of paradise.

There was no shortage of creativity within the plots. Sergeant's rows were ruler-straight, with vegetables planted according to height. His corn had been ''knee-high by the Fourth of July,'' a fact he hadn't let anyone forget, and now it was already inches taller. Pole beans climbed woodenstake tepees followed by two dozen tomato plants in wire cages. The garden was traditional. In a rare moment of nostalgia he had admitted that the garden was exactly the same as the first one he had planted as a young man.

Elvira's garden was a contrast. She had opted to plant herbs and flowers among hills and riotous clumps of vegetables. Cucumber vines snaked through clusters of marigolds, zinnias, and balsam. Ruffled purple basil fanned out from the base of eggplants. A former art teacher, Elvira had volunteered to help with the day-care children, and together they had poured concrete into sandbox molds to make memory stones. Some of the stones dotted her plot, set amidst creeping thyme that sent its savory fragrance to perfume the air whenever anyone stepped on it.

The Trans, a Vietnamese family from the housing project, had planted all the herbs they used in their cooking, such as ginger, Thai basil, and lemongrass, as well as tiny picturesque pepper plants that bore such a hot fruit the patriarch had put a hand-lettered warning sign beside them. A family of Polish descent had planted rows of beets for borscht and enough cabbages to make huge crocks of sauerkraut at the season's end. Jo Turner and her two little boys had concentrated on making their garden fun, including a circle of sunflowers that was almost tall enough to serve as a fort.

Mary Kate stopped beside Jake's plot. Jake's garden was much like his house, surrounded on all sides by the tallest plants and makeshift trellises, as if he couldn't trust his neighbors or tolerate the sight of them. She remembered what Sergeant had said about him. She had judged Jake without understanding his motivation, and she hadn't given him credit for the changes he had made since he had begun his garden here. She had been intolerant, arrogant . . .

Something crunched behind her. She turned and saw Jake on his hands and knees among the cornstalks of a poorly tended plot across the aisle from his own. A young family from the housing project had faithfully planted the rows, but between the illnesses of their children and problems with their car, they came too rarely and never stayed long enough.

Jake stood, dusting off the knees of his worn trousers. Mary Kate hadn't realized he was still here, but he was. She knew he had stayed longer than anyone else because he found a measure of peace in the garden. He had stayed to help a family who would never know and never thank him for it.

A cold wind seemed to blow from nowhere. Rain began to fall, a chilling autumn rain that soaked her to the skin. She didn't care. She was shaking uncontrollably. She tensed and squeezed her eyes closed, hoping to ward off what she knew was coming. Suddenly she was somewhere else, reaching for a doorknob. She opened the door in front of her and stared at the woman framed in the opening.

"I didn't do it to hurt you! Don't you see? I did it because I had to. I didn't have any other choice. You can't tell me what's right for me. You don't know who I am, what I feel! You can't keep me from living my life the way I need to and from making my own mistakes. Nothing you can do to me now can change what's already happened. Love me. Just once in your life forgive me and stop judging me!"

Mary Kate's eyes snapped open. As the garden came sharply into focus, nausea churned through her. For a moment she thought she was going to be sick.

"Mary Kate?" Jake came to her side and put his arm around her. "Didn't I tell you, you were overdoing it? Why don't you ever listen?"

She slipped her arm around his waist. "I am," she said, her voice cracking. "Believe me, Jake, I'm listening now."

16

THE ACT OF DRIVING A CAR HAD ASSUMED hideous proportions in Mary Kate's mind. Under the best of circumstances she was a terrible driver, but now, between the pregnancy and that afternoon's flashbacks, she didn't trust herself at all. She wasn't sure from one mailbox to the next whether she would suddenly have another traumatic memory and forget where she was. She drove well under the speed limit and parked on the outskirts of town so that she wouldn't have to battle even minimal traffic.

She was sweating by the time she turned off the engine. Despite the length of time it had taken to drive in, she was still early for her appointment at the hospital. Now she debated what to do.

The memory fragments had renewed her determination to discover the identity of her baby's father. She didn't know what the memories had to do with her present situation, but she was sure that they must be connected. Sometime in her life she had suffered the deepest despair. Sometime in her life she had begged for, no, *demanded* forgiveness of another woman. Somehow these two events had been powerful enough to remain inside her when everything else had been wiped away.

Mary Kate closed her eyes and forced herself to try to picture the woman in the second memory. She couldn't remember much. The woman hadn't even spoken. But she had been of medium height, with a nondescript face and a jaw of iron. She hadn't smiled; in fact, she'd looked as if words were beneath her, as if Mary Kate herself was a worm at her feet.

Mary Kate had longed to reach out to her, and longed, inexplicably, for comfort.

Mary Kate opened her eyes and stared blindly through the windshield. The woman could not be her mother, since Kathleen McKenzie had died when Mary Kate was a small child. But perhaps the woman was her aunt. Perhaps in the years before her aunt died, Mary Kate had done something for which she hadn't been forgiven.

But what? All reports confirmed that she had lived an exemplary life. She had to find someone who had known her, someone she could confide in, and discover the truth. Then, perhaps, she could understand what her memories were telling her and connect them to her present, maybe even to the baby's father. Only then could she make sense of the turmoil inside her.

She looked at her watch. She still had more than an hour before her appointment, enough time to discover some answers. She slid from her seat and locked the door behind her.

"Mary Kate?"

Mary Kate had hoped that Joanna would be at the department store this afternoon. Mary Kate had avoided the store for some time, not because she was ashamed but because she hadn't figured out how to get information from Joanna now that her reason for needing it was so obvious.

She still didn't have an angle. But she did have the truth. And on the way to the store she had decided that it was her best hope.

"I was hoping you'd be here," Mary Kate said. She watched Joanna's eyes flick lower, then resolutely up again. She didn't seem surprised, but then Shandley Falls was in most ways a typical small town with a small town's love of gossip.

"Yes, I'm pregnant," Mary Kate said. "I'm guessing someone already told you."

"I don't even remember who told me first," Joanna admitted. "How are you? I wanted to call, but I didn't know if you'd want to talk to me."

"I need to talk to somebody. Are you available?"

Joanna seemed pleased. "I've got a break coming. I'll tell my boss. We can slip across the street and grab a Coke."

In a few minutes they were settled at a table at one of the local fast-food restaurants, Joanna with a soft drink and Mary Kate with a carton of milk.

Mary Kate knew that she didn't have much time. She had decided to tell Joanna the truth, with a small lie attached. "Look, I know this must have come as a surprise to you."

"That's putting it mildly." Joanna stirred her drink with a straw, and the ice cubes clattered nervously against the sides. "I mean, everyone thought you were going to become a nun. Now you're about to become a mother."

"I don't know who the baby's father is, Joanna." Mary Kate watched Joanna's eyes widen. Just at the point where she knew Joanna was scrambling for something to say, Mary Kate continued. "It's not what you think. I don't know who the father is because my memory was completely wiped out after the accident."

Joanna tried to put that together. "But when we talked the last time, when you bought clothes from me . . ."

"I didn't have the faintest idea who you were." Mary Kate put her hand over her heart. "It's the truth. I'm a master at fooling people. Was I always this good at it?"

"You? Are you kidding? You turn bright red when you even think about telling a lie."

Now lying came as naturally to her as breathing. Mary Kate felt surprisingly discouraged. "Boy, have I changed."

"But why didn't you tell me the truth right at the beginning? Why'd you try to fool me?"

"Because I didn't want anyone else to know I was pregnant. I was hoping the baby's father would approach me before he discovered the truth. Then, once the pregnancy was obvious, I was afraid if he discovered that I'd lost my memory and didn't know his identity, he would think he was home free. He'd never have to own up to what he'd done."

Joanna nodded uncertainly.

"But he never came forward," Mary Kate said. "And once people began to find out that my memory was gone, I knew I'd lost my chance. Not everybody knows, but too many people do." So far everything she'd said was true. Now, reluctantly, she padded it with an exaggeration. "That's the bad news. The good news is that my memory's returning bit by bit. I imagine before long I'll remember everything."

"I can't even imagine this," Joanna said. "You're carrying a baby and you don't know . . ."

"I don't. But I will." She let that rest between them a few moments. "The problem is that by the time I do remember everything, the baby may already have made its appearance. And I'd like to know who the father is before it does."

"Of course you would. What would you put on the birth certificate?"

"I need your help."

"But what can I do? I certainly wasn't there when, you know, *it* happened."

"Well, that's a relief. At least I wasn't into kinky sex."

Joanna giggled. "Mary Kate, as far as I could tell, you weren't into sex at all!"

"Do you have any idea who the father might be? Have I ever discussed a man with you?"

"We were never that close," Joanna said regretfully.

"And in the last few years, you weren't around much. You stopped to say hello when you could, but that wasn't very often. And we never discussed anything personal. You were so happy and involved at Eden's Gate. I didn't think there was anything *to* discuss."

Mary Kate was disappointed but not surprised. "Please don't be upset with me for this next question. But could Pete be the father?"

Joanna didn't seem to think the question was strange. She crunched ice with enough energy to make Mary Kate's teeth numb. Finally she shrugged. "Okay, I'll tell you the truth. I thought of Pete the minute I heard you were pregnant. But even so, it's hard to believe. He's a married man. Not that that means as much to him as it should, but from what I could tell, you stayed as far away from him as possible after . . . well, you know . . ."

"After he married Carol?"

"Uh huh. You definitely aren't the type to break up a marriage. Has he said anything to you that . . . well, makes you think it might be him?"

"He's given some hints. I'd probably know already if he'd just finish a sentence every once in a while."

Joanna giggled again, then she looked at her watch. "I've got to get back in a few minutes. I wish I could be more help."

"One more thing before you go . . ."

"Anything."

"I remembered something today." Briefly, and as unemotionally as possible, she told Joanna about the woman in the doorway, describing her as best she could. "I was asking her to forgive me for something," she finished. "It seems important, Joanna. Do you have any idea who she was or what I felt so terrible about?"

"Well, it doesn't sound like your aunt. Until your cousin Tim died she was always laughing. She treated you like a daughter. I can't imagine her getting angry with you. For that matter, I can't imagine you doing anything to make her that angry. No, I don't think it was her."

"What did she look like?"

"A little like you. She was short. Her hair was curly, like yours, but blonde."

"Blonde?"

"Uh huh."

The woman Joanna was describing didn't sound like the one in Mary Kate's memory. Not for the first time she wished she hadn't so diligently rid herself of all worldly things. One look at her aunt's photograph was all she needed to confirm or deny . . .

She sat up a little straighter. "*The Cricket.*"

"What?"

Mary Kate tapped her milk carton on the table. "*The Cricket.* I can ask Jim to look up my aunt's photograph in their files. She was a prominent citizen. They'll have something there."

"Jim? You mean Jim Fagen? He works there now, doesn't he? He always had a crush on you in high school. Maybe he's the father."

Mary Kate filed that away, but it hardly seemed likely. She hadn't seen Jim for a while, but months ago he'd had trouble finding the courage to speak to her. She couldn't imagine him urging her into bed. "Look, will you keep this conversation private? I know it's a lot to ask."

Joanna got to her feet. "No it's not. I'd do anything for you."

Mary Kate smiled warmly. It felt good to have a friend. Particularly now that Casey . . . The smile dwindled. "Thanks. You know where I'm living if you remember anything."

Mary Kate told herself she didn't want to see Casey again. She'd said everything she needed to earlier that day. She didn't want to apologize, and she didn't want to reconcile.

She wished she hadn't been so uncharacteristically emotional—and, well, needy—but there was nothing she could do about that now.

Despite that, when she got to the *Cricket* office and discovered that Casey had gone out for the afternoon she still felt a pang of disappointment. She tried to forget him and concentrate on her reason for coming to the office, but she turned every time the main office door slammed behind her.

She recognized the woman at the front desk, who had put in some time at the *Cricket*'s garden plot, and several other employees came through and said hello before Jim came out front.

He didn't look happy to see her. In fact, he looked mortified. His eyes stayed steadfastly above her shoulders, but she knew he was all too aware of the baby. She was sure that here, as everywhere else in town, the word had gotten out.

She tried her friendliest smile. "Hi, Jim. I haven't seen you at the garden for a while."

"I—I've been too busy."

She nodded, sure his absence had had more to do with her swollen belly than a swollen appointment book. She remembered Joanna's words, and for the first time she really wondered if there was something to them. Could Jim be the baby's father? He was a sweet guy, but she wasn't attracted to him. On the other hand, she was beginning to realize that the woman she was now and the woman she had been were almost two separate people. At times the only connection between them seemed to be her all too expanded flesh.

She moved a little closer. "I need your help. May I talk to you privately?"

"Casey's gone," the receptionist said. "Use his office."

"I—I don't know. He might not . . . might not—"

"It's fine," the woman said with an impatient wave of her hand. "He won't care."

Jim's reluctance was obvious, but he'd been left with no choice. Without a word he turned and led Mary Kate

through a large room with half a dozen desks, some occupied, some with telephones ringing.

She stopped halfway through the room. She recognized
the weak feeling in her limbs, the buzzing in her head. She
gripped the edge of one of the desks as another memory
surfaced.

*A woman with heavy bangs chewed gum fifty beats to the
minute, cracking it loudly on even chomps. All around her
desk, telephones rang and people dashed by. The woman
had to lean forward and shout to be heard. "I'm telling
you, this isn't a good idea. We could get sued. You've got
to consider everything before you take this on. It's not like
it's the only story out there. You've got—"*

"Mary Kate?" Jim gripped Mary Kate's shoulder. "Are
you all right?"

The memory dissolved. She swallowed too hard and
coughed in response. "Sweet Jesus . . ."

"Let's get you into Casey's office."

He guided her the short distance. She stumbled once. Her
legs felt like rubber bands.

"What happened? Are you in pain?" He helped her settle
into a chair in the corner, then backed away.

"No. I . . ." She couldn't ask Jim if she had ever worked
here. If she did she'd have to admit she'd lost her memory.
And if she admitted that, it was as good as admitting that
she didn't know the identity of her baby's father. What if
Jim were that man?

Of course Jim might already know about her memory
loss. A lot of people did. The juvenile offenders had known
almost from the beginning, and so had everyone who was
connected to her recovery. The more contact any of those
people had with interested outsiders, the harder it was to
keep her personal life private.

She tried to probe without revealing her own confusion.
"I haven't been here for a while. The room just seemed so
familiar, like an old friend."

"It should."

She prayed he would go on, and after a silence he did. "I still think a-about that summer a lot."

"Do you?"

"I felt so—so lucky to be chosen to do the *Cricket* summer internship. There were so many other juniors who ... wanted it. And then I—I found out you'd been chosen, too." He shook his head. "I—I felt like I'd won the lottery."

"We were how old? Sixteen? Seventeen?" She hoped he had been talking about high school.

"Seventeen. I—I thought you were the b-best."

She was touched for a moment, then she remembered that this sweet young man could be the father of her child. "I'm not very good at names since I was knocked in the head. Who was the woman with the bangs?" She used her hands to mimic a short Dutch-boy bob. "The one who always cracked gum. Do you remember?"

He frowned and shook his head.

Mary Kate frowned, too. "Funny, I can still see her face."

"I don't remember anybody like that." Jim leaned against the edge of Casey's desk. He fluttered his fingers nervously, as if he were practicing scales on the piano. "Why are you here, Mary Kate?"

"I ... We need a photograph of my aunt, Jim. For an ... um ... exhibit we're doing on the history of Eden's Gate. I know it sounds silly, but I can't find one that's suitable. I wonder if you have anything in your files?"

"I—I can check."

"That would be great."

He didn't move. "Is that all?"

"Not really." She practiced several lead-ins in her head before she settled on one. "You've known for a while that I'm pregnant, haven't you?"

He looked away. "Yes ... I ..." He slammed his palm

against the desk. "Why didn't you tell me—me right away?"

For a moment she couldn't catch her breath. Why hadn't she told him? He was obviously upset. Clearly he felt that he'd had a right to know. She floundered for something to say. "I—I . . . well, I—"

"That night last December. We were so close! I—I poured out—out my heart. I—I thought you knew, you believed in me. I—I thought I—I mattered to you!"

"I didn't know how to tell you." She didn't add that she *still* didn't know. What had happened in December? Had they made love? The baby had been conceived that month, just before Antoine had attacked her. Was the answer this simple?

"How—how could you have kept it from me for so long?" he demanded.

"Jim, I was injured. For a long time I could barely function. You know that. I could hardly put two and two together."

"You—you seem to be putting two and two together with Casey just fine!"

She was sure her jaw dropped. "What are you talking about?"

"He—he's known about the baby, hasn't he? Right from the beginning."

"Is that why you haven't said anything to me? Because Casey and I are—were friends? Why? Were you afraid it would affect your job?"

"Do—do you think I care about that?" He pushed away from the desk and began to pace. "No, I could see you preferred him. You told him about the baby, but you didn't—didn't tell me. And after everything—after everything that had passed between us!"

She got to her feet and grabbed his arm as he stomped by. "Okay, look. I should have come to you. I'm sorry. It's just that—"

He shook off her hand and faced her. He wasn't stammering now. "What? You were ashamed? After everything? You thought I wouldn't help? How could you have believed that?"

"I don't know." She turned up her palms. He was on the verge of incriminating himself. She was almost certain now that he was the baby's father.

Jim ran his hands through his hair. "That night in December."

She nodded, encouraging him with her expression. "Go on . . ."

"You—you were so . . ." He shook his head solemnly.

"What?"

"So understanding . . ."

That wasn't exactly the lasting impression a woman wanted to leave with a lover, but at this point Mary Kate didn't care. "I cared about you," she said, knowing that much had to be true.

"Afterwards, I—I thought you, of all people, would think I was a bad person."

"How could you think that?"

"You were about to commit yourself to the sisters."

She nodded again, leaning forward.

"I—I was sure when I told you I'd decided not to become a priest . . ."

Her heart slammed against her chest once, twice, then skipped a beat. "And?"

"And when you said you understood my decision, I—I felt such relief." He released a deep breath. "I knew I could live with myself then. Thanks to you. You—you helped me so much that night, Mary Kate. More than you'll ever know. Why wouldn't you let me help when *you* needed a friend? Did you think I would judge you?"

Mary Kate was wrung out and discouraged by the time she got to the hospital for her appointment. She had never believed that Jim was the baby's father, but during their conversation she had experienced moments of hope. He was a fine young man, and the baby would have been blessed to have Jim's sweet temper and innocent passion. But Jim was not in immediate danger of passing on his genes. Not mingled with hers, anyway.

After his outburst they had talked at length. She had told him the truth about her memory loss. She had even confessed that she had suspected *him* of being the baby's father. He had been stunned, then deeply concerned. He had told her more about that night in December when he'd come to her to discuss his future, and how it had meant so much to him that she had supported his decision not to enter the priesthood.

Before she left the office Jim had found photographs of her aunt, who looked completely unfamiliar to Mary Kate, and even photographs of the entire *Cricket* staff taken during the summer that she and Jim had interned at the paper. She, he told her, had worked in advertising and sales. He had been a cub reporter.

The woman cracking Doublemint hadn't appeared in the photograph. Mary Kate guessed that she just hadn't been at the newspaper on the day the picture was taken, but that didn't explain why, in Mary Kate's memory, they had been discussing a story, a potentially scandalous one at that. Not if Mary Kate's job had been to smile brightly and ask the local dry cleaners and funeral parlors how many inches of advertising they could afford.

As she made her way through the wide corridors she shoved aside the day's memories to concentrate on the moment at hand. She had been dreading this ultrasound for weeks. As it was, it was growing harder and harder to ignore the baby. Until now she had almost managed to think of the changes in her body as just another physical trial, something that fell between a tumor and a pesky virus. Now, even though she knew the ultrasound itself was painless, she felt uneasy.

How long could she pretend that the baby was something other than what it was, another human being who would soon be introduced to the world, only to be placed in someone else's arms? Somehow, even though she remembered nothing about that moment, she had helped create a new life. But it was a life she wouldn't be part of. From the moment she had first known about the baby she had told herself the baby had nothing to do with her.

But she had been lying.

She stopped at the wide glass doors leading to radiology and wished she didn't have to go inside. Last time she had been able to ignore the screen, to ignore the magnified sounds and the murmuring of the technician. Now she doubted that she could ignore them again. Today she was going to come face-to-face with her son or daughter.

Her son or daughter.

She almost turned around, but after a moment of hesitation she forced herself to open the doors into the radiology waiting room. She was alone, except for one man.

Casey stood, studied her face, then walked toward her and held out his hand.

She gripped it without a word. He released a long, harsh breath, and pulled her into his arms.

"Let me stay with you," he whispered against her hair.

She wrapped her arms around him and relaxed into his embrace.

ᥩ 17

MARY KATE STARED AT THE CEILING AND didn't look at Casey, but he held her hand anyway as the technician prepared her for the ultrasound. Mary Kate had agreed to let him come with her, but now he wondered if she was having second thoughts. If she was, he couldn't blame her. He claimed to care about her, then he stayed away for weeks at a time. He kissed her, then he left her alone to wonder just exactly what the kiss meant.

How could he really explain his own confusion? He was a man who didn't understand love, who had devoted his life and talents to exploring surfaces, who had learned as a child that feeling deeply was asking for abuse. As an adult, if he had loved at all, he had loved a woman who couldn't love him back. Gypsy's life had been an escalator going up, with throngs of people on the steps below, shoving and urging her to greater and greater heights. If she'd ever had any desire to get off and take a long look at where she'd landed, she hadn't taken the initiative. She had set her sights so high that she had been unable to reconsider her choices.

And God help him, Casey had never asked her to reconsider them, anyway.

"Will you be starting soon?" Mary Kate asked the technician. The question told its own story. Her voice warbled slightly; the words were a plea to get the ultrasound over with quickly.

Susan, the technician, was a plain young woman with straight brown hair and the overly bright smile of a brand-new kindergarten teacher. She seemed to sense Mary Kate's anxiety, and she patted her on the shoulder.

"There's nothing to this," Susan assured her. "This is strictly routine. In a minute we'll see how your little one's doing in there."

Mary Kate looked as if she wanted to say something. She bit her lip instead. Casey leaned forward. "Katie, is there something I can do to help?"

She looked at him for the first time since she'd taken her place on the gurney. "I . . ." She sighed.

He made his best guess. "You don't have to watch the screen. You can look at me instead."

"But then she won't see the baby . . ." Susan stopped. "Oh. Don't you want to see? Are you afraid something's wrong?"

"No. I want to see," Mary Kate said.

Susan looked relieved. "Good. I'll give you a picture or two to take home with you, if you'd like." She busied herself on the other side of the room setting out supplies.

"You're sure?" Casey asked Mary Kate. "You don't have to make this any harder on yourself than it is already."

"I'm going to have a baby," she said softly. "I can't ignore it any longer."

He didn't sit back. He brushed her hair off her forehead, letting the wayward curls twine around his fingers. Her skin was rosebud-soft, and he could feel her pulse beneath his fingertips. "A little denial can be a wonderful thing. It's gotten you this far. Don't knock it."

Her green eyes were clear, but deep inside them he thought he saw shadows. "I'll be all right. It was nice of you to come, but you don't have to stay."

"Don't I?" He stroked her temple. "Really? Then why don't I stay just because I want to?"

"I don't understand you."

"That makes two of us."

"Are you going to ignore me for the next two months then show up unexpectedly at the delivery? Because if you are, I'd like you to leave now."

"Would you like me to be your partner during the birth? I'll clear my schedule to take the childbirth classes with you."

"Grace already volunteered."

"I think Grace will understand."

He watched as she considered his offer. He could tell she wanted him with her, but she was afraid. Not just because he had backed away, but because she had fears of her own.

"This isn't going to have a happy ending, Casey. I've already decided I don't even want to hold the baby. The minute it's ready to leave the hospital I want it to go right to its new home. The three of us won't be leaving the delivery room as a happy little family."

"I know."

"You don't like scenes. You don't like entanglements."

"You know that much about me, huh?"

"Sometimes I feel like you're the only person in the world I *do* know."

She hadn't meant to say that. He saw that much before she looked away. But despite his own attempts to remain at least a little detached, he was touched. More than touched. Because he felt much the same way. This woman, whom he had grown so slowly, so reluctantly, to care for, now meant more to him than he wanted to contemplate.

Mary Kate McKenzie had replaced Gypsy Dugan in his dreams. Now, when he had a nightmare, it was not a reenactment of Gypsy's death. In his nightmares he woke up one morning and found that Mary Kate was gone. And no matter how hard he tried to find her, no matter where he searched, she was lost to him forever.

"I'm not in this for a happy ending," he said quietly, still brushing her hair off her forehead. "And I'm not in this because I'm a do-gooder at heart. I'm just in this to be with you."

"You're a better man than you think you are."

"No, you're a better woman."

Susan joined them. "All set. Now let's slide your pants low on your hips and pull up your shirt. I'll squirt some stuff on you in a minute, then we'll get going." She assisted Mary Kate until her leggings were low on her hips and her top was pulled high.

"Quite a sight, isn't it?" Mary Kate said, looking down at the huge mound of flesh that had once been flat and fit.

"Quite a sight," Casey agreed. As Susan rose to adjust something on the monitor he stared at Mary Kate's pale skin, stretched taut over the baby she didn't intend to keep. For the first time he realized the full impact of her decision to have this baby. She had made a nine-month commitment, agreed to discomfort and eventually pain, agreed to a disruption of her life, the criticism of strangers, the pain of separation when she gave up the child. She had made the commitment when she hadn't fully recovered from her injuries, when she hardly remembered her own name.

At the time he had given lip service to Mary Kate's decision to have the baby. Now he felt the weight of that decision deep inside him, solid and warm in places that had nothing to do with his physical attraction to her.

"If women looked like this before they got pregnant, there wouldn't be a population explosion," she said sadly.

Casey rose and leaned over her. Then, with a wide-eyed Susan staring at him, he bent low and touched his lips to the thin barrier sheltering Mary Kate's child. A child who was nothing less than a testament to its mother's courage.

Mary Kate clutched the images of her baby in her hands. She hadn't looked closely at them, but she didn't need to. In her mind she could still see her baby floating on the ultrasound screen, hovering in space like the hummingbirds she had watched with Casey.

Her baby.

"She knew." Casey didn't take his eyes off the road. "I'm sure Susan knew the baby's sex."

"She'll put it in my file, in case it makes a difference when the agency chooses the adoptive parents."

"You've never called them that before."

Although the ultrasound hadn't been physically taxing, Mary Kate closed her eyes and leaned back against her seat. She was completely exhausted. "That's what they are."

Casey didn't respond, but she knew what he'd meant. Until now she had simply called the people who would take her baby "the parents."

"Adoption is a wonderful thing. I'm only one small corner of the triangle." She knew she sounded defensive, but she was too tired to temper her words.

"Is there a family in place already?"

"I'm scheduled for an interview with the agency in two weeks. Sarah arranged it for me. I've already given them a list of my requirements. I have a lot of control over the process."

"A list?"

She was almost glad to be talking about this. Perhaps if she could treat the adoption like a business decision, she could return to feeling that's what it was. "I want a two-parent family with a mother *or* father who can stay at home with the baby for at least a year. I want them to have enough money to be able to afford a decent education, but I don't necessarily want them to be rich. Mostly I want them to know how special this child is, to fall head over heels in love with it."

"That's hard to specify, isn't it? How can you be sure?"

"The people at the top of the list have waited and waited. They have to really want a child to get that close. And the agency checks them thoroughly. It's too bad every birth par-

ent isn't investigated the way these adoptive parents are before they're given a child.''

"Then the couple will know about you and the baby
ahead of time? They'll be waiting at the hospital?''

"No. This agency doesn't even warn the adoptive parents.
They don't find out anything until I sign the papers after the
birth. Once they get close to the top of the list they live in
an eternal state of preparation.''

"So if you changed your mind . . .''

She couldn't address that. "I asked for a family with a
garden. That's silly, isn't it? I thought the social worker
would drop the telephone receiver.'' She squeezed her eyes
tightly shut. "I don't want to talk about this anymore.''

She rested, trying not to think about what she'd seen on
the screen. The baby had been sucking its thumb. She'd had
the most ridiculous urge to reach out to it. Her baby lay in
a perfect watery world, warm and comfortable with none of
the terrors and heartaches it would someday face, and she
had still wanted to comfort it.

Sometime later she opened her eyes when Casey turned
off the engine. But they weren't at the convenience store
where she'd left her car. They were parked in the driveway
of his house. He was watching her, the expression in his
dark eyes warm.

She frowned and glanced at her watch. "Casey, I have to
get back. I'm already later than I told Marie I would be.''

"Stay for dinner. We can work on making something
together.''

"The sisters are expecting me back at Eden's Gate.''

"They'll understand if you call them.''

She dropped the pretense. "Why now, when I was just
getting used to you being out of my life again?''

"Because neither of us got used to it, Katie.''

He didn't kiss her, but he looked as if he wanted to. She
knew better than this. She parted her lips to tell him to take
her to her car. "I don't cook.''

"Don't you?"

"I don't even boil water. If I learned how, I've forgotten."

"Then I'll teach you." He leaned over and unbuckled her seat belt.

She was debating what to do as he walked around the car to open her door. She was still debating when he helped her out and led her inside.

Floppsy, Moppsy, and Cottontail greeted her like a long-lost member of the pack. She squatted low and fondled their ears while she decided what to do.

"Enough," Casey told them at last. He held out an arm and she pulled herself back up. He didn't release her. Instead he turned her to stand in front of him.

Once again she thought he might kiss her. She longed for his kiss, for the feel of him close against her, for the hard planes of his body against the mountain of her own. She had tried not to think of him, of the magic of their bodies touching, of the aching sweetness of his lips against hers. Life seemed like a circle when she was in Casey's arms, and they seemed part of something larger, something complete and whole.

Something altogether frightening.

She stepped back, nearly tripping over Cottontail, who slammed his oversized paws against her hip.

"Damned dog," Casey said. "He's the one who's always underfoot."

She pushed the dog down. "You're going to miss them when you go, aren't you?"

"I'm going to move into an apartment with a no-pets policy."

"I'm not sure this is such a good idea. I shouldn't be here. I mean, I know you're not planning to seduce me. That's out of the question, considering the way I look. No man in his—"

"You look like Mother Earth. I've never seen anyone more beautiful."

Her eyes widened; her heart fluttered. "I . . . What did you say?"

"I said you're the most beautiful thing I've ever seen." He shoved the dogs out of the way and started for the door. "Let's get something to eat."

She stood transfixed and watched Casey, trailed by the dogs, make his way through the hall. "Beautiful?" she whispered.

She followed him in a moment and found him in the family room letting the dogs out into the fenced-in yard. He closed the door when the last one made its exit. "You'd better call Eden's Gate," he said, without turning around.

She stopped trying to fool herself. She went into the kitchen and left a message on the center's answering machine. She was just hanging up when she heard Casey's footsteps behind her. She felt the warm weight of his hands on her shoulders, then the exhilarating brush of his fingertips against the sides of her neck.

"I . . . don't know what I can make for dinner," he said.

She realized she had been holding her breath. She let it out slowly. "I'm not hard to please."

"Aren't you?"

"Anything is fine."

"That sounds like an open invitation . . ."

She turned around, and he laced his fingers behind her neck. "Don't start something you're not going to finish, Casey. I've lost my patience."

"You never had any to begin with." He shook his head slowly. "But I'm not going to start anything. Not unless that's what you want."

"I don't know what I want. I don't want to chase you away again."

"Mary Kate . . . Katie . . ." He shook his head again. "You haven't done anything wrong. This is about me. I'm not good at relationships. I never told Gypsy I loved her, then when I had a second chance after the accident, she had changed so much nothing was the same again. I know a whole lot about sex and very little about love. And that's not what you need.''

"How do you know what I need? Have you asked me?''

"Do you know?''

"Better than anyone else.''

"What then?''

The words poured out of her. "I'm not looking for love. I'm not looking for a husband. I don't know what I want to do with my life, but *this* life seems alien to me. I'm not cut out for it, Casey. I want something different. Maybe nothing in the whole wide world will ever seem comfortable or familiar again, but I have to find out. After the baby's born, I'm leaving Eden's Gate and Ohio. I'm going to Chicago or New York or Miami, somewhere big and bright and bold. I have to see what's out there. And I don't expect you to come along. I don't know who I am anymore, but I don't think I'm going to find my answers here.''

"I've *been* where it's big and bright and bold. There's nothing wrong with that. But you won't find yourself any quicker, Katie.''

"You had to come here to start your search. I have to leave to start mine.''

"You're sure of that?''

She wasn't even sure of her own name. She was made up of nine parts confusion and one part instinct. But that instinct told her that Casey—despite his poor opinion of himself—was an honorable man. And he would continue to back away if he thought he might hurt her.

She took a step toward him to brazen this out. "I'm willing to take my chances out in the world. I'm willing to take them here and now with you. I've proved I'm tough, even if I don't know much else about myself.''

He rubbed his thumbs along her jaw. Deep in his eyes

she thought she saw the amber light of caution, and she wondered who he was afraid for. Her? Or himself?

He dropped his hands. "You must be starving."

She didn't know what possessed her to make a decision for both of them. She narrowed the space in front of her until there was no space at all. Then she rested her arms on Casey's shoulders and nudged his head down. He sighed and took her lips hungrily, as if he was the one who had initiated the kiss. He closed his arms around her, wrapping her in the warmth of his body, and the kiss went on and on.

They breathed at last, moving just far enough apart to look into each other's eyes. "I want you," he said. "I have for a very long time. But I don't know if you can—"

She placed her index finger against his lips. "Dr. Kane says I can. But do you want me this way?" She took his hands and guided them to the mound between them. The baby was moving. She could feel it, and she knew that Casey could, too.

"I don't want to hurt you. Either of you. I *never* want to hurt you."

"You won't. I won't let you."

"Then the question isn't *if* I want you. It's when. Now?" One corner of his mouth turned up in a self-critical smile. "Or now?"

She leaned forward. The baby rocked against him, but it felt right, somehow, as if the baby was a part of them both. Not a barrier but an addition.

"You deserve a romantic gesture. I'd carry you up the stairs, if I could."

"I think Dr. Kane might frown on that part." She took his hand, aware that he was still holding back. "I don't have to be carried. I just need to be sure you need me. Really need me, the way I need you. That's all the romance I want."

He brought her hand to his lips and kissed it, then pulled

her close again. When he released her, he took her hand and started toward the stairs.

She held back. "The dogs? They'll be all right?"

"They'll be fine. We won't be up there all night." His eyes swept over her, and his lips turned up in the same self-deprecating smile. "Maybe I'd better get them."

She didn't want to wait for him. She wanted him to believe she knew exactly what she was doing. She climbed the stairs without him, searching for the bedroom he slept in. It wasn't as easy as she'd expected. There were four rooms, and none of them was draped with shirts and ties or littered with men's underwear. She found a briefcase filled with papers in the room at the end of the hall, but it was the only sign that Casey lived in the house. In his own way he, too, had assumed a stranger's life, and there was nothing to suggest that he'd found it easy or comfortable.

Mary Kate sat down on the bed because her legs didn't want to hold her any longer. Her bravado had slipped. Not because she was afraid. Despite everything she knew about herself, this seemed familiar and right. Not because she had regrets. No matter what happened in this room tonight she was not the same woman who had nearly joined the Sisters of Redemption.

She hadn't lost her courage. She was just unsure that she could please Casey. She was not beautiful, despite what he'd said, but that didn't concern her now. In the months of her recovery she'd realized how little physical beauty mattered. She was no longer obsessed with the size of her boobs or the length of her legs, and she knew better than to believe that Casey was that shallow, either.

But without physical beauty to trade on, she had needed to dig for something more, something buried so deeply inside her that she wasn't certain she had found it. No one understood that. They looked at her and saw a woman who, if unorthodox, was also filled with goodness and strength. She looked at herself and saw someone else entirely.

"You found the right room."

She looked up to see Casey framed in the doorway. His hair was rumpled, as if he'd just run his fingers through it. His eyes smoldered with emotion.

Something inside her caught fire at his expression. She was sitting on his bed, in his bedroom, and he was looking at her as if he wanted to devour her.

She tried to sound casual. "You hardly live here, do you? You never moved in. Where are all your things?"

"In storage. I didn't want to be encumbered. I brought clothes, a few books." He shrugged, but he didn't move toward her.

She smoothed her hand over the navy-blue comforter and realized it wasn't quite steady. "I don't own anything to speak of. What *you* own you don't have with you. You live Watson Turnbull's life, I live Mary Kate's."

"You *are* Mary Kate."

"No. Mary Kate died in December. And the woman who woke up in her body is someone else."

"Do you really believe that?"

She stood on trembling legs. "Do I believe I have another identity somewhere? The way you said that Gypsy did?" She tried to smile. "Not really. But even if I don't know how it happened, I do know I'm not the woman I used to be. Either the injury made me more or less than I was, I don't know. I'll never know, I guess. But if that's who you're expecting tonight—"

"I never knew *that* Mary Kate. The only one I know is the one who nearly put me in the hospital the day we met. The one who cusses and storms and pretends she doesn't care about anyone or anything. The one who gets starry-eyed when lettuce emerges from the ground but can't bean a bunny to save her life."

She didn't move toward him. When she spoke, her voice caught. "I can give you that woman, if you're sure that's the one you want."

"I've never been attracted to saints."

Her hands rose to the top button of her shirt. "And sinners?"

"I'm attracted to *you*, a woman who struggles every minute trying to figure out who she is. A woman who still doesn't believe in herself."

She scooped her hand over the buttons, ending at the hem. "Then you should be helping me with these."

He crossed the room and brushed her hands away. Then slowly, his thumbs tracing a line between her breasts as he worked, he finished what she'd started.

As Casey parted her shirt she was aware of the utilitarian bra beneath it, of the protruding flesh which was still covered by her leggings, of the pale, taut expanse of her midriff. As he slid the shirt over her shoulders and down her arms she was aware of the spectacular anguish of arousal.

She covered his hands with her own, stilling them. "Can you say I'm beautiful now? I ought to be in a sideshow."

"You *are* beautiful. You look like a goddess."

Her eyes didn't leave his. "A fertility goddess, maybe. Goddess of the harvest."

"No. Goddess of love." Her hands dropped to her sides and he reached behind her to unfasten her bra. It fell over her arms.

She watched his expression change, but she wasn't sure what he was thinking. "I finally have boobs, and I have to get this stomach to go with them."

He laughed, a sexy, growling laugh, then spread his hands against her naked back. She could feel every separate finger, the callused fingertips, the slight flutter of his thumbs.

The bra drifted to the floor. He bent his head and kissed her, a supremely tender kiss that turned ripples of sensation into waves, and as it deepened, waves into breakers.

She felt his hand slip between them to rest against one breast. She moaned low in her throat, all too aware how swiftly her own response was building, how greedy she was already.

"You feel so good." He rotated his palm against her breast, and his fingertips grazed the tender skin above it. She leaned back, opening the space between them so that he could touch her with more ease.

His hands drifted slowly to her waist. He slid his fingers under the elastic of her leggings to urge them down. From somewhere Mary Kate remembered the photo of a pregnant actress, her huge belly flaunted proudly for the world to see. During the ultrasound Casey had gotten a close look at her huge belly, but he had never seen her entirely unclothed. She wondered what he would think when he did, if the circus-clown clumsiness of her body would cool his ardor. Reflexively she grabbed for the pants, holding them up as he tugged them down.

He covered her hands, laughter rumbling in his chest. "We have to undress. You may have forgotten, but that's how it's done."

"I know how it's done."

He slipped to his knees before she could say another word. He tugged harder, and even her best efforts weren't good enough. She could feel her pants sliding away. Embarrassment suffused her.

"My eyes are even with the evidence," he said. His voice deepened with every word until it was a husky rasp. "I still want you."

Her eyelids closed as he circled her with his arms and kissed her stomach. She could feel the faint scrape of his chin and cheek against the tightly stretched skin. The pleasure of it was enormous. The relief was enormous.

Something almost like tears filmed her eyes. She dug her fingers into his hair and held him against her. Evening light filtered through the windows, and shadows lengthened on the wall. He touched his lips to the most private part of her, and she arched backwards in answer.

"Casey . . ." She wasn't sure her legs would continue to hold her.

As he rose he slid his hands slowly up her sides. She grabbed the front of his shirt and began pulling buttons from buttonholes. He helped her remove his clothes, but neither of them took their gaze from the other's. When he was naked, too, they stood in each other's arms, still staring into each other's eyes.

"I feel as if I've been with you this way." Mary Kate reached up and cupped his cheek. "That's silly. I know—"

He cut off her words with a drugging kiss, parting her lips with his and draining all thought of discussion from her. "I know," he said at last. "I know . . ."

He took her to bed then, to the cool linen sheets and the firm smooth mattress underneath. She lay on her back and looked up at him. He was staring down at her as if he couldn't remember who she was. She understood that too well. She felt as if she were living a dream, as if this was both an aching, throbbing memory and something so new, no name for it existed.

Without putting weight on her he straddled her hips, and her huge belly rested against an erection that proved how aroused he was. He carefully cupped her breasts in his hands, as if he understood their acute sensitivity. She hadn't remembered how it felt to be touched this way, how impossible it was to remain locked somewhere inside herself, how grateful she would be.

His touch was skillful, yet she thought his hands trembled, as if experience had no dominion here. When he bent low to take one nipple between his lips, she gasped and surrounded him with her arms. She was instantly caught up in the pleasure of holding him, the erotic joy of running her hands along his naked back and savoring the lean, hard muscles of his chest as his body brushed hers.

The room seemed to dissolve around them. She could still

feel the splendor of his body against her, the delicious pull of his lips. Her body seemed to heat and she moved restlessly, murmuring low in her throat as he abandoned one breast to kiss the other.

The room was dark, which was unusual. She preferred light, and lots of it. She wanted to see a lover, every single inch of him. Sex was more than feeling. It was sight, taste, smell, and sound, and she milked it for all it was worth. She lived for those final moments when she could abandon all thought, all caution, all need to please a man.

But tonight the room was dark, and the man above her would not be so easily abandoned. He always wanted more from her. He wanted things that no one else could see, things she no longer believed she had to offer. He would not take no for an answer.

And somehow, still, she could not abandon him.

The memory evaporated as quickly as it had descended. She jerked, startled, and for a moment she was confused about where she was.

"Katie . . ." Casey stretched out beside her and took her in his arms. He seemed to know every secret place, every inch of flesh that ached for him, every caress she needed.

"Casey, I—" She stopped. How could she tell him she had remembered another lover? She hadn't, not really. She remembered being with a man, feelings and thoughts and a room as dark as night. But she hadn't even seen her lover's face.

He whispered against her ear, rubbing his cheek against hers. "Don't let me hurt you. Tell me if something's wrong."

"You didn't." She cradled his face in her hands. *He* was the man she wanted, not a phantom from another life, a man without a name or face.

The father of her baby.

She brought Casey's face to hers, kissing him with more passion. She did not want anyone or anything to intrude on this. Casey was not a substitute for a man she couldn't remember. At this instant in time he was the only man in the world, the only man she desired. His breathing quickened as she reached lower, to cup his erection in her hands. He was hot and hard, and she knew he wanted her just the way she wanted him. She could feel him pulsing, and she wished that he *was* the man in her memory, that he was the father of her baby, and that the essence of him, leaking against her fingertips, had impregnated her.

Casey rolled to his back and brought her with him. For a moment she didn't know what he wanted, then he guided his hips against her, and she understood perfectly. She rose on her knees as he entered her. She stared down at him and saw that his face was contorted, as if he was struggling to control his own impulses. For her. Because despite his own needs, he was desperate not to hurt her or the baby.

He filled her completely, and for a moment she couldn't think at all. The room seemed to recede. She closed her eyes and saw the shadow room once more.

She heard a sexy, rumbling laugh echoing from somewhere in the darkness. A thrill of anticipation worked its way up her spine, although she tried to deny it. She didn't want to be in this man's power. No man had captured her this way before or worked this kind of magic. She had always had a different plan for her life, one that didn't include this connection to another, this sharing of hearts and minds, this unintentional and unwanted merging of souls.

"No . . ."

Casey stopped moving. He gripped her shoulders. "Katie, I'm—"

She bent low and smothered his words. She could feel him throbbing inside her. She seemed to heat from within, to shimmer and burn with the power of her own response. "I'm all right." She moved against him, the full weight of her child rubbing against his taut abdomen.

He wrapped her in his arms, as if by holding her tightly

against him he could destroy whatever had caused her to cry out. She moved, and he tried to resist. She moved again, and resistance was impossible.

He held her hips and urged her against him once more. She felt herself dissolving again, but this time she knew whose arms were around her. She cried out Casey's name.

⌒ 18

"**O**KAY, MARY KATE. A LITTLE TO THE left, over there by the post just behind you. Great shot. Get her from over here, Stu." Casey motioned to the burly cameraman who was hauling all his equipment on a shoulder the width of a barn beam.

"Yeah, the sunflowers have her covered." Stu framed Mary Kate in his viewfinder. "Jes—jeepers, she looks like something right out of Mark Twain. Becky fucking Thatch— oh, Jes—jeepers, I'm sorry!" He clenched his lips. Stu wasn't having an easy time. He was aware enough of his surroundings to care how he sounded, but not enough to censor himself in time.

Casey was growing tired, and he knew Mary Kate must be exhausted. They had started the shoot for *Ohio Moments* early that morning, and now it was nearly dinnertime. Casey had almost wrapped Mary Kate's segment, but he just needed something to clinch it.

He gave Stu, whose smoothly shaven head was bent in embarrassment, an irritated wave. "Just get the shot. Let's see if you can keep it clean for another few minutes, okay?"

"Sorry," Stu mumbled.

"Katie, are you set?"

"Set."

Casey knew Mary Kate probably needed to sit down. She had been on her feet too much of the day, but she had never complained. In fact, she had obviously loved being on camera. And she was good.

No, she was better than good. Frighteningly perfect, in fact. And although Casey had only reviewed a few minutes of Stu's tape, they had confirmed something else. Even though she was less than a month from her delivery date, Mary Kate looked wonderful on camera. The pregnancy had been a challenge to hide, but she was so radiant that nothing blooming in the Garden at Eden could compare with her. And that radiance, combined with surprisingly photogenic features and a natural ease in front of the camera, translated to tape. She was amazing. In fact, if he didn't know better, he would be certain she was a professional.

Casey moved to stand about ten feet from Stu's side. He planned to be out of frame for this segment. He wanted Stu to focus on Mary Kate with the sunflowers bobbing gracefully in front of her. He would speak, but the camera would remain on her. The lighting was ideal; birds sang nearby. As far as he was concerned, the situation couldn't be more perfect for a wrap-up.

"Okay, Stu." Casey waited a few seconds until he was sure the tape was rolling. "Mary Kate, the garden's beautiful, and I'm impressed with how much you've harvested already. In fact, everything about this place is impressive."

She dimpled. "Thank you. The garden represents a lot of work by a lot of different people. It wouldn't exist without them."

"The day's coming to an end now. The sun's about to go down. Everyone else has packed up and gone home. The teenagers have put away their hoes and shovels and gone back to their dorms. What do you think about at the end of a day like this one? What do you hope you've learned from spending your time here?"

Her smile was beatific, and Casey knew Stu was zooming in on her face. Under any circumstances Mary Kate's smiles were spectacular, but on tape they almost seemed ethereal.

"I came to gardening reluctantly," she said. "I couldn't imagine why people wanted to play in the dirt. I was drawn slowly into the magic of it, but after my first seed germinated, I was hooked. At the end of each day I hope I've learned what seeds seem to know already. That there's a time for everything. A time to be still and silent, a time to break through barriers, a time to stretch toward the sun . . ." She paused. "And a time to let go and trust that what you've brought to fruit will enrich the world and bear fruit of its own. I hope that's what the teenagers who come here are learning from this garden. I know that's what we're trying to teach them."

He was left with nothing to say. For a moment Casey could only remember the Mary Kate he had first met. Then he realized that there was no reason to say anything at all. Off the top of her head, Mary Kate had given them the perfect ending.

"Stop tape," he told Stu. "That's all we'll need.'

He strode over to Mary Kate, who was still standing in position in case they wanted something else from her. Casey bent to kiss her, lingering over her lips for a long moment. He withdrew reluctantly. "Perfect. You were perfect from beginning to end."

"It was fun."

"Nobody's ever mentioned that you did anything like this before?"

She didn't answer right away. Then she shook her head. "No. I don't have any reason to think I've ever been on television."

"Katie?" He lifted her chin so they were eye-to-eye. He knew there was something more.

"Well, it just seemed . . ." She shrugged. "Natural. Easy."

"You made it seem natural and easy. You were terrific."

"Do you have to rush off?"

"Stu's taking the tape back to the studio. I'm going in

later to start editing, but we have time for dinner."

"I'd like that. Something simple, though. All I have to do is look at food and I gain four more pounds."

"I like every one of them."

"You won't like them when you're trying to help me deliver a twenty-five-pound baby."

Mary Kate had started childbirth classes, and so far Casey had gone to all of them with her. He already felt as if he could deliver the baby alone, if he had to. Even though they'd only just begun the breathing exercises, he was a whiz with a stopwatch.

Casey looked up at the sun, which was rapidly heading for the horizon. "Do you want to change?"

"Do you mind?"

"No, I've got a few things to talk to the crew about, then I'll send them on their way."

"I'll see you in a few minutes."

Casey watched her lumber off. She was huge now, and in his eyes, more beautiful than she'd ever been. Shooting around the baby had been a challenge, but he thought that they'd managed well. He had been less concerned for the audience than for Mary Kate herself. In years to come if she looked at a copy of the show, he didn't want her to be immediately reminded of the child she intended to give away.

He went to finish up with Stu and the other two crew members who had come for the shoot. As they discussed details of what needed to be done next, he helped them pack up their equipment. Then he slammed the van door in farewell and watched them drive away.

The garden was deserted now, and the sinking sun gilded the thick border of sunflowers. They were at their absolute peak and deserved a modern-day van Gogh to immortalize them on canvas. Casey stood in the stillness and thought about everything that had been accomplished at Eden's Gate. The sunflowers, although one small part of the garden, seemed to symbolize the hope and joy so many people had received from working here.

The clatter of gravel and a muffled curse brought him back to reality. He shook his head ruefully. He needed to watch this latent sentimental streak, or he'd never get another job in television news.

He turned just in time to see Tyson trying to merge back into the barn shadows. Casey wasn't sure why Tyson reminded him so much of himself as a young man. Tyson wore his anger like a badge; Casey had sublimated his so it didn't interfere with the con games he'd run as a teenager. Tyson acted as if he hated adults; Casey had charmed them to get whatever he needed. Tyson's approach was more honest, but Casey's had taught him skills which had boosted him up a career ladder.

Casey wasn't a boy in Hell's Kitchen anymore, but he remembered and understood that boy's pain. He supposed that he understood Tyson's, too. He wished there was some easy way to help Tyson come to terms with his life.

Casey started toward the barn, calling the boy's name.

Tyson, who didn't look happy he'd been spotted, stood his ground. "They all finished?" Tyson said.

"Yeah. Now we've got to edit the film."

"That hard to do?"

"Not very." Casey had almost moved beyond the conversation to the thousand and one details awaiting him, when an idea occurred to him. He considered it a moment. He had no favorites among the kids who worked on the newsletter, or rather he tried not to have any. But from the beginning he had been impressed with Tyson's intelligence. His writing skills were just average, but his ideas were exceptional. And the boy was a talented artist. He had designed a logo of the old Victorian home and a weeping willow tree that was simple, yet evocative. And he excelled at layout.

"How would you like to come along to the station?"

Casey said. "I could show you how it's done. You've got a good eye, a really good eye. I bet you can help me decide what to use."

For a moment the boy's eyes widened. The petulant slope of his lips relaxed, and he looked like any other teenage kid who had just been given something he really wanted.

Casey slung his arm lightly around Tyson's shoulders. "Come on, let's see if your counselor approves."

Tyson stood perfectly still for a moment, then he shook off Casey's arm. "Forget it."

"Why? I think you'd have a good time."

"They won't let me go. Forget it!"

"No? Why not?"

"They canceled all my privileges, that's why. Said I started a fight with Pfeiffer."

"Did you?"

"He came at me. I just let him know he'd better not do it again."

"Did you explain what happened to your counselor?"

"No reason to explain. This place don't mean shit to me. Nobody would believe me. Never did, never will."

"I believe you," Casey said. "Maybe they will, too."

"Get outta my face, man. I don't need your help."

Casey was stumped. Obviously Tyson wasn't going to let him intervene, and for that matter, Casey only had Tyson's story to go on. He hadn't been there when the fight occurred.

"All right, forget coming with me," Casey said. "But we'd better get you back to your dorm. You're not supposed to be out here alone. Especially if you're already in trouble."

"I'll go back in a minute. I gotta get some air."

"You'll get plenty on the walk back."

"I'm not going!"

Casey wasn't really a staff member, and he didn't carry a walkie-talkie for moments like this. He supposed if he was forced to tangle with Tyson, he would probably win. He was larger and just as determined. But their tentatively blossoming relationship would be destroyed forever. And for what? To enforce a rule he hadn't made? The moment the counselors realized Tyson was gone, they would come looking for him, and the boy would suffer the consequences of his own behavior. He would pay a price, but his relationship with Casey would be preserved.

"Promise me you're not going to try to run away," Casey said.

"Why do you care?"

"Because the next step for you is someplace where people always get to finish the fights they start, but somebody usually gets hurt or killed in the process. You're a good kid. You don't need jail. You need the chance this place can give you."

"Some chance."

"Promise me you won't run away, and I'll leave you alone."

"My promise don't mean a thing."

"I think it does."

Tyson was silent.

"If you're checking me out, I'll tell you right now you can depend on me to stay here until this is resolved," Casey warned.

"I won't run away," Tyson said at last.

Casey didn't know if he believed the boy, but he had gotten the promise he'd requested. "Don't do anything stupid." Casey turned his back and started toward his car.

Mary Kate got into the car and kissed Casey's cheek. She hadn't bought a lot of maternity clothes, but she had splurged on this dress. The tiny green stripes couldn't camouflage the vast girth bobbing under the dress's ample folds, but they made a valiant effort. At the last minute she had added small hoop earrings that Casey had given her a week ago, on the last night they had made love.

Casey gave a wolf whistle. "You look good enough to eat in that dress."

"Is that a figure of speech? Or are you planning to try to seduce me?"

"Don't tempt me. You think I'm the soul of patience, but if you really knew."

She touched her fingertip to his lips, then turned and buckled her seat belt—a feat that was growing more difficult every day. They had been lovers for the past weeks, but both of them knew they wouldn't make love again until after the baby was born. She was growing increasingly large and uncomfortable, and although they hadn't discussed it, they were both concerned about the baby.

She hated to lose what they had only discovered together. With no memories to guide her she had tried to imagine making love to a man. But imagination was a poor substitute for the real pleasure, the ecstasy she felt in Casey's arms. No words could describe the joy he had brought her. He was a tender, sensitive lover who mixed passion with obligatory restraint, but he'd never seemed to feel cheated by the things they couldn't do. When they made love Casey made her feel as if she was the most appealing woman in the world.

Although she had another month to go, she was already having contractions. Dr. Kane had assured her that the baby probably wasn't going to be early, but she felt surprisingly protective. She still spent hours in the garden, but she left the real work to others. She talked to the gardeners and helped them harvest, researched questions they had, and drew up tentative plans for next year. But she also took naps in the hottest part of the afternoon and took time all through the day to put up her feet and rest.

Tonight after dinner, instead of hours of pleasure at Casey's house, she would come back to Eden's Gate and go to bed early. But until then, she planned to make the most of her moments with him.

Casey negotiated the long drive and pulled out on the main road. "Where do you want to go?"

"I'm really not very hungry. Let's hit something in town."

"I know a place with the best pie in the world."

She did, too. "The Hometowner?"

"Uh huh. They make a mean meat loaf."

Months had passed since Mary Kate had been back to the restaurant where she'd first met Pete. She had returned for lunch several times, but the waitress who had seemed to know her so well had never been on duty. And she'd never seen Pete there again, either.

"Meat loaf it is. And whipped potatoes." She lowered her seat to a more comfortable position. "And green beans and hot rolls and salad with ranch dressing."

"Not hungry, huh?"

"That's not hungry."

"I'll have to stop and take out a loan on the way."

"Is there anything I can eat while I wait?"

He shot her a grin, and something stirred deep inside her. She refused to spend time thinking about Casey and what he meant to her. Her life was in flux. She didn't know where she would be in a few months or what she would be doing. But it was growing harder to tell herself just to enjoy him while she could.

On the trip to town they talked about *Ohio Moments* and continued the conversation after they found a parking place half a block from the coffee shop. Even though it was Saturday night and busy, they found a booth large enough to accommodate Mary Kate.

"The special's a fish fry." Casey pointed to a blackboard on the wall. "All you can eat, not that there are enough fish in the ocean . . ."

She stuck the menu behind the sugar dispenser. "Are you trying to kill me?"

"What?"

"I never eat fish. I hate it. One bite and . . ." She wrapped her fingers around her throat, and crossed her eyes.

"You're kidding."

She dropped the pose. "I'm surprised I haven't told you before. I break out in a cold sweat if someone opens a can of tuna a block away."

"Does fish make you sick?"

"I never get close enough to find out."

"Gypsy was allergic to shellfish. Once she almost died from a bite of shrimp creole."

Casey rarely mentioned Gypsy Dugan anymore, but mentioning her at all was too often for Mary Kate. She didn't like to be reminded that Casey had loved another woman. She changed the subject. "Anyway, I'm sticking with the meat loaf. And you'd better pray they have chocolate meringue pie, or prepare to see me weep."

"That would be a first. I've never seen you cry."

"It's so good I might cry if they *do* have it."

A familiar brassy blonde came to their table, pencil poised to take their order. "You folks decided ye—" She leaned forward and squinted at Mary Kate. "Mary Kate? I almost didn't recognize you."

Mary Kate's gaze flicked to the heart-shaped name badge. "Millie." It had been so long she had forgotten the woman's name. "I haven't seen you in a while."

Millie's gaze followed the inevitable path to Mary Kate's belly. "I've been wondering how you were."

"I'm doing fine, thank you."

"Baby due soon?"

"Uh huh." Mary Kate wasn't surprised Millie had asked. The truth was hard to ignore.

"I hadn't heard until a couple of days ago," Millie said. "I've been in Canada, staying with my brother. He had pneumonia. Took awhile to recover. He started smoking again as soon as he could take a real breath." She shook her head. "I got no patience with fools."

Mary Kate wasn't sure if Millie was shaking her head over the pregnancy or her brother's folly. But she took the opportunity to introduce Casey.

"This little girl's something special," Millie told Casey. "My baby died of cancer this past January. Mary Kate here was the rock of Gibraltar for the whole family. Most people who knew Robby didn't want to watch him die and they stopped coming to see him, but not Mary Kate. You meant so much to him," Millie said. "I know what a good person you are."

Mary Kate felt as if she and Millie were discussing someone else. Apparently Robby had been one of the hospice patients the Sisters of Redemption visited regularly. She wondered what he had thought after she stopped visiting. Had the boy realized that she had been injured herself? Or had he felt that she'd deserted him at the very end?

Millie took their order and left to carry it back to the kitchen.

Casey took her hands and folded them in his. "It still makes you uncomfortable, doesn't it, when somebody tells you what a difference you made in her life?"

"I don't remember Millie's little boy. I don't remember anybody. I still feel like I'm cheating."

"Is that part of the reason you want to leave Shandley Falls? Because you'd like to be someplace where you can start over?"

"I guess."

"And who will you be when you do?"

"I guess I'll just be me. Whoever that is now. It seems to change every day."

He lifted her hands to his lips and kissed them. "I like you, whoever you are at any given moment."

"When I'm with you, I can be me. I don't have to pretend. I don't have to wonder."

"Would it always be that way, do you think?"

She wasn't sure what he meant. "Always?"

"If we stayed together."

She felt as if somebody had knocked the oxygen from her lungs.

"We could," he continued. "Have you ever considered it?"

She managed to inhale. "What are you talking about?"

"Marriage. Living our lives at each other's sides."

"Casey, we'd probably live our lives at each other's throats. I'm pregnant with someone else's baby. Besides, after it's born, I'm taking off to see the world."

"That's what you've been saying. But is that what you really want?"

She pulled her hands from his. "You're trying to confuse me."

"I'd have to take a number, Katie."

"No, I'm not confused about that. That's what I'm doing."

"You made up your mind before you fell in love with me. Are you saying you can't change it now?"

She stared at him, and not one of her thoughts was clear enough to verbalize.

"You love me," he said. "And you love that baby. You could have us both . . ."

"You're saying you'd be willing to take . . . to keep . . . ?"

"I feel like the baby's mine, Katie. I want to be its father."

Mary Kate realized that Casey hadn't told her that he loved her. Her thoughts were like falling stars, brilliant and beautiful, but they blazed and died before she could really grasp them.

His beeper went off and saved her from having to give him an answer. He pulled it from his pocket. "Will you give this some thought?" he said.

She nodded. She would think of little else.

"I've got to find a phone and call the office." He slid

from the booth as if he was glad to be leaving. "I'll be back. Don't eat my dinner."

She watched as he asked Millie where he could make a call. Millie pointed to the sidewalk beyond the front window. Casey caught Mary Kate's eye and shrugged, then he disappeared out the door.

He wanted to marry her. She couldn't believe it. Casey wanted to marry her and help her raise her son or daughter. She didn't know what to think, and she certainly didn't know what to feel. She hadn't been this confused since she woke up to find herself at Eden's Gate without one single memory of her former life.

Millie arrived with lemonade. "You seen Pete lately?"

Mary Kate shook her head.

"I hear he and Carol split up."

If anything else could have gotten Mary Kate's attention, that was it. "Really? Do you know why?"

Millie looked as if she did know, but didn't want to say. "I told John to give you an extra portion of meat loaf. You're eating for two, you know." She turned to go, but Mary Kate grabbed her sleeve. "You know more about Pete and Carol than you've said, don't you?"

"Nothing worth talking about."

"Why aren't they together anymore?"

Millie shook her head, but her gaze flicked to Mary Kate's belly again, just as it had when she'd first approached the table.

"Oh . . ." Mary Kate understood. "Does Carol think that Pete's . . . ?"

"I heard them talking a couple of days ago, over in the corner. That's how I found out you were . . . you know. I guess this is one of the only places where Carol's sure she can find Pete. He nearly always has lunch here."

Millie fiddled with the cutlery. Mary Kate suspected she was waiting to be told it wasn't true. Mary Kate would have liked nothing better. But she couldn't. Not without lying.

"Rumors aren't worth repeating," she said, knowing it wasn't good enough.

"I've told everyone you wouldn't sleep with a married man."

"I hope you're right . . ." Mary Kate looked up and saw Millie's frown. "I mean, I hope you're right to even dignify those kind of rumors with an answer."

"I'll go check on your meat loaf."

Millie abandoned the table, and Mary Kate rested her forehead in her hands. She didn't know how long she sat that way before she realized she had company. She looked up, expecting to see Casey, and found Pete sitting across from her instead.

She wondered about the constellations at that moment. What stars were lined up, what planets had veered off course to force so many decisions in so few minutes? Since the moment she had awakened from an attack she didn't remember, she had struggled to redefine herself and every aspect of her life. She had fought with the world and fought with herself until even the simplest acts became complex and weighty.

And now she thought she was about to discover yet another facet of herself, one she didn't want to face. Because for the first time she realized how disappointed she would be to find that Pete Watkins was the father of her child. She didn't believe that she had been a saint, but neither did she want to find that she had been capable of that kind of destruction.

Pete was dressed in a polo shirt and wrinkled khakis and he needed a shave. His eyes were shadowed, as if sleep had eluded him for days. "Why didn't you tell me?" he said. "Why didn't you come to me right away?"

Mary Kate groaned. She felt as if someone had opened a new door into her psyche, and the view wasn't a pretty one. For a moment she considered telling Pete the truth about her memory loss, and asking outright if he was the baby's father. But a wilier part of her warned that she might never discover the true answer that way.

"What good would it have done?" she said.

"It would have explained a lot of things, Mary Kate. Like that visit to my office. Like the way you were acting. I know you got hit on the head and your memory's been fuzzy—"

"Do you?"

"Everyone knows. But you couldn't have forgotten . . ." He shook his head mournfully.

"No, I haven't forgotten some things," she said, glad it wasn't a total lie.

"Do you remember a certain night in December?"

Both times she had spoken to Pete he had talked about the last time he had seen her before her injury. Now she made her best guess. "You mean the last time we were together? Yes, I'm afraid I remember."

"I'm so ashamed."

Her heart sank. Foolishly she had begun to believe the things people said about her. Slowly and steadily she had accepted the possibility that underneath her temper and self-centered whims dwelled a good person. Not a perfect one. Not even fifty-percent perfect. But she had almost let everyone convince her she was a woman with strengths, a woman who could make a difference.

This time, the difference she had made in the life of the man in front of her and his family was a terrible one.

"Carol knows, doesn't she?" she said. She looked down at the table. "She left you because of what happened that night, didn't she?"

Pete shook his head. "No, Carol left because she thinks—" He swallowed. "She thinks *I'm* the father of your baby, Mary Kate. And I could be, that's the hard part, the part I can't argue with. If I'd had my own way, it might have been me. If you hadn't set me straight that night, I could be that baby's father."

Mary Kate had been so sure of what he was going to say

that it took her seconds to adjust. "I . . . I set you straight?"

"Carol and I have terrible problems. I don't know if we'll ever be able to resolve them. But that night in December you were right. I didn't love you. Not that way. I just loved the way you made me feel about myself. I love Carol, only I don't love the way we're living."

He tapped his fingers on the table. "I quit my job at the firm on Friday. I'm going to do my woodworking full-time. And I've already got orders for enough tables and headboards to keep me busy for the next six months. I won't make half as much money, but I'll be happy. And if Carol can see her way to forgiving me for that and for everything else I've done, then maybe we can start over. But only if . . ."

She realized Pete had expressed entire thoughts. Several of them in complete sentences. Unfortunately her own thoughts were in terrible disarray. "If what?"

"Only if you tell Carol that you and I never made love. Because if she goes on believing you're carrying my baby, we'll never have another chance."

Mary Kate looked Pete straight in the eye and saw he was telling the truth. He was *not* the father of her child. She was still in the dark about the baby's paternity, but she was overwhelmed with relief. "Why didn't you come to me sooner and tell me what Carol thought?"

"I had to sort this out. I had to decide what to do, like a real man. This wasn't about you. It was about me."

Mary Kate was glad, so very glad, that she hadn't destroyed a marriage. She covered his hand. "I'll write Carol a note."

"I'm not trying to get myself off the hook. Tell her everything, if you want. Tell her what a fool I was that night coming on to you the way I did."

"Carol doesn't have to know about that night, Pete. I'll tell her the truth, that she's the one you love. But promise me you'll get some help."

"I'm already seeing a counselor. I hope Carol will start going with me."

Mary Kate looked down at the table. "Pete, there's something I can't remember. That night in December, did I tell you I was involved with another man?"

"No. You didn't tell me a thing, but I'm not surprised. You were always good at keeping your feelings close to your heart."

"Better than you might think," she said. "Right now it's a baby who's close to my heart. And that baby's father is a secret, even from me."

⌒⌒ **19**

SO FAR CASEY HAD MADE SURE THAT MARY Kate didn't have a chance to bring up his bombshell marriage proposal during dinner. He had returned from the marathon phone call about an upcoming feature to find her staring blankly at a plate of meat loaf. She had looked shell-shocked, a state he understood, since he felt the same way. He had never planned to offer to marry Mary Kate. For weeks he had considered it, and every time the idea had surfaced he had talked himself out of it. Then, tonight, the invitation had flowed like a river of words, with no dam in sight.

The strangest part was that he didn't regret asking her. He regretted the way he had blurted it out. He regretted his unemotional tone and poorly chosen words. But he didn't regret asking her. He regretted asking in such a way that he had probably destroyed his chance of having her say yes.

And he wanted Mary Kate to say yes. More than he had imagined.

Since taking his seat across from her he had carried on a one-sided conversation about anything and everything, just to stall her. He had expounded on the rice in the salt shakers, the hum of the air conditioner, the corny jokes on their paper placemats.

He had talked with his mouth full, talked between swallows of iced tea, talked more than he had talked in days. But he had to pause for air eventually.

Mary Kate chose that moment to speak. "If I wanted to raise this baby, I could do it alone." She had withered visibly during his uncharacteristic stream of chatter. "Having a husband was never the point. All over the world women are raising children alone and doing damned fine jobs of it."

"It's easier with two parents." Casey realized he had suddenly run out of words. Now that he had something important to say, the river had run dry.

"Right from the beginning I've used being single as my excuse for giving up the baby. But it's not the truth. It's not even a very big part of it." Mary Kate propped her fork on the edge of her plate with great care, then turned it a degree, as if the fate of the world rested in getting the angle right.

"What's the real reason, then?"

She still didn't look at him. "Don't you know? I'd make a terrible mother, Casey. It's so easy to see. I don't have the skills. And I didn't learn what I needed when I was growing up. My own mother didn't—" She looked up from her fork masterpiece and suddenly her eyes widened. She grew visibly paler, and beads of sweat formed on her forehead.

She squeezed her eyes shut, and for a moment he was afraid she was going to faint. He soaked his napkin in his ice water and reached over to dab her cheeks. The paper shredded into a dozen tiny pieces and lint speckled her skin. "Take a deep breath."

She gulped in air, but her color didn't return. "Oh . . ."

"Are you having contractions?"

She shook her head.

"What were you saying about your mother? Did you remember something? Is that it?"

She shook her head so vehemently that her curls whipped

her cheeks. "No! My mother didn't live to teach me anything, that's all."

He was concerned about her. Her eyes were feverishly bright. He signaled Millie, who made a beeline for their table. "Can I pay you now? She's not feeling well."

"Fourteen'll do it. Don't you dare leave a tip."

He took her at her word and went around to help Mary Kate out of the booth. By the time they reached his car, she was a little steadier on her feet.

On the drive back to Eden's Gate he was silent, giving Mary Kate the time she needed to recover. He slowed down as they reached the house, but Mary Kate waved him on. "I still need some air. Will you take me out to the garden?"

"I don't want to leave you there by yourself, and I have to go in a little while."

"Just drive."

He knew better than to argue. If he didn't take her, she'd walk there alone. As strange as it was, these days the garden was the one place where Mary Kate seemed to feel she belonged. And obviously she needed to be there right now.

"We can look for hummingbirds," he said, desperate to say something to bring them closer.

"I've seen one hummingbird pretty consistently. But never two. Not since the night we saw them together. So much for your story of undying love."

He felt a jab of anger. "Look, I'll drop you off so you can be alone. I'm sorry I proposed. I didn't do it to upset you. If it will make you feel better you can pretend I didn't say anything."

"Why are you trying to mess up my life? I know what's best for me. I know what's best for the baby!"

"And what about me?" he demanded. "Do you know what's best for me, too?"

"This isn't about you! This is not your child. You don't have to feel responsible just because we've been lovers. I'm not putting the baby in a basket on a stranger's doorstep.

It's going to a good home. It's going to good parents!''

He was so angry he was having trouble drawing a full breath. As he pulled up beside the garden he told himself not to say another word, but he was too upset not to make some sort of statement. He reached across her and shoved open her door, making it clear he had no intention of getting out.

She sat very still. He turned his head and willed her to get out before his self-control vanished completely.

"Oh, God."

For a moment he thought she was going to apologize.

"Oh, Casey . . ."

Casey turned and saw tears streaming down Mary Kate's cheeks. She was sobbing, full wrenching sobs that seemed to issue from the bottom of her soul. From one heartbeat to the next he felt wretched. He had never wanted to bring her to this. He tried to take her in his arms, but she began to struggle with the seat belt.

"Katie, it's okay. Don't get out. We can talk this through."

"The sunflowers."

He didn't understand. She wrested the belt loose and swung her legs to the side. Then she began to run toward the garden.

He shoved his door open and followed her. And he saw what had finally wrung sobs from a woman who never seemed to cry.

The sunflowers, planted with such hope and love, lay in tangled heaps on the ground, hacked and mangled almost beyond recognition.

Tyson didn't look up when Mary Kate and Casey found him sitting beside the pond. They had searched for twenty-five minutes. Mary Kate had taken a walkie-talkie before she and Casey set off to find him, and now she used it to tell the others that Tyson had been found.

Tyson didn't say a word as they approached him. He didn't even turn his head. He stared at the water and ignored them completely.

"I'll take it from here," Mary Kate told Casey softly.

"Like hell."

She heard the fierce protectiveness in Casey's voice, as well as outrage at what Tyson had done. Obviously, Tyson was the one who had destroyed the sunflowers. Casey had recounted their confrontation in the garden. Tyson had gone back to the dorm, the way he had promised Casey that he would, but sometime later that evening, without his counselor's knowledge, he had left again to sit by the pond.

But he hadn't tried to leave Eden's Gate.

"I want to do this alone," Mary Kate said.

"What if he comes after you?"

"He won't."

"The kid who cut down those sunflowers is an angry kid, and he's probably capable of violence."

"The kid who cut down those sunflowers was making a statement. And I've got to tell him I heard him loud and clear."

"I'm not leaving."

"Go. If he thinks I'm afraid of him, that will change everything. Don't you see?" She saw that he did, but that he was more concerned for her than for Tyson.

She didn't want to love this man. She squeezed her eyes shut. Tonight her entire world seemed to be lying in pieces at her feet, like the sunflowers.

"Go." Before she could think again about all the revelations of the night, she turned her back on Casey and started toward Tyson. After a few seconds she heard the sound of retreating footsteps behind her.

"Tyson . . ." She paused at his side, then thought better of looming over him. With the grace of an elephant, she lowered herself to the ground, leaving enough space between them so that he wouldn't feel threatened.

"What're you doing out here?" he said.

"Well, this is one of the places I would come if I was feeling hurt or angry. I thought we might have that in common."

"Nobody asked you to come looking for me."

"I know. But I thought it might be better if I found you, instead of somebody else."

"Why?"

"Because facing me was going to be hardest of all."

"You think I care?"

Mary Kate leaned back on her elbows, trying to get comfortable. "I think that's why you're out here. You're not taking any pleasure in what you did. You're sitting here wishing you could start this day over and do it differently. I feel like that so often I know the signs."

"You don't know what you're talking about."

"I'm afraid I do. I have so many regrets, sometimes I think I'm going for a world championship. And I don't even remember most of my life."

"You don't know nothing!"

"Tyson, I thought things were going well with you. The other kids like you. You're a natural leader. Casey thinks you have real talent as an artist, and you're a hard worker. I—"

"Shut up! Just shut your mouth!"

Mary Kate was too startled by his outburst to speak.

"Tyson this and Tyson that. Who d'you think you're talking about? Some Tyson I don't know, that's for sure. Don't you understand nothing? I killed my brother! That's the kind of person I really am."

"You were a little boy when it happened. You did something any little boy might do in the same situation. You didn't mean to hurt him. It wasn't your fault someone left a loaded gun in reach."

"No?" Tyson turned, and his eyes were blazing. "He was a little kid. He was always after me. I was tired of him following me everywhere. I pointed that gun at him to scare him, so he'd leave me alone.''

''Those are normal feelings all kids have about their brothers and sisters. You meant to scare him, not shoot him. You just said so yourself.''

''That so? Well, I killed him anyway, didn't I? And what about the day Antoine went after you, Sister Sunshine? What did I mean to do that day? I could have stopped him, but I didn't!''

Mary Kate had never wished harder that her memory would return. She didn't believe what Tyson was saying, but she was sure that *he* did.

''Tell me what happened that day,'' she said, because wishing hadn't worked before and wouldn't work now.

''What for?''

''Because you were there, and in a very real sense, I wasn't.''

He gave a short, unpleasant laugh. ''You were there, just that your brain got scrambled.''

''Why did Antoine go after me?''

Tyson didn't answer.

Mary Kate pushed herself to her feet and walked to his side. ''Tyson, why don't you show me what happened in the greenhouse?''

He stood, crouching forward in a threatening posture. ''It would take three to show you, wouldn't it? And Antoine . . . well, he's off in some jail now, doing time. Just like I'm going to be.''

She wasn't afraid of Tyson. She didn't know why, considering what Antoine had done to her, but she wasn't afraid of this boy. ''Will you show me?''

''You'll tangle it all up if I do!''

''Maybe not.'' Mary Kate could see Tyson struggling. He wanted her to know what had happened that day in December, but something about it frightened him.

He seemed to make a decision. ''You were here.'' He

indicated a place on the ground. She moved to the spot. "Antoine was here," he said, pointing beside her.

"Where were you?"

"I started out here." He pointed to her other side. "But when the fight started, I was over beside him." He took his place.

"Were you and Antoine friends?"

He made a sound that cured her of that notion immediately.

"I see. Then why did I let the two of you end up so close together? I'm told Antoine was always a problem when he was here, that we were talking about releasing him from the program."

"How do I know what you were thinking?"

She chewed on her thumb, considering his question. "Okay, tell me this. Did I usually let the two of you stand that close together?"

He snorted, and it was answer enough.

"Okay, then. Obviously I wasn't doing my job very well that day." A possible reason occurred to her. She had started off well enough, but she hadn't fully concentrated on the boys that day in December, the same December when she had made love to a man and conceived his child.

She had been so preoccupied with her own life she hadn't been careful enough.

"What happened next?" she said.

"He jumped me."

"*He* jumped *you?*"

"Yeah. That's the way it happened."

"And what did I do?"

He was silent so long she thought he wasn't going to answer. Finally he looked away. "You got in the way."

Mary Kate wasn't sure she understood. "On purpose?"

His nod was so slight she nearly missed it. "Oh . . . I tried to break up the fight?"

"Stupid-ass thing to do, wouldn't you say?"

"Of course not. Because I'd do it again. Do you think I should have stood there and let him attack you?"

"Why not? When he picked up that shovel and went after you, I didn't do nothing. You don't mean nothing to me—"

She ignored him. "Let's see. I tried to stop the two of you from fighting." She moved to another spot, as if the boys were really there. "I'm told he was bigger than you are. And he was the one who jumped you, so you weren't prepared. Were you still on your feet when he turned on me?"

Tyson didn't answer.

"Were you still on your feet?"

He gave one short shake of his head.

"So Antoine knocked you to the floor?"

"I fell against the table."

"And while you were trying to get your balance and scramble away from him, Antoine grabbed the shovel and hit me. That's the way it happened, isn't it?"

He didn't answer.

"Tyson?"

She put her hand on his arm, but he shook it off. "You think you know everything! I wanted him to hurt you!"

"No . . ." Mary Kate knew she was right. Tyson was a master at concealing his feelings, even from himself. All these months the boy had suffered because he hadn't been able to save her. He didn't understand himself well enough to put his own feelings into words, but she could do it for him. "You didn't hate me then, and you don't hate me now. You *never* wanted Antoine to hurt me."

He sneered. "You think I cut down those sunflowers 'cause I like you?"

"No, I think you cut them down so you could prove you're a monster once and for all. It's easier when nobody cares about you, isn't it? Then you can't hurt the people you love when you make mistakes."

"Fuck you!"

"I'd tell you I forgive you, Tyson, but as far as that day in December, there's nothing to forgive. You couldn't have stopped me from getting hurt, even if you hadn't fallen. As for the sunflowers? Well, you're going to have to earn my forgiveness for that. And it won't come cheap."

"You think I care?"

"Funny thing . . ." Her voice cracked, and she cleared her throat. "But you know what? I do."

Tyson's counselor led the boy back toward the dormitory. Mary Kate folded her arms over her chest, but it didn't ease the ache in her heart.

"Between us, we understand him better than anybody else in the whole world." She turned to Casey, who was watching Tyson's retreat, too. "The county fair's in a few weeks. Luckily he didn't destroy the pumpkins, too. I put him in charge of our entry in the pumpkin-carving contest. Either he has to do all the work by himself or get the other kids to cooperate with his plans. They're furious at him right now, so it's going to be a challenge."

"He agreed?"

"He didn't say no." Mary Kate realized she was crying again. She angrily wiped her cheeks with her fists. "Life's so damned hard sometimes. And it's never going to be as easy for Tyson as it ought to be. He's always going to remember his little brother and his grandmother. What happened that day is always going to be there in the back of his head. I wish I could just scoop him up and jump-start his life all over again. I wish—" She couldn't go on.

"It's too bad, isn't it, that you don't care about anybody."

"Don't start on me, Casey."

"I don't have to start on you, Katie. Nobody does. You stay on your own case just fine."

She thought about all the things she had learned that night. Casey believed that she loved him, and because he was a good guy, he wanted to marry her and give her baby a home. Pete was not the baby's father, and although that was good news, she now had no leads whatsoever. Tyson, whom she had clashed with right from the beginning, was torn up with guilt over the incident with Antoine.

And there was one thing more. The memory that had flashed bright and clear in her mind during her conversation in the restaurant with Casey still haunted her. In those brief seconds she had seen the same angry, dark-haired woman again, and despite all evidence to the contrary, now she knew, deep in her heart, that the woman had to be her mother.

"You're no daughter of mine. Don't ever call me Ma again. I don't ever want you to remind me that I raised you, Mary—"

"Let me take you back to the house," Casey said.

Mary Kate thought about the sunflowers lying crushed and broken on the garden border. "No, I'm going to clean up the mess in the garden. I don't want anyone else to see it. The gardeners will find out what happened, but they don't have to see the evidence."

"It's dark, and you're exhausted. Get the sisters to help you first thing in the morning after their prayers."

"I'm doing it now."

Casey hooked his thumbs in his pants pockets. "There's no point in arguing with you, is there? You'll do what you want."

"I have to."

"And that's the way it'll always be, won't it? You'll make up your mind to do something, and that'll be it."

"That's not true."

"No? Well, I think it is. I think you make a decision, then you hang onto it like a life rope. That way you don't have to feel anything, Katie. And that's why you don't want to think about marrying me and keeping your baby. Because if you do reconsider, it might uncover a whole well of emotions you don't want to face.''

She tried to reason with him. "You can't be thinking about marriage right now. Not seriously. You don't know what you're going to do, where you're going to go. You don't need me and a baby to worry about, you—''

He cut her off with a wave of his hand. "I'm staying here in Ohio. Howard and I are negotiating a contract right now. That segment of *Ohio Moments* was to prove to him that I'm not just a pretty face, that I can produce and direct and do some writing. I've already agreed to anchor the local news, but if everything works out the way I want it to, I'll be working in production, too.''

"Here?''

"Cleveland. But I'm looking for a house near Shandley Falls. I'm putting down roots.''

She was tongue-tied. She didn't know what to say.

"My offer stands, Katie. But I'm not holding my breath. You'll have to rethink your life, and I don't know if you can do that.''

She was too emotionally exhausted to fight off the anger that blazed through her. "So what's in it for you? You're a good guy. You have a bigger heart than you give yourself credit for. But you're no angel. What'll you get in return for taking on a wife and a child you didn't even create? Am I penance for all your past mistakes? Or are the baby and I supposed to be window dressing for this new life you've created for yourself?''

A kaleidoscope of expressions passed over his face, and she wished that she hadn't added those last sentences. Because she knew, deep inside, that they weren't true. She looked away, because she didn't want to see his pain. "I'm sorry,'' she said.

"I've got a long night ahead of me.'' He turned and started toward the road where he'd parked his car.

"Casey?''

He stopped, but he didn't face her.

"Do you want me to ask Grace to attend the rest of the childbirth classes with me?"

"I said I'd be there, and I will."

"I really am sorry."

He gave a curt nod, but he didn't look back. She watched him get in his car and drive away.

ᕒᐢ 20

MARY KATE TOYED WITH HER FORK. SHE had forced herself to eat a muffin for breakfast, but with just a week until her delivery date, she had lost her appetite. Now she ate simply because she had to nourish herself and the baby.

"Finished?" Grace asked.

"Yes, thanks." Mary Kate stood to bring her plate to the sink, but Grace, ever sensitive to others' needs, took it and motioned her back to her seat.

"You don't seem to be feeling too well today."

"I'm not sleeping well, that's all."

"You're sure?"

"I'm not in labor, if that's what you're worried about."

"You seem sad, Mary Kate. You've seemed sad for days. Would you like to talk about it?"

Mary Kate rested her elbows on the table and plowed her curls with her fingers. "I . . ." There was so much to talk about she didn't know where to start. And what good would it do anyway? "No, I'm just tired."

"I imagine you're tired of a great many things." Grace stacked the dishes in the sink and began to fill it with water. "You've worked hard these last months to find answers to a number of questions, but the baby's almost here and you haven't found nearly enough."

"Are you reading my mind?"

"No, I'm making educated guesses."

Mary Kate couldn't discuss Casey with Grace, and she didn't want to discuss the frequent memory fragments that blindsided her several times a day now. She was confused and miserable, about to give birth to a baby she couldn't keep, a baby whose father she didn't remember.

She settled on that. "I would like to know who the father of this baby is, Grace. It would make things easier if I just knew."

"You haven't had any success with your search?"

"Dead ends, all the way."

"I'm sorry."

"I've checked out every possibility. I scoured my room, my office in the barn, every paper in my possession. I wasn't big on leaving clues."

"You were never a very introspective person. It wouldn't be like you to keep a diary. But you were forever writing in your gardening journal . . ."

"Believe me, I've gone through it with a fine-tooth comb. A lot of it's in my own personal shorthand, which is no help at all. Abbreviations, symbols." She gave a defeated shrug.

"Symbols?"

"It's taken me awhile to figure them out. Some are obvious. I drew little suns if the weather was good, raindrops if it wasn't." She managed a humorless laugh. "One drawing completely defeated me until I realized it was bunny ears. I guess that was my cheery little way of pointing out that we'd had crop damage."

"You were such a whirlwind, I suppose that saved time."

"I actually abbreviated the Latin names of plants."

"That was probably just a way to remember what you'd learned."

"I've been able to figure out some of them with Sergeant's help. C. Maxima is short for Curcurbita Maxima, or winter squash. A. Porrum means leeks. You don't know what R. Scilla is, do you? It comes up a lot."

"R. Scilla?"

Mary Kate had just been making conversation. "It doesn't matter."

Grace rattled dishes and sloshed water for a moment. "You know, I wonder if that one's a plant at all. We had a patient we visited named Robert Scillato."

"Robert . . ." Mary Kate wondered why that rang a bell. Then she remembered Millie. "Would that be Robby? Millie's little boy?"

Grace turned from the sink, her hands dripping. "Little boy? Hardly. But Robert's mother's named Millie. Do you remember her?"

"I've met her. She works in town at a little restaurant where I've eaten. She talked about her son, but she called him Robby. She called him her baby."

"I suppose that's the way she saw him. I think Robert was the youngest of her two children, but he was nearly thirty. It was a real heartbreaker."

"I must have visited him often. Millie said I was one of the few people who continued visiting after . . ." She didn't know any more than that. She hadn't paid that much attention. "His name's in my journal almost every single day for months, Grace."

"If you visited that often, Mary Kate, you didn't tell us."

Mary Kate's brain was now working double-time. "Tell me about him."

"He died at the beginning of January. We had all prayed for a miracle. He had leukemia, but he had rallied several times over the course of his illness. He was doing better for a while at the beginning of winter, but then he got worse quickly. From one visit to the next he was gone."

Mary Kate wanted to feel something. Something real and personal, but all she could feel was the sadness of any human being for the death of a stranger.

Grace smiled a little. "Robert was an artist, quite a talented one. He was a bit eccentric, I suppose. He kept to himself and lived alone. He was very intense, but never rude. Just internal, if you know what I mean.''

Mary Kate nodded, to keep her talking.

''I always liked him. Losing him was harder than I wanted it to be. We had become friends, I think, but he got very quiet at the end. He hardly talked at all.''

''Did he ever say anything about me?''

Grace didn't seem surprised by the question. Obviously she understood Mary Kate's thoughts. ''He was shattered when he heard what had happened to you, Mary Kate, but all our patients were. If you're asking if Robert's reaction was unusual, I don't think I can say for certain. But he did get worse quickly after that. He died before anyone could tell him that you were beginning to recover.''

Mary Kate didn't want to spend time in the community garden that day. Her head was spinning with Grace's information. The only thing she really wanted to do was go into town and see if she could find Millie. But surely if Millie suspected that she and Robert had been lovers, she would have asked Mary Kate outright if the baby she carried belonged to her son.

''Walking's good for you at this stage. You want to stay fit,'' Samantha said, slipping her arm through Mary Kate's. ''Come on, you'll be glad you did it.''

Mary Kate had grown used to Samantha's good cheer. In fact, she'd come to depend on it. She didn't want to think about leaving any of the sisters behind. She didn't want to think about leaving the juvenile offenders, the gardeners, or the garden itself. She was certain she had made the right decision, but somewhere along the way everyone and everything about Eden's Gate had become precious to her. She would miss them.

She would miss Casey most of all.

She didn't want to think about that, but burying her feelings was getting harder. As promised Casey had attended her final childbirth classes, and he still came to Eden's Gate to work with the offenders or, occasionally, to do his share in the *Cricket*'s garden plot. But they hadn't had a serious conversation since the night ten days ago when she had discovered the destruction of the sunflowers. He was polite and distant, and she hadn't had the courage to call him on it. Because what could she say that she hadn't already?

From a distance of a hundred yards, the garden looked deserted. Most of the gardeners had been so successful that their plots had been overrun with produce. In the last few weeks some had stopped coming just to avoid reaping what they'd sown. The sisters and the more faithful of the gardeners had harvested the extra produce and taken it to local hunger centers. And the residents of the Landsdowne Apartments and the housing project were all rich in tomatoes, zucchini, and green beans.

"Nobody seems to be here today." Mary Kate tried to turn around, but Samantha tugged at her arm and spoke. "Let's see for sure. I can't believe nobody's here on such a pretty day."

It *was* a pretty day. The first hint of fall was in the air. No leaves had turned or fallen, but the temperature was dropping steadily, and now mornings could be almost chilly. The pumpkins, which Tyson checked at least twice a day, were plumping nicely for their trip to the county fair next weekend.

Mary Kate let Samantha pull her along. Even without the sunflowers the garden was still lovely. The day-care center children were back in school now, but just before Labor Day they had made scarecrows to decorate the plots. Tyson had been convinced to help them paint faces on burlap-sack heads stuffed with straw, and the results ranged from interesting to spectacular.

Samantha swung back the gate, and Mary Kate stepped inside. A shrill whistle sounded, and suddenly the garden was flooded with people. Out of nowhere Garth Brooks blared from stereo speakers set up beside the barn, and everyone applauded.

"What?"

"It's a party, for you," Samantha said, squeezing her arm. "They planned it. By the time I found out, it was too late to stop them. They wouldn't take no for an answer."

"For me?"

Samantha smiled, but her eyes shone with sympathy. "For you, and the baby."

Mary Kate didn't know what to say. She hadn't shared her plans for the baby with anyone except Casey and the sisters. She realized that everyone else expected her to raise the baby alone. They hadn't even considered that she might give it away.

"I was afraid to warn you," Samantha said. She looked penitent, as if her sin was a huge one. "It meant so much to them, and I was afraid you wouldn't come if you knew."

Mary Kate had no time to think about what to do or say. She was instantly swamped with people, who wanted to wish her well. A table set up between the stereo speakers was laden with brightly wrapped gifts and trays of sandwiches and cookies. Someone had made a huge cake in the shape of a carrot, and there looked to be gallons of purple punch to go with it.

She was hugged and patted from all sides. Someone pressed a small gift into her hand; someone else gave her a bouquet of wildflowers. She was herded toward the table before she realized what was happening.

"Speech, speech!" someone cried, and everyone else took it up.

She was sweating, and her hands were shaking. The noise died down, and she swallowed. "I . . . I don't know what to say."

Everyone laughed.

"Were you surprised?" someone called.

She realized Jo Turner had asked the question. Jo Turner,

who was leaning back against Jim Fagen. Mary Kate had never noticed Jim and Jo cuddled together before, but obviously this wasn't the first time they had stood this way.

"Oh, yes." Mary Kate cleared her throat. "This is such a surprise."

"So what do you think?"

She recognized the voice as Jake's, then she saw him standing beside the Tran family, the littlest Tran hanging on to his shirttail.

"I think you're all . . . wonderful." She sniffed. She was going to cry again. She was getting much too good at it.

"Aw, don't cry, Mary Kate." Sergeant pushed his way to the front. "You'll spoil your pretty face." He handed her a handkerchief. "Come on, blow your nose. And let's have a party!"

She wiped her eyes. Everyone cheered, and someone turned up the volume on the stereo.

Somebody took her bouquet and handed her a plate of sandwiches. Somebody else poured her punch. People drifted in and out of the small circle around her, wishing her well and chatting about the baby.

"Do you have a name picked out?" Elvira asked.

"Not . . . not yet."

"I always liked Melinda for a little girl, and you could call her Mindy."

Half a dozen other people made suggestions. Lola wanted Mary Kate to name the new arrival Lourdes, after Madonna's baby. "And you were going to be a nun and everything," she said, in case Mary Kate hadn't gotten the connection.

Tyson was standing on the edge of things, but he dismissed Lola's suggestion with one of his milder profanities. "It's gonna be a boy. Too big to be a girl."

Mary Kate felt warm hands resting on her shoulders. She knew, without looking, who was standing behind her.

"Let's give Mary Kate some space," Casey said. "Or

she might have the baby right here and now.''

Everyone laughed and began to move back. In a few moments they drifted away.

She turned, but he didn't drop his hands. ''Did you know about this?'' she asked, when they had a little privacy.

''Not until this morning. I think they kept it a secret because they were afraid I wouldn't like the idea.''

''What am I going to do?''

''Try to enjoy it. They're doing this because they love you.''

''But I can't take their gifts.''

''You can. And you can send some of them home with the baby. The new parents will probably be glad to have things you sent along to show the baby later, when it's older.''

She nodded, swallowing hard. ''Okay.''

He stepped back. ''Can you hang in there?''

She nodded again.

''I'll stay with you while you open the gifts.''

For a moment she wanted to ask him to stay with her forever.

Mrs. Tran had made a rag doll with Asian features for Mary Kate's baby. Jo had hand-decorated a knit sleeper with rickrack and colored ribbon. The volunteers from St. Anthony's had pooled resources to buy six dozen cloth diapers, and Sergeant had painstakingly dried and hollowed out gourds he'd grown in his plot to make birdhouses to hang outside the baby's window next summer.

But the most poignant gift of all had come from Jake, who presented her with an heirloom-quality baby quilt that his wife had made for their son. ''I won't have grandchildren,'' he'd said. ''I figured it's time now to pass this on.''

She had embarrassed him with tears, and he had held her awkwardly. But he had kissed her cheek before he let her go.

Back at the house after the party ended, Mary Kate tucked the gifts in her closet, smoothing her hand over each one as she put it away. Wisely the sisters had left her alone. She stood at her window until Grace finally knocked at her door.

"Mary Kate?"

"Come in."

"I just checked our answering machine. You have a message from a Howard Larkin. He wants you to call him this afternoon. I have his number here."

Mary Kate nodded.

"I've been thinking about our conversation this morning," Grace said.

"So have I."

"I know Robert was close to his sister June. She lives about an hour away, but she visited almost every day. After he died, Millie was too upset to clean out Robert's house and sell it, so June did it alone. I thought . . . well, I thought she might remember something . . ."

"Do you have her phone number?"

"It's the second one." Grace held out a scrap of paper. "If you'd like to go and see her, I can take you anytime today or tomorrow. You shouldn't be driving."

"You would do that?"

"That and anything else."

Alone again, Mary Kate stared at the paper in her hand. Then she went down to the second floor to use the telephone in the hall. Of the two calls, the one to Howard seemed less risky. She punched in the number and made her way through an operator and his personal secretary before Howard himself came on the line.

"Mary Kate, good to talk to you."

They exchanged the requisite social chitchat before Howard got to the point. "I've seen Casey's tape of your interview."

She tapped her fingers on the telephone table. She was

already worrying about the next call. "I'm sure it's excellent. He's such a pro."

"He's good, no doubt about it. But I'm calling about you. You're luminous on tape, Mary Kate. Articulate, witty. You have a real presence."

She thanked him, then waited for him to end the call.

"I'd like to use you here, if I get the right project. But something better may work out for you. I have a friend who's producing a new garden show for public television, and he's looking for a host. He wants a fresh face, a woman who understands gardening basics, but he also wants somebody who can be genuinely surprised by the people she interviews. He's more interested in personality than experience. Some of these shows are deadly dull, and he's determined to make his snappy. If you're willing, I'm going to express him a copy of Casey's tape."

Howard had her full attention now. "He's really interested in seeing it?"

"Uh huh. I told Tony about you. He's intrigued."

"Where will the show be produced?"

"Well, he's living in southern California. If you got the job you'd have to move. But the filming will probably take you all over the world. So should I send the tape on?"

Her head was whirling. "Sure, I don't see why not. What can it hurt?"

"And the baby? You could do this with an infant?"

She closed her eyes. "The baby won't be a problem."

"Good. I've told Tony you're exactly what he's looking for. Now, we'll just have to wait and see."

They chatted a few moments about the Indians before she hung up, but in her mind she was already frantically going over what Howard had said.

California. And filming all over the world. If this Tony liked what he saw, she might have an audition in California. For months she'd been saying that she wanted to explore, to have new experiences. What better way to make it happen?

And she had loved taping *Ohio Moments* with Casey. She had loved everything about it. She had felt completely at home in front of the camera, as if she'd stood there a million times before. She would be a good choice to host the show. Whatever she didn't remember, she would . . .

Whatever she didn't remember.

Something clicked shut in her brain. She stood still, staring at a painting of John the Baptist that one of the sisters had placed above the telephone table. For a moment she had felt in touch with her entire life, with things that had been out of her reach for months. For just a moment she had known . . . something.

She sank into the chair next to the table and put her head in her hands. For months frustration had nibbled at her constantly, but now it devoured her. She had to settle things, and soon. She didn't know how much longer she could handle a life with more spaces than solid ground.

She reached for the telephone and dialed the second number. A woman with a soft, musical voice answered right away, and Mary Kate wasted no time or words telling June Scillato who she was.

June sighed. "Mary Kate, I hoped you would call me someday."

Mary Kate had no intention of explaining her memory loss. Not yet. She wanted to see June in person before she explained anything or asked questions. "June, I have to see you. Is there any possibility I could visit you today?"

They arranged to meet at four o'clock at June's house.

"I have something for you," June said, just before she hung up. "Something Robert wanted you to have."

June lived in Mentor-on-the-Lake, a quiet neighborhood of small cottage-style homes near Lake Erie. Her house was one-story and tiny, but it had a view of the lake that no amount of money could have duplicated.

June was a small woman, with blonde hair, like Millie's, and an olive complexion that was an attractive contrast. She didn't seem surprised to find that Mary Kate was hugely pregnant, and she led her inside to sit down as soon as they'd exchanged greetings.

Mary Kate was immediately attracted to the dark, moody paintings that covered June's plain white walls. She suspected they were Robert Scillato's work. In her untutored opinion Robert had been greatly talented. He had worked with the most ordinary subjects, trees and gardens, children and animals, but given each a new twist, so that nothing was ordinary after all. She could almost read the history of each subject at a glance and understand its secret torments and passions.

"Yes, he was remarkable," June said. "He had no idea how to market himself, but I made it a crusade of sorts after he died. There'll be a show of his work at a Cleveland gallery in the spring."

"I wish I could remember him." Mary Kate switched her gaze to June. "I don't, though." In as few words as possible she explained about her memory loss, about her recovery and the pregnancy. About working to discover the father of her baby and finding a series of dead ends.

When she had finished she was almost out of breath. June looked as if she wanted to cry. "I didn't know," she said. "I just found out . . . about the baby. My mother mentioned it. She doesn't suspect, of course . . ."

Mary Kate held her breath.

"But I didn't know that _you_ couldn't remember . . ."

"What can't I remember, June?" Mary Kate said.

June exhaled forcefully enough for both of them. "You and Robert fell deeply in love, Mary Kate. You didn't mean to. Neither of you meant for it to happen. But it was one of those things that was just meant to be."

"Could he have been . . . was he the father of this baby?"

June didn't answer directly. She smiled sadly, then she got up and left the room. She returned with a large flat parcel wrapped in brown paper. "This is for you." She put it in Mary Kate's lap. "I'll be in the kitchen making tea. Call me when you're ready to talk."

Mary Kate waited until June had left before she peeled back the tape and unwrapped the paper.

She stared at the portrait, so different from anything else Robert Scillato had done, but every bit as evocative.

She stared at her own image caught on canvas. She was standing at the window, her hair a tumble of red curls, her breasts half-covered by a sheet carelessly draped around her. Her eyes shone like stars, and she was smiling in invitation, as if the man she adored was standing right there looking back at her.

Because, of course, he had been.

Mary Kate clutched the portrait against her. But this time she couldn't cry.

Some things went too deep for tears.

ᴄᴏ 21

Rᴏʙᴇʀᴛ Sᴄɪʟʟᴀᴛᴏ ᴡᴀs sɪᴄᴋ ғᴏʀ ғɪᴠᴇ ʏᴇᴀʀs before he died, sometimes in remission, sometimes in acute crisis. During his final year the hospital social-services department had felt he would benefit from regular visits from the nuns. His mother and sister, who were trying to care for him and juggle full-time jobs, would benefit, too.

Mary Kate had sensed Robert's need for companionship, and she had made a special effort to spend time with him. Once they had become friends, she had gone to visit him more often than anyone else had guessed. They had fallen in love slowly. Neither of them had planned for it to happen.

On the day he received his diagnosis Robert Scillato had been told he had probably been rendered sterile by the disease and would certainly be sterile after the treatment.

That prediction had turned out to be incorrect.

Night was falling, and as she had for the past week, Mary Kate sat in the garden among a thicket of withering cornstalks. Another harvest had taken place that afternoon. Green tomatoes still lingered, a handful of leathery pole beans adorned vines, and a few peppers had been left until they turned a ruby-red. But much of the garden was empty now. Sergeant and Jake had both put their plots to bed and would come only to weed some of the less-tended plots to ready them for the winter. Sergeant had already informed Mary Kate that he was drawing up a list of rules for next year's gardeners. And he and Jake intended to spend the winter months building trellises and birdhouses to place along the fence.

The teenagers were back in school and living at home, but they still came to Eden's Gate to spend the weekends. Right now they were at their dorms carefully carving the newly harvested pumpkins to take to the county fair tomorrow morning. Tyson had created stencils of the faces of ten American presidents, and under his demanding supervision, the kids, armed with stiletto-sharp instruments, were about to create masterpieces or mayhem.

Mary Kate was glad she had declined to watch.

From somewhere nearby a whirring noise disturbed the silence, and she turned her head in anticipation. With disappointment she saw that the noise was only the crackle of a cornstalk in the breeze. She was waiting for the hummingbirds to appear, just the way she had waited for them every night that week. The trumpet vines Sergeant had planted along the fence posts still had a few blossoms, and the bright red flowers were a favorite of the hummers. But so far she hadn't encountered a single bird.

The baby shifted, as if settling itself more comfortably under her ribs. She wrapped her arms around it protectively and wondered if Robert's child would be born with its father's talent. She carried a special child inside her, a child who wasn't supposed to be conceived, a miracle child who was all that was left of Robert Scillato, except for the memories of those who had loved him and paintings that would live for many lifetimes.

Sometimes she thought the child inside her was all that was left of Mary Kate McKenzie, too. She did not remember Robert. All she knew of him was what June, and later, Millie, had been able to tell her. She knew that he had loved her. The painting was proof enough, and June had told her that he had said her name in his final moments.

But the Mary Kate that Robert had loved was no more.

For the first time she was convinced that she would not remember her former life. If discovering her love affair with Robert hadn't brought back her past, nothing would. She continued to have flashes of a different time, but now she thought they had nothing to do with her. Perhaps they were hallucinations brought on by her injury. All she knew for sure was that the flashes didn't relate in any way to the life that others recounted to her.

"I thought I might find you out here."

Mary Kate hadn't heard Sarah come up behind her, but the nun's words were so soft Mary Kate wasn't startled. She turned and put on a smile. "I was hoping I'd see hummingbirds."

Sarah was still wearing a suit from a meeting earlier in the day. "I think they may have started their migration."

"Can you imagine what a flight that must be? Those tiny little wings fluttering nonstop for weeks to carry them such a long distance?"

"All of us cover huge distances in our lives." Sarah gave a self-effacing laugh. "Sometimes I really sound like a nun, don't I?"

"Not that often. You've been so good to me, never pushing, never threatening my immortal soul if I didn't shape up."

"I've always thought your immortal soul was perfectly safe, although it could benefit from more frequent attendance at church."

"I'm as close to God here as I am anywhere."

"Very theological, coming from you."

Mary Kate laughed. "I'll miss you, Sarah. I'll miss all of you."

"You could stay. Not as a sister. I know that wouldn't be wise or even reasonable. But you could stay and continue your work with the teenagers and the garden. We could find the funds somewhere to pay you a small salary. You wouldn't have to live here at Eden's Gate, if you didn't want to. You could live in town.''

"And keep the baby?''

"If that's what you wanted.''

"Is that what you came out here to tell me?''

"No. I came to tell you that you had a telephone call from a man named Tony Bucci in Los Angeles. I took his number. He seemed to think he had to talk to you right away.''

Mary Kate hadn't forgotten that Howard Larkin had sent the tape of *Ohio Moments* to a west coast producer named Tony. The show had aired on Sunday morning, and without undue conceit she had seen exactly what had impressed Howard. But she hadn't given Tony and his program much thought. There were a thousand more experienced women who had lens appeal.

Besides, there had been too many other things to fill her mind.

She rose. "What do you know about hummingbirds, Sarah? Besides the fact that they fly south in the fall?''

"What do you want to know?''

"Does the female raise her young alone? Or does the male help her?''

"She raises them alone. The male's only good for . . .'' She stopped, as if she suddenly understood the significance of the question.

Mary Kate finished Sarah's sentence. "For procreation. I imagine he's not even faithful to her, is he? He probably goes after everything in shiny green feathers.''

"That's more than I ever wanted to know about the sex lives of hummingbirds.''

Mary Kate knew how stupid she was to care. But she wondered if Casey had lied to her on purpose. Why had it mattered to him that she believe in hummingbird fidelity? Why had he tried to protect her? He was a better man than

he believed himself to be, but not one who made a habit of
rescuing other people from the truth.

Why had he asked her to marry him?

Sarah put one hand on Mary Kate's shoulder and pointed
with the other. "Look, over there," she whispered.

The sky had grown so dark that for a moment Mary Kate
couldn't see anything unusual. Then she detected movement.

As she and Sarah watched, a hummingbird darted from a
trumpet-vine blossom to the one beside it. And as she and
Sarah silently said their good byes to the tiny bird with
thousands of miles ahead of it, a second hummer flew out
from behind the vine to follow the path of the first.

Mary Kate made the call to Tony Bucci at Sarah's desk.
The night was young, but she felt centuries old. After she
talked to Tony she was going straight to bed. Her back
ached and the baby was exerting pressure where none had
existed before. She knew she could deliver any time now,
and when the big event occurred, she wanted to be as rested
as possible.

She punched in Tony's number and, as she had with the
phone call to Howard, she navigated her way through un-
derlings before she was connected to him. The moment he
picked up the phone, the line began to crackle. He sounded
far away, and she forced herself to speak louder. This time
she engaged in only the barest minimum of polite dialogue
before she turned over the conversation to him.

"I've seen Howard's tape," Tony said, as if he were in
a hurry, too. "I'd like you to fly out here to audition. Sometime next month, so I can talk to you in person."

"Next month?"

"Yeah, I'm going to be in and out of town until then.
And I've got a thousand things I have to do before we bring
the host on board for this show. Is that too late for you?"

She was surprised at his conciliatory tone. What did Tony

care if next month was too late for her? She was a nobody.

Hope began to flicker. She had assumed that Tony had gotten in touch because he felt a duty to Howard. But maybe this was more than a courtesy call. "Next month will be fine," she said.

He actually sounded relieved. "Good. But look, you have to know something up front. You'll have to move here to L.A. when—if we hire you. You'll be traveling all over, but we want somebody who's on the scene here to help make decisions. We're looking for someone who wants to take an active role in shaping the show. So if you're not willing to leave Ohio, we'd better cut off the negotiations right now."

She opened her mouth to tell him that of course she would move. But the words didn't arrive as scheduled.

"Miss McKenzie?"

"Um . . ." She went at it another way. "Howard told me I'd have to move out there before he sent you the tape. And he told me I'd be traveling."

"Good. Just so you understand. Look, I'm not going to play games with you here. Get an agent. I'm not making any promises, but I liked what I saw."

She didn't want to sound as surprised as she felt. She kept her tone casual. "I'm glad. Exactly what part did you like?"

"You're a good Midwestern girl. That's what we're looking for. And we want personality, lots of it. No deadbeats or robots, and nobody faking smiles. We're looking for genuine, with a dose of sex."

She wondered what he would think if he could see her swollen body. "Sex? For a gardening show?"

"Sex sells. Look, you don't know my background, do you?"

"No, Howard didn't tell me anything."

"I started in DC, behind-the-scenes stuff on a local news show. I watched a lot of people come and go, and I know who made it and why. Gypsy Dugan got her start at the station about the same time I did, and from the sidelines I watched her knocking out the competition on the power of that smile.''

From nowhere, a picture of Tony Bucci began to form in her mind. Dark hair, a ruddy complexion, and thick glasses with stark black rims. When he got excited his Adam's apple bobbed so swiftly it had made her dizzy to watch. Tony had made one halfhearted attempt to take her to bed, but she had rebuffed him so sweetly that he hadn't been hurt. Those had been the days when she still had the inclination to be kind to people. Before—

She gripped the receiver in both hands. Her head began to buzz. Her imagination was working overtime. She forced herself to speak, but her voice emerged as a whisper. ''You're comparing me to Gypsy Dugan?''

''You've got the same smile, McKenzie. The rest of you is different, wholesome, girl-next-door stuff, but the way that smile lights up the camera? You can't teach somebody how to do that. Gypsy was born with it. You were born with it. So the way I see it, you're exactly what we need, a low-wattage Gypsy, God rest her soul.''

He stopped abruptly, as if he realized he was giving her too much leverage for negotiations. ''Just come out next month. We'll talk then.''

Tony put her through to his secretary, who promised to get back to her with flight schedules and hotel reservations. Then Mary Kate hung up.

She was trembling. The whole thing was preposterous. She knew how hard it was to find jobs in television. This one had practically been dropped in her lap.

She started to stand, to make her way up to her room, when her knees simply gave out. She fell back into the desk chair, and the room began to revolve.

She knew how hard it was to find a job in television.

She squeezed her eyes closed and tried to push away the

truth. But this time the truth was more powerful than she was.

"The truth, the whole truth . . ."

She knew how hard it was to find a job in television because she had been in television.

"Oh, God." Her cry wasn't blasphemy; it was a revelation, an epiphany. Suddenly, she knew why the past of Mary Kate McKenzie had always seemed like someone else's past. She understood why she hadn't felt the vital connections to people from Mary Kate's former life, why she hadn't felt Mary Kate's calling.

It had never been her calling, her past, her life.

The memory flashes she had experienced had not been slices of Mary Kate's life. Before the attack that had nearly killed her in December she had *not* been Mary Kate McKenzie. In fact there was no "nearly" about it. Mary Kate had died in the ambulance on the way to the hospital, and she had gone wherever souls go after death. But after the body that had housed Mary Kate had been revived, a new soul had moved in, lock, stock, and libido.

The soul of the woman the world had known as Gypsy Dugan.

She put her face in her hands. "Oh, shit!"

She had never remembered anything about Mary Kate's life, but now she remembered Gypsy's, as if it were speeding by on fast forward. She had been born Mary Agnes Dugan, one of seven offspring of a Cleveland steel-mill worker and his wife. She saw her childhood, with the dark-haired mother who was so strict and unforgiving that early in her teens Gypsy had given up trying to please her, and had taken to pleasing herself instead. She saw the pregnancy she had aborted late in her teens, her confusion and guilt over what she had done, then her mother's unforgiving fury. She saw herself running away from home, and all the compromises she had made afterwards to work her way into television news.

Now she understood why the world of television had seemed so familiar to her. She had worked hard at every job she'd been given, stepping on anyone who got in her way, clawing and fighting to win an anchor position on a tabloid news show. She had cultivated a hard-ass image so that no one would get too close to her.

But one man had gotten close anyway. Charles Casey, *The Whole Truth*'s best reporter. Casey, whom she had loved as much as Gypsy Dugan had been capable of loving anyone.

As Gypsy, she had taken one look at Casey and known that she had to get him into her bed. Their relationship had begun with a sexual attraction that had nearly incinerated them both. Neither of them had made enough time or room for love in their fast-track lives. But Casey had been different than her other lovers. She had never wanted to face her feelings, because if she had, she would have had to do something about them. And love would have slowed her down.

She had loved him then. But now, she loved him so much more. Sex had been the culmination, not the commencement of their new relationship. This time she had loved him deeply and completely before they made love.

She had learned so much.

Why?

She didn't remember anything about Gypsy's death. Her life as Gypsy had stopped at the moment when she had crashed the station limo into an oncoming Mercedes. She remembered running for her life that afternoon, afraid that someone was trying to kill her. But, of course, no one *had* killed her. By her foolish actions she had caused her own death and that of the woman in the other car . . .

Suddenly she realized that the part about the other victim wasn't exactly true, either. She remembered Casey's story. Gypsy Dugan had awakened after the accident claiming to be the woman in the other car.

That woman, whoever she was, had taken over Gypsy's

body *and* her life. But where had Gypsy's soul resided before it took up residence in the body of Mary Kate McKenzie? She waited for that memory, silently prayed for it, but nothing surfaced. She thought she remembered a white light drawing her closer and closer. She thought she remembered being bathed in warmth, in love and forgiveness.

She couldn't remember more than that, but she didn't need to in order to understand. Because if such a place existed, perhaps second chances existed, too. And she had been given this chance, this gift. She had been given this child to raise, been entrusted with its welfare. Somewhere the Mary Kate McKenzie who had given her heart and body to Robert Scillato was now with the man she had loved. And a different Mary Kate McKenzie was carrying their child.

Because this child had to be born.

She didn't know how that realization had come to her. Whether it was a logical conclusion from a completely illogical memory, or whether that knowledge was buried so deeply inside her that the reasons behind it would never surface again, she knew it to be true. This baby had to be born.

She didn't believe that she was carrying a messiah, not a Mozart or a Picasso, a Gandhi or a Martin Luther King. But she was carrying the child of two special and talented people. The child had survived tremendous odds to grow and develop in her womb. This child, in its own way and as all children do, would change the world.

She was so glad, so grateful now that she had brought the baby this far, that she had nourished it well and followed through with prenatal care. She had given it the only gifts she could. She had carried it to term; she had tried to provide for its future.

Her child.

The vision of a different Mary Kate McKenzie and a man named Robert Scillato began to vanish. Her own former life as a woman named Gypsy Dugan began to vanish, too. The room spun harder. She closed her eyes and a void opened in front of her. She clutched the baby, wrapping her arms around it to protect it from harm.

The room dropped away, and she tumbled into darkness.

22

"MARY KATE . . . WHERE IS EVERYBODY?"

Mary Kate heard a voice from far away, but she was resting so comfortably she only wanted it to stop. She tried to turn her head, but she couldn't move. Slowly she realized her head was cradled in someone's lap.

With a sigh she forced her eyelids open and looked up at Tyson's face. "What . . . ?"

"Don't move. You're all right. You are, aren't you?"

She had no idea. In fact, she had no ideas about anything. For a moment the world was a perfect blank.

"I found you on the floor," Tyson said. "On the fucking floor! I came in to . . . I don't know why I came in. I don't know why it matters. You're leaving, anyway."

Memories began to trickle back, then they flooded her mind until she remembered everything. Her telephone call with Tony Bucci. Her promise to go to California for an audition. Then the awful dizziness that had seeped through her until she had blacked out.

She had remembered something about her life.

Or had she? For a moment Mary Kate could almost touch something new she had learned, something profound. Then whatever it was slipped from her grasp. Her past was still a perfect blank. Even the tiny splinters of memory she had experienced in the past months seemed hazy and unreal, nothing more than the products of a vivid imagination.

358

She did remember that right before the world turned black, she had pondered her life. But now that seemed unimportant, because apparently she hadn't come to any conclusions.

She tried to sit up, and Tyson assisted her. When she was settled and obviously holding her own, he moved away and stood. "I've got to get somebody. Got to tell them what happened. You've got to go to the—"

"Tyson?" She pointed at Sarah's desk. "Is that one of your jack-o'-lanterns?"

"What's it matter?"

She gazed at the pumpkin, a unmistakable replica of Bill Clinton. The pumpkin face had exaggerated chubby cheeks and a bulbous nose straight off of an editorial-page cartoon. "It's amazing. It's spectacular." She clapped her hands together. "You're amazing. You used a stencil? You made a stencil?"

His lips curled in disdain. "So what?"

"But you could sell the stencils, Tyson. If the others are as good as this one, you could sell them and make some money. We could find somebody to help you with marketing. Catalogs maybe, or craft shops. We could find somebody who knows—"

"Stop this shit! You aren't gonna be around to help me do nothing. I heard what you told that man. You're going to California to do some kind of audition. Don't pretend you're coming back!"

Her chin dropped, then her eyes darkened. "You listened to my conversation?"

"We got the same line at the dorm as the one in this office. I picked it up. I was gonna call the other line here, to see if we could get you to come down and see what we'd done."

She realized now where the background noise on Tony's portion of the call had come from. "Tyson, I—"

"You're going away, Sister Sunshine. Well, don't let us

stop you. Gonna take that baby with you? Or maybe you'll leave it behind, too.''

"Is that why you came to find me?'' She got awkwardly to her feet. She had fallen to the floor from the desk chair, and now she used it to help herself stand. "To insult me? That seems like a long way to come just to get in a good jibe.''

He shook his head, as if she were crazy.

Slowly, she got her bearings. "Maybe it really matters to you whether I stay or not. Is that right? Maybe you're just the teeniest little bit sorry that I won't be around this next year if you stay in the program. Are you planning to stay? Because we want you to.''

"We? You aren't gonna be here, remember?''

"No?''

She didn't know how she could have been so stupid. She didn't know how she ever could have believed she would find what she needed anywhere else if she hadn't found it here.

But she *had* found it here. She had found a community of people who cared about her. She had found a job that, while not glamorous or exciting, was challenging and important. She had discovered that she had a talent for making certain that plans worked out and a talent for bringing about positive changes in the lives of other people.

She might never remember her past, but that no longer mattered. She had discovered qualities inside herself that had never been fully developed, and she had discovered that despite her own willfulness, she could put others first when that was needed.

And, dear Lord, she had found the man she wanted in her life forever. The lover she wanted in her bed, the friend she wanted by her side, the man who would make a wonderful father to her child. Because now, she *knew* that she couldn't give up this baby. Something inside her had changed after Tony's phone call. No, that wasn't right. Nothing had changed. She was the same as she had always been, except that for the first time, she was facing who she really was. Something inside her had shaken loose or tightened up, she didn't know which, but now the deepest desires of her heart had been revealed. She knew that she could not and would not give this child to anyone else to raise.

She would die before she gave this baby away. She wasn't perfect. She wasn't even close. But this was *her* child, and she would learn whatever she had to so that she could raise it to be a healthy, happy human being.

Her child. Her man.

And right now, here in front of her, one of God's other children, waiting for the world to kick him in the ass again.

"So when are you leaving?" Tyson asked.

"I'm not going anywhere." She looked Tyson straight in the eye. "I was tempted. I'll admit it. It's not every day somebody gets a chance to have their own television show. But you know what? I think I'll continue working at Eden's Gate instead, so I can watch you grow up. Because it's not every day somebody gets a chance to do something that important, either."

"Shit, you're crazy. You know that? Must have hit your head hard when you fell."

"It doesn't matter. I'm staying. Whatever the reason. And you can bank on it." She made her way toward him, her hand outstretched.

He didn't move away, although he looked as if he might at any moment.

She patted his cheek. One quick maternal pat. Then she stiffened, and her eyes widened. "Uh, just one more thing."

His eyes narrowed. Trust wasn't going to come easily to this young man. But some things were worth waiting for. "What?"

"You might want to get Sarah. And somebody might want to call the hospital. I think I'll be heading there soon."

He grabbed her, as if to hold her up. Hostility flew out

the window, and he looked like a scared little boy. "You did hit your head!"

"I think that's a minor point. More important, I think I'm about to have a baby."

Casey hung up the telephone and rested his forehead against his upturned palms. It was nearly seven o'clock and he still had a paper to put to bed.

"St. Patrick and all the saints!" His head had been pounding all evening, and nothing seemed to help. He had already swallowed every over-the-counter remedy he could safely take. He had rotated his head, flexed his shoulders, held a cold cloth to his temples.

Even the call from his agent hadn't reduced the hammering in his brain. Howard Larkin had met their terms. At the end of December, when Watson Turnbull came back to take over *The Cricket*, Casey would move to an office at Howard's station.

He had found a new home in television news.

Someone knocked on his office door, and he sat up reluctantly. "Come in." Through waves of pain he could see Jim's outline, a cockier Jim than the one he'd first met.

"Any news from Mary Kate?"

Casey started to shake his head, then thought better of it. "No."

"The baby's due any day, isn't it?"

"Could be, who knows. First babies tend to be late."

"Jo's boys were late. Both of them."

Casey knew Jim was talking about Jo Turner. "You and Jo are getting serious, aren't you?"

"I took her home to meet my mom, and now the two of them are best friends. My mom's making quilts for both the boys' beds. If I don't marry Jo, Mom's going to adopt the three of them."

Casey realized that Jim hadn't stammered once. He had a new confidence these days, and he actually seemed taller.

"I'll let you know when I hear from Mary Kate."

"You know, if you don't want to stay with her when she has the baby, I could do it," Jim said. "I've delivered a dozen calves. Once I helped our old sow—"

"No thanks!" Casey rested his head on his hands again. The image of some other man watching Mary Kate give birth didn't please him. He wasn't even sure he wanted Dr. Kane that close. A brand-new round of pain fired in his head.

"Well, I've known her a long time," Jim said. "Longer than you. And since you're not spending time with her anymore . . ."

"How do you know what I'm doing?"

"I'm a reporter. I pay attention."

"Pay attention to what you're paid to pay attention to."

"Feeling a little frustrated, huh?"

Casey tilted his head just far enough to glare at Jim. "Go away."

"I've known Mary Kate all my life. In high school she was one of the few friends I could count on."

"Okay, she's the Shirley Temple of horticulture. She's everybody's little cupcake. Please, I'm dying. Get out of here!"

Jim didn't move. "I wanted to be a priest. Or at least that's what I thought. When I realized I didn't really have a calling, I was so afraid I'd disappoint her. But, of course, she wasn't disappointed. She understood."

"What in the hell are you getting at?"

"She didn't come to me when she . . . uh . . . she fell in love. See, she doesn't know how to ask for anything. She tries to handle everything alone . . ."

Up until this point Casey thought they were probably talking about two different women. The Mary Kate he knew was not the selfless, saintly do-gooder. But his Mary Kate didn't know how to ask for support, either. She had taken on the burdens of an unfamiliar life and tried to shoulder them by herself. And for the most part she had succeeded, because she was a strong, intelligent woman with good instincts.

But damn it, she still needed him.

Casey's head throbbed harder. "I suppose there's some point to this, since you're refusing to leave."

"I always thought a good reporter never takes no for an answer. I guess it's different in television news." Jim turned on his heel and started to leave the room.

"What?"

Jim stopped with his hand poised on the doorknob. "I guess it's different in television. I guess you don't learn the killer instinct, huh? I mean, if you did, you wouldn't have given up so easily. You'd know you were right, and you'd keep after her until you got what you wanted."

He ducked out the door and closed it behind him before Casey could say another word.

"Damnation!"

Casey jumped to his feet and strode across the room to lock his door. He kicked it once, and the wood splintered against the toe of his loafer. He grabbed his foot, and made kangaroo leaps back to his desk, trailing curses as he hopped.

He didn't know what he was angriest about. Losing Mary Kate. Being accused of misplacing his killer instinct. Or the fact that Jim had been right. He *had* taken no for an answer. Somewhere along the path toward changing his life he had forgotten that some of his skills had a flip side. He didn't have to be a remorseless bastard, intent on getting what he wanted at any cost. But that didn't mean that he couldn't go after things that really mattered. He could pull out all stops when it came to Mary Kate. Because he knew, deep inside, that she needed him in her life.

And he needed her. He loved her.

He loved her.

He loved Mary Kate McKenzie, but he hadn't told her he

did. Because he was a fool. The truth had been staring at him. He was a journalist, a reporter, a vicious mad dog in search of spectacular scandals. He could sniff a story a thousand miles away. He could worm details from a corpse.

He just couldn't see what was right in front of him.

No wonder Mary Kate hadn't taken his offer of marriage seriously. He had made it into a charitable gesture. He hadn't even told her that he loved her.

"What's in it for you, Casey? Am I penance for all your past mistakes? Or are the baby and I supposed to be window dressing for this new life you've created for yourself?"

He hadn't told her he loved her because he had never admitted his feelings to himself. Love was so new, so precarious, so terrifying. He had offered Mary Kate a life, but he had never offered her his heart.

They shouldn't be together. They were both screwed up. Neither one of them knew what to do or think or say, not about something this important. Not about something that could tear both of them into a million pieces.

But that didn't matter. Because Casey knew he was disintegrating into a million pieces without her. Maybe they would have to try harder, argue longer, compromise more often, and practice patience until they finally got it right. And maybe they wouldn't make it.

But maybe, just maybe they would.

He released his foot and tried his weight on it. He could walk. If he had to, he could run. He crossed the room, barely limping at all, and unlocked his battered door.

"Somebody get a carpenter in here," he yelled as he hobbled through the office. "And don't expect to see me again tonight. Put the paper to bed yourselves. I'm on my way to the most important story of my life!"

Mary Kate didn't think she was in labor, but the fluid gushing down her legs at the end of her talk with Tyson had been a sure sign labor was about to begin. Now Grace and Sarah, who had teamed up to get her here, were in the emergency waiting room while a resident examined her.

"I'm sure Dr. Kane will want to admit you," the young woman said. "We've got a call in to him right now."

Mary Kate gritted her teeth until the resident had finished the exam. "I feel fine. But since my water broke, I knew you'd want to check me over."

"I'm certainly glad you came in."

"How long before he'll get here? Should I wait outside with my friends?"

The resident, tall, blonde, and bleary-eyed from too many hours on call, looked at Mary Kate as if she'd lost her mind. "No, the minute we hear from him, we'll be taking you upstairs."

"Well, I just hate to take up a bed when I don't have to."

The resident looked down at her chart, then back at her patient. "Mary Kate, right?"

"Uh huh." Mary Kate wondered if somebody ought to call Casey. He had faithfully attended all the childbirth classes with her, and she desperately wanted him at her side when she delivered. But wanting and asking were different things. She hadn't even decided if she should have Sarah notify him when she was deep in the throes of labor. He was a conscientious man, despite the things he believed about himself. And he would come to the hospital to be with her, even if it was the last place on earth he wanted to be.

But what if she couldn't find the words to tell him she wanted him in her life? What if she couldn't find a way to let him know that she loved him, needed him, wanted him forever? What if she cried or screamed, and he was so upset that he changed his mind about marrying her?

The resident said something, but by the time Mary Kate realized she had spoken, the young woman had parted the curtains and disappeared.

The pressure she'd been experiencing all afternoon was intensifying now. Although she wouldn't call the sensation pain, she supposed this could be the earliest stage of labor. She had been warned she was in for a long haul since this was her first child. She cradled her huge belly in her hands and wondered how her little one was doing.

Her little one. Her baby.

She pushed herself upright. "Oh my God, I have to have a name!"

She had not indulged herself in fantasy names for a baby she wouldn't keep. Instinctively she had stayed away from anything that would tie her to the child inside her. Now that she would be keeping it, the baby had to have a name. A name of *her* choosing.

"Miranda. Um . . . Becky. June." As much as she wanted to name the baby after Robert's mother or sister, she just couldn't. "Roberta?" No. That didn't work for her, although if the baby was a boy, she might name it Robert. "Or something Robert . . ."

She couldn't deliver the baby unless a name was waiting. She started through the alphabet. "Alice, Alex, Aaron . . . Um . . . Angela . . ."

"Mary Kate?" Sarah pushed through the curtains. A nurse tailed her, muttering under her breath. Sarah pulled herself to her full height and sent the woman a stare that would have squelched every parochial-school student in a packed auditorium. "I am going to stay with her no matter what you say, so if I were you I'd find a better use for your time."

"Whew," Mary Kate said after the muttering nurse made a hasty exit. "I thought that 'look' had gone out with habits."

"Do you want me to call Casey, Mary Kate?"

"I don't think so. Not yet."

Sarah frowned. "Are you sure?"

"I've got to think of a name for the baby, Sarah." She

grabbed Sarah's hand. "Look, I don't know how to tell you this, but I've made a terrible mistake."

"There's nothing terrible about having a baby. Besides, it's a little late to worry now."

"No, that's not it. Look, I'm keeping the baby. I made a mistake when I thought I could give it away. Will you call the agency and tell them I can't go through with the adoption?"

"Of course I will." Sarah hesitated. "But are you sure? You don't want some time to decide?"

"I don't! I'm not going to change my mind. This is my baby. I'm sorry, but at least the adoptive parents aren't waiting in the wings."

"Of course no one's waiting. Everyone suspected you would change your mind."

That brought Mary Kate up short. "Everyone did?"

"Right from the beginning. You'll be the best kind of mother. Devoted and practical. Everyone could see it except you."

Mary Kate gripped Sarah's hand harder in gratitude. "I . . . I've got to think of a name. Do you think you could go to the gift shop and buy a book? They'll probably have one. We can look through it while I'm waiting."

"I don't think there's time."

"I know I won't be down here long, but I'm sure they'll let you come with me when I go upstairs. And this is supposed to take hours."

"Hours?" Sarah covered Mary Kate's hand with both of hers. "Didn't the doctor talk to you?"

"She told me she was calling Dr. Kane."

"Mary Kate, you're already very dilated. She's not an obstetrician, but she's guessing it won't be long before that baby makes an appearance. The minute they get you upstairs they're going to prep you for delivery."

Mary Kate stared at Sarah. "Delivery?"

Sarah wrinkled her elegant nose and nodded.

"Mother of God! Sarah, get Casey now. I don't care where he is! I'm not having this baby without him!"

Casey pulled up beside the house at Eden's Gate. Few lights were on, but since the sisters were conscientious about every aspect of the environment, he didn't pay much attention. He knocked on the side door, then rang the bell. A few minutes later, after he hadn't roused anyone, he progressed to the front door with the same result, and finally to the back.

He was about to try the barns, then the dorms, when a car drove up. Samantha got out and waved good-bye to several women.

"Sam . . ." Casey limped toward her. "I'm looking for Mary Kate. Do you know where she is?"

"Isn't she inside?"

"No one answered."

"She's probably down at the dorms with the kids. They're carving pumpkins for the fair tomorrow. I'm going to check on them in a minute. Marie's supervising and all their counselors—"

Casey cut her off, aware that he could expect a complete rundown if he didn't. "I've got to find her. Would you mind looking inside first? If she's not there I'll check the dorms next."

"No problem." She beamed a sunny smile in his direction and opened the door.

He followed her inside and paced awkwardly as she went through the house calling Mary Kate's name.

After a few minutes she came back down the stairs. "She doesn't seem to be here. Let me see if there's a note in Sarah's office."

"Don't bother, I'll check—"

"Better wait. She could be at the hospital."

He went still. "Hospital?"

"That's usually where a woman goes to have a baby. Of

course in some cultures—'' She winked to let him know she was teasing. "Wait right here."

She returned with a scrap of paper in her hand. "I was right. That's exactly where she is. They took her in about an hour ago."

"An hour?" He couldn't believe it. Mary Kate had left for the hospital an hour ago, and no one had notified him?

To his credit he didn't say the next thing that popped into his head. "I'm on my way," he said. "If anyone calls here, let them know I'm coming."

"She'll need you. She doesn't want to give this baby away, you know. I hope you can talk some sense into her."

"So do I. But first I have to tell her I love her "

Samantha didn't seem surprised. "That might be a good idea," she agreed. "Then she'll know what the rest of us figured out a long time ago."

Mary Kate gazed around the birthing suite which was equipped with every possible luxury except the one she needed most.

Charles Casey, television's sexiest reporter.

"Nobody knows where he's gone?" she said, for the second time in a minute. "He didn't tell anybody?"

"We've got everybody looking for him," Grace said, stroking her hand. Since she had originally agreed to be Mary Kate's helper during the birth, she had volunteered to be present for the delivery. Sarah was back in the waiting room.

"Did you call Eden's Gate? Maybe he's trying to find me!"

"I told you, Sarah called. Nobody answered, but she left a message. They're all down at the dorms, and it's probably too raucous to hear the telephone."

Mary Kate squelched the word she wanted to say. "I'm not having this baby until he gets here."

"You may not have any choice," Grace said calmly.

"Watch me!"

"You're still feeling all right?"

"I'm not having this baby."

The nurse assigned to her arrived in time for the final syllable. "Dr. Kane's on his way. He should be here in a few minutes."

"It . . . doesn't . . . matter! I'm not having this baby until Casey gets here."

The nurse tucked covers around Mary Kate then grasped her wrist to take her pulse. "That's something new. A woman in no hurry to get this over with."

"Grace, do something!"

"Short of whipping out my rosary, I'm afraid I can't help."

"This is ridiculous!" Mary Kate closed her eyes. The pressure came and went in definite waves now, and it was ebbing close to pain. She felt nauseated and dizzy to boot, but nothing felt as bad as Casey's absence. "It's my fault. I should have called him right away."

The nurse dropped Mary Kate's wrist and turned to Grace. "If she gets the urge to push, come out in the hall and yell for me. I'll just be gone a moment."

"I . . . am . . . not . . . pushing!"

"I know. Not until Casey gets here," Grace said.

Casey would never have chosen the little American-made sedan that Watson Turnbull had bequeathed him, but he had contented himself with its dependability, if not its style. Now, as if in defiance, the car died at the first light outside of Shandley Falls, and refused to start again, no matter what he tried.

He slammed his fist against the steering wheel. Then, cradling his bruised knuckles against his chest, he got out. He abandoned the car and started into town.

The hospital was only half a mile away, but sometime in the last few minutes rain had started to fall. The raindrops were fine and cool, but as he hurried down the sidewalk, they fell harder, until by the time he had gone a block he was soaked.

He was going to be too late.

This was his fault. How many times had he told Mary Kate she was a fake, when *he* was the one who hadn't understood himself? He adored her. He couldn't imagine his life without her. He had loved Gypsy, too. He knew that now. But he and Gypsy had been star-crossed lovers, unable to surmount their personal barriers. He had nearly played that game with Mary Kate, too. But no more. If he was just given another chance . . .

"But how many second chances does one man get?" he muttered.

Cars passed, their headlights gleaming on the rain-slick road as he trudged on. He heard one coming up behind him, and he moved over so that he wouldn't get splashed. The car slowed, and in the gleam of the wet street he saw the undulating red light of a police car.

The police officer trumpeted one blast on his siren, then pulled up beside Casey and cut his engine. He opened his door. "Hey you, is that your car back there?"

"I broke down. I couldn't get it started."

The officer squinted into the darkness. "You look familiar."

Casey saw it was the same potbellied cop who had arrested him on the night of the fight at the Dew Drop Inn. His heart sank. "I'm Charles Casey, the managing editor of *The Cricket*."

"I don't care who you are. You can't leave that car in the middle of the road. Get in. I'll take you back and see if I can jump it for you."

"Officer, I'm on my way to the hospital."

"You sick?"

"No, I—"

"Then get in. Whatever's waiting at the hospital will

keep. But you've got to get that car out of the street.''

Casey knew he had two choices. One was to do what the cop requested. The second was to use his training as a rogue journalist, sprint across the vacant lot to his left, cut between houses and businesses on the next street, and make his way to the hospital through alleys and backyards.

''Fine.'' He started around the car, as if he were going to comply. The cop got back in and slammed his door.

Casey took off running as fast as his injured foot would carry him.

''You're not quite ready to push, Mary Kate,'' Dr. Kane said. ''But almost. Do you remember what you learned in childbirth classes?''

''I'll save her the trouble of answering,'' Grace said. ''She's not pushing.''

''Until Casey gets here,'' the nurse finished.

Mary Kate knew that Casey was on his way, but she didn't know what was keeping him. She was definitely in pain now, puffing and panting with the contractions, the way she had learned in class, but the labor had progressed so swiftly there hadn't been time for painkillers. And besides, she wanted the safest possible delivery for herself and her baby.

Her baby. And, God willing, Casey's baby, too.

''Where is this man?'' the doctor said.

''He left Eden's Gate twenty-five minutes ago,'' Grace said. ''He should be here any minute.''

''Well, it's raining out there. That might have slowed him down . . .''

''He'll . . . be . . . heeeeeeere!'' Mary Kate groaned and suddenly, gravity seemed to take over her body.

Doctor Kane took one look at her face and positioned himself between her legs for another quick exam. ''Sorry, but it looks like you and the baby can't wait another minute.''

The door into the birthing suite slammed against the wall as a figure in a green gown and cap came through it. Casey's forehead was beaded with raindrops. "Somebody in here about to have a baby?"

"Casey, you bastard!" Mary Kate started to cry. She had nearly given up hope that he would arrive.

"Make it quick, Katie, the cops are after me."

Grace moved to give him room, and he squirmed in beside her.

"Cops?" Mary Kate said.

"Don't worry, they won't track me here for a few minutes."

Another contraction began, and suddenly she couldn't think of anything except what was happening to her body. "Oh . . . Oh!"

He grabbed her hand. "I'm here. I'm always going to be here for you. Listen, I love you. I love this baby. You're going to be all right. *We're* going to be all right."

She groaned and pushed with all her might, as the doctor gave her directions she couldn't hear. All she could hear were Casey's words.

The pressure eased, and she realized she was crying. "What . . . what did you say?" she asked hoarsely.

"I love you. I adore you. I want you in my life forever."

"I . . . I'm keeping the baby, Casey."

"We're keeping the baby." He kissed her hand.

"I love you, too. I'm just . . . so stupid!"

"No, you're not. You're beautiful. Wonderful. The best. You're my heart."

She couldn't answer, because another contraction was beginning.

"This will do it," the doctor said. "The head's crowning. You're about to meet your baby, Mary Kate."

Casey came around behind her and helped lift Mary Kate the way he had learned in their childbirth classes. She pushed with everything she had, straining and gasping.

The reward was a thin wail.

"Congratulations, Mary Kate, Casey," Dr. Kane announced. "You have a beautiful baby girl."

Mary Kate began to cry again. She looked up and saw that Casey was crying, too. He continued to hold her as the doctor put the baby across her abdomen, and he didn't even wipe the tears from his cheeks.

"I'm guessing nearly eight pounds," the doctor said. "Her color's good. If I'm not mistaken, she'll be a redhead like her mom."

"Charlotte," Mary Kate said, "for you, Casey. Kathleen for my mother. Charlie, for short. What do you think?"

"I think I'm the luckiest man in the world."

"I'll tell you what I think," she said.

He bent low because her voice had dropped.

"I think I hear a siren," she whispered.

He kissed her then, and tasted the salt of tears against her lips. "Then you'd better let me be the first to hold our daughter," he murmured. "Just promise you'll bail me out as soon as they let you out of the hospital."

Mary Kate woke up from a peaceful sleep. For a moment she didn't know where she was, then she remembered. She turned over and saw Casey sitting in a chair beside the bed, still cuddling Charlie, who was fast asleep in his arms. She didn't think he was asleep, but his eyes were closed, and he was smiling.

She turned her gaze to the clock and saw that it was nearly midnight. She had been a mother for four whole hours. Casey, who had squared things with the police, was still here, and Charlie was still sleeping.

She tried to remember if she had ever been this happy. She couldn't imagine it, but she supposed she would never know for sure. Her past was a mystery and would probably remain so.

For the first time that thought neither frightened nor disturbed her. Months had passed. Even the illusory memory flashes seemed to fade away as she tried to recall them.

Somehow none of that mattered anymore. She didn't remember anything about her life before the injury, but she had learned everything else she needed to know. The past was less important than the future. Who she had been was less important than who she would be. She was a woman with strengths and faults, but her man accepted and loved her, just the way she was.

She wanted to tell Casey again just how much she adored him. She wanted to hold her baby close again, too. But there would be plenty of time to do both. A lifetime of opportunities.

Her eyelids drifted shut, but just before they closed she saw two shadows drift into the room, two shadows who seemed in some odd way to be connected. She was so tired that for a moment she didn't understand, then she realized the shadows were holding hands.

As she watched they drifted closer to Casey and Charlie, stopping to peer down at the baby. They drew closer together, and something almost like a sigh of satisfaction filled the room.

She was exhausted, drifting somewhere between wakefulness and sleep. She forced her eyes open to make the shadows disappear, but unexpectedly, they didn't. At least, not at first.

They merged, as if exchanging a kiss. Then, slowly, still holding hands, they vanished into her dreams.

Dear Reader,

Each month, Avon Books publishes the best in historical and contemporary romance. So be on watch for these upcoming Avon titles.

For historical romance fans, there's Julia Quinn's Avon Romantic Treasure, BRIGHTER THAN THE SUN. The Earl of Billingham, a notorious Regency rake, must marry before his 31st birthday or lose his inheritance. He thinks he's found the solution to his problem in marriage to Miss Eleanor Lyndon. But Ellie is more than he'd bargained for. Is it possible for this rake to become reformed?

In THE WILD ONE by Danelle Harmon, Julia-Paige— and her baby—arrive in 1776 England from America to confront devil-may-care Lord Gareth de Montforte. When Julia informs Gareth that his late older brother is the father, Gareth impulsively marries the beautiful mother. But is he truly ready to settle down and become respectable?

The romantic Scottish Highlands is the setting for Lois Greiman's HIGHLAND BRIDES: THE LADY AND THE KNIGHT. It's 1516, and Sara Forbes is on the run with a very special baby. Soon, she finds herself protected by Sir Boden, an irresistible and brave knight. But can their growing love overcome his devotion to duty?

Looking for a contemporary romance with a touch of humor? Then don't miss Barbara Boswell's WHEN LIGHTNING STRIKES TWICE. Rachel Saxon, a modern career woman, is swept off her feet by Quinton Cormack and must decide if it's time to put *pleasure* before business in this sizzling love story by one of romance's most popular writers.

Remember, each month look to Avon Books—for the very best in romance.

Sincerely,
Lucia Macro
Avon Books

Discover Contemporary Romances
at Their Sizzling Hot Best
from Avon Books

**LOVE IN A
SMALL TOWN**   *by Curtiss Ann Matlock*
78107-7/$5.99 US/$7.99 Can

HEAVEN KNOWS BEST   *by Nikki Holiday*
78797-0/$5.99 US/$7.99 Can

FOREVER ENCHANTED   *by Maggie Shayne*
78746-6/$5.99 US/$7.99 Can

ASK MARIAH   *by Barbara Freethy*
78532-3/$5.99 US/$7.99 Can

TILL THE END OF TIME   *by Patti Berg*
78339-8/$5.99 US/$7.99 Can

FLY WITH THE EAGLE   *by Kathleen Harrington*
77836-X/$5.99 US/$7.99 Can

WHEN NICK RETURNS   *by Dee Holmes*
79161-7/$5.99 US/$7.99 Can

Avon Romances—
the best in exceptional authors and unforgettable novels!